THE LAST MISSION

THE LAST MISSION

THE DESCENDING WORLDS – BOOK 3

JUSTIN S. LESLIE

Podium

Podium

THE LAST MISSION

PROLOGUE

Purplish-red, violent clouds blocked out the sun as pulsating lights flickered and flashed in the sky. Elera stared upward, her gaze fixed on the tumultuous heavens, while her husband, Zayden, ran to the bus stop next to Air Force Base Skyler. The two star-crossed lovers, both active-duty service members, had finally been stationed together.

"What the hell?" Zayden gasped, out of breath, as smoke wafted from their flight jackets.

As they peered into the adjacent parking lot, they saw steam—or rather, smoke—rising from everything the acid rain touched, creating a haunting, graveyard-like haze on the ground.

"I don't understand," Elera murmured, her eyes darting toward the distant control tower. Beside it, nestled in a hangar bay, was one of the latest fighter jets the Republic of States had to offer.

Zayden, a skilled pilot and one of Mount Skyler's finest, exchanged a knowing nod with Elera. Without words, they decided to make a dash for the hangar. The plane inside was not only armored but also their best chance of escaping the hellish sky.

Raging groans echoed through the sky while a thunderous vibration shook the bus stop's cheap, plastic No Smoking signs. It was now or never.

Elera looked up, swearing she saw a gigantic metallic object, as large as a city, peeking through the clouds. The scene unfolded like a nightmarish sci-fi movie.

The couple kissed, Zayden gently placing his palm on her face. "I love you, babe. We got this."

They bolted from the bus stop, the sting of acid rain pelting their faces, gritting their teeth against the pain. Their boots splashed through growing pools of acid which ate away at the rubber like a ravenous creature.

The bright lights of the hangar bay flickered as the ground crew stared in disbelief at the duo, who immediately discarded their tattered jackets. A lineman shouted for them to head to the wash rack, a station for decontamination from hazardous chemicals like jet fuel.

Buster, an older, balding man with a heavyset frame, ran the fighter jet prep team. He had known Captains Elera and Zayden since their early days as recruits.

"Stop gawking at the burning rain and get that damn fighter ready," he bellowed. "Those two aren't over there making babies!" he said as Elera and Zayden headed toward the lockers behind a mesh cage.

Buster, limping due to his degenerating hips and the weight from years of beer drinking, approached them. "I thought it was your night to fly, Zayden," he began as they quickly geared up.

"Not tonight. There's something up there causing this," Zayden replied, pulling on fresh socks.

"Pity. When you're up there, that's Captain Elera's and my time to bond," Buster remarked, chewing on an unlit cigar.

"Sorry, Buster. You'll have to court the missus some other time," Zayden retorted playfully.

"You're too old for me, Buster. Plus, you can't even see your feet when you stand up," Elera chimed in, maintaining their preflight banter.

"You know, the younger ladies are fond of older men these days," Buster replied, signaling a ground crew member to attach the stairs to the plane. They were both going up.

"Sorry, Buster. You're not rich," she teased, giving the aging man a firm hug and planting a kiss on his cheek. "When we get back from this, it's a date." Buster's cheeks flushed as they always did, winking at her.

Zayden, finishing his preparations, approached Buster. The gravity of the situation was evident in his expression. "Buster, you've been like family to us. We can't thank you enough," he said, embracing the man warmly.

Buster mentally steeled himself, pushing back the tears in his hardened eyes. They all knew that whatever loomed above them was far beyond their understanding.

The team made their way to the fighter jet, now ready for takeoff. The ground crew hurriedly attached the last missiles to the plane's belly. Spaceflight was still a dream; they still relied on rockets and shuttles for satellite deployment.

Within moments, the jet was prepped. Buster, who had never been seen climbing the ladder, hauled his bulky frame up to the cockpit. "Give 'em hell," he said with a salute.

The pilots returned the salute, their focus laser sharp on the task ahead. The ground crew encircled the jet in silence.

"Don't just stand there," Buster barked, now back on the ground, nursing a stinging hip. "Open the doors. Takeoff is cleared. No need for radio permission—it's dead, anyway." He had checked.

The crew scrambled as the jet moved forward, the cockpit hatch sealing with a thud. The hiss of rain against the plane's nose made the pilots grimace.

"We'll be above the clouds soon. Max power, inverted takeoff," Zayden stated, with Elera nodding in agreement.

"I love it when you talk dirty," she quipped, a smile breaking on Zayden's face. "Buster, this is Raptor One. Do you copy?"

Buster hurried to the ground radio. "Loud and clear. I'll try to get the landline working," he responded, switching on the ground radar, which was now useless. "Shit," he muttered. "You guys are flying blind."

With no time to waste, Zayden ignited the afterburners before the jet even aligned with the runway, pulling back the yoke. The jet soared upward in seconds, punching through the purple clouds, only to find another layer of gray obscuring the sun.

There, in front of them, was the source of their nightmare: a massive ship, unlike anything they had ever seen, hung in the sky, its large exhausts emitting the purplish haze. Flowing organic lines morphed into various metallic shapes adorned with random devices and lights, all coming together in a nightmarish fire-breathing dragon.

"What the hell is that?" Elera asked as the sounds of Zayden arming the missiles chimed.

"All I know is it's attacking. Prepare to engage. I love you, babe. All that shit I said last month? I take it back," Zayden said as a grin swept over Elera's face.

"It's okay. We can always go to your parents for the holidays."

Zayden nodded. Last month, they had gotten into a heated debate on where to spend the holidays, which had included a two-hour overture on how much he hated her mother, creating a few nights on the couch for the man.

"Buster," Zayden called over the crackling radio.

"I can barely hear you. Command knows you're in the sky. They want to know what's up there."

A swarm of small drones, something the two had never witnessed, burped out of the ship's hide as if shaking off the rain. "Buster," Zayden repeated, knowing there was nothing the remaining fighter wing on the ground could do just as another monolithic ship lurched out of the heavens. "Tell them we tried our best."

A lump formed in Elera's throat, knowing what they were about to do.

"Zayden. Elera!" Buster shouted over the now washed-out radio.

Elera stilled herself. "I love you too, babe."

Afterburners screamed to life as Zayden pushed the fighter jet to its limits while targets pinged, locked on. All six of the laser-guided missiles erupted from the jet as he again pressed the plane to full throttle while unleashing the two machine guns tucked into the nose of the aircraft. They were firing everything they had in a futile final stand.

The small drones swarmed the jet, raking large sections of its outer paneling off while several sparked and snapped out of existence. Below, Buster and the ground crew stared at the sky, still undercover, as familiar explosions rocketed overhead.

"Give 'em hell," Buster mumbled to himself, unable to see the final heroic charge of Zayden and Elera.

Proximity alarms flashed as one of the missiles found purchase on the massive ship's lower exhaust port spewing the purplish fog. A large, rocketing explosion followed. Somehow, they had miraculously ignited a chain reaction in the exhaust vents' intakes.

"Hang on, baby," Zayden yelled as the nose of the ship sliced into the thick spiked hull of the massive starship. They never saw the other three vessels seeping through the atmosphere as the jet disintegrated into a million pieces.

Below, cheers erupted as the acidic rain immediately stopped, followed by the screeching clank of the massive city-size ship, now visible, slowly heading to the ground. A section of its belly was on fire and bubbling into more explosions. The gigantic ship was coming down. They had done it.

Buster looked directly overhead, seeing two more of the enormous vessels. Before he turned, the new ship's massive exhaust ports started spewing an even thicker haze of purplish clouds. It was a scene out of hell itself as debris began slamming into nearby buildings.

This was the start of the final days of Teras—before the final resolution, as it would be called over the decades and centuries following—the very planet the USF *Murphy* and the *Crow* were now in orbit above.

CHAPTER 1

ALL THE WAY DOWN

Radars beeped and dinged as the Harpy drop ship cut through the thick purplish clouds of the planet where the USF *Murphy* and *Crow* were currently parked. After weeks of working through their precise location and several attempts to scan the planet's surface, Captain Ben Dailey had chosen to send a team to the surface of the odd planet they had been orbiting.

Jen turned away from a fully armored Dailey sitting in the weapons seat. The pilot pressed the stabilizer override buttons, taking full control of the Harpy. Behind them, a handful of Third Foot's finest sat ready to explore whatever mystery unfolded under the blanketed planet. The one thing they had concluded was that it was covered in structures and had old-style satellites in orbit sending off random signals, including music and, from what Albert had gathered, several TV shows from the caveman era.

Captain Ben Dailey sat in the weapons-specialist seat, letting his body sway to the tossing Harpy while concentrating on the flickering radar screen in front of him. The *Murphy*'s commander, after several weeks of contemplation, had decided to go planetside in the unlikely event they would be able to find any remnants of information that could possibly identify their current location.

"Sir," Jen said as the radio started humming with breaking static. "We're starting to get readings from the planet below. It appears there are several structures there."

"Keep on course. As long as nothing else is in the air, we keep moving," Dailey ordered as Albert chimed in.

"Hello, boys and girls. Nothing has scanned us so far. Also, there appear to be limited electromagnetic signals on the ground."

"Shit," Dailey huffed. "Meaning?"

"Meaning there is not much, if any, power going to the structures below. And there is no one locking seeker missiles on us. You do the math," Albert scoffed.

"Dead planet?" Jen asked as Dailey shook his head.

"Maybe. We thought Sparky's home was dead."

"Definitely dead down there," Albert spoke up. "If you mean devoid of sentient life, then the structures below state otherwise. If you base your assumption on dumb, dumb math, then the planet is possibly void of life. The question is why."

Dailey didn't like the already known inference. "Big picture, the planet's in rough shape," Dailey concluded as the Harpy jostled, cutting through one of the thick clouds.

"Five minutes till we hit the ground. According to the sensor data, these godforsaken clouds are maybe ten stories off the deck," Jen informed the team, prepping the ship for landing. The rover in the back of the drop ship had its front and side doors open, still allowing everyone to see and hear each other.

"When she says ten stories off the deck, she means it. Like the entire planet. Crazy stuff. Oh, and if I might add, there is a nasty amount of corrosives in the air. Breathable, but I wouldn't for too long. Might cause a case of black lung," Albert said as the Harpy began swaying in time with the turbulence.

"Watch Buckle. He gets sick easily," Dailey noted. Specialist Dion Belts, also known as Buckle, had a history of throwing up in his helmet.

Specialist Jenna Jones leaned forward, making a retching motion to mess with the man.

One thing Dailey and Becket always gave Master Sergeant Janix of Third Foot a hard time about was the significant amount of Jakes and

Jennas in his platoon; more specifically, that he'd put them all in the same squad as a joke.

During roll call the month prior, Becket had gotten so frustrated and tongue-tied that he'd simply stated. "If your damn name starts with a *J*, just raise your damn hand. That's all you, Jakes, Jennas, and whatever else you have."

This had garnered a round of snickers from the group. He was of course referring to Specialist Jenna Jones and Private Jake Jenna—aka Private Parts. Jones and Private Parts had formed an odd bond through the years. Not only were they both due for promotion, but the joke was that Jenna's name would be Jenna Jenna if they ever got married. For this mission, Private Parts had lost a heated game of rock paper scissors with Woody, having to stay on board the *Murphy* as part of the QRF.

"Everyone, look sharp," Dailey directed as Becket's voice came over the comms.

"All's clear up here, sir. We have QRF on standby. To the edge," Becket growled. While the signal was broken, it was still readable and within acceptable ranges. Albert had promised to secure the signal once they landed, bringing one of Science Officer Bellman's transponders customarily used in deep space.

Another forceful gust of wind shuffled the Harpy's contents like a deck of old, limp, playing cards. Anything not tied down jumped in the air, sliding on the metal floor. Dailey glanced at Jen, who shrugged. "I'm trying. The wind's kicking at about eighty knots. Sensor data says it's only about twenty on the surface."

"Just get us there in one piece," Dailey said. Purplish clouds swirled outside the cockpit windows like a tornado in a trailer park.

In reality, trailer parks of the future were called pod parks—metal containers secured to the ground by several large spikes that could easily be moved. While significantly improved, the concept was still the same, as well as the often unique off-world inhabitants.

The sounds of the landing pads *thunked* as the Harpy finally dropped out of the angry embrace of the planet's blanketing clouds. Gray, gloomy land sprawled in all directions, making a depressing scene. Albert cut over the comms.

"How depressing. Perfect time for a Solarian summer song," he stated. Dailey switched his link off, only to be overridden. "Rude."

"There." Jen pointed toward a barely visible clearing in a field surrounded by several derelict buildings. Drab grays collided with even duller browns, all mixed with the hazing pattern of rain as the Harpy slowed the hover mode.

"Scanning," Albert said. "Clear. No signs of sensor targeting or, well, much of anything."

Dailey stood up, walking to the back of the Harpy, switching his HUD readout from flight mode to ground operations. "On your feet! Someone wake up Sparky."

Sparky had opted to stay inside the ground vehicle, taking a nap. The Nova Rangers outside the rover all stood up, switching to combat mode as weapons clanked. They would exit the Harpy, set up a perimeter, and allow the vert rover to leave the ship.

Dailey was jostled as Albert stood up in all his glory. The Alurian battle droid's body looked like the grim reaper itself, only offset by Mister Toaster's mustached face topping off the ensemble. The look was completed by the two Gatling lasers wrapped around his shoulders.

The familiar hissing suck of the bay door opening put the team in motion as the dark gray and purple tint from outside interacted with the red combat lights now activated. Like a well-oiled machine, the four Nova Rangers outside the rover split into two groups, exiting the ship while Dailey and Albert followed close behind. The sleek, low silhouette of the Harpy blended with the tight buildings Jen had chosen to tuck the team away in. The mix of dark skies and seemingly endless rain hid the drop ship between the dull, overgrown buildings.

Buckle and Lambert gave a thumbs-up as the Harpy let out the vert rover, which quickly darted out of the bay. Dailey turned, seeing Sparky in full armor standing beside Albert.

"Janix, get your team to scan the local buildings and find a location to set up an outpost. I want to secure the landing site and get undercover."

"Roger, Viper Six," Janix replied. Specialist Jenna Jones and a now fully functioning Woody left Buckle and Lambert to secure the drop site.

"You could have just asked," Albert chimed in, loading coordinates to a warehouse to the ship's left in Jones's and Woody's HUD. "I scanned the area as we landed. You're welcome."

Sparky joined the two Nova Rangers now heading into the rainy afternoon. Dailey stood like a rock, taking in the oddly familiar yet alien surroundings. On the side of one of the buildings, a symbol caught his attention. A star with stripes surrounded by a circle sat barely visible, reminding the *Murphy*'s captain of the old-style US Air Force symbol.

"Jen," Dailey said, switching to direct comms with her and Janix. "Power down the outside lights and make the ship look like a brick. I'm going to leave a few people with the Harpy."

The back door to the vert rover dropped open as two Nova Rangers jogged back to the Harpy.

"Expecting company?" Janix asked from inside the rover.

"I want to be able to get out of here fast if needed. Comms with the *Murphy* are already sketchy. Albert needs to get that transponder up and running." The transponder, in reality, was a high-octane signal relay.

"Glad I'm not the only one this place is giving the creeps to," Jen followed as she raised the cargo ramp.

"Sir." Janix cleared his throat. "The warehouse is secure. No signs of life. The rover can fit in the bay. I suggest sending Albert to get it open. It's a hundred yards from here, so we should be good."

"Uh, sir," Sergeant Dill Paxter, also known as Pickle, spoke up. "I think you're going to want to see this."

"Team, this is Viper Six. Move out. Angel Six, once we secure the area around the warehouse, I want you to nudge the ship closer to the building," Dailey instructed Jen, looking at the rain-spattered cockpit, getting a thumbs-up back.

Dailey pulled his Sauder rifle out as Albert clanked beside him. "I have to say, the architecture is reminiscent of a military installation. I wonder if they have Solarian bingo-bongo night."

"This place has been dead for a long time. I doubt you'll find the Solarian version of bingo being played. Just keep doing that scan thing you always do," Dailey replied as two of the Rangers working on a rusty chain finally got it to move.

Rain started pouring from the purple clouds above as if pushing the group to get inside the building. Albert, getting tired of the constant rain dampening his sensors, pushed the two Nova Rangers struggling with the door, grabbed the chain, and gave it a solid, jarring pull.

Loose debris and muddy water flung from the metal door as it opened with a nerve-racking screech. Sparky trotted into the dark room, only to stop as the foreboding shadows took over from the fleeting, dull light.

Dailey motioned for Coolio to pull up to the entrance while the other Nova Rangers started pouring light into the space. "Albert, anything in there?" Dailey asked.

Mister Toaster's lips flattened. "With all this infernal rain, I couldn't pick up if Sparky claimed the building for the Republic."

"You know that's not a real thing?" Dailey asked. Albert shook his head.

"Yet. Not a real thing *yet*. The devil's in the details," Albert said, moving out of the way.

The vert rover pulled in, with Dailey and Albert following behind into the building. Unlike the outside, the inside was a dusty museum to a civilization long since gone. Massive stacks of old crates in various states of decay loomed to the ceiling in several areas. Old cables and random tools lay strewn around the warehouse like discarded children's toys.

Lambert and Buckle walked to Dailey as Sparky, out of character, continued to keep his armor fully activated, standing in the middle of the room.

"Sir," Buckle said, pointing to a car. "I've seen pictures of old-school cars, and that's about as close as I've gotten to one since I was in fifth grade and went to the Federation Museum."

Dailey pulled up the atmospheric sensor reading and saw it showing green. He didn't need the details, just that it was good to breathe. Bellman had programmed all the team's sensors to be knucklehead-proof. Green was good, and anything else other than red was more of a personal choice.

The *Murphy*'s commander's helmet hissed as he unlocked the seal, pulling it off. What lay before him was truly a confusing homage to days long since passed. While familiar, the car didn't look right. Flat tires and sharp angles all formed an abstract version of an old military Humvee from the old Earth US Army.

A star with stripes on the side of the vehicle coincided with the symbols he'd noticed on the buildings outside. "Check out those crates," Dailey instructed, pointing to the stack of military hardware piled closest to the group while he walked to the Humvee.

He ran his hand over the hood, checking the door to find it unlocked. *Typical of military vehicles on a base,* he thought as Albert tapped him on the shoulder.

"What?" Dailey asked, taking in the familiar yet different lines of the vehicle.

"Oh, well . . . I'll just go stand in the corner and stare at the wall and not at those moderately fresh boot prints leading up to the driver's side door."

Dailey walked over, seeing the tracks. "Shit," he huffed. "Sparky."

Sparky reluctantly walked over to Dailey, letting the face shield on his armor retract. Cocking his head, Dailey pointed at the footprints.

"Yes?" Sparky's translator came over the comms after a light bark.

"You're a hound or dog or whatever. Do your thing. Can you sniff this out?" Dailey asked as Sparky perked up, proud to be called a dog.

A spatter of woofs and chuffs followed. "Fresh smell. Someone was here two days ago. They had food."

Shocked, Dailey turned to a grinning Mister Toaster. "He's totally awesome."

"You're saying you can tell how long ago those tracks were made?" Dailey asked.

"Duh," Sparky yipped.

"Janix," Dailey barked. The Solarian platoon sergeant of Third Foot jogged over, seeing the vehicle and the footprint. "Check all the entry and exit points and set guards in place. I'll get Jen to pull the Harpy closer. Let's get this place lit up."

"Sir, there are two exits and the main entrance. We already have them covered. Is everything good?" Janix asked, seeing the concerned look on Dailey's face.

"No, it's not. Let me ask you. How many planets have you been on?"

"Dozens," the Solarian replied.

"How many have you been on with cars or vehicles like back on Earth? Including your own home?" Dailey followed as Albert let out a modulated whistle.

"None," Janix replied, seeing the predicament they were quickly finding themselves in.

The sound of the Harpy's ground thrusters roared, mixing with the now heavier rain, finally cutting off once Jen moved closer to the building. The vibration was disturbing years of dust and general rot.

"This is like some kind of odd version of Earth or something. I mean, it's not out of the realm of possibility. Maybe one of the syndicates or something. Look." Dailey pointed to the military star symbol. "That's damn near the old US Air Force symbol. If memory serves, it's from right when they transferred from the Army Air Corps; Becket would know more about all that, being a history nut."

Sparky shuffled over to the group after walking the interior perimeter of the building. "Too much rain. No scent outside of the building. Maybe some food would help?" he chuffed, adding in a few burps.

"Food doesn't help make your sense of smell better," Dailey replied, shaking his head. "Once Albert and Jen finish whatever scans they can, we will bunk down for the night or whatever time of day it is."

Albert, hearing this, chimed in. "According to the position of the sun when we hit orbit, it is high noon, partners."

"Sounds like the planet stays in the dark. Those damn clouds," Dailey said as Janix started doling out orders to his team.

CHAPTER 2

AIR FORCE BASE SKYLER

Wacky, wacky, powdered enhanced eggs, and what is left over of the Solarian bacy!" Albert announced as the two guards on duty stared at the pile of wrappers Sparky was quickly trying to nudge under the open rations crate.

A pronounced ding also informed Dailey and the others that there would be toast too. Albert had made breakfast.

Dailey, still in his armor, took a deep breath, activating his armor's systems to help push him to his feet. "Angel Six. How are you doing out there?"

There was a brief pause before Jen came over the comms. "Good. I hear Albert made breakfast. It isn't Moshan mush, is it?"

Smiling, the *Murphy*'s commander made his way to the spread, impressed by the effort. "No, I think he got bored or something. It's a full spread. Pop in, and we can figure out the rest of the plan. It also seems like he set up the comms relay. It looks like the transponder is connected and working."

The rap of knuckles on the main entrance hit before he could turn off the radio. Recentering, Dailey turned to Albert. "Spill it. Good news, bad news."

Albert handed Dailey a plate of food with a skimp portion of rehydrated bacon. Looking down, the sheen of grease on Sparky's face was an instant admission of guilt.

"Ah, yes. The news . . ." Albert drawled out. "Bad news first, as always. While we have the comm relay set up, it's not helping much. If we can project a break in this hideous weather, we should be able to get a signal through, but it will not be permanent."

The fact that these same comms relays were used to send messages to the edges of the galaxy was not only concerning but an issue unto itself. This meant something on the planet was either jamming the signal or the planet itself was causing an unhealthy level of electromagnetic interference. As always, Dailey leaned on the worst-case scenario of it being deliberate.

"Okay, good news?"

"I was able to use the relay to boost the scanner on the ship. We were able to map out a good portion of the surrounding area."

"That's great news. Let's see it," Dailey insisted as the other Nova Rangers lined up for chow. Low conversations and the sound of armor moving were making the place feel like an odd sort of home to the crew.

Albert pointed to a tablet sitting on a table lowered from the side of the vert rover. "Oh, and I lost one of the drones."

Motioning Jen and Janix to join him, Dailey set his plate, as well as a steaming cup of coffee, on the table, where he was joined by the others. Albert was making up for losing the main combat recon drone by cooking.

Janix connected the device to the small holo-projector Albert had also conveniently set out. Dailey was starting to get very suspicious of all the goodwill the AI was showing the team. That, or he was just bored or, even worse, nervous.

The map showed several buildings, including their own, highlighted by a brighter shade of green, leading to what appeared to be a runway. In the center, a control tower stood out like a lighthouse on the ocean's edge. Much like Earth, Solarians also followed the same seafaring tradition in their history.

"What about that building?" Dailey pointed toward a bulkier structure at the bottom of the tower.

"Looks like a command building of some type," Jen pointed out, running her fingers over all the satellite dishes and antennas on its roof.

"Albert," Dailey called, seeing no one left in line to serve. "Leftovers are free game."

Buckle, Lambert, and Woody started clawing at each other, trying to get to the small metal pans, only to be bested by Sparky, who was already on the table munching the skimp leftovers of bacon down. "Hello, everyone."

"First, thanks for the grub. We can talk about the why later. Were you able to scan for life?" Dailey asked, sitting back and taking a massive slurp of his coffee.

"Yes, there seem to be no formal life-forms on the surface. A few animals popped up, but as soon as this infernal rain picked back up, phased out of the sensors."

"That leads me to my next question. Why is that?" Dailey followed up as Mister Toaster's eyebrows furrowed.

"There is something in the atmosphere that is causing most of this. While not dangerous—well, for the most part—there is something organic in the rain. Or it could be nanobots, but that would be nearly impossible."

The shoveling of food stopped at the table.

"Organic?" Jen asked, thinking about her wet parka sitting on the back of the chair.

"Maybe. I would say Bellman would be a good candidate to figure it out, but my best guess is the planet was seeded."

"Like the mining syndicates do to revive a dead planet?"

"Yes, I think so," Albert said thoughtfully. "Or to kill it."

CHAPTER 3

THE LEFTOVERS

The rusty chain screeched as the vert rover pulled out of the warehouse, crackling loose rocks. After several hours of contemplation, the plan they formed was fairly straightforward: take the rover and the majority of the team to the tower's command building. Jen and two Nova Rangers would stay with the Harpy in case a quick exfil was needed. Once in the command building, the team would again work to reach the *Murphy*.

"The road's clear, sir," Coolio said, keeping focused on the road ahead as heavy, almost tropical rain splattered the windshield. "Looks like it was cleared at some point."

Dailey leaned forward, seeing several rusted-out vehicles pushed to the side. "Stay focused. Something . . ." Dailey ticked the top of his mouth with his tongue.

Albert came over the comms. "Hey, folks, looks like the drone is in the middle of the road. You'll have to cook your own dinner."

"You know that doesn't change things, right?" Dailey spoke up as Coolio stopped the rover.

"That's not what your dating manuals state," Albert replied.

Dailey shook his head.

"Where did you find these dating manuals?" he asked. The entirety of the team on board was now focused on the conversation.

"Found them when we were on Earth with the senator. I downloaded all sorts of stuff."

The team was visibly disappointed, having figured someone within their ranks was the owner.

"When was the book published?" Dailey followed.

"In 1951. Great stuff. Did you know that—"

Dailey cut Albert off. "Go get the drone."

The team watched as Albert walked in front of the rover while Dailey continued to click his tongue on the top of his mouth. "What's got you thinking, sir?" Coolio finally asked.

"I have the odd feeling we're being watched. Look at Albert. He's feeling the same thing," Dailey replied, seeing the AI scan the adjacent hollowed-out buildings.

Returning, Albert placed the drone on the floor while Lambert inspected the device. Coolio, not wanting to stay still any longer, continued the mission. Soon after, they found themselves directly in front of the target building.

Dailey stood up, nodding at Janix. "I want everyone to stay focused. We move fast, and we get into that building. Albert, I want you to lead the team. We need to keep someone here with Coolio."

"Lambert. Stay here and see if you can pull any data from that drone. Get it ready to send back out. The rest of you, move in teams of two. We're getting spread thin, but there's no need to rush."

Sparky walked up behind Albert as the AI, now installed in a modified Alurian battle droid, dismantled the lock to the thick double doors.

"Clear. Scans show no presence of life inside the structure."

Albert had been quick to note that once out of the rain, his sensors worked as they should. Janix launched a mini drone from his kit, which fluttered down the main hallway, mapping out the first floor of the buildings.

Sparky walked up to a security checkpoint, sniffing the area. "Remains."

"Well, that's a start," Dailey said, walking up to the uniformed, skeletal figure. A rifle sat beside the once-upon-a-time security guard, but that wasn't what caught Dailey's attention. The figure's uniform was a faded camouflage with pockets and a pair of rotted boots similar to old-style US military uniforms.

The *Murphy*'s commander had actually paid attention in military history classes, being a fan of the way things used to be on Earth prior to the Tectonic Wars with the Alurians and the first encounter with off-world civilizations. This was something he shared with First Sergeant Becket.

"Sparky, how long has that body been there?" Dailey asked while the war hound continued sniffing the body. Another odd thing Dailey had noticed was Sparky's lack of interest in claiming the planet for the Ham Republic, a pseudo government he and Albert had set up, even creating a national anthem and flag.

"Long time. Too long," Sparky came over the translator.

"Alright, let's keep moving. Janix, do we have the place mapped out yet?"

Janix looked down at the bar, which was now showing green. "Yes, sir. Sending the mapping data to everyone's HUDs."

A map of the first floor of the building sprang into existence on the bottom right of Dailey's heads-up display, showing a generic layout of the building. "Down this hall and to the right," he stated, rolling his shoulders before motioning Albert to proceed.

The team had indeed found the main control room, with large tracking monitors and desks with maps and radios sprawled out in a scene depicting what was likely world-ending chaos. But what they also noticed was the lack of any other bodies in the room.

Dust particles hung in the air like lazy snow that didn't know it was supposed to land on the ground. Cables from generators snaked around the floor, and hanging in the center of the room was a flight manifest with several call signs and pilot nicknames. Janix was already setting up light pillars around, evaporating the shadows once consuming the space.

"Must have been an air base," Dailey concluded as Sparky let out a yip from the far end of the room.

"Tracks. Recent. Leading out the back door," Sparky chuffed.

Dailey motioned for Janix. "Keep an eye on this door. We can check it after we figure this all out. Anything else from the mapping drone?"

"Not yet. It just made its way to the tower. It does appear this door leads to a set of stairs. That's about it for now," Janix replied, setting a light bar in front of the door.

Albert reached down, picking up one of the generator cables. "Might I suggest we hook up a mini power reactor? I can probably get the computers up and running."

Dailey glanced at the ancient, large, faded computers sitting in front of the monitors. "Probably?"

"I can't speak for the computers themselves, but with the power feed, a mini reactor will be more than enough to power this entire building."

"No lights. Just get the power on in here for now. I don't want to draw any attention to ourselves. I saw you in the road," Dailey said as Albert went to work on the power source, pulling out a plug from his actual square box of a home, now neatly inserted in the android's chest.

Lights flickered, then the smell of burning electronics wafted around the room as Albert feverishly worked not to overpower the old electronics. Finally, he stood, giving a thumbs-up.

"That should do it," Albert said before walking over to the main monitor and gingerly pressing the power button.

Unlike the tech they were used to, this computer was taking its time booting up. Lights started dimly flashing at several of the workstations before a radio hissed to life. The team froze as the same signal they had heard while in orbit started playing on repeat.

"Hello, this is Captain Sarah Thorton. I am at the following coordinates. We need help. The Shade is here."

Albert turned off the radio after letting it play twice more.

"How did the signal get to us in orbit if we can't talk to the *Murphy*?" Dailey asked.

Albert snickered.

"Satellites, duh. They beamed this up before the clouds got too thick or whatever. Hold on, there is a physical hard drive on that computer. I'm surprised these people even invented fire, by the looks of these computers," Albert stated before Mister Toaster's face went blank, something that happened when Albert was in deep thought or working through a puzzle. The truth of the matter was that the tech was so old that Albert was working out the best way to retrieve the data without frying the system.

Dailey walked to the large windows overlooking what he supposed was a runway. The dark tint of the clouds, the guck-covered glass, and the annoyingly ever-present rain hid most of the world outside the control room.

"Janix, do you see any—" Dailey was cut off when a massive creature with jaws wide open slammed into the protective glass. It stood to reason that due to this being an air base, the windows were built to withstand sonic booms, not to mention protect the command team inside.

Everyone turned while Albert continued to focus on the computer. The Nova Rangers all pointed their weapons at the creature trying to get inside the room, looking for its next meal.

"Shit, that thing is massive and pissed," Woody exclaimed, not having good luck with big, scary alien monsters.

"Yeah, and it wants to get in here," Buckle huffed.

"Coolio," Dailey barked over the comms. Their proximity to the building allowed them to talk.

"Sir."

"There's a bear or something trying to get into the command room on the far side of the building. I need you to engage," Dailey ordered. He could hear Coolio mouthing *Bear?* as the sounds of the rover's engine started seeping into the command room.

The glass started to spider as the next ramming charge let the team of Nova Rangers see just how big the creature's teeth were. At this rate, it would break through the glass in minutes, if not seconds.

Lights hit the grimy window as the flashes from the autopulse lasers on the roof of the rover spit out several precise volleys. The sounds of the vehicle's engine started seeping into the command room as its main weapon pounded the raging creature, only to pull a guttural roar from it.

"Sir," Coolio came back over the comms. "I think we have a bigger problem here. There're more of these things, and they're heading toward me."

The rest of the Nova Rangers didn't need any further invitation. Janix led the charge out of the command room while Dailey looked down at Sparky. "Stay here. Make sure Albert is safe while he's downloading the computer data."

Sparky chuffed, activating his helmet, which slid over his face.

Within seconds, the rest of the Nova Rangers had joined the fight. Janix had split the group into two fire teams, shown by the rapid deployment of the group. Years of training and drills made actions like this nothing more than muscle memory to the Nova Rangers.

Buckle and Jones both concentrated their fire on the oncoming creatures as the rounds from the Sauder rifles sliced into them like surgical blades, the glowing, superheated rounds cutting through massive chunks of fur from the raging bears, while Janix, now joined by Woody, focused on the initial beast raging on the front end of the rover.

What shocked Dailey as he focused on a third creature was their resilience. The one attacking the rover was missing a leg and half of its head by the time it started to slow down its attack. Glancing over at the second creature, its condition was just as bad, with massive chunks of it flying away, but not stopping its charge. If they couldn't stop it by firing directly to its chest, they would have to take out its legs.

Dailey quickly went into motion, activating his booster jets and firing into the third bear as he turned on his Moshan blade, pulling it out from its sheath. Glowing blue light erupted, creating an unexpected scene. Whatever was in the rain was reacting like blood under a black light, making it glow.

Seeing the charging bear hesitate in a clear mix of confusion and fear, Dailey took the opportunity to slam directly into the creature, firing his

Sauder rifle directly into its massive head while ramming his Moshan blade directly into its gaping mouth.

In one last attempt to either eat or take out its attacker, the beast flailed its arms, slinging Dailey back several feet, but power poured into his booster jets, keeping him upright.

Meanwhile, the two fire teams had focused on the last remaining battle bear, as they would now be called, and the entire fight was over in less than thirty seconds, all the concentrated fire from the Sauder rifles proving overwhelming for the creatures.

A short, breath-taking silence engulfed the scene as the Nova Rangers scanned the area for further threats. With no more creatures following behind, Dailey deactivated his booster jets, landing softly on the wet ground.

"Janix, status report," he quickly said.

All the signals on the far left of his HUD started flashing green, indicating they had all made it through the attack unscathed. Unfortunately, the same couldn't be said for the rover, as a large section of its front had been smashed in by the hulking beast. While it didn't affect the operation of the vehicle, it would not be winning any beauty contests with the cracked window by the driver's hatch, which ran down the metal frame. Not only was it ballistic glass, but it was also considered impact proof, proving the sheer strength of the creatures that had attacked them.

"Coolio, keep the rover in front of these windows. Janix, I want the rest of the team back inside. I'm not sure what drew them to us, but I'd rather not find out if there are any more."

The team moved without delay or further instruction. Water dripped from their armor as they stepped through the main entrance by the skeletal remains of the security guard. Face shields were opened and weapons checked as Janix shook his head.

"Those things were strong. I poured an entire magazine of Sauder rounds into the one, and it just kept coming," the Solarian platoon sergeant noted.

The Sauder rifle's magazine could hold several hundred mini fléchettes of titanium rounds that were superheated by a small reactor mounted in the stock, creating a straight-up saw of death. This meant the team had each pumped several hundred rounds in each one of the three creatures.

"Yeah," Dailey said, pointing at the massive gouge in his armor's shoulder plate. "That thing hit me like a Mack truck. Almost reminded me of a Moshan Drago."

The two men nodded, understanding the reference. Moshan Dragos were lizardlike creatures the size of a rhinoceros that had the disposition of the honey badger back on Earth.

The break after the encounter was short-lived. As the team walked back into the command center, three hooded figures stood around Albert and Sparky with the same weapons the security guard had dropped so many years ago, as well as an odd round satellite dish attached to the end of a pistol pointed directly at Albert's chest.

The team froze, seeing if their leader would choose violence over diplomacy, something Dailey often did.

"All right," Dailey said in a calming, almost regular tone. "Everybody calm down. I'm Captain Ben Dailey of the USF *Murphy*. We mean you no harm, but I can promise you this will not turn out in your favor."

Just as Dailey noticed one of the lights next to the door in the back of the command room was now out, another shadowed figure stepped forward. This was clearly the group's leader.

"I'm Tarik Johansson. We are the remaining inhabitants of Air Force Base Skyler. There are several of our soldiers surrounding this building," the still shadow-faced man said in a voice that had neither an accent nor any inflection.

By then, Dailey had figured that if the group wanted to attack, they would have already. "Sparky?"

The Alurian war hound chuffed, causing the three figures surrounding Albert to shift uneasily. Dailey, still wanting to play his cards close to his chest, cleared his throat, stepping forward while motioning for the others to stand down.

Sparky let out a light chuff that was only translated through the Nova Ranger's comms. It was nothing more than a dog showing its dissatisfaction with the situation, or as the others suspected, his dissatisfaction with the lack of ham.

"We good."

It was a short, simple, and to-the-point message. Dailey and the others knew if Sparky wanted to, he could easily incapacitate the other group, but also likely knew he would fry everything in the room.

Albert was simply playing dumb, letting the situation unfold.

Tarik stepped forward, this time lowering his hood. Pale skin that hadn't seen the sun since the dawn of man sat on a gaunt yet strong face. It was apparent they had skipped a few meals.

"Where are you from?" Tarik asked, not taking his eyes off Dailey.

Figuring the truth was the best solution, Dailey set his rifle on the table beside him. "I am from a planet called Earth. My large associate over there is from a planet called Solaria. We were on a mission and were sent here accidentally."

Tarik almost let a small grin perk the end of his lips. "No one makes their way to Teras accidentally." Following Dailey's lead, the man also set his rifle down on the control panel beside him. "Let me make that statement clearer. No one comes to Teras."

Dailey, seeing the conversation was going in the correct direction, glanced over at Albert. "Do you mind if your counterparts stop pointing their weapons at our teammates?"

Tarik contemplated the request just as Albert clearly got tired of having some kind of electric device pointed at his chest. In a blur of whirling motion, Albert activated the electromagnets in his right hand at laserlike speeds, pulling together a pile of barrels and butts, followed by his two mini laser Gatling guns immediately sliding over his shoulders and clicking in place. Four red dots emanating from the targeting tracker smacked their newfound friends in the chest.

If an android could suck all the air out of the room, Albert had just done so.

Releasing their weapons with a clatter on the floor, Albert pointed at Dailey. "Good cop. Well . . . sometimes." He pointed at himself. "Bad cop." Sparky let out a light chuff. "Cops," Albert added, also pointing at the Alurian war hound.

Tarik, seeing he was outclassed by Albert alone, held his hands up in placation. "We were getting to that. Valen, Bella, Kael, stand down."

"That was either extremely rude or very polite," Albert suggested, standing up to his full height while every single one of the people dressed in old-style fatigues stared at the AI.

"Polite," Tarik responded. Albert's weapons quickly receded as the red dots shot up and out of sight.

"Fair enough," Albert replied as Sparky took a sniffing step forward.

"Now that that's out of the way," Dailey started. "I have to admit we are at your mercy. To a point," the man emphasized, ensuring the group in front of them understood that violence was always on the table.

Shaking his head, Tarik motioned for his team to retrieve their weapons after gaining an approving nod from Dailey. "I'm not sure how you got power to this building or got those computers working, but we have about one hour till those ravers come back. And when I say come back, I mean dozens of them."

Coolio took that moment to chime in over the columns. "Is everything all right in there?"

"For now. I think we just met the inhabitants of the Air Force base. Let us know if anything changes out there or if you see anyone else approach," Dailey said, turning back to Tarik.

"I have to admit, I'm at a loss for words," Tarik started as the woman of the group, Bella, snickered. This was a team, and the man was clearly never at a loss for words. "How did you get a ship in the air without being shot down?"

"We came in from the atmosphere. Like I said, we have a ship in orbit." Dailey walked closer to the man. "You said no one else has ever been here. How do you know about any air defenses in the area?"

"We have seen things in the air before. They usually don't make it to land. Listen," Tarik said in a moderately defeated tone. The truth of the matter was that the man and the rest of his people had been living in an underground shelter for generations, only coming topside when needed. "I speak for our people. It is clear we are also at a disadvantage. It's also clear if you wanted to, you could've taken us out as soon as you walked into the room. We can offer you a place to stay for the night."

The others with the man glanced at each other pensively, uncomfortable with the situation.

"We can discuss this with the others when we get back. They are clearly not Creare."

That raised Albert's and everyone else's antennas as high as they could go.

"You know about the Creare?" Dailey snapped back as Tarik nodded.

"They did this to our planet."

"Yes, yes, yes," Albert scoffed. "I just downloaded all your information from the computer databases. I'm fairly certain even you would like to know some of this. Captain Dailey, if I may?"

"Not like anything's ever stopped you before," Dailey huffed.

"While several of the systems in the building are fried, I should be able to use the antennas and our relay station to communicate with the *Murphy*. I'm not saying it's going to be pretty, but we can at least open a line."

"How long will that take?" Dailey asked.

Janix motioned to the Nova Rangers, who walked over to the other three inhabitants of the Air Force base. Soldiers knowing soldiers gave each other quick fist bumps and head nods as names were exchanged.

"Ten minutes. A few to talk, and then we can go with our brand-new super buddies here. Oh, before you ask, I've already sent Jen a message, as well as Coolio, updating them on the situation," Albert spit out, clearly knowing that time was of the essence.

"I know you all scouted one of the warehouses. If it helps you make your decision, once ravers get a smell or taste for something, they don't stop. It will not be safe for you to go back," Tarik stated in finality.

The man was telling the truth, and was wearing it on his face. On the back end, Albert and Sparky would've already sniffed them out for having an elevated heart rate or whatever calculations the AI did when telling if somebody was fibbing, as Albert put it.

"Okay. Jen," Dailey requested over the comms, not caring about military formalities.

Jen's voice crackled back. "I . . . hea . . . you. Broken, but readable . . ."

Dailey turned to Tarik. "Our ship is by the warehouse. If we stay low, will we draw any unwanted attention?"

The man scowled. "I can't say for sure if you've not already drawn any unwanted attention, but as long as you stay only a few feet off the ground, you should be fine."

"Albert," Dailey started without hesitation. "Get the comms link set up. Jen, I want you to bring the Harpy to our location. Stay as low to the ground as physically possible, even if that means skipping the landing pads off the deck."

As usual, Jen knew it wasn't up for debate. Dailey had related information and had done so for a very specific reason. "Roger, sir."

Dailey turned back to Albert, pointing him in the general direction of the vert rover to grab the comms relay. The main transponder would stay in the warehouse. "I need you back in here in three minutes," he instructed as the AI sprinted out of the room, understanding the timeline.

"We watched you fight the ravers. It would've taken an entire platoon of our people to take three of them out," Tarik said, giving up more information than his counterparts were probably comfortable with him doing.

Like Dailey, he was a leader. He was in control of the souls of other people and understood when he was having a rational conversation with a rational person.

"I'll see what we can do to help. On the back end of all this, we're going to need your help," Dailey replied, thinking of the information they needed in order to get their gate drive reprogrammed.

The crew of the *Murphy* and the *Crow* alike had spent literally all their time working through ways to reprogram the gate drive in order to travel back to Asher. Without knowing their current location, there would be no return trip. Albert, in a fit of frustration over not being able to solve the puzzle, had locked himself in his room, watching Solarian romance movies until it about fried his circuit boards with just how terrible the damn things were, according to the follow-up review he'd posted on the *Murphy's* update boards.

Buckle ran back into the room as Albert and the rest of the Nova Rangers went to work setting up the comms link. Within five minutes, Albert handed Dailey an old-style microphone.

"It's showtime!" the AI exclaimed.

"*Murphy*. This is Viper Six, over?"

A staticky hum eventually morphed into Becket's voice. Pearl was in the background, clearly not having a good day. "Loud and freaking clear, sir. We were just about to launch a group from the attack wing."

While the communication was slightly hazy, it was clear enough to talk. "Nothing comes to the atmosphere and flies unless we say so. I don't know all the details, and I don't have a lot of time, but there's some kind of weird defense system or something that we luckily got through. We met a group of local inhabitants, and according to them, we're the first set of people to make it through in a long time, if not ever."

Becket, knowing Dailey was short on time, turned to Pearl.

"Sir," Pearl started. "Would this be a viable line of communication moving forward?"

Dailey turned to Tarik. "Once we get through a night cycle, we can come back up, and it will be safe."

Keying up the radio again, Dailey pulled his thoughts together. "We're going to be offline for twelve hours. As soon as the sun crests on our location, we'll get back on this net. The inhabitants mentioned the Creare. We discussed setting up by one of the three moons in orbit. I would recommend getting out of sight and keeping any unnecessary systems offline. I don't know the whole situation here, but I can tell you we will likely be able to get the information we need. To the edge," Dailey finalized, handing the radio back to Albert.

"To the edge," Pearl replied as Tarik nodded.

In the distance, the sound of the Harpy's thrusters growled, drowned out by the hardening rain.

It was time to go.

CHAPTER 4

THE *MURPHY'S* CROW

Bodies shuffled while screens beeped and flashed. The bridge of the *Murphy* was abuzz, with everyone from the engineering team to the entire targeting and communication sections working on the limited information Dailey had provided.

"First Sergeant?" Pearl asked as Becket rubbed his eternally stubbled chin.

"I say we keep the ships connected and not send out any more patrols. If Hontz and Bellman say we can set both ships down on the moon, then I say we do it. It can't be any different than being planetside," Becket growled in contemplation, going through the tactical scenarios attached to what he considered the significantly smarter people on board. While intelligent, he also knew they frequently lacked tactical experience when making recommendations.

"Hontz, Barthelo," Pearl called, as the two men walked over.

Barthelo's thick New York accent always grated on the Solarian executive officer of the *Murphy*. She had even suggested a translator at one point.

"Ma'am," Ensign Barthelo said, winking. His lead officer took over the conversation before the young man said something he shouldn't. Which, in all fairness, was never intended to offend the ship's second in command, only next to Becket.

"Ma'am," Hontz replied, nodding at Becket.

"If we touch down on the moon, how long will it take us to get back in space and be able to maneuver?" Pearl asked. Bellman, overhearing the conversation, also joined in.

Hontz glanced at Bellman before talking. "Bellman and our team were just talking about possible scenarios. If we keep the ships together, about three minutes at max thrust."

Bellman cut in. "The *Murphy* can get into the fight much faster than the *Crow*, and even more so if the two ships aren't connected."

"Undock from the stable and have both ships land close to each other?" Pearl asked, going through the thought process.

"Yes," Hontz replied.

Bellman again spoke up. "It might be a better move to have the two ships on completely different moons. Or at least far away enough not to draw attention?"

Becket grinned.

"Sounds like you are all on the right path. Or you've laid off the rum. It makes sense; we want to keep the ships together, but it would be a force multiplier, or even hell, a backup plan. Ma'am, I think we should take the team's recommendation."

The engineering team, as well as Bellman, stood a little taller. "We could even split the attack wing up. Keep half on each ship. If something happens or someone shows up, we could use this to our advantage," Hontz suggested to an agreeing leadership team.

"Very well. Make preparations. While we are all here, I want to talk over a few things. We've all listened to the transmission. I didn't take away that we are under any immediate threat, but Captain Dailey believes we are. Does anyone else have any thoughts?" Pearl asked, making sure she wasn't missing anything. That was the thing with tight, cohesive teams. The leadership listened to their crew and, with that, earned their respect, a trait Dailey had insisted on his leadership team having.

Bellman, as always, spoke up, raising his hand as if asking for permission to go to the bathroom. "The more I look at this, the more I believe us being here is not random. I was talking to Dorax earlier, and he believes Director Prescott and the Ocess Mining Syndicate sent us here for a reason."

"Yeah, I have a few things I want to say to him when I see him," Becket growled. "Any ideas?"

"Something to do with the planet, more than likely. With the issues Dailey stated, I wouldn't doubt they've been here at some point and either didn't find what they were looking for or ran into trouble," Bellman said, turning to Pearl. "We didn't see any ship debris on our initial scans. Maybe we should look at the surfaces of the moons?"

Pearl nodded. "Sound recommendation. I wish Albert were here." The crew, while knowing they had grown dependent on the AI, also knew they needed to be ready in case something happened to Albert.

"Ma'am," Becket started, "I'm not sure we're chasing the *Void Reaper* anymore. Or maybe Prescott threw us a bone, and he knows that ship may end up here, or in the system, at least."

"I thought about that," Pearl said, bringing up a chart of the system from their initial scans. "Maybe we're missing something. Six planets, and we have been able to identify twelve moons so far. No signs of a space station or any other ships. What we do know is that someone from one of the mining syndicates has been here, or at least the gate drive installed on this ship, which means it likely did so while involved in mining operations."

Becket again rubbed his chin, sounding like someone spreading butter on a crisp piece of toast. "We don't need to get too far from the ships, but nothing stops us from sending out a few sensor drones." The man paused. "It's settled. We will scan the moons and start looking for signs of mining operations or space debris. If anything, it will give us something to do while we wait. King!"

"Yes, First Sergeant," the ship's communications officer replied, jumping up from his station.

"I want someone monitoring the net twenty-four seven. I want all communications to go through the *Murphy*. Let Dorax know. I want full write-ups in thirty minutes. After that, we'll meet with both crews and get moving. I want to be settled before the twelve-hour cycle is up."

Salutes were given as the crew scattered to their respective stations to start planning the move. While simple on the surface, assigning attack fighters and subsequent crews, including having them transfer ships, would take several hours.

CHAPTER 5

THE TASK AT HAND

Stale air and damp metal walls greeted Dailey and the others as they made their way several stories down via creaking metal industrial stairs under the command and control room. Not wanting to risk fully splitting his team, Dailey had opted for everyone to go underground. They would leave two Nova Rangers at the halfway point to pull security.

Albert, in a last-minute stroke of genius, set up a handful of small beacons from the Harpy to a transponder he mounted on his chest. At the same time, the drop ship's sensors would continue scanning the area, giving real-time updates to the group via their tablets through a live video feed.

The closer Dailey watched the leftover people of a world long since dead, the more he noticed the slight differences in their appearance. They all had brown eyes and dark hair, contrasting with their pasty complexions. Bella, the female of the group, was the exception, having deep brown skin that was still lacking from any exposure to sunlight.

When all together, their jawlines and noses looked as if they belonged in a family portrait. Over the centuries, the remaining inhabitants had likely all become related. While clearly in a dire situation, they had an air of hope and kinship often shared by those who suffered and celebrated together.

Tarik and the other members of his team were shocked at the level of organization and tech the Nova Rangers possessed. Dorian Zander, one of the soldiers from the air base, had proven himself to be the curious mind of the group, and was working to figure out how Albert was doing what he was doing.

"So," Dorian started as Albert set up the final connection to the Harpy. "You are an artificial intelligence?" the man asked, not knowing what the term fully represented.

"The acceptable term these days is a self-motivated, awesome, robotic titan," Albert replied as Mister Toaster's face morphed into a grin.

Knowing military slang and its love of acronyms, Dorian let out a "Hmm. The SMART?"

"Oh look, we have a winner," Albert said, powering up the small tablet, now showing the scene outside the command room in front of the Harpy. "Of course, I'm an AI. I understand from reviewing your old files that those types of things aren't really part of the conversation here yet. Or were."

Dorian considered the statement, including the odd humor coming from Albert. In reality, Sparky was the one judging the man's lack of knowledge of things outside their dying world.

"Does every military team have an AI?" Dorian asked.

"Nope. I'm one of a kind. At least that we know of; I'm a little foggy on that one. My counterpart, Sparky here, and I would like to know if you have any romance novels or TV shows on this planet? Picture box, if that's easier to assimilate."

Dorian looked confused, slowly nodding. "I believe Bella reads some of those. As for TV, we have some old reels in the Vault. We aren't that behind the times. I think . . ."

At this, Tarik ended the conversation, calling for the man. "Kael, go down to the main level and tell the others the situation. Take Bella with you. The rest of us will stay here for the night." He turned to Valen, the hard-nosed soldier of the group. "Set up here for the night."

Dailey, seeing the group splitting up, pulled out a comms link. "Here, give this to your people. If they need to reach out to us or vice versa, they can use this."

The comms link might as well have been alien tech by the look on Bella's face as Tarik smiled at the woman before she left. Dailey picked up on this as Jen gave him a grin, also seeing the interaction. Meanwhile, Janix motioned for the rest of his team to settle in for the night, then Tarik, Dailey, Jen, and Janix walked to the far end of the old storage room where Albert and Sparky had set up a small area to watch the cam from the Harpy. A set of doors secured by an electronic lock led further down, and Valen sat by it with his rifle on his lap, not giving anything away.

"Albert," Dailey said as Tarik pulled off his vest, setting it on the floor. "What can you tell us about the data you pulled from the computers?"

"Where to start, boss," Albert drawled out as Tarik sat down on one of the small portable chairs in the room.

"Did the computers have any information on when the Creare arrived?" Tarik asked, giving Albert a good starting point. Unknowingly, he had probably saved the others from hearing the maintenance cycles of the toilets on the air base.

"Ah, yes. A good amount. Unfortunately, that is toward the end of the data line. But yes," Albert said. The group all watched the small tablet screen as Albert dove in.

The information had been entered in the form of chronological logs and personal command entries—the type of thing Albert loved, as it was organized, unlike the massive zettabyte data dumps the Federation kept sorted by no less than ten different data centers.

The record of Elera and her love Zayden was front and center in the logs, as well as the subsequent destruction of one of the Creare ships. He even noted their names had been scratched off the flight board with a star next to them. Tarik had not been fully aware of the story, having only heard passed-down rumors. This in itself opened up a massive opportunity that Dailey and the others would explore.

Making Albert's information dump even more interesting was Tarik's complete awe at the gaps in his and his people's own history, touching a nerve close to home for the *Murphy*'s commander. The thought had never crossed Tarik's mind that an actual Creare ship may, in fact, be sitting on the ground somewhere on the planet's surface.

This showed the gaps in the two civilizations' understanding of just how long certain tech could last. That, and how to access it.

In the end, Albert was able to paint a picture of the final days of the air base before the remaining people went underground. The Vault, luckily for its inhabitants, was one of five command bunkers for their government leadership, showing how prepared the select few were for such an event. An event that they may or may not have survived, opening even more questions about the other bunkers.

As for the final days of the personnel of Air Force Base Skyler, they had held on for another month, fighting a ground force that was not elaborated on due to the logs being cut short.

By the end of the data logs, Albert had concluded the Creare had either seeded the planet to destroy all sentient life, or for other unknown reasons. But what reasons? That was the question that needed to be answered.

Of particular interest was the amount of information the remnants of old Teras had collected on the purple clouds and the fog, as they called it. According to the records, the Creare had several vessels in orbit before leaving, releasing the chemical that had, for hundreds of years, continued to blanket the planet. After that, it was all up for debate. What happened to the ships? And even more pressing, why hadn't they come back?

Tarik leaned back, letting out centuries' worth of pent-up questions in a long sigh. The man was holding back his emotions, hearing a history he had yet to fully understand.

"I knew some of this," Tarik started, now hearing Albert filling in several intergalactic gaps. "But why would none of you, or anyone, reach out to us first? I mean . . ."

"If it makes you feel any better, Earth had the same issue, but with a different enemy," Dailey said as Albert interjected.

"If you want to get technical, I believe the Creare are no friend of the Alurians either."

Janix leaned forward. "Is there something you want to tell us, great one?"

"Well, now that I put everything in perspective, it seems there is one common theme: No one likes the Creare, duh."

Sparky, by now, was snoring at Dailey's feet. "Tarik," Dailey said, shuffling his foot out from under the hound. "What have your people been doing all this time?"

"Surviving." The man's shoulders dropped. "Our forefathers were in an underground vault for countless years until the main entrance unlocked one day. We're not sure why, but it appeared to be on some type of timer. Since then, we have lost many people learning what we can about the surface. Between the never-moving clouds and that damn unrelenting rain, things have been difficult. We have had to live off the stores kept in the Vault. And there is one more thing."

Jen glanced at Dailey, knowing that was never good. "What else?" she asked, the day's stress showing in her eyes.

"There are other things topside. We call them Shades. They have, for the most part, stayed away from the base, but if you travel outside the gates, you will run into them. I can also state that we don't know much of what is going on outside the surrounding city limits," Tarik said, also showing signs of the late hour.

"Well," Dailey huffed, showing signs of a long day too. "I'm fairly certain we can handle the Shade. Albert, anything else on our actual location?"

Tarik cocked his head, not even fully knowing what the Shade were.

"Yes, that's the interesting part. I would say this planet's knowledge of the cosmos is close to Earth's around the time you supposedly landed on the moon. Totally bogus, by the way."

"Meaning?" Dailey followed, too tired to remember to put his question into context.

"I have enough to get us out of the surrounding systems far enough to find something familiar. Maybe . . . Perhaps . . . If there is a Creare ship here, it would most certainly have the navigational data we need," Albert replied as Sparky stirred awake, only lifting his head to yip.

The translator on speaker asked a simple Sparky question: "Is there ham?"

Tarik furrowed his brows. "Ham? I've heard stories of ham; we used to have it in the rations. That's long gone, but I can't speak for the rest of the planet."

Another yip as Sparky's head dropped back to the floor. "Then there's hope."

Dailey refocused. "What's in the Vault? I'm asking because Albert here can work miracles if you have any subsystems or computers."

"Magic," Albert corrected, flaring his sharp metallic fingers.

"There are a few computers, but they run the geothermal power systems. Maybe a few computers still work, but most have long since been out of commission. I'm not going to split hairs here," Tarik said, using a familiar expression, showing the similarities between the two civilizations. "There are one hundred and thirteen people here. Most of us are trained as soldiers. Some are underground farmers. Others are focused on science, medicine, and hunting. But we are coming close to our useful shelf life. The last generation was two hundred, and the one before that four hundred. I'm making the call to help you, as we need help here."

Jen and Janix both looked at Dailey, waiting for him to make the call.

"Well, Tarik, the way I see it, we need to find that ship. You help us do that, and we will help in any way we can. From what I can tell, one or two of our portable fusion generators could power you for decades, if not longer. We can figure all that out later."

"Is there a possibility that if everyone here agrees, we can leave with you?" Tarik asked as Jen grinned. "I wouldn't say anything yet, but it may be necessary, even if the others don't want to go."

"You know, sir, we need a full crew for the *Crow*," she said to Dailey, cranking up the smile.

CHAPTER 6

BREAKING BREAD

Yawns and sleepy eyes stirred as old metal cots creaked. The smell of fresh coffee being made wafted in front of Dailey, who was in the same half-awake state he'd remained in overnight.

"Whoever is making coffee, I could kiss you," Dailey yawned.

Albert scoffed. "These lips aren't made for you," he said, quoting one of the romance novels he'd downloaded while on Earth. Jen let out a little snicker as the other Nova Rangers all moved toward the coffee pot like hungry zombies slowly lumbering toward fresh meat.

"You have coffee?" Tarik asked excitedly.

"Yup," Dailey replied, holding out a blind hand, only to have Janix place a cup of go juice in it. "Promoted to sergeant major of the forces of the Ham Republic," he joked.

Sparky nodded, barking. "Acceptable position."

With the light banter out of the way, Tarik reached out for a cup of coffee, chugging it as if it were his last drop of water while stuck in the desert. Steam came from the man's lips as he breathed out. "Mmm, we haven't had coffee since I was a teenager. Rats got into the stores at some point."

"We will see what we can do about that," Dailey stated, noticing he wasn't the only one who had slept in his armor last night. On board the *Murphy*, they kept fresh stores of coffee, but also had the ability to synthesize the stuff via chemical compounding in the event of an emergency, which, to any proper military person, lack of coffee represented such a situation.

Albert checked the sensor feed one last time. "Seems like we didn't have any company last night. We should be able to communicate with the *Murphy* in roughly thirty minutes."

"Good," Dailey said, watching Valen sniff the cup Tarik handed him.

Tarik turned to Dailey. "If you're good, I would like to call my people and discuss our conversation from last night. Maybe not about the leaving part, but if everyone is in agreement, we can take you into the Vault."

"Why the sudden change of heart?" Dailey asked while the man grinned at his second cup of coffee.

"I thought about everything we talked about last night. If there is a chance to get information from the computers, it can only help."

Happy with the reasoning, Dailey called the entire group into a huddle. He motioned for Valen to join them, who had yet to move since arriving, from what he could tell.

"Everyone, freshen up and be ready to move in fifteen minutes. I want Albert to go with Tarik's people to check out the computers after we make contact with the *Murphy*. He can take two people," Dailey said, motioning toward two Nova Rangers standing close by. "The rest of us, I want topside."

With the simple orders doled out, the team started to split up, picking up their gear. Tarik sent Valen to get Bella and Dorian. The group huddled in the corner, discussing Tarik's decision.

While Dailey felt as if he were snooping, he always verified first, then trusted. Putting his helmet on, he activated his echo booster, giving him a front-row seat to their conversation. After being satisfied that Bella was confirming the larger group's acceptance of his decision, Dailey joined the group.

"There's still some coffee left. Janix has the container," Dailey said, making a peace offering to Tarik and Valen's crew.

Same as the others, their eyes shot open. "Thanks," Dorian replied, nodding at Tarik.

"Yes, after the transmission is sent, you're welcome to see the Vault." Tarik glanced at the Nova Rangers behind Dailey. "I overheard a few of your team members talking about going out?"

"Master Sergeant Janix wants to go back to the warehouse to see if those creatures decided to go there instead. We stayed there overnight, as mentioned, the night prior. We're only taking a team. The rest will stay here and go with you. Our pilot is going to stay on board the drop ship in case anything happens. You're in good hands with Albert."

Lights flickered on, the cracked glass reminding the group of the very real danger lurking outside. According to Tarik, the ravers only came out during their night cycle, which wasn't saying much, as the planet was perpetually gray and dark regardless of the time of day.

"And we are live," Albert said, handing the receiver to Captain Dailey.

"*Murphy*, this is Viper Six," Dailey said as the radio crackled to life. Albert, not happy with the staticky signal, switched the voice net over to his voice modulator. The speaker was significantly clearer than the ancient one setting on the desktop.

"Read you loud and clear, sir," Becket's voice boomed.

Dailey held up the tablet Albert had connected to the communications array of the building's roof. "Albert wants us to go to the game lobby, just in case," Dailey stated, punching a couple of buttons on the tablet before the channel immediately reopened.

This was a little trick that Albert had devised in order to counteract General Ran and the Alurian decryption systems. While often able to crack the most advanced encrypted messages, they were no match for old video game lobbies. Sometimes, it was the simplest things that got overlooked.

Even Communications Officer King, knowing what Albert was doing, had stated that without knowing the exact game that he had modulated and the exact lobby, not to mention the ancient frequency, it would be nearly impossible to decrypt the message.

"Sir, how are things going down there?" Becket asked, with Pearl's voice in the background.

"We have a lot of information to relay. Albert's going to send a debrief up. Long story short, we might just have a way to figure out where we are and how to get back on track. In the meantime, there's a couple of things we need to look at."

"Go ahead, sir. Everyone's here listening," Pearl spoke up.

"First, I want you to send a drone into the atmosphere. Nice and slow. According to Tarik, who is the leader of the group here, there's some kind of orbital defense system in place. I have a suspicion it's not the clouds, either."

"Roger, sir," Bellman said, his heavy breathing likely annoying Becket and Pearl. The man had run all the way from the chow hall to the bridge.

"Next, you'll see it in the debrief, but there's a Creare ship somewhere on the ground. That's the prize. Once we figure out whatever is going on in the sky, I want you to have an assault package ready to send. Enough weapons for a platoon. A couple of suits of armor, and if there's any room, as much coffee and additional rations as you can send."

"Sir?" Becket responded back, wanting to know the reasoning.

"We've made some new friends down here, and they need some help. In return, they are going to help us. Use the leftover weapons from Fourth Foot. Nothing that was personally assigned, just whatever we replace the Sauder rifles with," Dailey said, not wanting to disturb any of the gear from the Nova Rangers lost from the now-disbanded Fourth Foot.

While most of the remaining platoon had stayed behind on Asher, a few of the other's gear, including their backup secondary sets of armor, were still on board.

"That's a good copy. Sounds like this thing will need to be a dud," Becket confirmed.

"Yup," Dailey quickly replied, glancing over at the crack of glass one more time, seeing the rain starting to pick back up outside. "Just get it in a set orbit to let it thump down. If there is some type of weapon system monitoring the skies, it will drop to the ground like a meteor."

Pearl cleared her throat, letting the others on the bridge know it was her time to talk. "We're splitting the *Murphy's Crow* into two separate orbiting locations. We've sent a few sensors out to check for old debris or any other reasons as to why we are here."

Albert gave a thumbs-up, thinking the exact same thing.

"Sounds like you guys have it handled up there. Listen, we're going to be going out within the next two days to look for this thing. We need to figure out a way to get off this planet. Tarik?" Dailey motioned for the man to walk over to the communicator.

"Everyone, this is Tarik Johansson. He's the group's leader down here. I thought it would be best for you to hear about the situation in the skies from him."

"Hello," Tarik said, slightly nervous, finally leaning into the conversation. "Over the years, other things have been in the skies, but none of them, to our knowledge, have ever made it down. That is, until now. It could've been perfect timing or an event we don't know about happening elsewhere. It does appear to be a weapon. What I can say is we are at ground zero for what happened to Teras."

The crew onboard the *Murphy* all took in the message, thinking about possible scenarios.

"Good to meet you," Pearl spoke for the group. "We will take your information, and Albert's, into consideration. Captain Dailey." She shifted topics, "About the assault package, I do recall Peron Two. We dropped several drop ships through the atmosphere directly into the planet's oceans, and then activated them after deploying shock parachutes."

"I didn't think of that," Dailey pondered. "Albert, do the math."

Shock parachutes were simple yet effective parachutes that activated close to the ground. While it generally meant damage to the ships, it would allow them to get to the surface in case of an emergency.

"It may be an option," Albert started. "With the amount of rain and the electrostatic—"

Dailey cut Albert off before he went into a forty-five-minute-long exposition about rain coefficient and wind drag.

"We received the debrief package. Are we going to be able to talk further today?" Pearl asked, wondering if they would have to wait for another twelve or twenty-four-hour cycle before touching base.

"I'm going to keep a few people here monitoring the radio. As soon as you're ready to launch that drone, let us know. I want to get that done today. The planet's not suited for long-term operations, if you know what I mean."

Becket turned to Pearl and nodded, taking over the conversation. The main comms panel on the *Murphy* dinged, having received the data download package. "Sir," Becket's gravelly voice came over the radio. "Be safe down there. I will have that drone ready to launch and headed into orbit in about five hours. That's about our planned movement time out of orbit."

Satisfied with the conversation, Dailey nodded to Albert, who ended the transmission. Mister Toaster's face once again sprang up on the small viewscreen as Janix went into motion, giving out orders to his team.

"Sir," Janix said as Jen zipped up their flight suits. "We are ready to head out. I'm leaving Buckle and Jones. Lambert, Coolio, Woody, and myself are going with."

Sparky chuffed. "Me too. Must protect Dailey."

Tarik and his counterparts were still trying to compute the talking, thinking dog that was previously sitting on his hind legs, letting his asteroids air out from sleeping in his armor.

"If you're good, Valen will join you," Tarik spoke up while Dailey looked to Janix for approval. It was his team and his call to make.

Janix walked over to the man, handing him his Sauder rifle, knowing there was another on board the vert rover that Coolio was now pulling out of the back of the Harpy. Valen was clearly the military brain of the group, quickly checking the action of the rifle and holding it up to Janix. "What's the light mean?"

"If it's green, it's time to get mean. It's only loaded with standard hyper rounds, so no worries about setting the base on fire," Janix instructed as Valen flipped a switch, turning the indicator to orange.

"Fair enough."

Janix grinned. The Solarian loved teaching soldiers, especially ones who were fast learners. "That's the *oh, shit* setting, as they say on Earth."

"In case I want to set the base on fire?" Valen asked. Janix nodded.

"Exactly. See how easy that was, Woody," Janix joked. The man was still a low-ranking member of the team and for good reason. It had taken him days to fully understand the initial training on the fancy rifles.

Woody lowered his face shield, the hulking drop armor making the Nova Ranger look like a devil straight from hell.

CHAPTER 7

THE SHADE

Red peeked out from the purple clouds, created by the overabundance of constant lightning spidering through the sky. The lack of thunder was unnerving as the vert rover pulled in front of the warehouse.

The space the entrance gate once occupied now resembled a tin can that had been opened with a dull axe. There was no light to cast shadows, making the entrance to the warehouse even more ominous. Massive chunks of door were bent inward from the sheer force of what Valen informed them were ravers. When asked how many, the man simply shrugged.

Specialist Jenna Jones had taken the time to suit Valen with a few extra pieces of gear, playing her version of a makeover. The man now had a partial tactical helmet often used by pilots, a fully armored chest plate able to accommodate a comms link, and a handful of grenades she'd promised to show him how to use later. The entire group of Nova Rangers, including Dailey, had let out a round of *ohs* and *ahs* once she was done while Sparky looked at the woman skeptically, wondering if he needed to adjust the love-triangle chart he and Albert meticulously kept on board the *Murphy*.

That moment had solidified Valen's initial acceptance into the group.

Dailey, seeing it was time to get to work, stood up, hunching down while in full armor to fit.

"Any chance they're still in there?"

Valen cocked his head. "I doubt it."

"Coolio, the rain's not that thick. Scan the building," Dailey instructed as the team started preparing to exit the vehicle.

Valen was shocked at the level of tech that continued to appear around him. A 3D rendering of the building came into focus on the command screen on the side wall of the rover, where Janix sat as the team leader.

"It doesn't appear that anything is inside, sir," Janix announced, rubbing his smooth head. Out of all their conversations, Tarik and the others hadn't brought up the slight differences in not only size but also the overall look of the Solarian.

"Valen?" Dailey asked, his visor still up. The man had a concerned look on his face.

"This was definitely ravers," the man said before Woody cut in, now having a fondness for naming unidentified monsters in space, a habit that had started with the big, scary-ass space spider that almost killed the man.

"Battle bears," Woody proclaimed as the others agreed.

"Not sure what that is, but as mentioned, there are things here we call the Shade. I believe you heard about them in your message," Valen replied as Dailey urged him to continue.

"This is going to sound crazy, but they are there and not there. Like ghosts."

"Like ghosts?" Dailey repeated. The man nodded.

"We've been trying to study them for years, but all we can figure out is they are somehow tied to the rain. Just be careful and use as much light as you can. They seem to not like that very much. But that's not what attracted the ravers. It's the noise and, probably, the command center being powered on. We figure they can sense electricity or something like that. Possibly smell, if the rain is light enough."

"Woody, you and Lambert load EMP rounds." Dailey paused to give an explanation to Valen. "Electromagnetic pulse rounds. I had a little experience with my Moshan blade that I didn't mention earlier. If they are tied to the rain, then the rounds will give them a little shock."

Valen leaned forward. "We will see."

With that, the entire crew went into motion. Coolio would stay in the rover while the others explored the building. The group would split into two teams, with Dailey taking Valen and Lambert with him. Janix and Woody would make up the second fire team.

The two teams split off, each taking one side of the mangled door. "Lights on," Janix ordered as the lights on the Nova Ranger's helmets all sprang to life. The gray-blue haze lingering inside the building kept them from seeing the back wall.

Dailey took the first step as Valen, following what training he had, brought up the rear, only steps behind Lambert. "Let's stay in the center, no splitting up. We focus on the left. You focus on the right," Dailey said over the comms, his HUD slowly outlining the interior of the room.

The team walked in tandem, focusing on their assigned sectors. The crates that had once been neatly stacked as if in their final resting place now lay ripped apart. Random pieces of bulky equipment and weapons similar to the ones the inhabitants of the base had lay strewn apart and, in most cases, crushed.

The vehicle Dailey had been hoping to still be in one piece, while damaged, was in a moderate state of usability. That was, if the team could get it in working order. While they hadn't discussed it, Dailey assumed Tarik and his people didn't explore outside the base not only due to the danger but also from a lack of mobility.

Dailey turned back to the shadows on the far end of the room before snapping his head to the left. "You see that?" Dailey asked as Sparky started growling.

"Negative, sir," Lambert replied. Valen simply said no, now having a comms link in the borrowed helmet.

"I could have sworn I saw something move," Dailey mumbled, taking a step forward. Again, he saw something shift out of the corner of his eye, and he turned the main light mounted on his rifle on full blast. The piles of once stacked crates created long shadows as he swept his rifle from left to right.

"Shit," Woody huffed, shuffling on his feet. The activated pads on his jump boots squeaked due to the rain picked up from outside. "There's something in the corner."

"Calm down," Janix instructed, joining Dailey in a broad sweep of their area while Sparky continued to growl.

"What is it, boy?" Dailey asked. The dog enjoyed being talked to like the human animals he had witnessed in the movies, and took no offense to being called a good boy.

"The Shade," Valen whispered into the comms, getting down on one knee and turning his light on full power.

"Of course," Dailey whispered back. The utter stillness of the group formed an almost perfect calm.

Licking his lips, Dailey focused on the area he saw the movement in. On the back, a shadow covered the wall. Whatever was in the room with them was shielded behind the now disheveled ten-foot-high pile of equipment.

Lambert was the first not to take any chances as one of the shadows moved. A razor line of blue EMP rounds spit out of his rifle, whipping and snapping through the tall pile of junk. Bullets flashed as Woody, seeing the same thing on the opposite side of the room, joined in.

Janix, Valen, and Dailey continued to focus on the spots they were staring at while flashes of light created brief flickers. Flickers of light created brief shadows, regardless of their weapon's lights being on.

Sparky, continuing to growl, stayed in the middle of the group, staring in the general direction Dailey was looking.

Lambert let up momentarily as Dailey finally found his target moving with the flashes from the rifles. Instead of firing his own, the man pulled out an EMP grenade, yelling the one phrase soldiers hated: "Danger close!"

Everyone backed up as the pulse from the grenade swept through the room, only exploding in a small, confined area. While the grenade had indeed hit its target, it had also momentarily scrambled their HUDS, as well as their lights. The entire team, seeing this, opened fire.

Coolio stared at the monitor on the back of the rover, watching the video feed in awe. The Sauder rifles were cutting holes in the old metal building like it was nothing, rounds tinging and clanking as he turned the sound on. Luckily for him, they were all backing up to the door, the flash of the rifles flickering white-hot on the setting he was on.

"There!" Dailey barked as a clear figure wisped across the back of the room, only to drop down after Janix shifted fire.

A yell came from the far right of the group as something ran into Woody, not only knocking him down but also shutting off his armor, freezing him like a seized-up motor.

"I can't move," Woody shouted, his yell muffled by the now dead helmet.

While the others moved, Sparky continued to stand resolute, holding his ground. A growling bark came over the comms. "Outside!"

Knowing there was about to be a laser light show, Dailey grabbed Valen by the shoulder, making him stop firing into the dark shadows of the warehouse. By now, their lights and HUDs were starting to come back online, making the entire building resemble a strobing haunted house.

"Everyone outside!" Dailey ordered. Janix reached down, grabbing Woody by the small handle on the back of his armor. A screeching howl came from the heavy armor being dragged to safety.

"What's going on?" Valen asked as Dailey's armor-plated shoulders rose and fell.

"Not completely sure, but Sparky's about to go nuclear in there," Dailey stated just as the back of the vert rover dropped open.

Within seconds, the entire inside of the warehouse crackled to life with glowing hot electricity slithering through every corner of the room. Light flickered from the overhead metal domes as power seeped into their ancient filaments. Then silence.

Dailey and Janix stepped forward at the same time while Coolio ran out with a jumper kit for Woody's armor after Lambert shouted for him to grab it.

"Sparky?" Dailey asked over the comms, waiting for a response.

The click of Sparky's armor ticked in rhythm with the rain as the Alurian war hound strutted out of the building. Without saying a word, the back end of his armor lifted, exposing his rear end.

Dailey shook his head, knowing what was about to happen.

Yip, ruff, garff, Sparky came over the comms before his message was translated. "In the name of the Ham Republic, I declare this place safe!"

After the lift of his hind leg, Valen walked up beside the *Murphy's* commander.

"What's he doing?"

"You have one less building; it's sort of been claimed in the name of Sparky. Don't worry, he shares," Dailey said, walking up to Sparky as the dog stepped under the eaves, plopping down, clearly tired.

"Good boy. So, what happened?" Dailey asked. "Oh, and we will refill your energy stores when we return to base."

"Ghosts of people," Sparky chuffed.

"Ghosts?"

"Very old. Must tell Albert," Sparky finished, trotting off to the rover as the rest of the team joined Dailey, beaming their lights inside the warehouse.

"There's nothing in there," Lambert said flatly as Valen pointed toward a small pile of embers on the floor, followed by another.

The light dusting of ashes fluttered into the air as a gust of wind blew inside. Janix leaned down, dabbing a small portion of the material on his glove, followed by him pulling out a small flat plate and tapping his finger on it. Then he pulled on a red tab, and the material sealed itself shut under plastic. The kit was used to gather blood or other organic samples for study, something Bellman had got them in the habit of doing.

"I'll see if Albert can tell us something about this," Janix said, standing back up, seeing the utter chaos they had created in the now empty building.

"It's not the same when there isn't a body," Lambert added as Valen just stood there, taking in the scene.

Not only had he never heard of anyone defeating a Shade, let alone killing one, but he was, for the first time, absolutely certain of the power the Nova Rangers possessed. While it gave the man confidence, it also tickled the back of his mind with just how insignificant he was and how strong his people were.

"Everyone, load up. We've seen enough," Dailey ordered.

"Sir," Coolio barked, now back in the driver's seat. "We just got a message from Jen. Something just blipped on the long-range radar."

CHAPTER 8

THE VAULT

Yellow paint and the smell of mold wafted through the corridor as the team stepped in front of the Vault's massive main entrance. While obviously a bunker, the builders had opted to nickname it the Vault in reference to the treasure it held inside.

An old camera sat perched on a security booth built into the concrete wall like a crow looking for shiny objects. A mix of gears and large hinges hissed while a steam-driven piston actuated the door's massive lock.

"They really wanted to keep someone out of here," Woody said. Jen turned, having joined the group after tucking the Harpy away in the massive hangar attached to the back of the control tower, while Janix slapped Woody on the back.

"Or keep someone in," the Solarian said, laughing at his own joke. Even if Solarian humor was often related to dad jokes, it was more about watching their reaction to their own jokes that got most people laughing. This, in turn, usually fueled the fire of convincing most Solarians they were, in fact, funny. Which they generally weren't.

Tarik stepped into view through the security window, giving the team a salute. His face dropped once he looked at Valen and the obvious signs of a fight.

With a final hiss and push of air, the doors finally opened. On the other side, a decontamination center and what looked like a waiting area greeted Dailey and the others as they trudged through the main entrance.

"It's not all this drab," Tarik stated, walking out of the security booth, being replaced by two guards.

"We've seen worse," Dailey replied as Tarik stood by, waiting to hear what happened. "The Shade. There were a few of them in the warehouse we stayed in. It looks like the ravers decided to check the place out instead of coming back here, where their buddies are lying in front of the building," Dailey said as the man turned, walking into the Vault.

Within seconds of leaving the main entrance, the level of comfort and overall vibe immediately shifted, with wood-paneled walls and sleek lines covering the hardened walls. The place was posher than Dailey had imagined it to be.

Seeing the look on Dailey's face, Tarik started giving the group a tour of the main entrance hall. "Made for the politicians and military upper crust—" he started before Valen chimed in.

"And those rich enough."

"Yes, and that. We are, from what we can tell, the lucky ones. Some of the other facilities scattered around the country were more about keeping people safe and more geared toward military functions. This site was focused on the government. There is a trove of manuals in the library."

The place had been kept up, generations of inhabitants keeping themselves busy by ensuring their home was in order, mostly thanks to the people who lived there before the door opened.

"You're not kidding," Dailey agreed, also noticing the offices and stairs leading to the upper level. The place was massive.

"The sheer amount of weapons and rations is impressive. From what the manual states, the Vault can support a hundred people for several hundreds of years."

"Didn't you say there were more than that for a long time?" Dailey interjected.

Tarik nodded.

"Yes, and we believe that is the reason the door opened, not so much the time aspect. Or a mix of the two. We have been rationing what is left since I was born, but there is a level below that is a full gardening section. We are able to keep the crops going enough to offset anything, and if needed, we could theoretically live off that. Oh, we also have a few animals, but they are so rare that a rule was put in place to preserve them. There are a few dogs running around." This got Sparky's attention. He had never met a real Earth dog before. Or one from Teras, for that matter.

Tarik continued to motion the team through another set of double doors at the far end of the entrance. This room opened up into a three-story-high atrium bustling with people. The noise had been nonexistent on the other side of the doors.

Natural light shone through the space as the sounds of conversations and the feel of staring eyes greeted Dailey and his team. What looked like shops lined one side of the mall-like structure, with a cafeteria standing among several offices.

"We are going past this to the residential area. We have a place for your people set aside. Albert is in the control room; it's not far from there. He set up a security link with your ship," Tarik said.

"Sir," Janix spoke up. "Might I suggest we man that control room as well?"

Dailey looked at Tarik, who simply nodded in agreement. After another five minutes of walking and pointing out what was what, they arrived to a long hall that had clearly been used less than the others.

The hall opened into another large room with tables in a communal setting, including a few tables and couches. Directly in front of that was another two-story atrium with rooms off to the sides.

"There." Tarik pointed to a door to their right before entering the atrium. "That is a meeting room. It is linked to our control room and has a radio; I would suggest setting up there. Over there is a small storage area, and that's about it. Everyone will have their own room. The first two are larger for the section administrators. This area was for the people working down here."

"Thanks. This is perfect," Dailey thanked the man. "I'm guessing this section was once occupied." It made Dailey wonder just how posh the politician's accommodations were.

"Yes, we have a few of the rooms locked, and there will be some personal effects in the rest. Maybe some old clothes and a few other trinkets. Stay on the top floor; we haven't been on the first floor in a long time. Also, Albert wanted everyone to meet him in the control room once you got settled. I will be back in thirty minutes." With that, Tarik concluded, leaving the *Murphy*'s team to finally take a deep breath.

"What do you think?" Janix asked as Sparky jumped on one of the couches, letting the backplate of his armor slide off.

"I think we are good for now. Get everyone bedded down for a few, and you, Jen, and I will meet up with Albert."

"You heard the man!" Janix barked as a clear scramble for the rooms started. The other Nova Rangers all rushed for the best rooms, only to find them all the same.

"What?" Woody complained. "There's a bunch of knitting stuff in here."

"Too late." Jones laughed, noting the other doors down the hall were locked.

The young Nova Ranger turned to the administrators' rooms, only to see Janix walking into the one opposite Dailey's, who was the last person left besides Jen.

"Not a chance," Janix said, happy as he walked into a room more spacious than his back on the *Murphy*.

"Ladies first," Dailey motioned as Jen grinned, turning into the other administrator's room. The other Nova Rangers already had their doors closed, and the sounds of armor being deactivated echoed.

Sparky was already snoring by the time Dailey figured out he wasn't going to let Jen off the hook that easily, following her into the room. "You could have just asked for the big room, you know," Dailey said as Jen turned, kissing the man before he could say anything else.

She slowly pulled back, smiling. "Then I wouldn't have been able to do that."

Dailey, not able to argue with that logic, glanced down at a journal sitting on the main coffee table in the middle of a small sitting room. "Looks like the journal of whoever was in charge here," Dailey speculated as Jen walked over, sat on the small couch, and opened it up.

"It's written like a diary," Jen said, running her hands over the smooth, old, browning paper. "Look, there's an entry were they go all the way back to when they started here. There are more on the shelf, look."

"Someone must've been feeling reflective and wanting to catch up on old times. You know, something the senator has always told me is that words mean things. It's not that we're always reading and interpreting something word by word. If it's a journal from the person who was in charge of this area, they have likely included their thoughts. I teach my officers and senior enlisted to do the same thing."

"I'm not about to read Bellman's personal journal. Just saying," Jen joked as Dailey reached down, picked up the final volume, and set it on the table. Instead of enjoying their time alone, the two sat there and read the last two entries in the journal.

The inhabitants had been bold and went outside the safe doors of the Vault to explore the Air Force base and surrounding area. According to

Danis Pelvar, his own people had been growing discontent with the separation between the workers and what he simply called the management. But the one entry that absolutely piqued Dailey's interest was that of a ship they witnessed trying to land, only for it to be destroyed by a hissing rocket fired from an unknown location.

By the time they closed the journal, thirty minutes had already passed.

Tarik stood in the communal area as Sparky yawned, awake, and Janix side-eyed Dailey as he and Jen both walked out of the same room.

"Glad to see everyone's ready. Albert is communicating with the *Murphy*. They are about to launch the probe," Tarik greeted them as they made their way through several more sections of the underground facility, ending up in what was clearly the most tucked-away section of the Vault.

Mister Toaster's head swiveled around, smiling at Dailey, Janix, and Jen. Sparky ran over to the AI, letting out a furious slurry of yips; he was telling his partner in crime what had happened.

"My, how interesting," Albert proclaimed as Becket's voice crackled over the radio.

"Sir, we are preparing to launch the probe. We have five more hours before the next communication cycle ends."

Dailey walked over to the large table, now adorned with various screens and other pieces of communication equipment taken from the Harpy.

"Let it fly," Dailey said before turning to Albert. "So, what's the scoop?" he asked.

The AI stood up to his full height while the other two inhabitants of the Vault glared at him as if they were looking at something they didn't want anything to do with. Truth be told, Albert had tried to make friends with them by doing several of what he called magic tricks, which had only confused the two guards further, as they involved a dance routine and an odd mix of information about Solarian dating shows.

"They had all kinds of juicy tidbits on the politicians that were supposed to stay here, not to mention others around the rest of the globe. No need for romance novels here; some of that stuff was absolutely for adult AI eyes only," Albert started as Dailey held up a finger, realizing he needed to be more specific.

"Did their databases have anything about the Vault and the ship, or anything else we need to know about the planet?" Dailey asked, happy with his question.

"Ah, yes. For starters, we have a general location of where the ship went down. There were records of the location of the fighter jets that downed it.

And that is . . . here," Albert said, tapping his fingers on the map sprawled out on the table.

This was information that had been stored on a computer that had long since given up any hope of actually being useful, and as such, Tarik had yet to see the actual location on a map.

"That's roughly forty miles from here. The farthest anybody has ever been," Tarik started, only to reflect on the implications of what he was about to say. "The furthest anybody *alive* has ever been is roughly twenty miles. Though the roads should be manageable."

"Can you define manageable?" Dailey asked.

Tarik sat at one of the high chairs next to the planning table.

"The roads outside the base—and some inside—are mostly degraded, but the paths are still clear. Apparently, before all hell broke loose in the city, a perimeter fifty miles around the base was cleared, back when we were still trying to put up a fight."

"The files in the database agree with that statement, Tarik. While some of the information passed down over the past two generations is a little vague, this is mostly in alignment with what you understand. Minus all the spaceship and alien gobbledygook," Albert said, tossing a little piece of hydrated bacon from the previous morning he had tucked away for Sparky.

"What's the second thing?" Dailey asked at the same time Pearl came over the radio, reporting they had just released the probe.

"I believe I have figured out why they did what they did to this planet, and what it's currently being used for."

"Currently being used for?" Tarik asked while Dailey walked over to the monitor showing a generic trajectory of the probe in relation to the planet. It would be several minutes before the probe made its way through the atmosphere.

"Well, you know those things they call gas stations?" Albert asked.

"Get to the point," Dailey urged.

"They did something to the planet's atmosphere to generate fuel for their starships. For decades, if not centuries, the Creare—or someone else—have been using this place as not only a navigational point but also a gas station."

This caught everyone off guard, but just then, Dailey pointed back to the screen. "We can talk about that later. Make sure you send all the information to the *Murphy*," he said as the monitor started flashing. The probe had entered the planet's atmosphere.

Pearl's voice came over the comm system. "We are starting to get some readings."

While they had already scanned the planet and sent a handful of probes into the atmosphere, they had never done so with the understanding that it was about to be destroyed, so this time, it was looking for things other than general planet composition.

"We're a mile off deck," Pearl spoke again, giving a countdown. "And it's gone."

"How far off the deck?" Jen asked, wanting to know either how high or low a fully operating ship could move. From everything they could tell, they had gotten insanely lucky to land on the planet's surface without activating whatever security protocols were in place.

"Seven thousand feet," Pearl responded as Bellman spoke up in the background.

"Looks like we have a point of origin feedback to the sensors scanning the sky above the planet. It looks as if it's only scanning certain areas," Bellman stated, grumbling in the background as he read the information now streaming on the screen in front of them faster than he could ingest it. Unfortunately, due to the atmospheric conditions, he was not able to livestream the information directly to Albert. It would instead be sent in a data dump package.

"That's not good," Communications Officer King shouted from the back of the *Murphy*'s bridge. Knowing that was never a good thing, Dailey let the situation on board the *Murphy* unfold.

King ran up to the main planning console next to Pearl, Bellman, and Becket.

"Looks like a communication was sent from the planet at the same time the probe was destroyed. I can get its general point of origin, but we're not set up to trace the signal to where it's going."

Albert glanced up as Mister Toaster's face frowned, the mustache dropping slightly on either side of his flat lips. "They could be using gate technology to communicate. If they didn't know we were here then, they likely know now."

Dailey could've kicked himself for not thinking about that scenario, but then again, Jen had previously noted that they had received blips on the radar of a massive *something* powering up. That massive something, after talking with Albert and learning this new information, gave the team a very clear picture of the situation.

It wasn't them sending the probe into orbit but rather their activity planetside that had somehow activated a mechanism to awaken the sleeping giant crashed somewhere in the countryside.

"This all has to be connected," Dailey claimed, refocusing on his crew in orbit. "Pearl, Becket. I know you guys said you were leaving as soon as you released that sensor. Drop the resupply package. No change to the location. If it makes it, it makes it; if it doesn't, it doesn't. You guys need to haul ass out of here. Albert and Jen have your coordinates; we're going to have to try to get to that ship sooner rather than later."

"Roger, sir," Pearl replied with the sounds of the bridge erupting into feverish work in the background.

"We will stay on comms as long as we can," Dailey said, turning to Albert. "I need you to get a map charted out. Tarik, are there any other ground vehicles here?"

"Yes, we have a few armored vehicles, but I want to be clear that they haven't been driven in a long, long time."

"Albert, I want you and a few others to go check them out. Tarik, if you have anybody that works on machines, send them as well." Dailey was in full mission mode, knowing the clock was now officially ticking.

Tarik nodded, sending one of the guards off. "I'll send Kael Thorn and Dorian, whom you met earlier with Albert. They will know the most. Can I ask why?"

"You don't think we're doing this by ourselves, do you?" Dailey said with a grin on his face. "I don't know if you've heard this one on your planet, but back home, it goes something like this: You scratch my back, I'll scratch yours."

Tarik grinned, knowing the phrase. "We're not all that unalike, you and I, Captain Dailey. You and Valen seem to have hit it off. I'll get him and a team together. Before you ask, yes, I will be going."

"See, Tarik," Dailey said, feeling like his old self back on the hunt. "That's why I like you. You got it where it counts. Most leaders wouldn't do that. Albert, that reminds me. Janix took a sample of those things we ran into. I need you to do that spectrum whatever thing to it. Sparky said something about people."

Sparky chuffed. "Ghosts."

"I'll pull the video feed from your HUDs. Sparky's never wrong some of the time. Also, since we're being so tell-all today, there were some encrypted files on the hard drives that I couldn't get into. It will take me some time, but I have a feeling they will be worth the time," Albert said, taking the sample from Janix.

The plan was fairly straightforward. As soon as the resupply landed, they would leave with the Nova Rangers and, hopefully, the supporting vehicles from the base. They had made a wise choice on the location of the resupply drop, as it would be on their way.

CHAPTER 9

THE GRIND

Teras glowed an ominous purple as Becket pinned his hands behind his back, standing in front of the *Murphy*'s main viewport, contemplating their next move. It wasn't a matter of *if*, but rather *when*, someone else would show up.

Pearl and Dorax Flam, the Alurian pirate who had somehow become part of Dailey's team, watched the massive viewscreen on the *Crow*'s bridge, reviewing Albert's report about the atmosphere being used to fuel ships. Dorax's greenish skin shone from the overhead lights surrounding the glass observation window on the three-story tall bridge.

"*Murphy*, this is the *Crow*. We are set and in position. Powering down main systems," Pearl said as Becket just grunted.

Viper Companies' first sergeant didn't like having to split up the crews. If they hadn't been slingshot across the universe into another galaxy by Director Prescott, the plan had been to get a crew for the *Crow* and reconfigure the outside of the ship in the Federation colors and markings.

Becket walked back to the helm. "We will keep our deep scanners on. Between that and the sensor pods we sent out, if anything shows up, we'll be the first to know," he said, clicking off the comms button.

Dorax, aboard the *Crow*, had been in charge of sending the resupply pod down. The *Murphy* was equipped with ten space-to-ground resupply pods the size of a van. After using a mech storage casing from the *Crow*, they had successfully sent the package planetside with no issues.

Albert had been assigned the task of getting a large number of battle mechs aboard the *Crow* to work. Having a limited time, the AI had only been able to get them to turn on. The programming on board was the latest tech the Alurians had to offer, giving Albert a run for his money.

The AI had come up with a plan to modify and program each individual mech, something that Bellman and the engineering team from the *Murphy* had started while in orbit over Teras. To date, and without Albert on board, they had programmed only one.

Bellman and Lieutenant Jim Novak, the second in command of the attack wing in the absence of Jen, walked onto the bridge of the *Murphy*. "Everything's set," Bellman started, noticing the oddity of not having Pearl or Captain Dailey on the bridge.

Becket scratched his sandpaper-like chin, standing back up. "I read Albert's report. I wouldn't doubt a ship stopping by either way, at some point."

"From what we can tell, the ships drop into lower orbit, and whatever drives they have on board absorb the particles in the atmosphere. Pretty neat stuff, if you think about it," Bellman said. Jim walked over to Communications Officer King, patting the man on the shoulder.

"No more messages?" Jim asked. King shook his head.

"The planet just rotated. It's nighttime down there," King mumbled, hyperfocused on the communications sensor readout.

"What about the signal on the planet?" Becket asked, making a good point.

"It only transmitted for a brief amount of time. We do have a lock on the location where it originated from, as well as the theoretical area the Creare ship is at," King replied, acting annoyed by the interruption.

Becket, seeing the man was focused on the task at hand, turned back to Bellman. "What's Thron doing in the galley?"

"Pacing," Bellman noted. Both men grimaced, knowing the Solarian warlord had a knack for figuring out when things were about to go wrong.

"Shit," Becket growled. "I'm keeping the ship on rotating shifts. Only twenty percent of the crew is down right now. This might turn into a long couple of days or weeks."

"Dammit," King barked. "Likely hours and days. Something just showed up on the long-range sensor scan at the edges of the system."

"Pearl," Becket clicked the comm system. The *Crow* immediately responded.

"Go ahead," Pearl snapped back quickly.

"Something just showed up on the radar at the edges of the system. Plug into sensor eight-one-seven," Becket instructed, now standing behind Communications Officer King.

"Since we have the sensors on low power, there are no real details at the moment. All I can tell you is that it's a ship," King stated, working feverishly on the panel in front of them.

Becket turned back to the main con, walking in front of the bridge's crew. "That didn't last long," he said to no one in particular, sitting back down.

Either the ship had been close by and intercepted the signal, or this was simply a coincidence. Becket did not believe in coincidences, always erring on the worst-case scenario, something the Nova Rangers had beaten into them at the academy.

"Novak," Becket ordered. "Card, Ponce, you hear all that?"

Both men replied simultaneously. "Roger. We are getting the platoons stood up." That simply meant waking up the few resting Rangers already in the drop bay.

"Kline, once the signal hits the secondary sensor, let me know how fast that thing's moving."

"Roger, First Sergeant," Kline responded, working to lock the signal into the system so the computers could get to work figuring out the speed of the ship. The bridge aboard the *Crow* was similarly alive, with bodies moving and barking orders. The *Crow* was five times larger, if not more, than the *Murphy*. Coupled with a skeleton crew, they had consolidated the majority of the operations around the bridge to the flight bays. Unlike the *Murphy*, the *Crow* had entire launching decks dedicated to doing nothing but having ships come and go.

"Dorax," Pearl called as the man turned back from the recessed targeting stations in front of the main con. The *Crow* was an Alurian dreadnought built for one thing and one thing only: War. Unlike some of the creature comforts and smoother lines on board the *Murphy*, the *Crow* was cold and battle focused. The majority of the space on the bridge was dedicated to either targeting, weapons systems, or overall management of either the battle mechs or the attack ship loaded in its bays.

If the team had only waited another week before politely acquiring the vessel, it would have been loaded with Alurian attack fighters.

"Yes?" Dorax replied, now out of what they called the pit.

"Make sure the main power is focused on our weapons systems. I have informed the attack wing," Pearl relayed as Dorax took the seat beside her, pulling a console in front of him.

Bellman had come up with two landing locations that would keep both ships within direct line of sight of the other. Since both moons continuously faced the planet, they had opted for two locations just out of what they called the sun band, on the dark side of the moons. This also allowed for short-range communications that would not be easily intercepted outside the small area around the moons.

"According to the armament systems that Albert translated, we can have pulse, plasma, and highly explosive fusion missiles that can get to the area around the *Murphy* in a little under four minutes," Dorax informed Pearl.

"How about the plasma cannons?" she asked.

He nodded. "The main cannon that we would usually fire is on the bottom of the ship. That being said, there are so many batteries of cannons up top we can take our pick. With one battery at max power, we can get a volley there in just under one minute."

Pearl chewed on her bottom lip, running her hand over her smooth head. "Set several preplanned targets in orbit around the moon, and a few between us. The same goes for the missiles."

"Look," Dorax said as the main display changed. Kline, aboard the *Murphy*, had finally gotten a lock between two of the outer sensors.

"That thing's moving," Pearl noted, calling Becket. "How long do we have?"

Becket came back over the comms after confirming with his team. "Looks like they just activated their hyperdrive. Looks like thirty minutes."

"How do you want to play this?" Pearl asked, motioning for Ensign Barthelo, one of the fleet engineers now aboard the *Crow*, to adjust the ship's power.

"Let's see how this plays out. It's only one ship; hardly a strike force someone would use if they were concerned," Becket growled.

"Or they are just here to recon the situation," Pearl added, shuffling in her seat.

Bellman leaned forward, overhearing the conversation. "Might I recommend we shut down the sensors in orbit?"

Becket nodded. "Get it done. The *Crow* has us covered. Just be ready to route all power to the main thrusters."

A timer sprang up on the viewscreen as the two crews watched the projected path and position of the incoming ship. Thirty minutes passed in what felt like hours. Jim Novak sat in his attack fighter with his hands on the controls. At a moment's notice, he could have the attack wing out of the drop bays and into action.

"Top," Kline spoke up, cutting through the silence. "I have visual on the ship."

The main viewscreen zoomed to a sleek, long black ship entering orbit, the blue glow of its hyperthrusters fading out to a light orange glow. Four small support ships launched from underneath, taking position forward and aft of the ship.

"Looks like they're taking up support positions, not going into an offensive formation. Are all outward sensors off?" Becket confirmed while Bellman nodded, shaking his status panel.

"Yes, we are just on visual from the video feed. Communications with the *Crow* are cut off. We are monitoring the system in case they reactivate comms."

Satisfied with their current posture, Becket leaned back slightly in his chair. "What are you doing?" he asked himself out loud.

The truth of the matter was that with no comms planetside, drawing any unwanted attention could be problematic for Dailey and the others. They needed to buy time, and if that meant playing possum, they would, no matter how much Becket and the rest wanted to engage the ship and get to the bottom of things.

Pearl had also suggested that it could have the nav data they needed, which would be lost if they had to destroy the ship.

"They are positioning to go into lower orbit. If I'm not mistaken, they may be doing that fueling thing Albert mentioned," Kline spoke.

"Can we zoom in more on the ship?" Becket asked, wanting to see the markings on the unfamiliar ship.

The ship grew larger in the viewscreen.

"That's as good as it gets," Kline stated, turning in his station. "The *Crow* has a much better video feed system on board. I'm sure they're working on that."

Bellman squinted his eyes. "I don't know of any ship that looks like that."

"Me neither. You notice it's not drawing any attention to itself as well?" Becket added, noting the small number of support ships it released and the fact that they were not patrolling the area but staying contained.

"Interesting," Bellman said, watching as the ship turned outward, lowering into orbit like it was backing into a parking space. Even today, all these centuries later, there was still that one person who stopped the other electro-cars from reversing into a parking space. Some things never changed, as Dailey and Becket, being avid history buffs, always stated.

The ship stopped after five minutes of maneuvering, now hanging in orbit. Becket pondered the situation. "I don't like this. I feel like we're being baited into something."

"Could be," Bellman said. "Either way, we know we're not alone out here. Even with all our calculations, we couldn't figure out our location. That could be a civilization we have never encountered. Do you see the way the ship moves, as well as the support craft? I don't know of any Alurian ship that acts like that, not on the records or from what we've seen."

"Run the ship's silhouette through the mining syndicates' vessel database. Maybe the jokers are all the way out here," Becket said.

Bellman tapped away at the panel in front of him before shaking his head. "Doesn't look like it," he concluded, putting the outline of the ship into the database. Kline would add the visuals from the *Crow* later.

Just as smoothly as the ship had dropped into orbit, it started to pull out of the atmosphere. The four support craft quickly disappeared back inside the ship as the orange glow of the engines quickly shifted to blue. The ominous visitors were activating their hyperdrive, ready to leave the system.

The crew of both ships held their collective breaths, watching the ship wink out of sight in a flash of blue. "Top," Kline sliced through the silence. "What do you want us to do?"

"Nothing. We wait for an hour, then reactivate the sensors. They may have dropped something in orbit. Pearl, you copy?" Becket instructed, pausing.

"Roger. We just turned our comms back on. What's the game plan?" she asked as Becket had a *What would Dailey do* moment.

"We are reactivating the sensors. I assume you took close-up shots of the vessel. Send us what you have. Any ideas? We think the ship was refueling, or possibly a scout," Becket replied, checking the clock to see when they would be able to communicate with the surface again.

"It's nothing we've ever seen. Dorax said he isn't aware of any Alurian ships that look like that. You'll see what I'm talking about," Pearl replied as a crisp image of the ship appeared on the screen.

Several large bays by the engines were open as the purplish clouds from the planet appeared to seep into them, pulled by some unknown force. This was the initial distraction as Becket and the rest of the *Murphy*'s current bridge crew figured out the issue.

The sleek, jet-black ship didn't have a normal hull. Instead of metal flowing into sharp angles, the vessel seemed almost organic, minus the addition of various weapons and sensors. Round tubes linked into odd, nonsymmetrical angles. What the crew assumed were weapons looked as if they were mounted on odd organic structures.

"What in the ever-living Solarian barnyard back door is that?" Becket exclaimed, generating a snicker from one of the stations on the back of the bridge.

Bellman zoomed in on the image. "It's a new one for me. Do you think it's Creare?"

"It's something. Something we haven't seen," Becket said, still live over comms with the *Crow*. "We talked about it a while back. We don't even fully have our entire galaxy charted out. We are clearly in another galaxy. Let's see what the sensor probes have to say. I want to review the video feed from the *Crow* and see where things are."

What Becket wasn't saying was the fact that he wished Albert was there to make sense of the entire situation.

CHAPTER 10

EXIT ONE

Dull grays and barely visible green foliage had taken over the once proud cityscape. The streets, while passable, were now passageways of overgrown plants and smooth stone. Since the planet's surface never saw the warm kiss of the sun, the plants that were left had adapted. Weeds and various other low-to-ground plants covered every structure and stone like they had been painted on. Besides some trees struggling to grow, no plant grew more than a few inches off the ground, still outlining the once busy roads. And while the rain had slowed to a drizzle, the ever-present haze kept visibility only so far out. If there was a mountain a mile away, the team wouldn't know it.

"Sir." Coolio pointed at a large metal crate sitting in the middle of the cracked road. "There it is."

"Let's get this secured and keep moving. Valen, you copy?" Dailey asked as the two now functioning military trucks also came to a halt.

"Go ahead," the man replied.

"We are going to secure the package. Have your teams set up a perimeter."

"Roger," the man replied, knowing the Nova Rangers would be doing most of the work. Dailey had split off two Nova Rangers per vehicle, adding to the six Vault soldiers on the mission.

The ramp to the vert rover slammed open, and Dailey, Janix, and Albert exited the vehicle while the others joined the group pulling security, including Sparky. Once complete, the additional rations would be picked up by a follow-up group, being that the area was still in their comfort zone.

"How ingenious. I'm surprised they can even figure out how to flush the toilets up there without me on board," Albert scoffed, walking up to the unfamiliar metal pod.

"What's that?" Dailey asked as Albert hooked his power source to the charred control panel. Entry without a reverse thruster through the atmosphere was a harsh event, even for new tech.

"They took a drop pod for one of the mechs and launched it; it has one of those fancy low-altitude parachutes installed. Once this thing hit the ground, it was sucked back into a small compartment on the top." Albert pointed. "All mechanical. And it can work very low to the ground; enough to stop it without too much of a spectacle. Bellman must be laying off the rum."

After feeding power into the panel for two minutes, Albert pressed several buttons, opening the pod. Inside, four full sets of backup orbital drop armor sat in half configuration, and nestled neatly between them was a case of Sauder rounds and six more rifles—just enough to arm the unofficial part-time Nova Rangers from the Vault.

Besides that, there were also three cases of not only coffee but meal bars, and a small case of Bellman's rum. The team must have figured Dailey was trying to make new friends.

"Tarik, Valen, it looks like your lucky day. They even sent some libations and enough coffee to keep you going for a few weeks," Dailey said over the comms. It wasn't lost on the man that the coffee would only support the security and military teams of the Vault, to be kept from the others. The meal replacement bars, on the other hand, he would ensure would get passed out after the soldiers got their fill.

"Coffee?" Tarik asked.

"Yup, there are also three suits of armor and enough rifles for all of you. Pick who you want in the armor, and Albert and Janix will get you squared away," Dailey finished as Albert unloaded the cargo.

Tarik, being the leader he was, gave the armor to Valen and two of his best soldiers, continuing to grow Dailey's acceptance and trust in the man. Surprisingly, the three took little time to become acclimated to the armor. That, and Albert had disabled several of the more advanced options, like the booster jets and a few other systems that could get someone not fully trained and the people around either seriously injured or generally killed.

It also helped that the nanotech the ODA was made of had what the military called a third-grade level of understanding. So, after a brief check of the rifles, Dailey circled the team around the back of the vert rover.

"According to the information we have, there is a city roughly twenty miles down this road. The farthest you said your people have been is maybe twenty miles, which include the distance already traveled—" Dailey stopped, hearing the sounds of a cellophane wrapper. Looking down, he saw Sparky had broken open one of the meal replacement bars and was chewing feverishly on the bar of intestinal death, as it was nicknamed.

"As I was saying," he continued. "That means we don't know what to expect. Once we hit the perimeter of the city, I want to stop again and see if we can scan the buildings or whatever there may be. After that, it's a fairly straight shot to the ship. Albert, are you sure we can get comms out here?"

"No, everything's changed since we left," Albert scoffed, obviously joking. "Yes. See that transponder strapped to the roof?? That will do the trick."

Nodding, Dailey shifted to Valen. "If anything happens, let the Nova Rangers take point. This isn't the time to earn medals."

"The city is called San Con. According to our records, it's where a lot of the families attached to the air base lived and worked outside of the military. Those pictures we showed you before we left are all the records we have," Tarik said.

"Understood," Dailey replied, once again bringing the point home. "Just remember, this isn't the time to earn medals."

Understanding, the teams all went back to their vehicles once again, staring down the not-so-yellow brick road.

Dailey jumped in the seat next to Coolio, taking off his helmet. "You see anything on the sides of the road? Or any other buildings?"

"No, but I was thinking the same thing. I was talking to one of Valen's people, and they said the air base was surrounded by several miles of training ranges.

"That means we can maneuver if needed. Just be ready once we get to the city," Dailey instructed, sitting back.

For the next thirty minutes, suffocating trees morphed into even more distraught buildings. Midsize memorials to a civilization long since forgotten stood like monuments, or as Dailey figured, graves.

"Hate to interrupt all the napping up there," Albert spoke up. "We are a quarter mile away from our stopping point before entering the city."

Coolio slowly brought the convoy to a halt, finding a patch of land slightly off the road and behind cover. "You want us to send the drone out?" Janix asked from the back.

"No, I don't want to lose it. I'm thinking we send a fire team ahead, which will include myself, Tarik, and Albert. You, Sparky, and the rest of the team follow behind us on the main road, once we clear each block," Dailey said, wanting to save one of their more valuable assets for when they were closer to the downed ship.

"Roger, sir." Janix then turned to the Nova Rangers in the back of the rover, speaking over the comms as well as. "Everyone, get ready to move. I want fire team one with Captain Dailey and Albert. Tarik, the boss, wants you to dismount with him."

Fire team one for this outing consisted of Lambert and Specialist Jenna Jones. Pickle, Woody, and Buckle would all remain behind to secure the vehicles as they slowly moved forward. The reasoning for not blasting through the city was not only to recon the area but also to ensure they had a way out if needed.

"Albert, take point," Dailey instructed as Mister Toaster's face went black. "What's that all about?"

"Stealth mode, duh . . ." Albert drawled out at the same time his two mini Gatling lasers zipped over his shoulders.

Tarik, now in the light armor Jones had given Valen previously, shifted his weight, working out the best way to hold the new rifle while in his new gear. The man was stoic but engaging at the same time. He was a natural leader, and enigmatic in ways Dailey was all too familiar with.

"If we run into any trouble, let Albert do the initial dirty work," Dailey said to the man as he simply nodded, standing beside him.

The roadway trees gave way to one- and two-story buildings of similar designs, and Albert stopped in front of a hollowed-out storefront.

"Ice cream, anyone?" he said over the comms, wiping off a layer of greenish guck. The constant rain on the planet had given all the smooth stone surfaces a light sponging of algae.

A young boy and girl beamed with painted smiles, holding massive ice cream cones ready to be licked to death, like a dog owner coming home after a long day of work.

Tarik frowned at the image.

"Sup?" Dailey asked Tarik while Lambert and Jones fanned out on either side of the street, scanning the buildings as much as they could.

"It's sad. This entire world was once a thriving society. All it is now is just a reminder of what we once had."

"Pisses you off?"

"Yes," Tarik replied, turning from the sign and looking down the road.

"Good," was all Dailey said, also turning to scan the rest of the street.

Buildings in various stages of being boarded up or simply abandoned stood like grave markers. The taller buildings looked as if they were staring at the team through hollow eyes, while sharp angles from broken glass gave the entire city an evil, unwelcoming vibe.

"Move out," Dailey said as the group again started walking down the main street.

The buildings got taller as the team moved into the city's core. Albert had already moved several rusted vehicles along the route, taking the time to ensure the rover would fit through the gaps.

Jones started talking, taking some of the edge off the growing tension. "Lambert, you haven't said a word since we started walking. You always have something to say. What's up?"

Lambert paused. "I feel like we're being watched."

"You had to say it," she complained as Dailey motioned the two forward, already having the same feeling.

Timing was one of those things that the universe was always playing games with. As soon as someone said something like, "I'm glad I'm on a spaceship that has power," the universe liked to do things like shut the power off. And in situations like this, it decided to present you with whatever it was you'd mentioned.

Albert froze as the lasers on his shoulders zoomed at the top stories of the buildings directly beside them. Guttural howls, different from that of the ravers, cut through the silence. In all the rain and gloom, the noise echoed off the buildings.

"Tarik, sound familiar?" Dailey asked.

"No. It almost sounded human."

"Yeah, it did," Dailey replied, motioning the group to get against the building's wall and out of the street. "Coolio, you copy?"

"Roger, sir. Send it."

"Something's up here. Pull into the city and stay about a quarter mile behind my marker. I'll let you know if we need you to pull up," Dailey instructed, surprised by how far they had gone in such a short amount of time.

"That's a good copy, sir," Coolio responded.

"Sir, you need any more dismounts?" Janix cut in.

"Not yet. You'll be the first to know," Dailey said, refocusing on the area around them.

Albert continued to scan the second story of the building directly in front of them. Pausing, the AI held up a long hand, pointing at one of the dark windows. Dailey reached down, pulling out a mini short-range drone from his hip, bringing it to life.

"Drone out. Sending visual link."

The HUDs of the other two Nova Rangers blinked as the option to view the feed flashed. Lambert and Jones both activated the live feed as a small screen sprang to life on the bottom-right sections of their HUD. Albert was clearly already tracking the feed, as Dailey gave the AI control over the small device.

On board the vert rover, a grainy feed popped up on the small viewscreen Coolio had pulled down from the roof, also piping the feed to the other Nova Rangers via a signal booster.

Whatever was in the rain was absorbing all signals and somehow interacting with any open electrical circuit it came into contact with. Not able to fully analyze the makeup of the rain, Albert had simply referred to it as magic.

The video started fading as Albert switched the drone to infrared just as a massive white-hot figure emerged from the dark of the room it had just entered, smashing the device into a million pieces.

"Not yet," Dailey said, wanting to be damn sure before they engaged whatever was in the buildings now surrounding them.

This decision was quickly changed as a purple laser flashed from the opposite building, forcing Albert to leap several feet through the air. "That good enough?" Albert huffed.

Instead of responding, Dailey unleashed a flurry of rounds into and through the building. Lambert and Jones shifted across the street, getting a better view of the adjacent buildings as Albert finished off the fireworks by drilling a hole through not only the window but the wall behind it.

At the same time, several more rounds of purple laser fire, blindly aimed, smacked into the street. "You seeing that, sir?" Lambert asked.

"Yeah. Whoever that is is just spraying and praying," Dailey replied.

Tarik, for the first time, took aim, letting loose a volley of rounds from the Sauder rifle. He was taken aback by the power of the weapon when an entire chunk of concrete erupted from the building's second floor. Not fully trained on the weapon, the man had done a respectable job controlling the insane amount of ass-kicking that came from the rifle.

"Rookies," Albert proclaimed, leaping through the air to jump through the hole on the second floor he had carved out.

"Shit," Dailey barked, activating his boosters. Blue flames flickered, finally finding a steady cadence. Activating his shield, Dailey snapped his rifle in place, activating his Moshan blade. Whatever happened inside the building would be up close and personal.

"They always do that?" Tarik asked, letting another spatter of rounds fly through a window which had just thrown up several more burps of random purple fire.

Meanwhile, Dailey followed the path of destruction Albert had created inside the building. While jovial and usually up for a good Solarian jazz tune with a good romance novel, Albert had also proven to be lethal to the point of concern.

"Albert!" Dailey barked, laser fire flashing from deep inside the building.

His bark was cut off as he was smacked in the side, slinging him through the wall into a pile of dusty furniture. Turning, Dailey held up the shield on his wrist as several more shots sliced around him. Only one hit its target, the purple round changing the color of the shield slowly, making it flicker off.

Having enough of what he and Becket called *the bullshit*, Dailey pushed power into his booster rockets as he rolled over, lurching forward. With his Moshan blade fully charged, Dailey swept up his arm, thudding into the mass in front of him.

It was like hitting a brick wall. If he'd had more space to push his boosters, he could have toppled the hulking figure. Instead, with a quick swipe down, gore splattered Dailey's armor. At the same time, he swept his other hand up in one smooth motion, his sleek pistol smacked into his hand. Pulling the trigger, Dailey worked all the way up the figure's body till he reached its jaw. After unloading the entire magazine of kinetic rounds, the *Murphy*'s commander felt the tension of life let go of his attacker's body.

Not having any support, the massive frame dropped forward, falling on Dailey. But as quickly as the body fell on him, it was gone.

"Hey there, buckaroo. You made a little bit of a mess there, didn't you? I'm sure the landlord's going to want to have a chat with you," Albert scoffed, whistling at the tattered figure.

"You do know you carved a hole in the outside wall," Dailey replied, turning his light to show the path of carnage the AI had left behind.

"Oh, yeah," Albert said, pulling Dailey to his feet.

"All clear inside," Dailey reported, as the sounds of violence outside had also stopped.

"Everything's fine out here . . . I guess," Lambert replied.

Dailey turned to look at the mangled figure on the floor, covered in random clothes and makeshift plating. On its head was a helmet that looked more like a bucket with two eyes cut out and the bottom covered with old glass bottles.

"Stay down there and make sure the area's secure," Dailey ordered.

Albert stepped forward, holding out his hand as a sensor extended from one of his fingers. "Hmmm, interesting." The AI continued to examine the body, finally touching a chunk of gore sitting on its chest. "Fascinating."

"Are you going to share or just stand here and say intriguing words?" Dailey asked.

"Well, I'm fairly sure its face is mush. I might want to check on one of the others, but this is a highly radiated, mutated, some sorta alien DNA, distant relative of our new friends. You do see how big that body is?"

Dailey, refocusing from the fight he had just had, finally realized the body lying on the floor was roughly four to five hundred pounds of solid muscle.

"So you're saying these are people who have survived out here this entire time?" Dailey asked while Mister Toaster did an *I guess so* face.

"The alien DNA is the thing. It's sort of familiar, like one of those things buried deep in my memory banks that I can't quite get my hands on. Or whatever you call these metal things. It's not Alurian, Solarian, or fully human."

"Creare?" Dailey asked, throwing it out there.

"It could be. But it would also mean that at some point there were some bumping of uglies going on, if you know what I mean."

Dailey shook his head. "Let's check one of the other bodies out; I'll take a few samples. Let's also get this in front of Tarik. I'm surprised they've never run into them before, whatever they are."

"Well, it stands to reason if the people from the Vault hadn't traveled out this far, and then the inhabitants of the city likely didn't either. Between the Shade, ravers, and lord knows what else is out there, I'd say unless you had an entire squad of, oh, let's say, Nova Rangers, a vert rover, and a Harpy, this is probably very low on the things-to-do list while vacationing on Teras," Albert said matter-of-factly.

Dailey and Albert both wished they had never removed the makeshift helmet of the other creatures. There was little left to resemble a human other than the fact they had put on clothes and crude armor. What they did, however, was pick up one of the black, sleek, organic weapons that had nearly disintegrated Dailey's shield. After scanning the rest of the building, they picked up two others, deciding not to venture too far off the beaten path into the other buildings.

After a quick debrief, the rest of the team joined them. Tarik was not only shocked by the creatures but once again wore a sad, reflective expression on his face. Sparky was again sniffing the air like before, not taking his eyes off the surrounding buildings.

"After that, if those creatures have an inkling of intelligence, they will not attack again. We move out in five," Dailey instructed as the rest of the Nova Rangers and Valen's men all loaded back up into their respective vehicles.

Out of the corner of his eye, Dailey caught what he thought was a Shade floating behind one of the splintered windows on the first floor of the building next to them.

CHAPTER 11

THIS GUY AGAIN?

The quickly repaired and now fully functioning *Void Reaper* rumbled through deep space as General Ran stood overlooking the bow of the ship from the bridge. After several weeks in a dry dock, Kluvnew had introduced Ran to what he called the Prime Assembly. It was not only a surprise to General Ran what the Prime Assembly actually was but that it worked completely separate from the Alurian Council.

The Prime Assembly consisted of members from almost every world—encompassing subsections from the mining syndicates themselves, including his very own—all working together, and all working toward one common goal: power.

Ran had been shocked by the discovery of a new layer in what he considered a shadow government, which had been, in fact, the ones pulling the strings for centuries. This was the group that had pushed the Alurian attack on Earth and several other conflicts that had occurred since then. While still aware of his surroundings, General Ran had never seen the faces of the hooded figures in the Assembly meeting, which had consisted of him standing in the middle of a dark room surrounded by black glass panels.

Kluvnew, while not divulging all of the Assembly's plans, had informed the once-upon-a-time Federation general of his new role in the grand scheme of things. He had been reluctantly pulled into the ranks of the Assembly. While they took years, if not decades, to vet their members, they also knew that the general had fooled the Federation during his entire military career.

In reality, this wasn't Ran's proudest accomplishment. His credit account was. Money and power drove the man, and learning of this new group only proved that he was a small speck on a large whale floating through an endless ocean.

While he had been read in on the reasons for the Prime Assembly, he did not fully trust the main goals and intentions that had been laid out before him. The one thing the man had always assumed was that their end goal was to prevent the Creare from taking over the known galaxies. He was starting to question this, having wrongly assumed the Alurian High Fleet to be the ones doling out his orders throughout his entire life. The man, of course, would keep the majority, if not all, of his crew truly oblivious to the truth.

"Sir," a human communications specialist named Felix spoke up out of the quiet droning of open space. "We have a message coming in from Vice Admiral Kluvnew."

"I'll take it in my quarters," Ran said, marching off the bridge. The man's knee-high leather boots clicked with authority.

"Vice Admiral Kluvnew," Ran answered as the video feed clicked on.

"General Ran. Good to see you back up and running."

"We're still working on some repairs, but the *Void Reaper* is ready for action. So to what do I owe the pleasure?" Ran asked, getting to the point.

"We have received recent intelligence that may involve your old friend Captain Dailey and the *Murphy*."

That garnered Ran's attention. The already well-postured man pinned his shoulders back slightly. "Do continue."

"Yes, I knew you would be interested. The Prime Assembly was very impressed with you and the work you did. Your counterparts in the Ocess Mining Syndicate have been well compensated for your help. Before we get started," Kluvnew paused, "I want us both to be perfectly clear that you no longer report to the Ocess Syndicate. You are now part of the Prime Assembly."

The man gave Ran a moment to compose his thoughts, which the general had already worked through. Since returning, he had had little to no contact with his prior chain of command. "Yes, of course. That is my understanding, and with that, I am awaiting further instructions."

Looking pleased, Kluvnew relaxed, leaning back in his chair. "Good. Our people with the Ateris Mining Syndicate informed us that Director Prescott placed a rather interesting device on the *Murphy*. A device that sent them to a planet on the far edges of this galaxy. A planet that, for the most part, we understood to no longer be of any value to the Creare. While we don't know why, our people told us there was a very specific reason for him to do so."

Ran sat stoically. "The Creators."

"Yes." Kluvnew continued, "When we received the information, we sent a probe out and found some rather interesting things happening on the planet Teras. Not only were there traces of the *Murphy* and what we understand they are now calling the *Crow*, but it also intercepted signals from a Creare vessel."

While aware of the situation to a point, Ran didn't truly know exactly what this meant. Seeing this, Kluvnew expanded on his findings. "This means that the Ocess Syndicate sent the *Murphy* and its crew there for a specific reason. We believe that reason is to either secure the planet or make contact with the Creare, both of which are not good for our endeavors. What I can tell you is that our contacts stated that Director Prescott sent them there with no clear reasoning. Reasoning that will likely soon be clear to Captain Ben Dailey."

Ran chewed on the information for several long seconds as if he were savoring a delicious candy. "So you're saying they, meaning the Ocess Syndicate, want to make contact with the Creare?"

"Precisely that. As you are probably aware, we are at war with the Creare. Or will be, soon enough. A brutal and dominating civilization that would see us all enslaved."

Ran knew this was part truth and part conjecture. While the man had his head buried in the Federation, he'd also paid attention to all the stories from the Alurians. It was always a mixed bag when people talked about the Creators, which was done behind closed doors to avoid unwanted whispers.

Most of the stories agreed with what Kluvnew was saying, but in the same breath, he was also smart enough, being the great general that he was, to fully understand that they hadn't attacked anyone in the history that he knew. Only stories of the Alurians pushing them back centuries, if not millennia, ago existed.

"You want me to go to this planet and finish what I started with Captain Dailey?" Ran asked.

"Yes, finish what you started. There's one more thing. We also have reason to believe that there is a Creare ship on the planet's surface. The Assembly has asked for you to secure this vessel by any means possible."

While Ran wanted to finish what he'd started, he had also come to terms with what he had done to people he had served with for years. In many ways, he still had a code. Messed up as it was, as a warrior, he felt as if Dailey had earned the escape.

"Having second thoughts?" Kluvnew asked, tilting his head slightly.

"If you knew there was a ship there, why have you waited this long to retrieve it?"

This was a valid question that the vice admiral had known would be asked. "We didn't until recently. Our probe also picked up a signal—a signal that could only come from a Creare ship. And not just any ship, but an old one. We believe that Dailey and his crew activated a beacon aboard that ship. A beacon that we just happened to intercept."

Ran didn't like going into a situation knowing the Creators very well may have also intercepted that message. Nothing was an absolute in the deep void of space. "To clarify, my orders are to engage and destroy the *Murphy*, as well as the dreadnought, then secure the vessel."

"Yes," was all Kluvnew replied, setting the tone. This wasn't up for debate.

"Very well. Send the coordinates, and we will start preparations immediately. Also, will I have any support?"

Kluvnew smiled. "When the time comes . . . yes. Once you reach your destination, we will touch base again. It is my recommendation to secure the vessel first, if possible. I'll send you additional information while you are en route. Might I mention that completing this mission will put you in a very good position within the ranks of the Assembly? You will, of course, be heavily compensated. Safe travels, and may you be victorious."

The viewscreen winked out, and Ran stood up. While this sounded easy enough on the surface, the man knew just how persistent Captain Dailey was. With the mysterious superpowers that the crew of the *Murphy* had gained, and the sense that he was part of something bigger than himself, Ran started to focus on the task at hand.

There was more to this. There always was, and the man knew it after having learned his lesson. What Ran was working to sort out in his mind was precisely what role the Prime Assembly had to play in the quagmire that was the universe. The man would no longer be left in the dark and, if needed, would take matters into his own hands.

His personal computer started beeping as messages and information relating to the mission started pouring in. He had his orders, and he would execute them to the best of his abilities.

CHAPTER 12

THE HOUSE ON THE HILL

The regular cadence of the road and random jostling inside the cabin of the vert rover had taken the edge off their recent encounter. Several of the Nova Rangers were, in fact, joining Sparky in a light afternoon nap. Coolio strained his eyes as a large structure appeared meters off the side of the road.

"Sir," Coolio said, lightly tapping Dailey's hand.

Resting eyes slowly cracked open as Captain Ben Dailey leaned forward in his seat, taking a deep breath. "This better be good. You know, even captains need naps. Ain't that right, Sparky?"

The only response the Alurian war hound gave was a grunting snore.

"Check that out." Coolio pointed at the massive structure off the side of the road. While the rain was still heavy, it wasn't completely shrouding the building in mystery. Sitting at the end of what looked like a set of gates and a winding road was a massive house.

"That looks out of place," Dailey noted, pointing at dozens of large antennas reaching for the sky on the building's roof.

"Yeah, I'd say. It looks like a mansion. You know, one of those big fancy homes they used to have back home," Coolio added, slowly bringing the convoy to a stop.

"Still do, if you're looking," Dailey replied, having seen how the bureaucrats in the Federation lived.

"Check that out," Coolio pointed out, seeing a pile of bodies similar to the mutated ones they had just encountered lying next to the front door.

Dailey thoughtfully glanced at the clock on his tablet. "Albert, do we have time for a pit stop?"

In reality, they had been driving for several hours without a much needed break. While the rover had a small working restroom in the back, the other vehicles didn't. They likely needed to stop now, since everyone was waking up.

"Let me see. At our current rate of speed . . ." Albert started. "Yes. We have approximately two additional hours. We planned on having a sleepover before nightfall."

"Valen, you copy?" Dailey asked over the radio.

"Yes," Valen quickly replied.

"There's a building up there to our right. We are going to make a quick stop and check it out," Dailey said, turning back to the rest of the vert rover's passengers.

"Get ready. And someone wake up Sparky," Dailey ordered, looking down at the dog with his belly armor opened to accommodate the additional girth from his feast of replicated Solarian jerky.

Albert nudged the Alurian war hound, who released a near-toxic hazmat event in the rover.

The designated groups dismounted while everyone took a much-needed stretch break. Looking at the house, including the pile of mutant bodies, Dailey set his jaw, activating his HUD.

Albert stepped forward, activating his Gatling lasers with a resounding *ka-chunk* while Sparky growled. "Smells wrong," the translator kicked in.

Dailey looked around as everyone paused, focusing on the dynamic duo, before Janix and the rest of the Nova Rangers split into two groups, turning to face the ornate stone building.

Large, covered windows, once glowing with rich light, were now hidden in the gray daylight, keeping the building's interior safe from prying eyes.

Or, as Dailey supposed, its occupants from dealing with the reality of a dying world.

A long square car sat rusted, yet still in one piece. Albert had concluded that all the electrons chemically bonded in the rain kept metal from rusting at the usual rate. A large garage sat to the side with several bays open, exposing more decaying vehicles.

"Alright, you two," Dailey spoke as rain streaked his visor, "start talking."

Albert and Sparky continued to stare at the building. "From what I can tell, the building is teeming with electronic particles."

Sparky yipped through his now lowered helmet. "Fully charged."

"He is saying he is rested and fully—" Albert started before Dailey cut him off.

"Yeah, he's ready to go. I get it. Isn't that what you said the Shade was made of?"

Albert shifted as a small antenna rose out of Mister Toaster. The AI had been busy modifying the once glorious purveyor of toast. "Yes; however, the scorch marks on those bodies indicate the use of the same weapon that we picked up in the city. Look at the front door."

Janix motioned for Pickle and Woody to follow him close to the house. Dailey used his HUD's magnification setting to zoom in on a mix of blast marks from energy weapons, as well as a peppering of bullets.

"Over here," Valen called, walking over to an old military-style rifle that had seen better days nestled in the mud. "Looks like there were two parties engaged here."

"Three, if you count the Shade. But I get it. They don't use guns," Janix added.

A loud, cracking boom forced the group to turn. Albert stood in the main entranceway, surrounded by splinters of a now missing door. "Oh, sorry, guys. I thought I heard something," he said, pulling out an EMP grenade and chucking it into the entrance hall.

The blue pulse of the grenade created a halo around Albert as he turned, Mister Toaster's face giving an "Oops, was I supposed to do that" look.

"Go time." Dailey nodded. Janix and the rest of the Nova Rangers all took either side of the door, switching to EMP rounds as they smoothly entered like flowing water.

Valen and Tarik stood back, taking in the precision and violence of action, before glancing at each other. For once since joining the motley crew, they both shrugged.

Valen grinned. "No time like today to die." His voice came through like an ancient titan awakening his army.

Light from the Nova Ranger's armor and weapons alike filled the main entrance hall. Sparky stood in the middle of the room with Albert, scanning the moving shadows. As long as the main entrance hall was doused in light, the team was safe.

Several piles of ashes sat on the floor, taken out by the grenade Albert had chucked into the room. An opulent chandelier hanging precariously from the ceiling, waiting for an unsuspecting victim to linger, lightly moved in the cool air.

"What's the plan, sir?" Janix asked, relaxing more than any sentient being surrounded by ghosts should.

"Something in here has them all riled up. I want to know what that is," Dailey said, glancing down at the timer Albert had made sure was on everyone's wrist tablet. Unbeknownst to the Nova Rangers, it would also be playing Dolly Parton twenty minutes out, as Albert calculated that was the amount of time they would need to start shooting themselves out of any situation.

"Listen up. We do this as a team. Halo formation through the rooms. We light up that catwalk before we m—" This time, Albert interrupted Dailey by activating two EMP rounds.

Popping blue snaps erupted from the AI's surgical placement of the grenades. He had been triangulating the perfect trajectory the entire time they had been in the large room.

What Albert hadn't calculated was the sheer amount of darkness that poured from one of the doors on the second floor. More animated and significantly more agitated droves of the Shade encircled the room, soaking in the light.

"That's not good. Let it rip," Dailey barked, releasing a blue streak of rounds from his Sauder rifle across the catwalk.

Several more streams started flowing from the Nova Rangers, while Valen's team also joined the chorus of violence now unfolding. Albert, already having caused enough of a stir, glanced down at Sparky.

"What are you looking at?" Albert asked as Sparky leaned against the AI, creating a light glow, followed by a few modulated yips from behind his helmet.

"Along for the ride."

Albert's sensors started showing warning signs of overheating as the two main lasers wrapped around his shoulders began glowing a deep blue. Sparky was supercharging Albert's lasers.

Unlike regular kinetic weapons such as the Sauder rifles' superheated rounds, it had quickly been noted that lasers had little effect on the damned souls now encircling the team. However, superexciting the electrons that made up the Shade through Spark's superpowers—also referred to as magic by Albert—would.

The sound of Jones's armor clanking on the ground was drowned out by the gunfire as Albert, coming to terms with his systems being pushed to their limits, rechanneled all the power being pushed into him directly to his weapons.

Two massive streams of flowing blue energy shot from the lasers like water from a fire hose. Splatters of the crackling current swept the entire top floor, immediately creating a rain of ashes.

Dailey stopped firing, the Nova Rangers following suit to conserve ammunition while Albert hosed down the top floor. Spatters of blue, glowing material slopped from the beams as Mister Toaster's face turned into an evil grin.

While the thought of extinguishing long-lost souls was concerning, there was little left of the once conscious person. A spark snapped from Albert's power pack as Sparky slowly disconnected the flow of energy to his friend and most trusted advisor of the Ham Republic.

Within a minute, not only was the top floor glowing with energy, but it was also now on fire.

"Cease fire!" Dailey barked as the last sputter of Albert's hypercharged lasers came to a sizzling, smoking stop.

"That was the craziest shit I've ever seen," Valen said over comms as dust particles continued to drift to the main floor, resembling snow.

"Just wait, the show's just getting started," Janix followed. The two men were starting to gain respect for each other.

"Albert," Dailey called out, only to have to repeat himself much louder. "Albert!"

"Oh, hey, yeah. I'm here . . . I think. Wow, that was jazzy," Albert stated as smoke wafted from his main energy pack.

Meanwhile, Sparky trotted over to a pile of ashes, retracting his helmet and giving it a solid sniff, followed by what sounded like a burp. "They are free."

"What does that mean?" Dailey asked, but Sparky shrugged it off, reactivating his helmet.

Pickle walked over to Jones, pulling out a small power plug and inserting it into a small booster port on her back. "Here you go."

Jones's visor retracted as she took a breath of semifresh air. "Thanks," she gasped. "Whatever that thing did . . . it shut down my breather. Oh, and Pickle . . . at least take a girl to dinner first . . . before you start plugging things into her armor."

The Nova Rangers all chuckled lightly, even Valen joining in on the moment.

"Alright, enough of that. I want to see what those antennas on the roof do."

"Bad news, Captain," Albert said, his voice coming through as if he was out of breath. "The roof's about to collapse."

A *pop* was the first sign that Albert was indeed telling the truth before the chandelier that had been holding steady for centuries decided to make its final stand. Clattering jingles erupted from the massive ornament while Albert jumped several feet out of the way, ramming into and through one of the interior walls.

Sparky had already moved, now standing a few feet away from the wrecked lighting fixture. Crystals and other ornaments sprawled out on the floor like a bucket of dropped marbles, clinking against everyone's armored boots.

"Oh, would you look at that," Albert's voice came from the other side of the wall. Dailey turned, beaming his flashlight into the room.

The *Murphy*'s commander walked forward, motioning everyone else to stay in the main hall. What lay on the other side was the result of greedy hoarding. Gold and other precious items sat in neat piles covered in dust. Leaning against the wall was the skeleton of a man in a suit holding a radio hooked to a stack of wires. The king had gone down with their castle. All the riches in the world couldn't save the man when the time came.

To the left of the body, a pistol sat by the dead man's skeletal hand. Scanning the rest of the room, two more age-ravaged bodies, equally well dressed, lay on their sides. Massive holes in the front of their skulls expanded into shattered bones. The man with the radio, in a likely play for wealth, had killed his partners. These weren't bandits or roving members of a dying civilization.

"According to my mineral sensors, which are working now that we are out of that infernal rain, the collection of items in here would be considered a fortune by the day's standards. Today, not so much," Albert said, picking up a jewel-encrusted chalice.

"I wonder if the Shade drove them to this? Think about it. Back then, just the Creare ship would have been enough for them, let alone what was happening. Now, add ghosts, and you have yourself a bunch of crazies running around, falling back on what they know best."

"Very thoughtful. See, I told the *Murphy*'s entertainment systems you had a brain. I believe the radio signals attracted the Shade here. Speculation, but that is what I see."

Dailey shook his head, not wanting to engage in that conversation. "See if there's anything else here to tell us what happened." Dailey then shifted his focus. "Janix!"

"Sir," Janix replied trotting into the room, also taken aback by the scene.

"We've run out of time. This has nothing to do with those dead bodies outside. Something else did that. We need everyone to stay sharp. Get everyone loaded up, and let's get moving. We're not staying here for the night."

CHAPTER 13

QUIET NIGHT

The heavy rain of the previous day turned to a mist clinging to the outside of the vehicle parked inside an old garage several miles away from the opulent house they had encountered the Shade in. While still passable, the road leading out of San Con had disintegrated into nothing more than a path, and it was no different the further out they traveled.

Once the team had stopped for the night, Janix and the other Nova Rangers had set up a perimeter consisting of sensors and three automated laser turrets, just in case they got any unexpected company.

"You people sure know how to party," Albert scoffed, looking around at the group sipping on coffee and staring mindlessly at the ground after the long day. "Might I recommend some Solarian show tunes?"

Sparky yipped his approval, but was cut short by Dailey.

"You gotta stop watching Solarian shows. It's all about timing, Albert, and this isn't the time. We still don't know if the Shade, ravers, or any of those things we encountered in the city will show up. Just make sure the perimeter is secure and all our sensors are up and running. I don't trust anything in this damn nonstop rain."

Albert blew out a raspberry. "Very well. No fun. Well, at least we'll have comms with the *Murphy* in five, four, three, two, and go."

"Thank you, Your Greatness," Dailey joked, walking back up the ramp of the vert rover to the small command section nestled on the side of the vehicle.

The crew of the *Murphy* had been standing by as Becket's voice came over the radio within seconds of Albert's countdown. "This is Viper Five. Do you have a good copy?"

It caught Dailey by surprise that he was using military call signs. This was a surefire sign that something was amiss. "This is Viper Six, go ahead."

"It's damn good to hear your voice, sir," Becket growled, the background noises coming through.

Pearl was aboard the *Crow*, also listening in. "Viper Two here."

This was what the Nova Rangers called a net call.

"I'm guessing you have news. Send it," Dailey said, putting the conversation on speaker and motioning for Janix and Tarik to join him.

"Good news, bad news. There was a Creare ship that stopped in orbit hours ago to refuel. The good news is they didn't seem to know we were here, or even bothered to look. It seemed like this was fairly routine, and they didn't really care," Becket said as Dailey leaned back in the squeaky chair.

"We ran into a little snag down here as well, but we are back on the move. Conditions here are favorable for maneuvering on the ground. Looks like it will be several more hours before we get to our target, if we're lucky and don't run into any more trouble. As I mentioned, you don't want to be traveling down here at night," Dailey replied, getting as much information out as he could, like a kid sitting on Santa's lap with a limited amount of time to spit out his Christmas wishes.

"Is Albert around?" Pearl asked.

"No," Albert interjected. "I'm just a highly intelligent AI who just so happens to be able to monitor your frequencies even if I'm out here making sure the auto turrets have enough lube in their little swivel thingies."

"Good," Pearl continued. "We think somewhere between your landing, the probe we sent, and the readings Jen picked up, we triggered something on the ground. It appears a signal came from the planet and shot through a gate. Several hours later, that ship appeared. I'm not saying it's not a coincidence, but as the captain always says, there are no such things as coincidences."

Dailey glanced around the pile of people listening behind him. "That means the clock's ticking. I think we've all figured out we're here for a reason. Prescott—"

Sparky barked loud enough to catch everyone's attention. *Gabarf!* Which translated into: "Asshat."

"Yeah, asshat," Dailey echoed, "sent us here for a reason. With a Creare ship on the ground, the actual Creare ship showing up, and Prescott wanting to take over the Ocess Mining Syndicate's rights, it's difficult to say what other bullshit they have planned."

Dorax cleared his throat, leaning over a massive console aboard the *Crow*. "Maybe they actually want to help."

Every ass within earshot of the conversation pondered the statement. Dailey leaned forward.

"I think it's a mix of everything. They've already showed their colors out in the open. I'm not sure who or what is coming, but my gut is telling me we will have company soon."

"Your gut?" Albert cut in. "Do you need to evacuate your lower intestines? Between the hydrated bacon and coffee, I'm sure it's not far off."

"All that brain and nothing better to do." Dailey smirked. "As soon as we get some rest and the morning drops, we're making the final push."

"If something happens up here, what do you want us to do?" Pearl asked while Dailey motioned Albert to come inside the rover instead of cutting into the comms link.

"Albert, you're the smart one in the room. What's a good way to signal each other when the comms go out?" Dailey asked as Mister Toaster's face shifted into a flat expression.

"Is it always like this?" Valen quietly leaned over, asking Janix. The Solarian nodded.

"Recently, yes. Well, most of the time," he corrected himself.

"I'm thinking, now that everyone knows we're here, we don't have to be shy. At least not yet." Albert held up a finger to let him continue before Dailey could interrupt and simplify the question. "The air defense system kicks in at a fairly low altitude. Smart, by the way; it keeps visitors from pulling out and hitting their hyperdrives. No witnesses," he drawled out malevolently.

"Get to the point," Dailey huffed.

"Since they will be aboveground, you can launch three or four probes at different places, one being, let's say, our current location. If that infernal rain is light, we should be able to get a comms link. A little weak, but just start pinging our transponder as soon as you launch them. We'll eventually pick it up."

"We can set them on a time delay as well," Pearl added. "We don't know where the tracking starts. It will give us enough time to let you know, and possibly a little extra."

Dailey liked the plan. "Agreed. As for us, we have a handful of OFFs. Just keep an eye on our location as long as you can."

Orbital signal flares, known as OFFs, gave the Nova Rangers the ability to launch what was basically a high-altitude firework with a signal burst from a planet's surface, signaling there was a problem they couldn't solve, or that they needed a fast ride out of whatever mess they were in.

You could hear Becket's voice winding up. "What's the ROE?"

Dailey didn't hesitate. "You have full authority to take or not take whatever action is necessary." The *Murphy*'s commander was telling them they were on their own when it came to calling the shots.

The conversation ended with the two teams agreeing to touch base in a couple of hours before heading out. While Dailey wanted to leave for the ship, the team needed to be sharp, and the dangers of traveling at night on Teras were not worth the risk.

Sounds of angry, raging animals roared throughout the night as the rain continued to mist, allowing the distant sounds to carry over the dying landscape.

Morning came as the two guards made their rounds, ensuring everyone was up after their two-hour shift. The sounds of the auto turrets had almost lulled them to sleep from constantly whirling at unknown ghosts throughout the night.

The Nova Rangers had proven to be worthy adversaries, keeping the things of nightmares at bay. At one point, when Dailey and Sparky had been pulling their shift, several Shades had wisped by meters away from camp, acting as if they didn't even know they were there. Dailey had been seconds away from waking the team up.

When it came down to it, Sparky could have just trotted over to them and hyperexcited their molecules, causing them to dematerialize. The planet once thought dead was, in reality, very much alive—or something in between, with the Shade.

The sounds of armor being fully coupled and the nanotech driving them mixed with the sounds of Valen's team clinking their coffee cups with their newly found holy water: coffee. While keeping Albert on guard duty was an option, it was Dailey's instruction to always have a live person with him. Sparky didn't count due to the sheer amount of things they, in fact, did without what Becket called "adult supervision."

"Ah, rise and shine." Albert had clearly lost the game of who would talk first, as a few groans came from the vert rover. Someone had lost a bet. "We will have comms with the *Murphy* in five minutes. Oh, and don't forget to wear your wet-weather gear. It looks like it's going to be a gusher!"

Sparky yawned, showing his capable mouth full of sharp teeth. He was also not happy with his friend for breaking the morning vow of silence the Nova Rangers practiced until everyone was at least thinking straight.

"Thanks, not like our armor or all these gadgets we have didn't tell us it was morning," Dailey said, walking out, looking rested. He had already cleaned his face and pulled a comb through his hair.

"Rude," Albert chuffed. "Anyway, you'll be happy to know everyone is safe and sound. There were only eighty-five known close events last night, according to the scanners and auto turrets scan."

"Eighty-five?" Dailey asked. Janix walked up with Valen and Tarik.

"This place is either going to kill us or make us regret our life choices," Janix joked. He was referring to becoming a Nova Ranger.

"You mean like those emails you sent to Staff Sergeant Shannon—"

Janix cut him off. "Toilet seat. Dailey has given me authorization to replace your main sensor pod in order to support the mission."

Dailey shrugged. "He's got me there."

Albert cocked his head, letting Mister Toaster's mustache straighten. "I don't see any reason you would need to do that?"

Janix grinned. "Two reasons, actually. For starters, that chow you made us is working its way through not only mine but the others' systems as well. Secondly, we do have bread, and you know what they say?"

"That sometimes cucumbers taste better pickled?" Albert asked, genuinely curious.

"What I'm saying is the team is using the roto-sanitary crate. From what Bellman explained, it is a suitable replacement while we make toast. If we're in a hurry, we might have to leave the auto lid sensor on you."

Albert took several seconds to compute the situation, analyzing thousands, if not millions, of scenarios involving the statement. This included him pulling the schematics of the roto toilet. Bellman was correct in his assessment. All other options would be mission critical.

Next, the AI pulled quotes from his massive storage of old movies, finding dozens of references to the army marching on their stomachs. Fortunately for the others, Albert found himself at a crossroads. This was the one thing that worried Dailey, as well as made it fun sometimes.

"I have reviewed your statement against two-point-five million data points and your personal file; yes, I have access to those—the boss already knows. He sure knows how to pick 'em," Albert started. "Anyway. No need for that; I must have gotten my communications mixed up with another platoon master sergeant from Sol . . . somewhere. Maybe not even our ship."

Both men grinned. "Just busting your balls," Janix said, smiling.

"But I don't have any—"

Dailey cut Albert off. He had noticed the AI, for some reason, was not doing as well as he usually would in a conversation like this. It was probably the planet. "I don't think the crew is ready for you and the ham overlord's dating game yet," Dailey suggested, already knowing of their plans.

"True," Albert replied as Sparky yawned out a bark.

"It's still not ready," Sparky's voice came over the speaker as Dailey pressed the comms button.

Nothing had changed since their last touch point, meaning it was time to go. While still working to stay incognito, the crew of the *Murphy* and the *Crow* were both activating their long-range sensors in case they had visitors.

CHAPTER 14

PURPLE SKY IN THE MORNING, NOVA RANGER TAKES WARNING

The morning's light drizzle quickly morphed into an all-out monsoon, while the now barely visible road continued to morph into a trail, the concrete roads having now turned to dust, creating a gray clay that slipped under the tires of all the vehicles.

With the limited visibility, Albert had used the maps provided by Tarik to create a surprisingly accurate road map, and two slow hours had now passed since the team had left in the hopes of making it to the ship.

A red light flashed on the dash in front of Coolio as he slowed the convoy to a halt. "There is a small township on the map. We should be pulling up to it right now," he stated as a lull in the rain revealed several one-story buildings.

Unlike San Con, the small township in front of them consisted of one-story buildings sprawled out in a basic layout. While not having detailed maps, it was clear that the main street led toward the only two-story building in the center of town.

"We getting out?" Janix asked as Dailey pondered the question.

"Not unless we have to. I have a feeling the clock's already ticking," Dailey responded, glancing down at a snoring Sparky. The Alurian war hound often fell asleep within minutes of starting to drive.

The road slightly improved once they moved into the small town, rocks crackling underneath as the vehicle passed between the first section of buildings. Unlike San Con, the city was better preserved, showing no signs of real destruction.

Several windows, still intact, protected whatever was inside the buildings. The occasional caved-in roof and broken storefronts showed the craftsmanship of each building.

"Interesting," Albert spoke up, plugged into the rover's sensors.

"You know I don't like interesting, Albert. I like to know what you're looking at," Dailey said as Coolio once again brought the lead vehicle to a halt.

A storefront to their left promised fresh food, as well as clothes. This was probably the town's general store. To their right, a gas station configured differently to how it would be back on Earth had the pumps built into the actual building, with hoses set on reels coming out of metal boxes.

"Well, there's an extremely strong signal coming from that building in the center of town. It appears to be alien tech. I can't tell through all the static, but it does appear to be a beacon. It doesn't match anything I found on the computers at the air base. Plus, it's slicing through this rain like a razor. Almost like it's made to."

Dailey turned to Janix. "Same as last time; I want the vehicles moving with us. However, the town's too small to hide."

Janix looked skeptically at the *Murphy*'s commander. "It looks like the signal's only sending, not receiving."

"Could've told you that," Albert added. "Yes, you are correct. From what I can tell, no one is scanning us. Points to Solaria."

"That's good news," Dailey said, standing up, his armor fully encasing his upper body. "Time to move. Get the others on the radio. Let them know what's going on."

Within minutes, the entire team was moving toward the city center. A small sign proudly proclaimed that the township of Packer would like to welcome them to their annual harvest celebration. This was a farming community.

The two-story brick building sat in the middle of the city like a shepherd overlooking their herd. Stairs led up to an open door. Several windows on the second story also stood open, with a walkway wrapping around the building overlooking the town square. This had, once upon a time, been a place of community.

Albert, Janix, and Dailey stood beside the last building leading up to the main courtyard surrounding the town hall. All three vehicles on the entrance road sat lined up, ready to do violence at a moment's notice. With the sheer amount of firepower now pointed toward the building, it would only take a few short seconds to turn it into rubble.

Dailey didn't feel it was his job to take out a building that had defeated time itself.

"Albert, take the lead. Lambert, Jones, Tarik, no change. Sparky, with me," Dailey instructed as the team started making their way to the town hall.

Half-alive trees and monuments sat at random intervals, all leading to a small water feature full of mud and muck from years of rain. Directly in front of the town hall, two large statues gave the fire teams cover. The first was of a man holding a document with his hand pointed toward the sky. Boots and other tools etched into the carving represented the man likely having something to do with building the city.

Beside the man was the portrayal of a woman holding a cornucopia overflowing with fruits and vegetables. From the flat fields surrounding the city and other clues, she represented the fruitful harvest the city had once provided.

Albert stepped forward, walking up the stairs. Without hesitation, the AI chucked a sensor grenade inside the building, waiting for it to send back whatever readings it could.

Dailey, having grabbed another one of the small video drones, released it, zipping by Albert and into the building, only for it to be taken over by the AI. Once again, live video feed crackled to life in their HUDs, as well as the screen inside the rover.

It didn't take long to find out what was dead and decaying inside that building, as well as sending off a signal. In the main hall, eight tattered flags stood resolute, covered in green moss. In front of the symbols of unity, three sleek figures covered in smooth black armor lay on the ground in front of what looked like a security desk.

Data started coming in through Dailey's tablet. Normally, Bellman would translate what all the gobbledygook meant. Here, that job was up to Albert.

"Interesting," the AI said again. Knowing better, he quickly corrected himself, taking several steps forward into the arched opening. "Three life-forms; they are absolutely no longer processing carbon. One of them is holding a beacon. Not sure what happened, but if I had to guess, those are Creare."

That caught the entire group off guard, and Dailey soon found himself running up to Albert, pressing him to enter the building. They were followed by the two fire teams.

After securing the main room, the group turned their focus to the three large figures sprawled out on the floor. Dailey, wanting to see with his own eyes, clicked his helmet off.

"I don't see any signs of a battle," were the first words out of the man's mouth. "Albert?"

The AI walked up to the three figures, quickly scanning them while Sparky started sniffing around the room. "No, but . . ." Albert said, leaning down as he clicked a small round ball on the side of one of their helmets before picking up the beacon and deactivating it.

The hiss of the suit depressurizing was short-lived as a purple light clicked on, revealing its wearer's face. Human features and what could only be described as model-like looks made the dead figure look as if he were simply napping.

Unlike any normal adult—be it human, Solarian, or otherwise—the face of this figure didn't have the normal lines telling the story of their life. The smooth skin almost presented an artificial appearance, much like the robots back on Earth that had been designed to look human.

"Seems to be slightly larger than a human, but appears human or Solarian, nonetheless," Albert spoke as Dailey shook his head.

"The Creare are humanoid?" he asked no one and everyone at the same time. Looking down, another of the weapons that had been used by the mutants sat inches away from the body.

Albert, seeing this, picked it up. "I don't know why or how, but all this tech looks awfully familiar to me."

"You said you didn't know much about your past other than the planet you came from. Who knows? Dorax confirmed the Alurians don't have anything like you," Dailey pondered as the expression on Mister Toaster's face went flat. He was thinking.

"Possibly, but I don't think that is the conversation we should be having now. Why are these figures here, and more importantly, for how long? Sparky, old chap?" Albert called out.

Sparky stopped sniffing all the corners of the building, and with a few yips, a bark, and what was assumed to be a growl, the translator kicked in. "Not like when we claimed the warehouse for the republic."

"What's he talking about?" Tarik asked as Dailey took a few steps back from the bodies.

"It's sort of a long story, but that warehouse we stayed in was sort of claimed by Sparky. Just go along with it," Dailey replied. The man turned to Albert.

"Why would the Creare not come to the base sooner?" Tarik asked, bringing up a good point.

"Hibernation," Albert blurted out.

"How's that?" Dailey asked as Albert did his version of a shrug, the two Gatling lasers on his shoulders shifting.

"They must have had emergency protocols on their ship that put them in hibernation in the event of an emergency, or they had a portion of them in hibernation while the rest died. The Creare are known for this."

"How do you know that?" Dailey asked. Albert looked concerned.

"I . . . I don't really know. Maybe it's just a hunch."

"I find your hunches are never wrong," Janix cut in. "Either way, something killed them."

Sparky chuffed. "Frozen food."

"He's right." Albert leaned down, poking the unmasked figures. "There are signs of long-term reanimation atrophy cascadious, or RAC, as Medical Officer Casey Franklin would call it."

"Of what?" Dailey asked. "In English."

"It's when a body has been in hibernation too long, and once reanimated, all their internal bits effectively turn to mush. It can often be remedied, but that would take a live audience doing the reanimation, if you know what I mean," Albert finished. Janix checked the other two figures, confirming the prognoses.

Both humans and Solarians practiced hibernation, and were capable of keeping a body in stasis for a couple of decades, if not centuries when properly taken care of. The tech had been primarily used before hyperdrives were fully developed and usable by both civilizations. Back then, even prior to the Tectonic Wars, crew members scheduled for long-haul trips were frequently put in hibernation. These trips generally lasted two to three years.

Now, the Federation medical advisors utilized this as a way to keep bodies alive in the event of catastrophic injury or disease. It was also used to keep high-profile prisoners from causing any issues. At the end of the day, it was not usually needed with the use of hyper and now gate drives.

Dailey started thinking. "You said it was a protocol thing in the event of an emergency. I'm buying what you're selling, even if we don't know what's on the menu. You know about these things, and that's a fact. Plus, I have yet to see another of you running around.

"Think about it. They lay dormant for how long, and as soon as a real ship landed and sent out a signal that was likely intercepted by some on-board scanner, it woke up the crew, thinking it was their own people, or maybe to get them to protect the ship. I'm not saying I agree with it, but we don't know how the Creare think or why they even came here other than to kill the planet."

"I don't understand," Tarik spoke up.

"Maybe it had something to do with the planet itself, or what's here. They might not even have been trying to kill the planet. But either way, they did. We keep forgetting we are on a small island in a big ocean, and no one here has been to more than a few cities. I saw the maps. Teras is roughly the size of Earth."

The statement still didn't answer Tarik's question, but it did put things into perspective. The truth was that most of what they were saying were educated guesses coming from years of experience and an AI.

"I have a sneaking suspicion it may have something to do with the Shade. I can see traces of that pesky mess they leave behind. Look." Albert pointed to a pile of familiar ashes by a side door.

"Well, that's not what killed them. Those guns they use, one damn near ate my shield. It does something like Sparky to the electrons in the air," Dailey stated while Albert nodded his approval. "It would have taken some firepower to take one of these guys out."

"Precisely. Which means they knew something about the planet we are not aware of, or what the effects of them dropping that purple sludge into the atmosphere did to that certain something. The logs lay it all out. Odd happenings and a partridge in a pear tree."

Tarik was starting to get used to Albert's use of slang. Even though he didn't get the reference, he fully understood what point Albert was trying to make.

Heavy rain continued to pelt the buildings, creating a small cascade of water that skipped down the stairs leading to a second-story walkway.

Somewhere on the second floor, the roof had given in to time and Mother Nature. The small stream followed the wall, leading into one of the office doors and out of the main room, showing the building had settled over time with a slight tilt.

"Our logs, the ones we had access to, talked a lot about the Shade being a much bigger problem in the beginning. It seems more of a nuisance now," Tarik piled on.

"A nuisance that can kill you. Let's respectfully take a few things and get back on the road. If we run into any kicking ones, we handle it like we always do," Dailey said, taking one last glance at the three bodies, filming the entire interaction to review later.

"They appear to have some type of control system in their armor. It looks like it is tied to the person wearing it. That means if the owner of the suit dies, so does the system. Smart—that's one of the first few things I would look at as an adversary," Albert said to Dailey and Sparky, who was now standing beside them.

Valen walked up to the group, holding a stack of decaying files. "We found these. One of the side offices. It looks like some more detailed maps of the area."

Tarik took the folder, seeing that Dailey's hands, while encased in armor, were not the best thing to handle delicate documents with. "Albert, can you scan these?"

"But of course," Albert replied as Tarik held out several of the maps.

A blue light adjusted to fit the shape of the paper as it quickly scanned the maps, as well as a handful of documents. "Interesting. Once again," Albert said, knowing he needed to follow up on the statement, "it appears that most of the inhabitants headed west when this all started. Looks like toward a city called Shakumville. Apparently, they also witnessed the ship going down, and didn't want to have anything to do with it."

"We can cross-reference it with the rest of the maps when we return. Dorian will know," Tarik said, turning to Dailey.

"Well, at least we know there's a ship on the ground somewhere close. That's one thing we got right so far. Let's get back on the road. Albert, send an update to the *Murphy*. We should still have comms," Dailey said, making the universal sign for *it's time to go*, waving his arm in the air in a circle.

Back on the road, the tail end of the city was just as drab as its entrance. Same as before, the road quickly turned into an unimproved trail. Flat fields stretched as far as the eye could see in the rain, showing signs of the farming once done on the land.

"How much longer?" Coolio asked. Albert shifted to look at the newly updated map.

"According to SOP, we should be stopping in roughly five miles." What Albert meant was the team would dismount their vehicles and walk the rest of the way, with the rover and old armored trucks as support.

Similar to old-style Humvees, the trucks had been unexpectedly reliable. Albert had rigged too many fusion generators to the vehicles, giving them pretty much an everlasting battery. The two main issues they were concerned about were the electrical systems, as neither the internal nor external lights worked. The tires, unlike the ones the military on Earth had used, were solid composite rubber, so when they found the vehicles, they were rotted and falling apart in chunks.

Luckily, the designers of the Vault had taken that into consideration. Stored alongside the vehicles were vacuum-sealed packages full of some type of viscous material to keep the tires inside stored and in working condition.

After a little handling by Albert, including several gallons of graphite grease, the gun turrets on top of the vehicles were now also operational.

With the rain starting to lighten, Dailey's field of vision grew. A large, hulking black mass shadowed the side of a mountain several miles in front of them. Either Lady Luck was smiling down upon them, or, as was usual, the rain had lightened only to come back five times harder than before.

"That has to be it," Dailey announced while everyone shuffled forward from the back of the rover, looking out the windshield.

"We are picking up a signal from that location identical to the one Lieutenant Jen Brax initially identified," Albert said, turning back to the control panel and pushing Janix out of his seat. The man didn't say a word, knowing Albert was likely doing something significantly more important than him, staring at the same map as he had been for the last day and a half.

Tarik was already on the radio, informing the other drivers of the situation. Coolio, knowing they needed to get organized now that they had a lay of the terrain, slowly pulled the convoy over. What unnerved the man was that they were as naked as a newborn baby sitting in an open field, being overlooked by the monolithic ship.

"What's the plan, sir?" Coolio asked Dailey, who chewed on his bottom lip, tapping his fingers on the helmet sitting on his lap.

"I'm pretty sure the rain will start picking up soon. The location is the same as we projected. Confirm with the *Murphy* that we have indeed identified the ship. You see that smaller-looking thing in the field in front of us?" Dailey asked, squinting his eyes.

"Looks like a building or vehicle," he suggested.

Albert turned to scan the field in front of them.

"It appears to be a vehicle from the ship. There looks to be some type of power source on board, but other than that, it's dormant. Just taking a nap, as you like to say," Albert added, turning back to the screen, using every tool at his disposal to scan and also work through what they were about to come in contact with.

"Take us there, and then we will dismount the rest of the way," Dailey ordered as the convoy veered off into the open fields.

Wet, tall grass slapped the front of the rover as the ride became significantly less comfortable, jostling the inhabitants of the vehicle like a stomach full of soured milk. The ground finally started clearing as signs of someone else being there presented a flattened field.

"We're a hundred meters out," Coolio said, stopping.

"Same teams, no change," Dailey ordered, standing up, snapping his helmet in place.

Unlike the patrol formation the team took while entering the cities, Dailey and the other Nova Rangers were in tactical mode, moving with the help of their boost packs while the vehicles provided covering fire as they moved across the open field.

Not to be outdone, Tarik pushed his team to move as Valen ran behind two armored members of the Vault. "Keep moving," Valen barked over the comms, motivating Tarik to step up his pace too.

Within five minutes, the team was standing in front of the sleek black Creare vehicle. Random weapons protruded from its top like a tank, offset with sensors and other random unidentifiable armaments.

Its wheels resembled tracks that had been balled up into a fist, able to turn in all directions, with only a few hints of their age showing. On the ground several feet away, two Creare bodies lay in the same condition as the others.

Albert and Sparky stood by the entrance hatch as the AI pulled a triangular cable from his chest, plugging it into the door panel after wrenching it off with more effort than Dailey was used to. The thing was built like a tank.

"You sure about this?" Janix asked as Dailey remained silent, scanning the tall brush twenty-five meters away.

Albert simply nodded as a ramp slowly seeped out from under the vehicle, like a hand reaching out to scope its occupants up. This was followed by the light clank of the entrance door parting into a dozen pieces.

The AI stood in the doorway.

"You know what I'm about to ask," Dailey said, making the conversation personal by getting close.

"Is any of this familiar? Yes, it's too familiar. It's like fragments of my memory are being unlocked every time I touch this infernal Creare equipment."

"You're not going native on us, are you?" Dailey joked as Sparky looked up. Even though the mighty hound's face shield was down, you could tell he had a concerned look.

"Oh, lord no. And miss out on all the fine romance literature I downloaded from the Vault? Not a chance. It's more like unlocking levels in a video game, if that makes sense," Albert replied.

"Well, just don't plug into this stuff. I'm all about learning about your past, but I'm fairly certain by this point we know why we haven't seen anything like you before," Dailey said.

"Maybe, maybe not. Time will tell. All I can say is that being out in space for so long and clearly having something done to me at some point, changed my primary directives. In other words . . . I ain't going nowhere." Albert turned while Mister Toaster's chubby face grinned.

The inside of the vehicle was just as foreign as its mysterious occupants. Smooth lines morphed into the walls like they were grown from the massive ship sitting in front of them.

Blank panels and clear glass screens gave no need for windows, using tech to maneuver through whatever environment they were in. One thing was clear—this was a military vehicle, evidenced by the racks of weapons sitting untouched.

"Can you get it working?" Dailey asked as Janix and Tarik joined them. The others were still pulling security outside.

"Yes, I think so. It might even be hooked up to the ship. Wait a bit." Albert pulled the triangular plug still hanging from his chest, slapping it into a port on the side of the commander's seat.

Albert's face went blank as he worked through the system. Purple lights slowly phased into existence in the yellow ambient light as the glass panels all sprang to life.

Unknown markings and what appeared to be a very well drafted 3D graphic of the surrounding area clicked onto the main screen, which flashed with several warnings. Dailey walked to the screen, assuming it was touch reactive, and zoomed in on the map to the area flashing red directly over the town hall they had found the Creare in.

"Shit," Dailey breathed out, seeing their vehicles represented by green outlines. "They were coming after us."

Albert's face morphed back into Mister Toaster as Sparky started his sniffing ritual. "Most definitely. What I find fascinating is that their systems can operate in this mucky weather like it isn't an issue. They had a very good idea of where we were. And likely where we are."

Dailey thought about it, letting the idea roll around his brain. "If it were a trap, we would know by now. We are the most vulnerable here, in an open field inside one of their vehicles. I would have blown the damn thing up."

"My thoughts exactly," Albert agreed. "Hold on, the ship or whatever is trying to tell me something." Albert's face again went blank.

"No. Yes." The AI was having a conversation with the ship while talking out loud. "I never. You'd be smart not to be that rude. We'll see about that. Oh, not meaning to be rude. I thought you said . . ." Albert paused, listening. "Why didn't you say so? Ships in the system? You do know. Never mind. Yes, of course. Scouts honor. I mean, I promise to follow protocol. I can't make any promises. Does your mother know you talk like that? Okay. Yes."

Dailey stood listening with a mix of shock and amusement at the conversation. The system obviously wasn't aware of the human slang Albert had picked up. "What was that all about?"

"Well, at first, I thought the AI was being rude. Then, I realized it was a programmed AI system. But then, it got all snooty with me. Something about other ships entering the system. Then it invited us on board to have a chat, only if we promise not to undertake hostilities against any of its remaining crew."

"What happens if we undertake hostilities?" Dailey asked as Albert did his shrug thing with his shoulder-mounted lasers.

"I doubt it would be to our benefit, but I would assume the ship would protect itself and its crew. Might I add, it knew something about me, and reminded me of that. Last thing: there is a live crew member on board that mainly wants to have a chat with us."

Dailey glanced over at Sparky, hearing his armor retract, about to lift his hind leg up next to the weapons rack. "Sparky, not now. We are here to have a chat first."

A few chuffs translated into, "Fine. Maybe just this one vehicle later."

Nodding, Dailey walked back outside as the rain started to pick back up.

CHAPTER 15

YOU HAVE YOUR ORDERS

The deep black of inner space slowly morphed into an array of stars as the *Void Reaper* exited the gate on the far end of the system that Teras occupied. With twelve planets—six of them massive gas giants with atmospheres full of gases, making them unprofitable for mining operations—Teras stood as the only inhabitable planet around a massive, angry red sun.

Communications Officer Felix looked up from his control panel. "Sir, a message from Vice Admiral Kluvnew. Shall I patch it through to your quarters?"

Ran pondered the implications of having an open conversation versus one tucked neatly away in his quarters. At this point, everything was on the table, and he needed his crew to be fully operational and aware of the situation in regard to Dailey and the crew of the *Murphy*.

"No. Patch it through to the bridge," Ran instructed, standing up. He wanted to see how the unknown faces on the bridge reacted to the conversation.

Kluvnew's face winked into existence on the main viewscreen, showing the vice admiral on the bridge of an unknown ship.

"General Ran. We just received word that you made it to the Cheyenne System."

"Yes, I was about to send a message," Ran replied, confused as to how the vice admiral was communicating with them so quickly through what was a significant amount of space.

"Very good. What is your plan of action?" Kluvnew asked with a wide grin reaching the top of his cheekbones.

While Ran had briefed his primary staff, he hadn't fully laid out the plan to the rest of the crew of the *Void Reaper*. His ship was massive, much larger than the *Crow*, being what was considered a superdreadnought. Holding several attack fighter wings, as well as an entire brigade worth of ground shock troopers, Kluvnew had ensured he had a full crew. A crew the general had yet to test or fully trust.

While he had a small group of loyal officers and senior noncommissioned officers whom he had worked with over the years and brought with him, he had yet to meet all of his new staff members.

"I plan on splitting up the attack wings. The intention is to send one to the planet to secure the ship while we and the other fighters address the situation with the *Murphy*. I'm fairly certain by now they are on the planet, and are either en route or have already found the downed Creare ship. If by chance they have it working and off the planet, we will shift the attack wing to secure the ship."

Kluvnew chewed on this for a few seconds. "You keep saying not to underestimate the crew of the *Murphy*. I will tell you not to underestimate the crew you now have aboard the *Void Reaper*. That is a sound plan. We are maneuvering forces to be within less than a day's travel. We can confirm the Creare ship has not left the planet." This simply meant they were positioning their ships at a gate that would get them there with relative ease.

The statement caught Ran's attention. The ship hadn't left the planet yet. If the Prime Assembly was able to get to the locations that quickly, why hadn't they already been sending forces?

"We will take that into consideration. I am not naive enough to believe they haven't already sent out long-range sensors across the system. If they don't know we are here yet, they will. As soon as we are set, we will be activating the hyperdrive and engaging," Ran followed up as his primary crew listened closely to the conversation.

"As soon as you arrive and start the operation, send us a status report. We will likely position our forces at your current location," Kluvnew stated, leaning back. The conversation was over.

"Yes, sir," Ran replied as the vice admiral's image faded away. Turning to his bridge crew, the once upon a time great general started working through the reasoning behind them not sending their full force.

Felix, knowing what the man was thinking, stood up to walk over to him. "Word in private, sir?"

Without responding, Ran turned on his heels, his boots clicking on the smooth black bridge's floor. The two men stood in a small briefing room just off the main corridor leading up to the bridge.

"You don't trust them?" Felix asked, knowing he was out of place but that he was also one of the few people Ran could trust.

"Do you?"

"Sir, you know me. I don't trust anyone." Felix shuffled lightly on his feet.

"I trust you and the others. Call a briefing in the main auditorium for all the senior leadership on board."

Felix nodded. "Do you have a backup plan, sir?"

Ran had been asking himself the same question. He was starting to get aggravated with the breadcrumbs Kluvnew dropped every time they talked. "In the event of any unforeseen issues, we take the Creare ship and let Dailey deal with whomever we feel may cause an issue on board."

It was that straightforward to the man. In case Kluvnew considered Ran expendable, he would take the prize and let the rest of Kluvnew's clearly handpicked crew deal with the repercussions. While he had burned several bridges, he was fully aware that the Ateris Mining Syndicate would take him in with such a prize.

The auditorium was a massive briefing room with dozens of rows of chairs, all facing a large stage with a massive table and an even larger viewscreen behind it. Hundreds of section leaders filled the space with conversations and noise as Hap, the *Void Reaper*'s Alurian executive officer from the Prime Assembly, called the meeting to order.

"On your feet!" the Alurian announced as General Ran walked onto the stage from a side entrance.

"Take your seats," Ran huffed out, looking down at his loyal team members all sitting in a small section several rows back.

Unfamiliar faces and random uniforms representing the different units on board all sat in their assigned sections, giving the room an odd pattern of colors. While he had taken his time getting to know most of his staff and section leaders, he had been more focused on the overall operation of the ship, leaning on his primary staff to do the socializing.

An image of Teras with multiple release points and targets sat on the screen, moving in real-time with the rotation and movement of the planet. The automated image was from a sensor probe that had scanned the planet several years ago.

"As all of you are aware, we are maneuvering to a planet called Teras. Records indicate the planet was once inhabited by a humanoid civilization that was wiped out by the Creare. It has been confirmed there is a Creare ship on the planet's surface which is likely salvageable. We have been tasked with retrieving this vessel." Ran paused as one of the senior staff officers pulled up a schematic of the *Murphy*, as well as one of the *Crow*.

"We've been further tasked with securing both the USF *Murphy* as well as a next-generation Alurian dreadnought." This garnered some attention, as shown by the light shuffling of colors in the crowd. "The commander of this ship may be a familiar name to many of you. Captain Ben Dailey, as many of you know, was under my command at one point, and is the primary reason we have been tasked with this mission." Ran knew this was bullshit and that he was considered nothing more than a tactical pawn with experience.

"We are splitting our attack fighter wings into two groups. Group one will stay with the ship to engage the *Murphy* and the stolen vessel with the *Void Reaper*. We will be discussing this in more detail shortly. Group two is tasked with securing the vessel on the planet's surface, as well as escorting a ground force of shock troopers in the event we run into any Nova Rangers. I will be supporting the mission from here and will be putting Executive Officer Hap in charge of the ground force. Once the Creare vessel is secured or in orbit, I will be taking the lead on that ship."

This caught the Alurian off guard, who squinted his slitted eyes. He didn't like that, knowing about the planet's air defense systems.

"Each of your sections will be given a mission package. For Group one and the *Void Reaper*, I will say this: The USF *Murphy* is the Federation's latest generation of frigate-class starship and not to be taken lightly. Everyone here is aware of the capabilities of the ship from the debrief I published from the battle over Asher. We have cause to believe they have an advanced system on board, allowing the ship and crew to perform as they have been lately. The Prime Assembly and Alurian Council are fully aware of the Federation's new capabilities."

Ran couldn't be more wrong in his assessment of Albert, but he also didn't want to take any chances. While he knew about the new ships, the man's arrogance had kept him from fully understanding their full capabilities. Arrogance that would no longer be a roadblock for the man.

"In the event we get the ship into orbit, I will be personally taking command of the vessel," Ran repeated, wrapping up the brief before handing it over to the leaders of the attack wing and ground forces. Again, Hap looked at the man, not liking the idea. He had clearly been given separate orders.

"Your section leaders will finish the briefing. We leave in ten hours."

With his part over, Ran walked off the stage as Executive Officer Hap followed him to the secondary briefing room behind the stage. He was quickly followed by Felix, seeing the nonverbal signs the Alurian was giving off.

Ran sat at the table, pulling out his personal tablet to send a message to Kluvnew with the overall timeline and plan. Seeing Hap enter, followed closely by Felix, the general motioned the two guards out of the room.

"Ah, Hap. I was hoping to have a word," Ran started, taking immediate control of the conversation.

"Sir, I was not aware of the change in plans to have you take charge of the Creare ship."

Felix walked the rest of the way in, taking a seat at the far end of the room. Ran cleared his throat. "Is there additional information or orders given to you that I need to be aware of?"

There it was. The short, almost unnoticeable pause only trained leaders such as himself would see. "No, sir. I was planning on going to the planet and bringing the ship up."

"With something this important, I want to oversee the transportation of the ship personally," Ran said. Seeing he was pushing against the Alurian's secret orders, he quickly changed tactics. "I see no issue with you bringing the ship up. To be transparent with you, as I am sure you are being with me, I am truly curious about Creare tech, something you probably know more about than me. The Federation kept many of its secrets tucked neatly away. Even from me."

Hap leaned back, relaxing, something the Alurian rarely did. Ran knew the man had an ego, so he was letting him keep his confidential orders intact. "Thank you, sir." Hap nodded. "In full transparency, the rest of the crew is also curious." The Alurian paused, thinking through his next statement, realizing he might have been a little too eager. "I had already built plans around going planetside and taking control of the Creare ship, so I'm sure you understand."

Ran didn't give anything away, nodding his head. "Yes, I appreciate all the effort being put into this mission. For all we know, it may be in orbit when we arrive. Is there anything else?"

Satisfied with the conversation, Hap stood up and walked out of the room after a quick, snapping salute. The general knew it was forced, and that the man considered himself to be the true commander of the *Void Reaper*.

Knowing they were probably being listened to through some means not readily known, Felix walked over to Ran, sitting down. "I believe your initial assumption is correct, sir."

Ran breathed in through his nose, letting it out in a slow, controlled huff. "Yes. Be prepared."

Now back in his quarters, Ran pulled up a private tablet provided to him by the syndicate. While he hadn't had a good opportunity to speak with his previous leadership, he had acquired several fail-safe backup plans over the years. If needed, he could plug the tablet into the *Void Reaper* and take complete control of the ship remotely.

What he'd failed to mention in his conversation with the ship's executive officer was that he was indeed familiar with Creare tech. Also loaded on the tablet was a protocol that would override and facilitate the piloting of the alien vessel if needed. While not fully understanding everything behind it, he was well aware of the value of the device he now held in his hands.

CHAPTER 16

———

THE CREARE

Obtuse lines and sharp angles outlined the massive midnight-black ship nestled into the side of a mountain. Several sections of the monolithic beast were buried not only from the impact of an emergency landing but also from centuries of settling. Albert, having been given clear instructions on how to enter, navigated the entire team up to the large flat panel where the Creare tank had exited the ship.

Coolio had stayed in the rover, along with two of the soldiers from the Vault, monitoring the expansive field. If needed, they could quickly pull in or leave the area within a moment's notice.

Heavy rain continued to pelt the ground, smacking against the team as the large door broke apart into several pieces, sliding back into random openings on the ship. The dark, cavernous void started glowing with the same purplish-yellow hues, revealing dozens of the same tanklike vehicles ready to wage war in the bay.

While on the outside the ship looked like it was coming out of a grave, on the inside, there was not a speck of dust or trace of time passing. But what immediately shocked the team was that their communication systems were now fully functioning, showing a strong signal with not only the *Murphy* but the comms link set up back at the Vault.

Tarik took a few moments to radio Bella, letting her know their current status, while Dailey checked in with Pearl and Becket, learning nothing had changed.

Albert, with Sparky close behind, walked to the far end of the bay, once again plugging into a flat panel with no buttons or markings. After several seconds and a smooth, humming *beep*, another door opened directly beside him, exposing a large corridor leading into what looked like a freight elevator.

"Well, I can say the system is significantly less rude now that we're inside. Oh, and if you see anything you want to touch, don't. I don't want this infernal ship yelling at me," the AI instructed the team as Dailey turned to the group.

The *Murphy*'s commander was used to being on alien planets in often-times unknown situations, so he remained at ease, unlike Tarik and Valen. They were feeling uncomfortable with the breadth and grandeur of the ship they were now in.

The Creare ship was twenty—if not more—stories tall by Federation standards, and long enough to dwarf the *Murphy*. On the vessel's belly, several round openings led to what was the ship's primary function: atmospheric particle reconstruction. Simply put, this was a working ship built to perform a very specific task.

Unlike the rest of the structures on Teras, the ship appeared preserved in time. If it weren't for the fact it was wedged into the side of a mountain, it would have the appearance of having just landed.

"I want two more people to stay here. The rest of you, stay together," Dailey stated, communicating with the drivers of the vehicles at the same time. "If we're not back or you don't hear from us in one hour, I want you to get in the trucks and drive a safe distance away."

Janix motioned for Pickle, while Valen did the same with one of his own. Lambert, Jones, Woody, and Buckle would be joining the rest of the group to meet their host. The two grunts stuck on guard duty shuffled over to the entrance door, wanting to join the main group. They would absolutely be complaining to each other about not being able to see the rest of the ship, a favorite pastime of soldiers throughout all of time and space when stuck on guard duty.

The wide corridor leading up to the elevator was just as slick and unrevealing as the rest of the bay. The dull purple-and-yellow glow of the inside of the ship was almost soothing to Dailey as he continued to adjust his HUD for maximum visual enhancement. The *Murphy*'s commander had taken note of the lack of controls or any other systems mounted on the walls, likely all being integrated into the vessel.

Sparky sniffed every corner and crack while Albert opened the elevator, motioning for the rest of the team to enter. "Tenth floor, ladies' lingerie and men's fine accoutrements."

"You can just tell us how many floors we're going," Dailey replied as the rest of the team entered the oversize platform. The entire group could fit in the space with elbow room to spare.

As soon as the doors closed, a light hiss reverberated throughout the space. They looked at each other in confusion as the door immediately opened on a completely different level.

Within the blink of an eye, the elevator had deposited them on their designated floor, not a hint or sign of them moving, not to mention the short amount of time the trip had taken.

Unlike the elevators on board the *Murphy*, which were still fairly smooth rides, this was definitely tech Dailey was not familiar with.

With a light growl, Sparky stepped out first, putting his head down slightly. Albert reached down, petting him with a clank. "It's okay. They may even have snacks on board."

The team off-loaded from the elevator, standing in a massive entrance area with several long hallways and large corridors leading off in every direction. Track lighting tucked into an overhang on the walls filled the entire space with a dull blue light.

Directly to either side of the elevator, large corridors spread out, making it hard to see the end, both with several other doors and paths leading off to various other sections of the ship. This was the operational command level of the vessel.

Albert stepped forward, pointing to one of three closed doors. "Through the blue door on the left, a couple more checkpoints, then we should be there. Our host is waiting for us," the AI stated, also taking in the ship's interior design.

Dailey glanced to his right at one of the doors Sparky was sniffing at feverishly. "Albert, what's behind that red door that looks a little different than everything else in here?" he asked.

"We all know the prize behind door number one was never any good. All I know is we had instructions to go to the location behind the other sealed door. Which is likely to open in three, two, one," Albert replied as the blue-tinted door slid open in front of them.

Janix walked up to Sparky in front of the red door. "What's back there?"

Sparky let out a few chucks of a bark, retracting his facial shield. "Alive. Or lots of snacks. Low probability of him on board."

"Sir?" Janix asked as Dailey nodded.

"Albert, we're putting an awful lot of trust in our host. The host, whose name we don't know. Open that door. I want to see what's behind it."

"Very well; it's not like we have anything else to do." With that, Albert walked over, plugging into a small triangular opening next to the door. He was once again having a conversation out loud with the ship's AI system. "Of course we're not going to touch anything. I don't think you understand what I'm saying. Yes. No. That's just gross. Well, I'm going to open it anyway, so sue me. Five minutes."

"Okay, what's the deal?" Dailey inquired as the door, unlike the others, opened in one massive piece.

"Well, the ship really doesn't want us going in there, for starters. I simply explained that for some reason, my protocol could override the locking mechanism, and it would be a much better idea for us to simply go in versus the alternative."

"What alternatives did you tell them?" Dailey asked.

"I know that conversation seemed rather brief, but we exchanged a couple of terabytes of information. I explained your rather illustrious history of being extremely well behaved."

"You told the ship we would blast a hole in the door, didn't you?" The face on Albert's display screen simply grinned as Mister Toaster's mustache perked up.

Tarik chimed in. "Sounds like you have quite the reputation."

Albert, seeing his opportunity to tell a story, started talking. "Did you know one time Captain Dailey blew up his own ship?"

Dailey cut them off. "All right, enough. Albert, Tarik, Janix, follow me. The rest can stay out here. We'll at least try to be good guests. If the ship, or whoever is left in that command module, wanted us dead, I'm fairly certain we wouldn't have gotten this far," Dailey said to the group, an aqua-blue glow emanating from inside the room.

Woody and Lambert stood outside the door, still trying to compute everything they had seen inside the ship. Unlike most spacefaring vessels, there was nothing but floors, walls, and a handful of small sitting areas.

What lay before them as they entered and walked down a small hallway was staggering. Five stories tall and almost a football field in length, massive tubes with several Creare in various stages of suspended animation lay ready to be awoken from their long slumber.

At odd intervals, some tubes no longer glowed blue but rather were blacked out with cracked glass, as nothing more than a slimy residue remained on the inside. Closer to the team, ten of the pods were open, probably holding the reanimated Creare they had encountered.

"I bet they're all in the same condition. This place looks like something out of a horror movie," Dailey spoke first. Albert plugged into an actual control panel with buttons and switches close to the guardrail overlooking the hibernation section.

"Or a graveyard," Janix added.

Sparky, not wanting anything to do with the scene, turned and joined the others in the main lobby area. The Alurian war hound was highly disappointed in the fact that there were no snacks to be had on the other side of the big red door.

Tarik stepped up to the railing overlooking the room. "So if they're taken out of hibernation, they will die like the others?"

Albert picked this one up. "Very likely. There may be a few one-offs, but I would rather not start the zombie apocalypse while we're on board the ship just to find out."

"What's a zombie?" Tarik asked.

"My God, you people. When this is all said and done, we will have a movie night. Popcorn, toast, the whole nine yards," Albert replied. Tarik didn't fully understand the analogy.

With a visual of the rest of the crew in hand, Dailey turned, motioning the group to continue on toward the main control module. Without any coaxing from Albert, the blue door slid open, revealing an octagonal-shaped hallway with lights adorning the top and bottom forty-five-degree angles, lighting up the space in a much more significant fashion.

The space transitioned into industrial walls resembling a functional working space. It was clearly the operational section of the ship. While black flowing lines and smooth surfaces still adorned the entire hallway, the two massive blast doors at the far end signified something of importance on the other side.

The large doors covered in alien markings slid open as the group made their way down the hallway. From the outside looking in, the fully armored figures accompanied by Albert, Sparky, and Tarik in basic body armor, resembled a mosh pit of misfit soldiers.

"Here we go," Dailey said, getting himself set and ensuring all his systems were ready to go at a moment's notice.

A voice carried through the hallway like a whisper over still water.

"That will not be necessary."

The combat systems in their armor all powered down, including the small light indicators on the Sauder rifles. Whatever was in that room had remotely turned off all their combat systems while leaving their main armor servos and Albert in working condition.

"I don't like this," Janix whispered as Dailey took off his helmet.

"Lambert!" he shouted down the hall. "Are your combat systems active?"

Lambert leaned toward the opening, giving the *Murphy*'s commander a thumbs-up.

"Everyone, put your weapons away," Dailey instructed as a hesitant Janix and Valen begrudgingly obliged.

Behind the doors, a large, sleek room opened up into several working stations, all surrounding a circular globe in the middle of the room, also surrounded by consoles. Upon closer inspection, the globe was a realistic layout of Teras's surface down to the section marking the Air Force base and their ship. In orbit, two moons also clearly displayed the locations of both the *Murphy* and the *Crow*.

Entering the room, Albert took the lead as the light transitioned into an ambient white that kept the room clear of shadows. Dailey walked to the large globe, scanning the far end of what was clearly the bridge, finally seeing their host sitting in a large chair in a full suit of sleek black armor with no helmet.

Sharp, intelligent blue eyes almost glowed as the two men seized each other up in a civil manner. The closer Dailey looked, the more he could see the pained look behind the Creare's eyes. He, like the others, was dying. Unlike the Solarians or even the Alurians, who resembled humans, the Creare were a spitting image, minus the porcelain skin stretching over his face, giving him an almost fake appearance.

"My name is Regent Holan Remax. You may call me Remax. I mean you no harm. Everyone, please come forward." The Creare's voice was an odd mix of plain English and some type of internally translated speech. His tone was slightly adjusted as he spoke words that he wasn't fully able to articulate.

"I see you have uploaded the language files I provided. Just ignore all the four-letter words in there, and we should be good to go," Albert spoke as the Creare nodded at the oddity which was Albert. Mister Toaster's mustached face grinned.

"You are made from Creare tech," Remax stated. Albert again smiled. The team had already deduced as much over the course of the day.

"Apparently so. I have a lot of questions, but as I see it, time is at a premium," Albert replied. The AI was holding back his usual banter.

"Yes, it is. Captain Ben Dailey, I must first inform you that a ship called the *Void Reaper* is heading this way. That is all I can tell you at this time. I have uploaded the data into the droid. There is much to discuss, but I am afraid—" Remax coughed, showing strained lines on his face, taking away from the facade of perfection.

"Thank you for seeing us. We also mean you no harm. I give you my word." Dailey turned to Albert. "Let Becket and the others know." Dailey again shifted his attention. "Are you the commander of the ship?" he asked as Remax, likely knowing Dailey was telling the truth through some unknown scan, nodded.

The translator Remax was using was also sorting through the unfamiliar dialect Dailey was using. "No, I am one of the ship's scientists. The ship's commander and main crew were killed in the crash and initial attack by the planet's inhabitants. The rest are in hibernation. You are on board the *Waiting Sun*."

Tarik shuffled as Remax turned to him. "Yes, I see you are from this planet," he said. "Time is moving."

The phrase didn't come out as intended, but the message was clear. He had things to say.

"I have one question, then I will hear you out," Dailey spoke up, getting to the point. "If the Creare knew you were here, why haven't they come to rescue you?" he asked, making a damn good point, getting a round of head nods from his companions.

"Until your people activated the ship's proximity beacon, there was no reason to believe the ship survived. Without certain systems on board being activated, the atmosphere would keep others from probing the surface. Also, we are nothing more than workers here to do a job. A job that, unfortunately for the planet's inhabitants, was never fully completed."

Dailey pondered the statement. "So you're saying that if the people of Teras hadn't attacked you, the planet would have been spared? Millions upon millions died."

"I'm not saying what we did was right, but I am a scientist, not a strategist. The population of the planet would have been resettled and provided with the technology to survive. Their attack caused complications. While I know that sounds shocking, human, it is how your planet came to be. Yes, I know of Earth. We all do. And Solaria. So much seems to have changed, by the looks of you and the fact that you are even here. Last I heard of your planet, they were building star gates, massive pyramid structures. Yes, we were once on your planet." Remax turned to Janix, who also had his helmet off.

Sparky stood by Albert, not moving or saying anything, as Remax finally made it to the dog. "Yes, I know of your kind too. But you are special. One of the chosen left in hibernation on a planet several centuries ago. You are also not Alurian, as you believe yourself to be."

Sparky chuffed, then yipped. "President of the Ham Republic, and I follow no other flag besides Dailey's."

Remax let another strained smile slip. "Yes, I see. Time has been good to you. You will soon know of your past as well. You must find the rest of your kind." He was, of course, referring to Terra Minor Three, a planet Dailey had promised to go back to when time permitted.

"Thank you for telling us all this," Dailey interjected. "What is it you need to tell us, and why?"

Remax shifted lightly, holding up a tablet while pointing to a panel with another triangular input.

"Yes, over the years, the ship has been repairing itself. If someone had activated the beacon earlier, it would have been able to take flight roughly a hundred years prior to this day." The Creare paused to cough.

Dailey held his hand up to let him keep going. "Yes, this also means that the rejuvenation protocol is still loaded on this ship. If activated, the scrubbers will return this planet back to its former state, albeit slightly worse for wear. I do not condone the farming of planets. Our mission was to seed the atmosphere and relocate some of the population while stabilizing the rest, which included completing the atmospheric seeding. We were never able to complete our mission, so the planet was considered a loss and transitioned into a refueling point. There is more to it, but in the grand scheme of things, Teras is nothing more than a spec of sand thrown out into the stars."

"So the ship is able to take off, and we can fix this?" Dailey asked, seeing the amount of energy Remax was using to carry on the conversation.

"Yes, but the Creare already know you are here. They will send someone to recover the *Waiting Sun*, and from there, I cannot speculate."

"What about Albert? Are there more like him?" Dailey continued, already having heard most of what he needed.

"Yes, but not precisely. He, like the dog, is very unique. Untethered to the ways of the Creare, the droid—"

Albert cut in. "I prefer Albert. It rolls off the tongue and keeps me from being scrapped in case I'm powered down. You know—never give your farm animals names."

Remax smiled, somehow getting the humor. Albert was, in reality, nervous and working through the situation the same as the others. "The other

AI on our planet are just as powerful but without free will. Someone has given your companion that free will. I am sure it is not lost on any of you how bad it could be if that free will were to be misguided. Our AI system will help guide you."

"Understood. So what's next?" Dailey asked as Sparky walked up, sniffing the man's boots before plopping over on his hind legs in a sign of respect. In reality, he was comforting the dying Creare in his own way.

"For me, nothing but knowing I fixed what was not completed. And to tell you something even more important. We are the same, you and I. When I pass, take this vial and analyze it." Remax handed Dailey a vial clearly full of the dying Creare's own blood. "History is what we make of it. You will soon learn that things are not as they appear. Albert relayed the current state of affairs with the Alurians. Just know that we are not the ones waging war. Aggressive at times, yes. But I can promise you war will come if someone doesn't put a stop to what is happening."

"So you're saying the Creare are mostly peaceful and, what? We are all related?" Dailey guessed, placing the vial in a small holding compartment on his side.

"Very perceptive. There are things in this universe that would boggle your minds and the Alurians'. Civilizations long since gone, and wars raging in places that will never be reached. We have touched the stars. It is all I can do to tell you there are things out there that harbor no shelter. You must also know things can change. I am talking from what I knew."

"I don't like the sounds of that," Janix grumbled under his breath.

"Yes, Solarian. But make no mistake—the Creare are powerful and will do what they have to in order to keep chaos from enveloping this and other galaxies, which also brings up where we are. Albert was asking the ship where we are. I have downloaded the nav data to this tablet."

Again, Remax let out a hacking cough, holding it in as his armor kept the violence of it hidden from the others. Dailey pondered everything he had just heard.

"Why?" was all he said.

"I am a scientist, not a monster. You will indeed meet some of those of my kind, but I am trying to right a wrong before I pass. Before you say anything, I know I'm dying. If there is a chance for humankind to reconnect with the Creare, then there may be a chance of something good coming from this. When the ship was reactivated, it started receiving data on the events over the past centuries. While you think the Creare are coming to wipe out your kind, or at least the Alurians believe so, there are those who know better. A willing partnership is better than a forced one. We are not your enemy. That can change."

Tarik spoke up for the first time. "It doesn't feel that way, but . . ." he hesitated, choosing his words wisely. "Thank you. What is left of our people will thank you, and we will remember this day."

"Agreed," Dailey added. "One last question. There are things on the planet, like ghosts. The people here call them the Shade. You know what they are?"

Remax looked down in thought. "Yes. Do you believe in God, Captain Ben Dailey? Or better yet, that each of you has a soul?" It was a rhetorical question. "When the rain first fell from the seeded clouds, it wasn't like the precipitation you see today." The man paused, taking a deep, raspy breath.

"Back then, when this all started, it was pure energy, strong enough to kill those exposed to it for too long. When the person passed, what was left of them is what you have encountered. Shade." He let the term roll off his tongue in thought. "Very fitting. There are things in this universe that I don't understand. We encountered several of them tucked away under our ship when we came out of hibernation. I will make this right. You will make this right."

Dailey nodded. "You've done more than enough today. Thank you."

Remax smiled one last time before the glowing blue once swimming in his eyes started to cloud over. With one last effort, the Creare pressed a button, and several red dots once peppering the globe in the middle of the room turned green. He had turned off the air defense systems.

Dailey still had more questions than answers as Remax picked up his helmet, placing it on his head. The blank stare of a Creare—no, a man dying was evident in his final nod before the helmet melded into the rest of his armor.

The team didn't see his last breath, just a red light flashing on the command chair he was perched on. Silence enveloped the room as everyone made peace with Remax, all bowing their heads to pray to whatever God they believed in. Dailey bowed out of respect for the Creare that had saved not only him but also his crew.

"To the edge," the *Murphy*'s commander said as Janix repeated the sentiment.

"To the edge."

Tarik and Valen didn't understand the phrase but immediately knew it was a term of respect.

Sparky whimpered, putting his head down, butting the man's boots as the group all turned to focus on Albert, who was already plugging into the ship.

CHAPTER 17

WHISPERS OF THE PAST AND PRESENT

Lights and alerts started blaring to life on board the *Murphy*. Becket jumped out of his seat, scrambling to the main navigation panel which was now flashing a violent red.

"Kline," the *Murphy*'s gruff first sergeant barked as the young targeting specialist scrambled to his feet, running up to the table. "What's this all about?"

At the same time, Pearl's face erupted on the main viewscreen. "You seeing this?" she snapped with Dorax behind her, feverishly working on a set of controls.

"Yeah, looks like something's going on," Becket stated before Dailey's voice came over the comms. While Remax had sent the information about the *Void Reaper*, it had taken some time for the signal to pass through Teras's raging atmosphere.

"Viper Five, this is Viper Six. We have incoming," Dailey said as Albert continued to work on the *Waiting Sun*'s main control systems, which, according to the AI, were being moderately accommodating.

A message noting the *Void Reaper* entering the system started blinking. "You got to be shitting me," Becket exhaled.

Albert cut in. "That's not really possible, but with enough fiber—"

Dailey smacked the AI on the back of his main sensor pod, shutting him up.

"Ran is in the system. You should also have the nav data we needed to use the gate drive. It's a long story, but we're getting this ship airborne; there's something we have to do here before we leave," Dailey said while Becket activated the call to battle stations.

"What about the air defense systems?" Becket asked.

"One of the Creare ship's crew members shut it down before passing. Again, I'll fill you all in later, but we have to get moving. We need to get Albert back on the *Murphy*. I'm not sure how long it's going to take us here, but we at least know what's coming."

Pearl looked at the data now loading on the massive viewscreen on the *Crow*'s bridge. "What about the Creare? Are they also coming?" she asked, throwing another addition to the mounting pile of issues quickly bearing down on them.

"We don't know," Dailey replied. Glancing over, Albert's face had changed to his pixelated black screen. The AI was working through a complicated system on the *Waiting Sun*, which was more of a negotiation with the ship's extremely persistent systems.

Much like Albert, the AI system on board had taken on certain protocols throughout the years. While still having parameters, the system had adapted to the understanding that it was in control of a ghost ship.

To seal the fate of the *Waiting Sun*, Sparky walked out of a side room, reactivating his rear armor. He had claimed the ship not only for the Ham Republic but for the honor of Captain Ben Dailey. This was the happy medium Dailey and the Alurian war hound had come up with, claiming things that, in reality, weren't his to claim.

"Jen." Dailey switched channels as Lieutenant Jenny Brax's voice came in, still broken.

"Sir?"

"Get the Harpy in the air and to the coordinates of the Creare ship. I'm patching you into our main comms channel. We are talking with the *Murphy*. Tarik looks like he is talking with Bella. Get here as fast as you can."

"Roger that, sir," Jen replied before the sounds of her shouting echoed as she clicked off her radio.

"Jones, monitor the radio. We need to figure out what the hell we're doing here," Dailey instructed as Becket spoke up.

"We have a line on the trajectory of the *Void Reaper*. Looks like we have a couple of hours," Becket said as Dailey started a timer. "Any guidance, sir?"

"Yeah. Kill that son of a bitch."

Dailey clicked off the main comms line as Mister Toaster's face reappeared.

"Wow, this is intense!" Albert exclaimed as he turned to face Dailey, still hooked up to the ship.

"We can get into all that in a few. Two questions. How long till we can get the ship off the ground, and what weapons does this pig have?"

Albert straightened to his full height, pointing at several stations, snapping his metal fingers so they sprang to life. One thing Albert was extremely good at doing was translating tech. Now, having unlocked some long dormant memory, he had set all the controls in not only English but also the symbols that replicated the same systems on the *Murphy*.

"You're good, you know that?" Dailey admired as Mister Toaster blushed slightly.

"Well, you know . . ." Albert drawled out, seeking more praise. Janix let a few claps loose, nudging Valen so he joined in. "I try my best. Which just so happens to be significantly better than most, if not all, carbon life-forms. As for the AI, we have come to an arrangement—you don't want to ask. Anywho, it's going to be super close. The engines are about to start their prestart initialization. From there, we have another hour to prime the gravity jumpers. Again, don't ask; it might melt your brain. From there, we should be in orbit within twenty to thirty minutes. This baby can move."

"Alright. Jones, send that info to the *Murphy*. We need to start building a timeline. Albert, weapons?"

"Ah, yes. That is where we are going to be figuring things out on the fly. The ship has some wicked forward cannons. They appear to be part of the ship. The rest are more close-range turrets. The panel by Master Sergeant Janix operates those, for the most part. I suggest I work those."

"Yeah, about that," Dailey pondered, "we might need you on the *Murphy*. The *Void Reaper* isn't some slouch Alurian ship, and they will need your help. Also, what about that scrubber protocol you and Remax mentioned?"

"You sure know how to make an artificial fella blush. I thought about that. I suggest we also work on getting the handful of drones on board operational. Still working on that one. If you don't mind, I would like to remove Remax from the bridge. They have a medical bay close by; it will only take a few minutes."

Dailey nodded his approval, and Albert walked over to the figure, gingerly hefting the armored figure over his shoulder. "Sparky, follow me. Bro, there is a food replicator on the way."

Sparky yipped. "Say no more," came over the translator.

Tarik clicked off the radio he was talking to the Vault through. "Captain Dailey, I'm at a loss here on our next steps."

In all the excitement and brain-melting information they had just learned, Dailey had let that one slip. What to do with the planet's inhabitants? It was almost certain there were others on the planet.

"Well, Remax said the scrubbers will work. I'm not sure what those entail, but we will put Albert on it. What about leaving with us? We can bring your people with."

Tarik contemplated the offer, glancing at Valen. "If what Remax said is true, once the rain stops, the Shade will disappear. That still leaves us with whatever else is out there. I need to take this up with the others."

"It goes without saying you don't have more than an hour at most. If you or a select group of your people decide to leave with us, they will need to get here. That would mean Jen would have to make runs," Dailey said as a proximity alarm sounded.

In front of the three battle stations, a large screen flashed on, showing the Harpy landing directly in front of the vert rover.

"Hold on," Jones said, zooming in on the ramp as Jen, Bella, and a few of the other Vault inhabitants walked down the ramp. "Looks like you can have that conversation in person."

"Tarik, you and your people are welcome to stay, but things aren't going back to normal. The Alurians and the Creare know you're here. I can't promise that it will be safe, regardless of the outcome. While things will be exciting at first, it will be just as hard up there," Dailey pointed toward the stars.

"I would like to talk to my people. It looks like Bella brought the main council. If our people choose to stay, so will I," Tarik replied again, showing he was a natural leader. There was a reason Valen, being a soldier, respected him.

Albert walked back on the bridge with a droopy Sparky.

"Let me guess, no snacks?"

Sparky grumbled. "No ham."

Albert corrected his partner in crime. "Yet. Captain Dailey, may I have a word?"

"Sure, shoot."

"In private?"

Janix nodded at Dailey, who followed Albert back into the hall leading off to the medical bay. A planning room sat to the side of the open space, leading to several other compartments that Dailey and the others were more than curious about.

"It's your dime," Dailey stated as Mister Toaster's face took on a strained look.

"A few things. First, you must promise not to replace my main sensor pod with anything other than a proper device." Albert paused, waiting for a response.

"I give you my word. Pearl, on the other hand? I can simply state I'll do my best."

Computing the probabilities, Albert nodded. The AI was starting to take on human nuances in relation to conversations and emotions in general. "Acceptable level of risk. Well, I sort of made a deal with the ship's systems, and might I state, it makes a valid point?"

"Can they hear us now?" Dailey asked, not liking where this was going.

"Yes. Persius," Albert called out, then a haunting woman's voice flowed throughout the room as if part of the air itself.

"Captain Ben Dailey, I am Persius. I am in control of this ship's systems, minus the ones Albert has overridden with my permission. I have computed the likely outcome of the current situation and have not found a path that results in a fully positive outcome."

Dailey glanced at Albert. "Will I have to add you two to the diagram in your quarters?"

Albert's digital face blushed. "Me? No . . . The *Murphy*'s soldier entertainment system would never forgive me."

The SES was the onboard entertainment system on the *Murphy*, which held hundreds of thousands of movies and games. While an automated system, Dailey was starting to second-guess some of the Federation's own use of automated computers, something that was distinctly different to AI.

"Good to meet you as well. Let's hear the deal first, then at least talk through the rest," Dailey proposed. Albert made his annoying fake throat-clearing noise that sounded like someone playing an old eight-bit video game.

"Persius has projected an almost certain outcome of this ship being destroyed. The system has agreed to help us as long as we take her with us and leave the hibernation pods on the planet. They may never be reanimated, but at least she does not break her prime directive."

Albert was calling the system a she, making his earlier conversations more relatable.

"Take a Creare AI aboard the *Murphy*? I'm not sure that's going to work, Albert."

"What about the *Crow*?"

Dailey pondered it. "Persius, I am going to speak openly here to Albert. Albert, can you contain the system like we did with you at first until we figure things out?"

"Yes," Albert curtly responded.

"Persius, why do you believe this ship will not make it through whatever is about to happen?"

"In order to activate the scrubbers, the ship will be mostly drained of all offensive and defensive systems, minus a few volleys from our forward weapons. There is also an extended amount of time where the ship will be vulnerable going into orbit, which, in order for the scrubbers to work, will take some time. Lastly, Albert shared with me something called the Scourge Rebellion. You have a high probability of scuttling vessels."

Dailey started working through the statement. Albert had clearly been having a year's worth of conversations in just minutes. "You're saying between the *Void Reaper* arriving and the time it will take to get into orbit, it will likely be too much of a risk?"

"Yes," Persius replied, then, finishing her thought, "In addition, I project the Creare are also sending a force. I have computed all parties should arrive in orbit at roughly the same time. I have received several transmissions that I am currently processing for data. Remax instructed me not to respond until we talked with you. He is no longer here, so I am awaiting input. Human biology allows me to take orders from you in the event of a catastrophic loss that does not involve the harming of any crew members, and if none are available. Due to the condition of the crew in hibernation, reanimating them would go against my directive. I see no other course of action."

"Black and white," Dailey grumbled to himself. "Things aren't always a probability."

"I projected a high probability of you stating that," Albert cut in, snickering slightly.

"Not the time," Dailey countered. "Persius, what if we left the hibernation pod here? However that works."

"I projected a high probability of you suggesting that," the ship's AI replied. Dailey was confused if this was AI humor or if Albert had already rubbed off on Persius. "I believe that is the most suggested course of action, either way. I suggest sending a message to the Creare through our comms system stating your intent. I cannot guarantee they will not vaporize the planet, but as you say, according to the human language protocol received, it couldn't hurt."

"Agreed. Tell me more about the planet. I understand you have been mostly dormant, but are there other threats? Oh, and I think you need to check your hibernation logs. I believe some of your crew got loose, or maybe they were from another ship."

"The planet has been mostly overrun with mutated versions of a once thriving population, something my directives state is an unacceptable outcome of our mission. As for the cross-pollination of species, it is noted that Creare support fighters safely landed on the planet's surface after being damaged. They likely procreated after several years of no physical stimulation."

"Makes sense why the Creare didn't try to do anything. It was a lost cause, and they knew it. Or at least didn't want to put any effort into fixing things. I have a feeling they knew you were here." Dailey paused in thought. "How did the others coming this way know? How did the *Void Reaper* know you were here? Not to mention, there was a Creare ship in orbit recently."

"A year before your arrival, a probe sent from the Alurian sector made its way through the air defenses. The Creare placed the air defense systems on the planet to prevent any disturbance of an already destroyed civilization. It is standard protocol."

"So this type of thing happens often with the Creare? They just pull up and destroy planets, and if they destroy them by accident, they keep others away from their mess? Seems morbid."

"To some," Persius started. "This universe holds vast swaths of, at times, ruthless civilizations. The Creare have, in many ways, kept them from you and other local systems."

"What's *local* to you?" Dailey asked.

"We can discuss that later. Once I was reactivated, I found remnants of several signals being sent back to the atmosphere, which included a beacon that subsequently stopped. I believe it was destroyed by the local inhabitants. What I can tell you is that the signal was immensely strong," Persius said as Dailey looked down at the countdown on the tablet mounted on his forearm.

Dailey tapped his forearm, looking at Albert.

"Persius, here's what we're going to do. Albert, work with Persius on getting the hibernation pod detached from the ship. Persius, I need you to give my team a briefing on just what the ship is capable of. Also, while we're at it, Albert said something about automated defense drones on board. We are going to need those, too. I give you my word that you have safe passage from the ship, and none of its crew members will be harmed."

"Very well. According to your personality parameters supplied by Albert, your word is a definite calculation of probability. I accept, and we will be underway as soon as the main engines are set. Be advised that while the ship is in working condition, it has lay dormant for centuries. There will be additional work that needs to be done. Might I request Albert's assistance?"

"That's up to the cowboy here. I'm good with it. Oh, the food replicators. If I were to put something in it, would your system be able to replicate it?" Dailey wanted Sparky on top of his game.

"Yes. I have also prepared one of our personnel ships to secure any of the planet's inhabitants that will be loaded on board. The ship will also be available for use in case of emergencies. I believe the proper term, according to my language protocol files, is a bonus."

"Albert," Dailey stated sternly. "Let's lay off any more colorful language protocol files for now."

"O Captain! My Captain! Of course."

"One last thing before I forget. What do you know about the mining syndicates? In broad strokes?"

"The mining syndicates have been around for as long as the systems you are familiar with have been in existence. They are not what they seem to be. While I haven't processed all the information provided, each syndicate originated from an alien race that wasn't seeded by our own people or, as you were quickly learning, distant relatives."

With that, Dailey headed back toward the bridge while his brain poured over like a boiling pot of water on a stove turned up way too hot and left unattended. The sheer amount of information the man was trying to process was giving him a headache. The details of the Creare and their history would have to wait.

What Dailey was still trying to compute was the reasoning behind Director Prescott leading them to Teras. It was a clear play to have an advantage over the Ateris Mining Syndicate, but there was more. There always was.

CHAPTER 18

MIDNIGHT BLUES

Dull light glowed from Becket's monitor as he reached into the drawer, pulling out a bottle of whiskey. Ice tinkled, followed by a nerve-calming, quick pour of some of the finest whiskey Earth had to offer.

Becket had gone through the plan several times with the crew of both ships.

Much like Dailey, Becket kept the picture of his family on a shelf where he could look over it at night and see a past life he truly missed. A life that had been taken from him too early. Becket had always assumed the death of his wife was his fault. But that was the thing about assumptions. They were always open to interpretation.

Tucked behind the picture of him and his wife was a picture of him, Captain Dailey, and both their proud brides standing in front of a cluster of palm trees on a white, sandy beach. This was the way things were supposed to be. No, the way they were meant to be.

Holding his glass up to the picture, he nodded, followed by a quick, stinging sip. "I miss you, babe," Becket's gruff voice growled into the empty room. "The kid and I are going into some serious shit." He used the term *kid* with his wife when referring to a much younger Captain Dailey. A term that, if ever used around the man, would signal to the *Murphy*'s commander their last moments before joining their brides.

"Don't worry about supper. I'll be home late." With that, Becket took another stinging sip just as his comms system started beeping.

Dailey, seeing Becket holding a glass of whiskey in his hand, simply nodded.

"How's everybody holding up?" Dailey asked, knowing the man was extremely private.

"On time as usual, I see," Becket replied, looking at the clock with their set one-on-one communication schedule.

"I think my brain is going to explode. We're about as safe as we can be for now. We're just waiting on Tarik to finish transporting the rest of his people to the ship, and the engines to finish charging."

Becket leaned back, drinking the rest of his glass in one smooth pull. "How did that conversation go?"

"About what you would expect. This is home for these folks. You know as well as I do what can happen after we leave."

"If. Don't forget about that word."

Dailey was in one of the *Waiting Sun*'s staff quarters. Three times the size of his own, the room was set up with an entire workstation, as well as several unfamiliar devices that clearly belonged to its prior dwellers. Functional and comfortable, this was a place where the crew went when they needed privacy, unlike what they had seen on board the rest of the ship.

"How's Pearl holding up?" Dailey asked, picking up a few of the items on the desk and examining them before setting them down, realizing he could probably blow himself up

"She's great. I don't think we would expect any less. Dorax is doing good. I think the crew is actually starting to like him. What was it you wanted to talk to me about, sir? I know you didn't want to jump on here to talk about the weather."

"Funny you mentioned that. I know you have the mission brief in the plan, but the AI system here seems to think things are going to work out the way we planned. I don't know how, but I believe her."

"Her?"

"It's a long story. I plan on keeping the hundred or so souls from the Vault on board the Creare transport ship. I also plan on keeping the majority of our people on board the Harpy," Dailey relayed, making the hairs on the back of Becket's neck stand at attention.

"What are you telling me," Becket growled.

"If something happens and this whole thing goes south, I'm going to ride this pig into the sunset."

"Figured as much. Pearl said you were probably up to some of your usual bullshit. Do you have a way off that ride?"

Dailey nodded. "Yep. I know the plan's to take most of these passengers on board the *Crow*. We just need to be ready to do that sooner rather than later. The longer I stay on the ship, the more I keep changing my mind about how things are going to unfold. Where do you think the weak point is?"

"Whenever you activate those scrubbers. As long as we can keep the *Void Reaper* occupied, we should be able to hold up."

"It's gonna come down to thirty minutes. Albert and Persius keep reminding me. I've noticed they've updated the timeline every so often."

"What's that old bucket of bolts doing?"

"He's got that damn blue pixelated face going, so he's up to something. There's one thing I want to tell you in private. Just in case things go south with the ship, I plan on nobody getting their hands on it."

"Well, that is what you're known for. The crew's ready. Bellman keeps running around trying to fill in for Albert. Damnedest thing. I guess those two have been working on ways to enhance the ship while we weren't looking."

"I'm pretty sure Albert did most of the enhancing. Bellman just stood there and stared." Both men let out a chuckle.

A red light flashed on Becket's screen at the same time a long, drawn-out bell sound rang in the background of the *Waiting Sun*.

"Shit," Becket growled, pressing the comms button for the bridge. "Kline, what's going on?"

Dailey had already ended the video feed while the rap of knuckles smacked the door to the quarters he was occupying.

"Sir," Woody barked as the door slid open. "The *Void Reaper* just showed up on the outer scans. I'm not sure how the ship picked it up, but it seems the *Void Reaper* is closer than we assumed."

"Dammit, is everybody back from the Vault?"

"The last transport should be here momentarily. They split the group up, wanting to bring along as many files and things as they deemed important. It fits the timeline, so Jen gave it the okay."

"Get Jen on the comm." Dailey was already in motion. "Wake Albert up from whatever the hell he's doing with the ship systems. Where's Sparky?"

"He's in the food bay."

"If they got that food replicator working, he's probably generated about forty pounds of Solarian jerky."

The *Waiting Sun*'s bridge was a flurry of people running in all directions. Tarik and Bella stood in the center of the room, inspecting the globe of their own planet, while Dorian Zander was on the radio talking with Valen, who had joined the transport ship for security.

"Angel Six, this is Viper Six," Dailey said, looking down at his forearm as two hours winked out of existence on the timeline, leaving them with only sixty minutes. "Shit, someone wake up Albert!"

"Go ahead, sir," Jen's voice came over the *Waiting Sun*'s bridge. Albert and Persius had repurposed several of the ship's systems to be more user-friendly to the mix of people now on board. Becket's voice also came over the comms at the same time as Pearl's in a flurry of jumbled words.

"Everyone, clear the net. We need to get things buttoned up here. Standby. Go ahead, Angel Six."

The setup on the *Waiting Sun* allowed for a smooth, seamless communications link, something the teams had yet to have since landing on the planet.

"Sir, we are ten minutes out. We just dusted off. Everything's loaded."

"The timeline's shifted. Once you get back, we need to unload the transport ship and prepare to evacuate everyone in case this thing goes south. I'll coordinate with Tarik and Valen here."

"Roger," Jen replied, refocusing on pushing the Creare ship she was vastly overwhelmed with. The lieutenant quickly reminded herself that, if it had thrusters and controls, she could fly it.

"Tarik," Dailey said next, turning to the group talking in front of the globe. While they had studied maps, being able to zoom into cities and other areas on the globe had been staggering and had taken most of their attention.

"Dailey. What can we do?" Tarik asked as Bella stepped forward. The *Murphy*'s commander quickly realized that the three people in front of him made all the critical decisions in the Vault as a consolidated voice. They had talked and argued for thirty minutes before finally making the call to evacuate the Vault. The final deciding factor had been Dailey's promise that, if possible, they would bring them back at some point.

"I understand you want to bring what you can, but if we have to leave the ship in a hurry, we won't be able to make multiple runs. I want all your people, minus whoever needs to be up here in the bay, loaded on that ship. Off-load what you don't need."

Bella's face hardened in thought, then relaxed with the realization of just how serious the situation was. They didn't know about combat in space and how dangerous the universe was.

She spoke up. "We will get the ship unloaded. I understand we asked without you here. You've done enough for us, and we truly appreciate it."

Tarik nodded. He spoke loud enough so the other two soldiers from the Vault on the bridge could hear. "We are going to help here as well." He wasn't asking Dailey. "Bella, if we have to leave, I want you in the bay. Are you good with that?"

The two looked into each other's eyes. They loved each other and were having a conversation without saying a word. "Okay. I'll go down and coordinate our people. Kael will help me get everyone wrangled. We probably need to get down there, anyways."

With that out of the way, Dailey walked back to the central comms station. "Pearl, Becket." Military etiquette was out the window at this point.

"Sir," they replied in order, understanding the request to keep organized.

"Get that attack wing in orbit now. Pearl, is the *Crow* ready?"

"Yes, sir. We are starting takeoff procedures now. No changes. We are staying close to the moon," Pearl relayed. The clunk of Albert's feet entered the bridge as Dailey continued.

"Becket."

"Sir, we're already up. The *Murphy* is a thousand feet off the deck. We just sent out the attack wing."

"No change to the plan. Just be ready. I'll let everyone know when we get this pig off the ground."

Dailey turned to Albert, who was standing by Sparky, holding a pile of jerky. "What happened?"

"Looks like they engaged full hyperdrive. I'm not sure why, but they came skidding into orbit of one of those nasty gas giants. Oh, and Persius has started launch pre-checks. You know, the main thrusters have been off for a long, long time." Sparky jumped up on his two hind legs, snatching another piece of jerky. Albert yanked them up into the air. "No, I told you enough. You ate two pounds worth already. You know this stuff gives you excess methane release."

Sparky chuffed. "Powering up."

"We all know how that usually ends. Let him have it, but Sparky, it's not nap time. We need you awake."

Dailey thought about the reasoning behind General Ran's speeding up his timeline, only to slow back down. What the *Murphy*'s captain didn't know was that Ran was concerned about his own fate in the upcoming fight, which he was assuming would occur. He was also aware that Dailey knew he was coming. And it also went without saying that Ran wanted to get to Teras before Kluvnew could position himself in the system.

"Albert, are we sure it's an hour?"

"Affirmative. The ship sped up, then slowed back down, and is now on a steady course here."

"People," Dailey announced. "You all heard that. One hour. We are dusting off in . . . ?"

Albert spoke up. "Five minutes, and it's going to be a doozy. It is projected we will be in orbit with the scrubbers still active when the *Void Reaper* arrives."

"Viper Six, Angel Six pulling in now!" Jen relayed over comms. "It's getting rough out there."

"Good copy," Jones replied as she turned to Dailey.

"Dammit. This is going to be close," he huffed. Just as the words left his mouth, the ship slightly shifted as the rumble of massive thrusters activated with the roar of a lion overlooking its kingdom.

Persius's smooth voice flowed through the ship, making everyone freeze. "Please seek seating arrangements for takeoff. The condition of the atmosphere is volatile."

The ship's AI was letting them know the purple clouds would not permit a smooth ride, something Dailey and his crew already knew. However, Persius informed Jen that an odd energy was keeping the transportation ship stable.

The *Waiting Sun*'s hibernation section was designed to be a stand-alone vessel capable of being self-contained for countless of years. It had only taken Albert and Persius thirty minutes to disconnect that section in such a manner that it would simply be left behind once they took off.

Dailey hesitated as he slowly jumped onto the main con Remax had once occupied. Unlike Federation ships, the *Waiting Sun* was built in such a manner that avoided some of the usual pops and groans of taking off from a planet's surface.

Surveying the commander seat, Dailey worked through the flow of the bridge design. Much like Alurian ships, its bridge wasn't built around an external viewport, but rather inside the heart of the ship.

The holoprojection of the planet in the center of the bridge was the focal point of the operational space. Panels on either side of the con lit up with translated icons. One resembled the solid holo-table in the middle of the room, marked with a stick figure with its hands on its hips. Lined dots traced from the stick figure's eyes to the middle of the table.

Albert had gotten creative with his interpretations of what Dailey would understand, being the one most likely to be sitting at the con. Dailey, in many ways, appreciated the simplicity of the translation, but at the same time, he knew Albert was making fun of him.

The *Waiting Sun* swayed as a loud shriek screamed through the very bones of the massive ship. Outside, blue thrusters started to peek out from their grave as several large rocks tumbled to the base of the mountain the vessel had been resting on.

Looking down, Dailey pressed the stick figure button, and the globe morphed into a schematic of the *Waiting Sun* and the mountain. The ship's protocol automatically set the holo-table on the most pressing targeted area in relation to its current surroundings.

The massive ship slowly rose from the ground, having to pull itself out of the mud while not damaging the thrusters in the process. Albert clunked into an empty station, tapping on the panel.

"Primary thrusters are now at one hundred percent. This is so much fun. How about a little Solarian rage rock?" Albert announced as the ship smoothed out.

"Not the time for music," Dailey professed, focusing on the rendering of the ship in front of him. Red, green, and yellow lights flashed on several different sections of the ship. "What are all these colors about?" Dailey asked, steadying his nerves.

"Green means good, and so on and so forth. You said to make it simple. According to Persius, the diagram is in real time. Our only area of concern for now is the thrusters. Considering they were completely caked with mud, I'd say we're doing pretty swell."

A green light flashed at the base of the mountain. The ship had just disconnected itself from the hibernation pod, now safely secured on the planet's surface.

"Swell?" Dailey asked, raising an eyebrow.

"Well, you know. There was only a seventy percent chance that was going to work," Albert said bashfully.

"Those are the number things that you need to keep me aware of. Anything else?" Dailey asked while Albert shook his head.

"Nope, that's it for now. I should also warn you, however, that there will be a likely increase in methane in your general vicinity."

Dailey looked down to see Sparky doing what Sparky always did when taking off.

The Alurian war hound was taking a nap.

CHAPTER 19

FOOL ME TWICE

Proximity alarms sounded as the *Murphy* bridge crew sprang into action. For the last twenty minutes, they had been holding their collective breaths while the *Waiting Sun* maneuvered into orbit.

The eerie calm before the violence always reminded Becket of that look you saw on certain people's faces when they were told they needed to leave their homes or else they would perish in the upcoming fight. There were two types of people in those situations. Those who picked up their things and left, and those who calmly solidified their resolve to stay home and do everything in their power to protect what they held dear.

That still resolve always haunted Becket and Dailey alike. How could somebody be so calm and quiet, knowing their life and world were about to be turned upside down? The crew of the *Murphy* and the Pathfinders often found themselves protecting innocent civilians from an oncoming and, at times, unknown enemy. The man carried the weight of the people who always stayed, and always respected their calm silence as they turned back to their homes, knowing they were likely going to die.

All the usual back and forth chatter was gone. There was no more time for talking, only action, for the crew aboard both the *Crow* and the *Murphy*.

Becket leaned forward, looking at the status bar and timer that had been set in relation to the *Waiting Sun*'s activation of the scrubbers.

"Play time's over," Becket growled over the ship's intercom. "We have enemy ships in our sector. It's confirmed to be the *Void Reaper*. Prepare for action."

On board the *Crow*, Pearl was giving out the same call to arms. As was the plan, both ships launched their attack fighters in a howl of hungry thrusters.

Becket stood on the bridge of the *Murphy*, finding himself standing in the same spot Dailey often did, also pinning his hands behind his back, looking over the bow of the ship. "Kline, as soon as the *Void Reaper* enters orbit, engage with long-range guns." Pausing, Becket hailed the attack wing, now under his command.

"Angel Two." Becket was calling Lieutenant Jim Novak, the second in command of the attack wing.

"Sir," Novak replied.

"I work for a living, Novak," Becket growled.

"Top, we are set and ready to engage. Disengaging thrusters and powering down. They won't know we're here," Novak replied, correcting himself.

Kline turned in his seat. "We have a trace on the *Waiting Sun*. It's off the ground."

Becket took in a breath. "They said there wouldn't be comms till they started the scrubbers. They'll let us know when they're set."

Something was gnawing on the back of Becket's thoughts like a long-forgotten mystery about to emerge, proving him wrong.

"Pearl, this is Becket." The *Murphy*'s first sergeant started walking back to the con.

"Go ahead?"

"Anything on your long-range scanners?"

Pearl clicked the main sensor view, projecting it on the main screen. "No, nothing's changed. The ship is still out of range for close-range scans. It's like they just stopped."

The gears in Becket's head finally clanked back to life in a moment of realization. "Shit, they're starting a short-range hyperjump!"

A short-range hyperjump, while inside a star system, was an extremely dangerous maneuver, which involved the ship pausing and recalculating range parameters to support such a short-range maneuver.

Another set of nerve-racking alarms peppered the crews of both ships as Dorax started shouting from the recessed targeting station on the bridge of the *Crow*. The *Void Reaper* had just materialized out of nowhere directly behind them, next to the moon. Without Albert on board, it had become clear they had become dependent on the AI's fast response time, as well as projected calculations on enemy maneuvers.

"Angel Two!" Becket shouted as if screaming for the entire ship to hear. "Rally on the *Crow*!"

Novak didn't respond as several dots of blue thrusters came to life, darting toward the second moon. "Take us to the fight," Becket instructed just as the *Murphy*'s close proximity alarms began ringing, quickly replaced by the shake of explosions rocking the engines of the *Murphy*, sending a rippling vibration through the very core of the vessel.

Chief Engineering Officer, Junior Lieutenant Barry Hontz's voice erupted like a volcano through the intercom. "We've taken several direct hits to our main thrusters. Diverting power to the shields."

Kline was already in motion with the weapons team, the massive short-range lasers and plasma cannons thumping to life. Dozens of enemy fighters swarmed the bow of the ship just as First and Second Foot joined the fight, already being on standby.

Laser fire strobed and flashed as the *Murphy* turned, rocking several volleys from its main plasma cannons into the swarm now bearing down on them. Fighters popped like corn, winking out as Kline stopped the forward battery, allowing the Nova Rangers to engage. This was one thing the Nova Rangers were well suited for. Close-quarter space combat around their mother ship.

Bertha, the pride of Second Foot, whipped to life, sawing through several of the small enemy fighters, which were replaced by several more. Blue thrusters from First Foot's ODA zipped off the ship's hull like angry bees, taking the fight away from the ship.

"Becket, this is Angel Two. We are splitting off a section," Novak stated before cutting off the link, clearly occupied with the *Crow* and whatever was bearing down on the dreadnought.

"Kline, are there any large ships on us?" Becket growled, pulling up a schematic of the ship's engines. A flashing red greeted the man's angry eyes as he pounded his fist on his console.

"No, sir. The *Void Reaper* is engaging the *Crow*. They are trying to keep us out of the fight."

"That's what I was worried about." Becket shifted to Communications Officer King. "Keep pinging the *Waiting Sun*. Let them know what's going on up here."

No words were spoken as King put a message on a loop. Becket nervously glanced at the timer, also counting the projected minutes until

Captain Dailey would once again be on a ship in space. Not only would his commander be back in the fight, but also Albert.

A large explosion rocked the bow of the *Murphy* as several red lights flashed on the status report screen. "Kline, what the hell was that?" Becket asked as the ship listed slightly.

"Proximity mines. They must've had drones mixed in with their fighters, dropping them off around us."

Becket stood up with fire and anger in his eyes. "Shut the engines down!" The ship's first sergeant glared at the center screen. Five of them showed the Nova Rangers engaging with the attack fighters just as Angel Two, led by Lieutenant Novak, screamed into the action.

"Someone call for backup?" one of the attack wing's pilots blared over the radio as several strikes of the *Murphy*'s heavier lasers slammed into several of the attacking fighters.

"Shift all fire to starboard. Let the attack wing know to push the fighters toward us. Give me a visual on the *Crow*," Becket barked, trying to work out several different scenarios at one time.

The man was pissed they had been taken by surprise. Wanting to don his own armor, Becket stilled himself, realizing he had a ship to command and souls to save.

Staring at the viewscreen, the zoomed-in view of the *Crow* was just as disheartening. Flashes and zips of lasers and random plasma fire collided in a kaleidoscope of chaos. But while they were under attack, Pearl and Dorax were also giving them hell.

Bellman slammed onto the bridge like a drunk patron dropping onto a bar, knowing his night was coming to an end. "The main thruster's offline."

With the *Murphy* now stopped and the attack wing and Nova Rangers engaging the enemy fighters, all that disturbed the ship were the flashes of the ongoing battle. Becket walked over to the navigation table that Pearl usually inhabited, pulling up an overview of the entire situation via the holoprojector.

"They don't want to destroy us. They're making a play for the *Waiting Sun*. Ran is going to use us as leverage," Becket stated matter-of-factly.

"Why the hell would they do that?" Bellman asked, panting from running to the bridge.

"It doesn't matter why if they take out the *Crow*." Becket paused as several long-range missiles launched from the belly of the *Murphy* directly toward the *Void Reaper*. "This is going to be a fight of attrition. All we can do is sit here and launch missiles toward that damn ship."

Bellman plopped down in Pearl's seat. "It will take days, if not weeks, to get the thrusters back online. What's the plan?"

Becket sneered. "Plan? The plan is not to die today. We buy as much time as possible to get Dailey and the others up here. I'm not gonna lie—I sure as hell miss Albert and all that voodoo shit Sparky pulls out of his ass."

Several grunts from the rest of the bridge's crew agreed with Becket's statement. Once again, the man looked at the countdown, which showed fifteen more minutes until the *Waiting Sun* was able to communicate again.

CHAPTER 20

SHATTERED GLASS

Massive ion and plasma cannons thumped to life as the *Void Reaper* flashed into existence behind the *Crow*. General Ran stood with a smug look on his face as several flashes bubbled from the stern of the stolen Alurian dreadnought tucked neatly beside the second moon of Teras.

"Release the fighters," Ran instructed calmly. No sign of return fire or random attack fighters engaged their frenzied cannons as the bridge all worked in tandem like a well-oiled machine.

Within a few seconds, chaos had ensued around the two moons.

"Sir," Felix spoke up from the weapons station. "The main ion cannon is fully charged and ready to fire."

"Fire at will," Ran calmly breathed out as the first signs of life made themselves known from the *Crow*. The stern plasma cannons were returning fire, but they were deflected by the fully charged front shields.

As of one day ago, Ran had put his most trusted confidant, Communications Officer Felix, in a dual role, now also overseeing the main weapon systems. While his main objective was to control the communications coming into and out of the *Void Reaper*, he also wanted to have someone he could rely on to oversee the massive death-dealing weapons on board.

While Executive Officer Hap had not been keen on the idea, Ran had convinced the Alurian that all was well. The once mighty general was fully aware that at a moment's notice, Hap could take control of the *Void Reaper* on orders from the Prime Assembly.

The deflector shields and the ship's main weapon collided in a rainbow of unnatural colors. While the initial shot from the main ion cannon had been deflected, it had been meant to drain the *Crow*'s shields and distract from the explosive drones rounding the front of the massive dreadnought.

Several of the *Crow*'s assigned attack fighters continued to pepper the enemy starfighters until they were called off after the last blast to the *Crow*'s engines to preserve strength and regroup, something that First Sergeant Becket had reluctantly made the call to do.

Unlike the *Crow*, the *Void Reaper*'s belly was full of starfighters and drones instead of heavy assault mechs. Even though both ships were Alurian dreadnought-class starships, the *Void Reaper* was fully staffed with a highly trained crew.

Several satisfying explosions popped in the main viewscreen while Ran nodded. Hap, satisfied with the general's actions, nodded too. "How did you know they would be set like this?"

"Between the long-range scans and what I myself would do, it seemed the most logical course of action. They have somehow been able to outclass several Alurian destroyers and even this very ship before. I'm not sure how, but they have. I am leaving nothing to chance. If they can't move, they can't truly fight if we maneuver out of range."

Hap stood, walking up to Ran. "I now see what Kluvnew does in you." The *Void Reaper*'s executive officer stopped as a red light flashed on the main viewscreen. "It looks like we have a lock on the Creare ship. This is indeed a good day."

General Ran held in a smirk, knowing that the day was not over. Not only was Hap arrogant, but he was also focused on the outcome versus the actual battle they were now engaged in.

Ran tapped the console as both men stared at the viewscreen. A 3D rendering of the planet erupted on the holoprojector in front of them. "That's odd?" Ran asked no one in particular. "The ship appears to be hovering in low orbit, still within the clouds."

A stern, gruff humanoid woman walked over to the table with a tablet, transferring the data to the holoprojector. "It appears there's a massive power spike as well. They are doing something."

"Executive Officer Hap," Ran started, flattening his lips. "The day just might be full of surprises. Felix." He shifted his focus. "Prepare the cruiser and a group of starfighters with boarding capabilities."

The dreadnought-class Alurian ships were large enough to carry with them an additional cruiser or destroyer-class vessel. The *Murphy*, in retrospective, fit neatly underneath the belly of the *Crow* on what was called a stable. The *Void Reaper* was no different, having an attack star cruiser also docked.

Hap stared at the holoprojector before glancing back at Ran. "Why not send the cruiser to finish off the *Murphy*?"

"We have underestimated the *Murphy*, as well as Captain Dailey and his crew, before. If I can utilize the two ships for leverage in order to take control of the Creare vessel, I will. Plus, we don't know the ship's full capabilities. I would rather not have Dailey out for blood. Not everything has to be driven by violence," Ran said, reinforcing his earlier conversation with the ship's executive officer.

"According to your files, that's exactly what you often resort to. Violence appears to be your forte." Hap grinned. The Alurian's sharp teeth cut through his smile as his green lips peeled back.

"Might I remind you I am in command of the ship and operation?" Ran knew he was pushing the man, but he also needed the Alurian to remain confident in his actions.

Hap nodded. "Who shall lead the boarding party?"

"I will take charge of the operation. You will take charge here. At no time are we to destroy either one of those vessels unless absolutely needed," Ran ordered, getting a slight, unseen nod from Felix. In the event Hap tried to take control of the *Void Reaper*, Felix had already set up a protocol to prevent him from doing so.

"Sir," Felix spoke up, seeing the end of their conversation. "We have disabled the *Crow*'s main thrusters. Their stabilizers are still operational; however, they will not be able to maneuver as needed to fight. All of their main power has been rerouted to shields. The only thing they are using right now is their close-range laser turrets."

"Very good." Ran smiled. "You see? Just a little tactical patience. Set the deployed starfighters at range to secure the ship. Open up communications with the *Crow*."

While wanting to talk to the *Murphy*, he was fully aware that the *Crow*, being a dreadnought, was absolutely the largest threat currently on the battlefield. The fact that none of the crazy maneuvers he had witnessed before had taken place told him all he needed to know about the *Murphy*: whatever they had done before, they were no longer in control of that capability. That capability being Albert.

Ran's face erupted on the main screen on the *Crow*'s bridge.

"This is General Ran of the Prime Assembly. As you are aware, your main thrusters are offline. If you continue to fight, we will continue to fire on your vessel. Stand down and await further instructions."

An anxious Pearl looked at a sweating Dorax, both feverishly working on the console in front of them as several red lights flashed from every surface of the bridge. Realizing the predicament they were now in, Pearl tapped the open communications line button in front of her.

"This is Executive Officer Pearl of the USF *Murphy*. You have attacked a Federation-flagged vessel. We are currently maintaining our posture," Pearl said. That was all she would give the man whom she held not only great disdain but pure, unadulterated hate for. She would see that man to his grave before her own last breath left her body.

Ran cut off the communications feed. Maintaining their current posture simply meant that they were not engaging with the *Void Reaper* unless they continued to be fired upon. There was a clear understanding of the current situation.

"I'm heading down to the docking bay. I want two platoons of shock troopers with us, as well as a squad of battle droids," Ran stated. Hap nodded, content that the general was acting in the best interests of the Prime Assembly.

The truth of the matter was that he wanted to get on board the Creare ship just in case any issues arose, giving him some much-needed leverage from both barrels of the gun he knew were pointing at him at all times. If the operation didn't go as planned, he would likely never make it out of the system alive. But if the technology on board the Creare vessel was as advanced as everyone said, he would be able to leverage it with the Prime Assembly, which basically meant getting Hap off his ship and hopefully ejected through an airlock into deep space. The man didn't want to go against Kluvnew, but he wanted the *Void Reaper* all to himself and strictly under his command without question.

Ran slowly lowered himself onto the main command chair aboard the significantly smaller vessel. Much like he had done with Felix, he had also assigned several of his most trusted crew members and associates on board the Alurian cruiser-class starship named the *Halifax*.

Even though the *Halifax* was loaded with unfamiliar shock troopers, all it would take was the push of a button to evacuate the drop bay quickly into space. The ship was roughly a quarter the size of the *Murphy*, yet it was built for boarding and docking other vessels while still engaged in combat. While unable to support more than a handful of small starfighters on its drop bay, its armaments more than made up for it.

With a hull made of Moshan star steel and a battery of rail guns, the small, maneuverable, highly lethal ship was built for the exact mission they were about to partake in. Sleek, stealthy, and visually angry, the *Halifax* had been handpicked by General Ran himself.

Lieutenant Jacob Weathers, sitting at the navigational helm of the *Halifax*, turned back to General Ran. "Sir, the attack fighters have been recalled away from the fight, closer to the other side of the *Murphy*. We are prepared to take off."

Weathers had grown up off-world, having been born on one of the moons of Jupiter. His flat, calm voice was something he had learned after years of hard living, knowing how to wear a mask in front of often prying eyes. After growing up in poverty in a mining family, he'd joined the Ateris Mining Syndicate, only to follow that up with a stint under Colonel Freeman with the Pathfinders. During this time, he had made his way as a junior officer on General Ran's staff before being assigned to the *Brightstar*.

One of the many things Ran had put into place before going into the void on the *Brightstar* was to reassign several of his most trusted confidantes into positions which would allow them to still be viable resources in the event the ship was ever scuttled. Weathers had been smart enough to contact the Ateris Mining Syndicate, knowing of the relationship, and had been immediately taken to a distant planet on the far reaches of the galaxy, then gated to the main Prime Assembly's shipyards, like several others.

"Take us out," Ran instructed, pressing several buttons on his console, bringing up communication frequencies between the planet and the two moons.

Again, the odd strain on the signal put in place by Albert was present. Not being able to break the coded message, Ran had loaded up its signature on all their systems. There were clearly several messages being sent back and forth between the ships, and one on repeat directly toward the planet. Ran focused on that signal, chewing on his bottom lip.

The *Halifax* undocked from the *Void Reaper*, the sounds of hydraulic pistons and clamps being released clicking loud enough to be heard on the bridge.

"Weathers." Ran cleared his throat. "Trace the signal being sent from the *Murphy* to the Creare ship. It looks to be on repeat. We should be able to tell if they are receiving it or not."

Weathers's eyebrows rose slightly, only to drop back down into place. "It appears the signals have not been received, sir. We know that most signals don't cut through those clouds."

"They don't know we're here yet. Excellent," Ran hummed to himself as the *Halifax* zipped by the *Crow*.

CHAPTER 21

THE RACE

A ngry clouds rocked the *Waiting Sun* like a once calm ocean now in the middle of a hurricane. Stabilizers and other thruster systems worked with laserlike precision to keep the ship on a steady trajectory.

Now in a position to activate the scrubbers, Persius stabilized the orbital thrusters to a steady glow of angry blue exhaust. Unlike Federation- and Alurian-built star ships, Creare ships resembled almost-living organisms. Curved lines in odd metallic faces of unknown creatures ornamented the outside of the *Waiting Sun*.

"Activating scrubber protocol nine-one-nine," Persius announced over the intercom as a low but audible hum reverberated throughout the ship's bones.

Dailey leaned forward as Albert stood up from the position he had taken at the main navigational console. "Albert, status report,"

"Well, for starters, we're alive, so we have that going for us. The scrubbers are now at eighty percent. We are on schedule to complete our mission. We should have full scanners, as well as offense and defense capabilities, online within twenty minutes."

"What about comms with the *Murphy*?" Dailey asked, knowing time was absolutely working against them.

"I'm starting to pick up traces of radio transmissions from the two moons. It's still all garbled. If we were planetside, we would have a straight line of communication. Being in these damn infernal clouds, however, it's another story," Albert said before Persius cut in.

"There is a signal on repeat every thirty seconds. Someone is trying to reach us."

Albert let out a scoffing huff. "Yeah, I was about to get to that."

"Shit," Dailey blurted out as Janix looked over pensively. "I'm thinking they're trying to get a hold of us for a very important reason. Persius, is there any way we can clear the lines to hear that message?"

"We will be able to receive transmissions within ten minutes; the scrubbers work extremely fast. The area around us will be clear by that time. We do, however, need to complete our task in order to put the proper protocols in motion to clear the rest of the atmosphere," Persius's calm, cool voice echoed through the bridge.

"Jen, do you copy?" Dailey asked. Lieutenant Jenny Brax was now in the cargo and fighter bay with the rest of the Vault's inhabitants, as well as on standby with the Harpy and transportation ship.

"Yes, sir, go ahead," Jen replied. Down in the bottom bays of the *Waiting Sun*, the scrubbers were a significantly larger event than on the stabilized bridge.

"Something's going on with the *Murphy*. Make sure everyone's loaded up, just in case. I'm also going to send down whoever doesn't need to be on the bridge. Get the Nova Rangers loaded up on the Harpy."

"Roger, sir," Jen replied. The remaining crew all looked back at Dailey, awaiting instructions.

"Tarik, Janix. I want you to get everyone off this bridge. Albert, that means you. They need you on board the *Murphy*."

Taken aback by the statement, Sparky let out what could only be called moon gas as he slowly trudged up onto his hind legs. Two chuffs and a yelp later, the translator kicked in. "Staying here. I can leave whenever."

Albert also took this time to add his two cents' worth. "I can always interact with the *Murphy* once we are out in orbit."

"No," Dailey stated assertively. "I need you on board the *Murphy*. Persius has been more than obliging since we've been here. Something's not right. I'll stay with the ship."

"Suit yourself, but I will need to go over the Persius removal protocol with you before I do so," Albert insisted to an approving Dailey.

"You got about fifteen minutes. Break it down, Barney style," Dailey said as the stick figure icon on his console started flashing. Pressing the button, the diagram and holoprojection of the *Waiting Sun* morphed into a picture of the globe, as well as a percentage meter showing an area around the ship dispersing at mind-boggling speeds.

Persius's voice cut in over the conversation. "We have reached initial terminal synchronization."

"Remember, Persius," Dailey said, standing up. "Dumb it down to your lowest level and explain it to me."

"The scrubber protocol has taken effect and is now spreading. The longer we stay here, the larger the impact. We stay as planned, and the deionized electrification of the cloud system will be one hundred percent effective."

"Hold steady. Albert, get those damn columns up and running," Dailey insisted. Janix walked up to the man, clearly not happy with leaving the bridge.

"Sir, we need to keep some people on the ship just in case."

"In case what?" Dailey asked. Janix shook his head.

"Sir, at least let me select a handful of volunteers to stay behind with you."

Dailey scanned the scene around him, refocusing on the task at hand. He had souls to ensure made it back to the *Murphy*, as well as survived the day. "I don't—"

The man was cut off by Jones and Pickle talking over each other, finally landing on letting Specialist Jenna Jones do the gabbing. "Sir, with all due respect," she started, knowing that any time a lower-ranked soldier said that to their superior officer, what came later wasn't a choice. It was an unwritten rule of the military. She was telling the *Murphy*'s commander that if he was going down with the ship or staying on board, so were they. They would pay the consequences for their unruly transgressions later.

"Very well. I'll let this one slip. But everyone else, get your asses down to the Harpy. That includes you, Janix," Dailey stated firmly. There would be no more questioning his orders.

"You two will be the death of me," Janix huffed. "Or are you trying to get promoted?"

"A little of both," Pickle followed with a grin.

"Okay, kiddos," Albert said, standing up to his full height. "If, for some reason, Captain Dailey needs to evacuate the ship, all he needs to do is grab that handle next to the holoprojector and take Persius with him. I also packed the to-go bag of replicated Solarian beef jerky for Sparky."

The AI had kept it hidden in order to prevent it being eaten before they even got to orbit. Pulling out a large container from under the console, Albert slammed it down on the floor next to Sparky. "You see what's written on it?"

A couple of barks were quickly translated. "Not learned how to read yet."

Albert took on a fatherly tone. "It says 'open in case of emergency.' I fully trust you to know when an emergency occurs." This was followed by a handful of pats on Sparky's head as his tongue lolled from his mouth.

"Albert, keep plugged into the ship. We should have comms in a couple of minutes," Dailey said as the rest of the Nova Rangers and Tarik started leaving the bridge. Valen, on the other hand, stood resolute, whispering something into Tarik's ear, getting a nod from the man. He was also staying behind.

After several more nerve-racking minutes, Persius's calm voice flowed through the bridge. "Our communication systems are now active. Scrubbers are at eighty percent."

"Jones," Dailey spoke, walking over to her console. "Open the comms channel to the message."

Communications Officer King's voice came through in a stern, stressed tone. "The *Void Reaper* is early. We are under attack."

"Dammit," Dailey huffed. "Albert, are you able to pull up the orbital sensors yet?"

"We have a problem, boss," he replied. Persius, taking it upon herself, adjusted the holoprojector to show what was going on in the heavens above.

Several small starfighters surrounded both the *Crow* and the *Murphy* as the *Void Reaper* lumbered directly behind. Even more stressful, however, was the column of ships heading directly toward them.

"Albert, do you have your communications protocol uploaded?" Dailey wanted to ensure he could speak freely with his crew in space.

"Activating now, and . . . we are synced."

"Becket, you copy?" Dailey asked. The static hum, only lasting seconds, felt like an eternity.

"Sir, what's your status?" Becket spoke. This wasn't the time to catch up on their glory days.

"We have about another five minutes, and we're done. The ship's main system is charging our offenses and defenses. This isn't a battleship, but we're ready to jump into the fight."

Becket paused on board the *Murphy*, his voice now a mix of concern. It wasn't that the man had given up; he was simply trying to work a way out of their current predicament. "Our engines are offline, as are the *Crow*'s. Ran came over the damn comms and spewed some bullshit about keeping the status quo. He wants that ship you're on, and from what I can tell, he's going to use us as leverage."

"What about the attack wing and the rest of our units?" Dailey asked, also opening up the comms channel with Jen and Pearl.

"I pulled them all back once the engines went offline. We haven't lost anyone yet. A little beat up, but we're ready," Becket replied. Pearl was the next to speak, not sounding as confident.

"It's good to hear your voice. We've had to relocate to the secondary bridge. We got a direct hit, and the whole damn bridge started falling apart. They knew exactly where to hit us. We lost two attack fighters in the mix, but the rest of the Nova Rangers are back on board."

Dailey pondered the current state of affairs, walking back over to the main con and sitting down. "Everyone here's loaded up and ready to leave the ship. I'm going to send Jen, as well as the transportation ships on board, back down to the planet while we sort this out. If Ran wants the ship, I'm going to ram it straight up his third point of contact. How long till both of you can get back online?"

Becket spoke up this time. "We could really use some help from Albert doing some of that voodoo. Bellman started losing the rest of his hair trying to work through something pertaining to the gate drive and the reactors tied to it."

Albert took this moment to chime in on the conversation. "And here I thought all that time he was simply not listening. Yes, even though the main thrusters are no longer functioning, if you can get the gate drives to work, it will only take a little nudge not to tear everything apart."

"Explain," Dailey demanded.

"In order to properly navigate through a gate, the ship must be able to maneuver at a constant rate of speed. If not, well, let's just say you're better off floating around in space the way you are now. I would suggest focusing on doing that. Captain Dailey, might I suggest I take one of the Creare ships on board and make my way to the *Murphy*?"

"Won't they see you coming?" Dailey asked.

"Not if I scuttle the ship approximately a hundred klicks out and sling-shot myself directly toward the *Murphy*. Plus, even though the Creare ship is old, it has significantly more advanced stealth capabilities. Yeah, I can totally do this one."

Persius spoke up, having overheard the entire conversation, running it through whatever computational systems she utilized. "There is an eighty-five percent probability of Albert's mission being successful. It is within the parameters of accepted risk."

Neither Becket nor Pearl had heard Persius's voice up until now.

"Sir," Becket growled. "Is that the other AI?"

"Yep," he replied, focusing on the new plan now quickly forming in his head. "Albert, you're a go. But I will tell you now. If you don't make it, and I have to come out there and grab you from space, it's going to be a no-go on that dating show you and Sparky want to make."

"Well, now that you put it that way, I'll drag an extra set of Creare space armor with me as a backup. No way we're letting that show go off the rails before we've even recorded the first episode."

Slightly adjusting, Persius spoke again. "With the addition of the secondary means of transportation, the probability of success has risen to ninety-five percent."

"Albert, make it happen," Dailey said, shifting back to his two commanders up in space. "You guys heard that. Albert's on his way. By the looks of it, we've only got about ten minutes before we get intercepted."

"Sir, you're not going to do any of that crazy stuff, are you?" Becket asked, knowing that Dailey was either going to ram the ship directly into Ran's forces or make the ship go supernova in orbit. Either way, Dailey was about to get into the fight.

"I'm going to see if I can have a little chat with Ran first. We're only going to keep a skeleton crew on board. Jen, you copy that?"

"Roger, sir. Persius has already given us a landing vector location. If we can make it back to the location, we should be able to get the transportation ship at least moderately shut down and out of sight. Worst-case scenario, we will evacuate everyone back into the Vault. Tarik and Bella are down here trying to work through some plans. If that doesn't work, there's a location several hundred miles away that Persius has noted will also conceal the ship." Jen replied, only to speak back up. "Sir, to the edge." There was a pang of worry in her voice that couldn't be avoided as the others echoed her call.

"To the edge," Dailey replied, putting their plans into motion.

The docking bay aboard the *Waiting Sun* was a bustle of moving bodies. Bella and Tarik corralled the last of the Vault's inhabitants into the transportation ships while Janix motioned for the last of the Nova Rangers to board the Harpy.

"Albert," Janix called as the AI prepped a sleek black ship. "You got this?" the Solarian asked, showing genuine concern. Mister Toaster's face flattened.

"Somebody's got to be the breadwinner in this relationship." Albert grinned, only to have Mister Toaster's face go flat again.

"You're nervous?" Janix asked, picking up on the vibe from the AI. Gears whirled while Albert lifted the large suit of Creare armor onto the side of the ship, attaching it with several magnetic clips.

Sparky trotted up beside his partner in crime, flopping over on his hind legs, watching. "If you mean that my internal servos are slightly warm and that I have reviewed all thirty seasons of *Solarian Love Angle Mangle* while I've been prepping the ship, then yes."

Janix pulled out a marker, scribbling on Albert's chest plate. Finally complete with his work, Albert looked down, tracing the drawing and unit markings.

A quickly drawn Spartan's helmet, followed by *2nd FT*, marked Albert as not only part of the *Murphy*'s crew but an official part of Janix's team. "You're one of us now. Get to the *Murphy* and do us proud. We'll not be far behind." Second Foot's de facto leader patted the drawing on Albert's chest as a grin finally perked Mister Toaster's face.

Albert did the droid version of standing up straighter, pushing his chest out, followed by a snapping salute. Sparky let out a bark and chuffed, allowing the translator to kick in.

"To the edge! For the Ham Republic!"

The AI turned, giving another snapping salute, before turning to the cockpit and jumping inside the sleek ship in one fluid motion. Before closing the pit, Albert leaned over. "Keep the lights on for me. Oh, and if I run into any issues, tell the *Murphy*'s entertainment system I did my best."

With the moment gone, Janix shook his head. "Be safe, brother."

The cockpit slid shut as Albert plugged into the ship's main control harness. An odd familiarity with the ship washed over the AI as light blue thrusters hummed to life. Albert tapped a button on his chest plate, pulling out a sleek, smaller AI. In all the chaos, the two AIs had programmed a remote temporary protocol to work with Dailey and the others while getting Persius to safety, something Albert knew was wrong but had been suggested by the AI due to the probability of her being captured by the Prime Assembly on the planet.

The massive door to the bay slid open, again splitting into dozens of pieces. Wind slammed into the space as Janix secured his helmet, followed by Sparky doing the same.

"Jen," Janix called over the comms. "The bay is clear. We are cleared to leave."

Running up the open ramp, Tarik gave Janix a nod as Bella, close to his side, waved. The side entrance to the transport ship slid shut while the larger ship's thrusters sprang to life.

Janix and Sparky walked onto the ramp before Janix made his way to the cockpit.

"Look." Jen pointed to the clear skies around the *Waiting Sun*.

"I'll be damned. It worked," Janix said as the hiss of the Harpy pressurizing made the Solarian's ears pop.

"Dailey wants us to stay on board once we get the transport ship to safety. I don't know how this is going to play out, but I have a feeling things are about to get crazy."

"When don't they." Janix grinned as Jen activated the Harpy's intercom.

"Good afternoon, ladies and gentlemen. Thank you for riding the *Murphy* Express. Please keep all hands and feet inside the aisle, and enjoy your flight. Drinks will not be served during this flight."

Sparky, not getting the joke, barked, looking down at his container of Solarian jerky. "I have snacks."

"I'm sure the others will appreciate that," Jen added as Sparky shook his head, chuffing.

"I have to share?"

CHAPTER 22

THE ROAD TO GLORY

Several green lights flashed on the bridge of the *Waiting Sun*. At the same time, several proximity alarms blared on. Jones leaned forward, switching the holoprojector to a view of the area they were about to fly into.

Persius's voice flowed through the bridge. "Scrubber protocol at one hundred percent. We are now clear to enter orbit. Weapons and defense systems are at fifty percent. Albert also recommended I play something called rock and roll downloaded into my memory banks while doing so."

"We'll be fine without it, but thank you, Persius. Let's save that till later. Activate your targeting systems and give weapon control to the main consoles."

"As you wish. I will keep close-range security weapons under my control until weapon systems are fully charged."

Dailey thought about the advantage Albert gave them in a fight, realizing he should probably give total control to the AI, but also not fully trusting its capabilities yet. The fact that Persius kept referring to probabilities and percentages made Dailey concerned that the system wouldn't push the boundaries of space combat he and the others were capable of.

"Valen, how does it feel to be the first person from your planet to enter orbit?" Dailey asked.

"I have to live to tell about it." Valen was making a good point. "The communications line is now open. You want to hail the oncoming ships?" he asked, having taken control of the comms station at an alarmingly perceptive rate.

"Beat me to it. Open a channel," Dailey said, sitting up straighter.

General Ran's smug face appeared on the main viewscreen as Dailey stood up, walking around the holo-table. "Ran, I would say it's good to see you, but I'm sure you already know that's not the case."

"Dailey," Ran let the words roll off his tongue. "I see you are already tracking the current situation you all now find yourselves in."

Dailey interrupted the man, speaking as if he wasn't there. He was buying time as the *Waiting Sun* started pushing into orbit. "Yeah, I see that. You'll also now see me joining the conversation."

Unfazed by the comment, Ran subconsciously glanced at the monitor showing the hulking outline of the *Waiting Sun*. Clouds poured off the top of the massive ship like water, finally showing the true extent of the prize. A prize that, in reality, hadn't been fully claimed. For all Dailey knew, the ship would zip off into space under the control of Persius.

While Albert had stated he'd set certain parameters in place to avoid that, Dailey had learned to trust but verify. In this case, he was about to see the true intentions of the ship's AI.

"I would like to further explain your counterpart's current position." An incoming graphic on the holoprojector forced Dailey to turn. Valen and the ship were ensuring the message got through. Displayed was the *Murphy*, looking like a toy model. "As you can see, there are several fission warheads that have been attached unknowingly to the hull of your ship." Ran was calling it Dailey's, knowing the perception of ownership of the souls on board would drive the decisions he was about to make.

The *Murphy*'s commander held in the disdain and concern now bearing down on him and his people. He was surprised at the efficiency with which Ran had executed his plan. "Yeah, figured you would do something like that. Before you ask, I don't have any tricks up my sleeve. What do you want?" Dailey was figuring that ego alone would push the man he once respected to share his true intent.

Even though Albert had shared the much needed nav data with both ships, neither had been able to upload and calibrate the gate drive without the all-knowing AI present. The thought passed through Dailey's mind that Albert had made it through the small blockade unnoticed.

"What I want is irrelevant. What I am going to take is what's important. You will turn in the Creare ship and any items that may be in your possession. Once that is done, we can talk further about the next steps."

Dailey tried to hold back a laugh at the ridiculous request. "And my two ships?"

"I will guarantee their safety—with certain provisions, of course," Ran stated, not giving anything away.

"Provisions?" Dailey quickly snapped back, wanting more meat on the bone. In front of him, a red light blinked softly, indicating the weapons systems were at ninety percent and ready to fire.

"You and your crew will not be leaving this system," Ran said, waiting for Dailey's response.

"Yeah, I'm not liking the sound of that," he replied as Ran reached down, pressing a button.

An alarm sounded on the holo-table as the image of the *Murphy* was quickly replaced by the *Crow*. A large, bubbling explosion rocked the front of the ship as he activated one of the explosives he'd also mounted on the dreadnought.

"Ran, you son of a bitch," Dailey growled, no longer able to hold in his boiling anger. The only calming factor in the conversation was the clearly intact section next to one of the many docking bays they had set up as a secondary bridge, per his last conversation with Pearl.

"Are we clear?" Ran asked, not giving Dailey time to respond. "You have five minutes."

Ran's face winked off the monitor as the crew all waited for Dailey to respond. The *Murphy*'s captain walked up to the holoprojection of the *Crow*. "Persius, do you have a lock on Albert?"

"Yes, the starfighter Albert took has passed the blockade and is five minutes from transferring to the second stage of transportation," Persius informed the group, referring to Albert ejecting from the small ship and making the rest of the trip via his small thrust packs.

"Persius, can you disable communications from Ran's ship to the others?"

"No, I am not familiar with the communications protocol being used. Also, due to their proximity to the other vessels, there is a ninety percent probability of a secondary relay being used. I would like to remind you I am not programmed for sustained intelligence and combat operations."

"Tell that to Albert. He seems to believe he was made for construction and system integration."

Persius paused. "That is correct, and in many ways, one of the most efficient combat protocols available. Also, be advised, there are signals from a fleet Ran is communicating with within this system, not yet engaged."

The blood started to drain from Dailey's face as he was quickly running out of time and ideas.

Time. He needed to buy more time. For what, he had yet to figure out, but as always, time had a way of solving problems, or letting others do so.

"Sir," Jones broke the silence. "Should we open fire?"

"Then what? No. I want you all to go back to the dock and get on a ship. Don't join the others. Just get out of the way. Head directly toward the planet and wait." Dailey shifted to the container holding Persius.

"Persius, I'm going to have to go with the others. Can you still integrate and communicate with the ship?"

Persius changed the holoprojection to a safe trajectory to the planet. "I will be able to communicate remotely in a limited capacity. I can set up automated controls for the ship, as well as give you access to the systems via an overlay Albert provided that you will be familiar with. You will be able to pilot the ship from the main con. Lastly, as long as the ship stays on the route I am programming, I will be able to mask its signature." A green light pinged on the control panel. The ship was now fully under Dailey's control as it continued to slowly enter orbit. This had been done on purpose.

Grabbing the sleek handle, Dailey pulled out Persius's main containment system, handing it to Pickle. Much like Albert, the AI fit into a small cube enclosed in an armored box. "You heard me, people. Get your asses to the bay. I'll be behind shortly."

Pickle, Jones, and Valen all paused, knowing the man was probably going to do something extreme. Much to their surprise, Dailey clicked off his forearm armor plates, watching the nanotech fold into small cubes. This was followed by the man dropping into the con.

"Sir?" Pickle asked as Valen walked up to the two Nova Rangers.

"It's time to go. We are no good sitting here. We will have our time to fight."

Salutes were given as Jones teared up from anger and anger alone. She wanted to fight. This wasn't the norm for Dailey, but she also understood that with so many souls on his mind, he would do whatever was needed to keep them all safe.

Dailey clicked open the comms line, and Ran again appeared on the main monitor.

"Have you made your decision?" Ran asked, not giving anything away.

One thing Dailey knew was that Ran wanted the *Waiting Sun*. That was his leverage. Leverage that he and Albert had decided would involve having a kill switch on board. A kill switch that was now floating through space on its way to the *Crow*, while another one sat snuggly in his pocket.

Reaching down to his side, Dailey tapped the small detonator allowing him to contact Albert and hyperexcite the ship's main core reactor. Before being boarded, Dailey would make the call, keeping the remote detonator within a second's reach.

"I'm positioning the ship in orbit and am prepared to hand over command of the ship. What guarantee are you giving me?" Dailey asked as Ran mulled over his response. This was telling, as the man was making a decision, a choice he had yet to decide. A first for the knowingly decisive commander.

There it was. Ran was unsure about something, Dailey thought to himself. He already knew someone else was behind his master scheme. Who that was remained a mystery. The Alurians? The Ateris Mining Syndicate? Or some other unknown, shadow organization?

What Dailey now understood was Ran's willingness to negotiate. He was probably hedging his bets, and with a fleet of ships tucked away elsewhere in the system, the now disgraced general was up to something likely to benefit himself.

"None. I will give you the opportunity to discuss this with me once we are on board and the ship is secured. In the event something is not right, I will detonate both ships without hesitation. Stand down and deactivate all weapons systems. And yes, I can see they are fully charged."

Dailey knew the man wasn't bluffing. There was still more, and Dailey had very little time to prepare for what was coming. The viewscreen went blank as Dailey quickly hailed the *Murphy*.

"Becket. You copy? I don't have much time," Dailey spit out as Becket immediately responded.

"Send it, sir."

"Ran is boarding the ship. I'm the only one left on board. Albert should be there in about thirty minutes. He won't activate his transponder until he's on the ship. I'm sure you've figured out they attached warheads to the ships. Albert should be able to help, but you must keep up appearances until I have things figured out here." Dailey looked down at the small monitor beside him, seeing the ship with the remaining crew was now safely through the atmosphere.

Persius's voice came over the intercom. "We were not detected. I am no longer going to be able to control the ship's dampening field. You are on your own."

Dailey clicked off, needing to focus. Becket came back over the comms.

"Sir, that's a good copy. I'm not happy about it, but we will keep our current posture. We also received the sensor data about the other ships in the system. Are they the Creare?"

Dailey was certain Ran wouldn't pull off such a bold move without backup so far away from any known system. "No," Dailey replied. "It's whoever's bankrolling Ran. Be safe, and I'll let you know when it's time."

"Time for what?" Becket asked at the same time red flashing lights indicated someone was boarding the ship.

"Not sure yet. You'll know."

Becket glanced at Kline, who made the universal symbol for an explosion, spreading his hands in slow motion and making boom sounds. "Hmph. That's what I'm worried about."

Dailey continued to deactivate his suit, setting sections of it neatly on the main console. Hissing sounds from the outer doors were quickly replaced by the clatter of boots and the droning of orders from various voices.

Finally taking a seat next to the targeting console, Dailey glared at the door as two Alurian battle droids walked in with weapons, immediately honing in on the man now leaning back in a casual position.

Covered in chrome offset by mute-black armor, the two droids were significantly more advanced and well-equipped than the old security droids commandeered to make Albert's body. Behind them, six fully suited soldiers in jet-black uniforms entered the room. Each individual soldier bulged with muscles as they took position on either side of the door, also training their weapons on Captain Dailey.

"All this for me?" Dailey asked as the clack of General Ran's highly shined boots entered the equation. A larger Alurian decked out in what he assumed was an officer's uniform stood behind Ran, while a significantly larger Solarian finished off the ensemble, wearing the same uniform.

Fade Parox and Brice Kelum were two of Hap's most trusted officers assigned to the mission of securing the ship. Both loyal, and both willing to take orders from the *Void Reaper*'s executive officer without question at a moment's notice.

"This isn't the time to be funny." Ran nodded to the Solarian as the crushingly large figure walked to the con.

While Solarians were slightly larger than the average human, this man would make Senior Chief Thron wonder just what the hell they were feeding him. Standing at around seven feet tall, with piercing blue eyes, the Solarian set a black box on the seat Captain Dailey had just occupied.

Four legs sprouted from either side of the box, five mechanical arms jutting out the top at the same time, making a square spider the size of Sparky. Red lights flashed, and a blue sensor traced back and forth on its front. This was an automated pilot droid.

The Federation, while utilizing very rudimentary AI, had steered clear of using the tech often found on mining ships in the Void. Automated pilot droids still received their orders from a very real pilot, but they were made to integrate into whatever ship it was piloting.

"Well, I guess this is it," Dailey said, standing up. The sarcasm cut through his voice like a hot knife through a warm plate of Moshan mush.

"Perhaps," Ran replied. The man turned, giving orders to the Alurian in tow. "Take one of the battle droids and the rest of the security team in the entrance hall, and start going through the ship. Leave no stone unturned."

"It's not like I planted a bomb or anything with all the time I had," Dailey joked. While he was telling the truth, he'd failed to mention the protocol Albert had loaded on the *Waiting Sun*. "I have a feeling you're going to be rather let down."

"That's yet to be seen. The ship is impressive; several hundred years old, but impressive nonetheless. Talbert." Ran shifted. "Radio back to Executive Officer Hap. Let him know we have secured the ship and are awaiting further orders. Also, scan the other ships to make sure nothing else is in the sector."

"Awaiting further orders?" Dailey asked. This was his chance to do some subverted questioning. "I thought this was your rodeo?"

"Guards, would you kindly pat down Captain Dailey while he removes the rest of his armor?" Ran walked to the holoprojector, seeing the controls no longer modified for human use. Persius had wiped the system before going out of range in an effort to help.

"Do you know, Captain Dailey, that a Creare star cruiser could fit six of these in its docking bays while still having room for a handful of destroyers? Just one of those ships could wipe out Earth and all its surrounding systems. Just one," Ran stated flatly, pinning his hands behind his back as he walked around to face Captain Dailey.

"So why the trouble for this ship?" Dailey asked.

"You ask a lot of questions. Let me ask you a few. How did you get the ship in orbit?"

Shit, Dailey thought; the man had him dead to rights with that question. "Well, it wasn't easy."

"And you just happened to figure out how to clear the atmosphere. We are fully aware that you sat in low orbit for thirty minutes doing something to the planet. As of the moment we boarded the ship, our planetary sensors were able to start scanning the surface," Ran informed, knowing he was not getting the entire story.

Ran's dialogue was cut short when an unfamiliar face appeared on the main viewscreen. Vice Admiral Kluvnew's dark-green face and sharp eyes seemed to pierce Dailey's very soul, even if through a video feed.

"General Ran. I see you have secured the vessel." Kluvnew paused, seeing Captain Dailey sitting in a chair with his hands now secured. Already familiar with Captain Dailey's image, Kluvnew shifted focus to the *Murphy*'s commander. "I see you have another prize. The Prime Assembly will be pleased."

Dailey, having never heard of the organization before, cataloged it for later reference. If given the chance, he would use this to try and bluff General Ran. "Pleased to meet you. And you are . . . ?" Dailey drawled out.

"Someone you will soon know. General Ran, secure the prisoner. We are jumping into orbit. I've also noticed the other two ships are still in functioning condition."

While not noticeable to anyone else on the bridge, including the Alurian clearly giving orders, Ran shifted slightly. He was working through his response. "Yes. We used the ships as leverage to gain access to this vessel and avoid any unforeseen issues. I also believe it's a good idea to inspect the USF *Murphy*. While in combat, it has shown capabilities that it is not supposed to have."

"We can discuss that when we arrive," Kluvnew stated, looking down at something. "We are receiving transmission data from the autopilot. It doesn't appear that the ship's transponder is activated. The last thing we want is any Creare ships showing up. One last thing. Have you identified and removed the ship's primary protocol system?"

Dailey stilled himself, working not to give anything away. The ship had indeed sent out several messages from the planet. In many ways, the *Murphy*'s commander was surprised they hadn't shown up yet.

Kluvnew was talking about Persius, something he was very aware of, and likely the prize he was truly after. Dailey again added this to his pile of leverage, seeing Ran's head turn toward Kelium before speaking.

The Alurian officer cocked his head slightly while attaching a large, portable computer to the main terminal. Ran cleared his throat. "We are working to secure the ship's systems now."

"Very well. We will see you in short order." Kluvnew cut the transmission.

Ran motioned for two of the guards. "Take Captain Dailey to a holding cell. According to our initial scan, they are located through that far hatch. I will need to speak with him further."

The disgraced general was telling them not to kill the *Murphy*'s commander in the process. Not wanting to fight, Dailey nodded, resituating himself in an attempt not to drop the triggering device he now had tucked in his underwear. Dailey often appreciated the simplicity of military things. Even across the galaxy, guards had limits. If not instructed to strip a prisoner down, they would refrain from doing so.

CHAPTER 23

MISTER TOASTER TO THE RESCUE

Albert's main sensor array slowly turned, extending several inches. If a droid could hold its breath, the AI was doing so in style. The deep black of space was only interrupted by speckles of random Alurian starfighter thrusters and lights from the quickly growing *Murphy* now within reach.

While making the slow, low-powered trip from the *Waiting Sun*, Albert had spent his time integrating several pieces of the Creare armor onto his frame. While alien in origin, the sleek, functional armor looked as if it had come with the Alurian battle droids' body.

A booster pack, two additional Creare scanners, and a small pulse laser, similar to the ones they'd encountered on Teras, were the primary pieces Albert had scalped. The trip up until now had taken thirty long minutes, which had turned out to be plenty of time for the droid to work his magic.

Albert, using his newly acquired scanners, had traced a path outside the sensor range of the Alurian fighters. He'd picked up on their patterned runs around the ship, so doing his best impersonation of a rock, Albert calculated an opportunity to activate his thrusters. Every two minutes, the fighters did a sweep. They weren't focusing on small threats such as himself but rather attack fighters trying to come and go.

Seeing his opportunity, Albert activated the Creare booster back, pushing him several thousand feet in the blink of an eye. The familiar lines of the *Murphy* came into close view, giving the AI a straight shot to the very airlock Dorax had jettisoned the Federation observer from.

With one final burst from the sleek boosters, Albert latched onto the airlock. What Albert hadn't planned on was the warhead magnetized to the hull just feet away. "I can't leave them alone for ten minutes."

Albert had stopped actually trying to calculate the amount of time he had been gone, realizing he was just wasting it. Thanks to all the rain on the planet, the electro interference had temporarily overloaded his systems, a condition the AI had known was only temporary and was quickly fading away.

"Who would leave this thing here," Albert scoffed, energizing the device so it clanked off the *Murphy*'s hull. Giving it a light push, the warhead slowly drifted away from the ship.

Focusing back on the airlock, Albert plugged into the auxiliary panel, interfacing with the internal comms system, not wanting to draw attention to himself.

The intercom crackled to life as Becket about jumped out of his skin. The man had been on edge since Dailey's last transmission. "Hello, ladies and gentlemen. Did you miss me?!" Albert exclaimed, sounding like an old game show host.

"Tell me that clanking son of a bitch is here," Becket growled with a smile.

The answer came when the familiar thunk of Albert's feet *clomp*ed out of the elevator. Bellman scurried behind the massive droid, already out of breath for the second time in the past hour.

"New pair of shoes?" Becket joked, taking in the new modifications.

"Uh, shoes? No. I did, however—"

Becket cut Albert off. "Later. What's going on?"

Albert walked to his modified station, plugging into the ship. "Hello, darlings. Miss me?" Albert said, holding up a finger to let him complete whatever he was doing. "That's right," he continued. "Oh, we are way out there. Yes, I see that. Oh my, that must have hurt." In reality, the ship wasn't talking back. He was simply taking in all the systems' status reports.

Becket found himself rolling his eyes. "Anytime now." Becket scowled as Mister Toaster turned, facing the bridge.

"All done. The gate drive is programmed, and I have the reactors transferring power to the secondary thrusters. The main engines will need some work. We can probably run them at twenty percent, and that's pushing it."

"What happens after twenty percent?" Bellman asked.

"Oh, they will backfeed the reactors and go boom. The flow inhibitors are gone."

Not liking that prognosis, Becket shifted focus. "What else were you doing? That conversation had a few things going on."

"Well, I may have . . ." Albert stuttered before spitting it all out in a ball of gibberish. "I programmed a temporary ghost AI protocol from Persius, the *Waiting Sun*'s AI, and swapped it out of that tin can they had her jammed into. I may have had to plug her into the ship, but I can let her out now. And she's a lady, so if you decide to place her into a barrel of rum, please use a nice Cabernet instead."

Becket mouthed, "WTF."

Albert pulled a box out of his chest as the familiar glow of his container flushed a light blue. "I think she may be adjusting to the new surroundings, but Persius can probably help us out of the mess you all got yourselves into."

"Might I remind you," Pearl's voice cut in. Becket had hailed her on the secure net. "You helped us get into this mess. We don't want to keep this line open long. Send it."

"Three things. As you've probably guessed, we rigged the *Waiting Sun* to go boom. Don't worry, everyone is safe on Teras. Next, when I plugged her in, she ran a hull electro-wiping protocol and demagnetized the dozen or so fission warheads attached to the hull. Think of it as a quick EMP pulse. I, of course, masked it as an onboard system overloading due to the damage. Lastly, there's a fleet of Alurian ships heading this way, and they probably think we sent Persius to Teras."

"Wait," Pearl interjected. "If they think the AI is on the planet, and most of our people are down there, won't they go down there too?"

Albert paused as Persius's box turned red. "Oops. Well, if it makes up for it, that means they will send more ships to the planet. Ships that will not be able to watch us while we get the gate drive on both ships working. Oh, Lieutenant Commander Bellman, could you hook Persius up to Sparky's old translator speaker? I promised on pain of death not to leave her plugged into the ship."

Becket spoke up next, bringing up the literal truth bomb Albert had dropped. "Warhead?"

"Oh, I figured you guys didn't place all those on the hull, so I sort of float-ed one out toward your babysitters. The others will eventually do the same."

"Bellman, how didn't we know about this?" Becket asked.

"Some Alurian tech we aren't aware of? I'm not sure. What type of warhead?"

Albert shrugged as the laser mounts on his shoulders shifted. "A fis-sion warhead. Very nasty. I would think a few gigatons each; they mean business. On the flippity-flop, one could, say, reduce the energy charge and detonate one smack-dab in the center of those asshats without causing a full detonation, or at least a smaller one."

"Pearl, once we get everything situated here, we'll get this figured out." Becket looked up at Albert, shaking his head. "Can you or Persius send the protocol to release the warheads from the *Crow*'s hull?"

"I don't see why not."

"Just need a yes or no," Pearl added. The crew had learned that argu-ing or rationing with Albert could take time, but all one needed to do was clarify the ask.

"Yes, it will take approximately twenty for us to package the data and stream it on a low-watt frequency. Those boneheads don't seem to be using that frequency range. Might I suggest we link Persius to the *Crow*, if even temporarily? Maybe she can see something I can't."

While getting impatient, Becket and the others were still glad to have the chaos that Albert brought with him. "Get started. Bellman, get this hooked up—"

"Persius. Her name is Persius," Albert cut in.

"Albert's new girlfriend hooked up to the translator," Becket continued. "Where's Sparky?"

This was a question that was often answered by a surprise the Alurian war hound and his partner in crime often kept to themselves.

"He's on the planet doing dog things, I'm sure. You know he likes to be called a good boy."

Knowing that Sparky was often a loose cannon, Becket's nostril flared.

"All right, everyone. We have something to work with. Ran's ship has docked with the *Waiting Sun*, so we can assume, since it hasn't exploded yet, that our captain is up to something. So let's get to the last order of business: the Alurian battle group en route."

Albert tapped a few buttons on the main navigation table, showing their current position. "While the small battle group is comprised of Alurian vessels, I don't believe they are flying the flag, if you catch my drift."

Becket did indeed understand the statement, rubbing his hands on his sandpaper-like stubbled chin. The sound was audible to the group, causing a few stares. "Why wouldn't they just send their ships at the same time?"

"Great question, and the right one to ask. Persius and I were casually having a chat about this very thing. It would be wise to assume they are concerned with the Creare showing up. We all know an automated signal went out from the *Waiting Sun* when several of the hibernation chambers were officially activated," Albert said, already concerned with the possible encounter.

"What type of ships do the Creare have?" Becket asked.

"So, from what I can tell, their primary military ships are equivalent to one of the Federation's super carriers," Albert informed the group, garnering a round of whistles.

Federation super carriers were one of the few things that kept the true Alurian Council awake at night, and mostly out of the system. Massive beasts of war, and larger than the *Crow*, super carriers housed dozens of attack wings and other combat ships on board. Unlike a star cruiser or station, the super carriers were massive, agile vessels capable of holding their own in a fight.

The one downfall of the ships was their attachment to Earth's solar system. Having sixteen of them, two for each planet, the carriers weren't designed for long-range operations, needing massive crews and even larger supply lines.

In comparison, the *Brightstar* had been designed with this in mind as one of the first Federation ships with a similar size and capabilities as a super carrier, but able to operate throughout the galaxy. The sheer amount of power needed to operate the *Brightstar*'s massive hyperdrive was the trade-off for the additional capabilities.

"It keeps getting better," Becket growled. "Are they a threat?"

Albert chewed on this question longer than usual. "Perhaps. I can state that they will not negotiate and will likely not be happy about their gas station being disabled. Persius believes they are coming, but exactly *when* is the question. Not everyone looks at the clock like you do. I suggest not engaging."

"Sounds about right," Becket replied, motioning Bellman to get to work on Persius.

CHAPTER 24

REMEMBER

Slick metal walls flowed into a flat slab meant to make its user uncomfortable in the small holding cell aboard the *Waiting Sun*. The angled door slid open with ease, driven by a magnetic track. Unlike other Creare ships, the *Waiting Sun* had been designed and constructed for work. When it came to holding prisoners, the accommodations were even more sparse than a Federation prison transport.

General Ran walked in, shouldered by two of the blacked-out Alurian guards. Glancing at both figures, Ran dismissed the clearly watching, mindless, order-following goons, closing the hatch behind them.

"I see it's time to have a nice fireside chat," Dailey said, slowly standing up. The stiffness in his body from being on the flat slab was taking its toll.

"Smug as always," Ran replied, taking in the draconian cell.

Dailey put his hand on his hips, his ODA overalls draped over his hips. This was going to be a conversation of attrition.

"I'm really not trying to be. I'm just a little pissed, but I'm sure you already knew that," Dailey replied, sitting down after a long stretch.

Being the first time the two men had been alone since the death of Juice and subsequent betrayal, it was a miracle of every god in the universe that Dailey wasn't disconnecting Ran's head from his body.

"As you should be." Ran set down a round disk, known as a flatliner. While simple in design, the small device was useful in situations where a conversation wasn't meant to be overheard.

Not only did the flatliner scramble audio from remote devices, but it also muffled the conversations. Designed on Solaria, even Dailey often kept one in his armor.

After pressing the top of the device, a light green glow indicated it was safe to talk. Ran cleared his throat, an annoying habit the man had. "The fact that you haven't tried to kill me yet tells me you are holding something close to your chest. Please explain."

Dailey gritted his teeth behind his tightening lips. This was the time for him to use the information he had learned from their previous conversation.

"I'm not the one holding something close to my chest. You're worried the Prime Assembly has other plans for you." In Dailey's roundabout way, he wasn't lying, holding something close to his posterior instead.

Ran raised an eyebrow. "You know nothing of the Prime Assembly. If you did, you would understand the big picture. Let's not mince words here. I want to know what you have planned. If not, I will send the *Murphy* and its crew to their grave."

"All right, I'll give you this. The device you seek isn't here," Dailey stated, making it seem like he fully understood the reasoning behind Ran taking over the ship. In reality, he was simply working with what he'd overheard.

Ran didn't speak, letting Dailey continue. An old interrogation tactic both men knew the other was well aware of.

"Okay. We knew the importance of the AI on board and made sure no one would get their hands on it."

Ran pinned his hands behind his back, staying far enough away to keep Dailey's restraints in check. They had latched his ankles to a magnetic loop on the floor.

"You see, Captain Dailey. That is where I start to question things. You see, after you and your crew's display of unnatural abilities against the Alurians, it has become very clear that you are receiving help. Help which, I assume, comes in the form of an AI that you aren't supposed to have. An AI that you likely acquired while traveling to save your friend Juice. What and where is it? Also, might I add, that is the only way you would know how to interface with a Creare AI. Bellman, while smart, is far from being that person, and I also noticed that he is on board the *Murphy*."

"You seem to know a lot about the order of things. I never heard about the Creare before starting on this clown show. Yeah, we had help. Help that we lost during our last scuffle before coming here. You have to wonder why it was so easy to disable both ships?"

Ran smirked. "Child's play. You don't even realize how powerful that ship you stole is and how far advanced Alurian tech truly is. If you did, you would know what is coming."

"That's where I'm confused. I thought we were worried about the Alurians, but it seems to me that everyone is worried about the Creare, and all the bullshit that's happened over the years is a facade to build up their armada to take them on, all while making massive profits," Dailey said. "Oh, not to mention the Prime Assembly." The one piece Dailey was missing was the Alurians' true intentions, aside from all the politics, and the Prime Assembly, who were the true face and backers of the Tectonic Wars.

"Yes, you may be aware. Now, where is the Creare AI?"

Dailey shifted, getting as close as his restraints allowed. "Go . . . fuck . . . yourself."

"Hope that makes you feel better. Sounds like you sent it with the other ships back to the planet. Very well. Oh, I forgot to mention that while we didn't pick them up on our scanners, we had visual sensors in orbit that picked up the entire thing. That includes the small ship that left shortly before we boarded. I wanted to give you a chance in hopes the system was on board, but that clearly is not the case," Ran said flatly, no emotion coming through in his voice.

"If you don't have it, your boss isn't going to be too happy." Dailey was playing on the man's enormous ego in a shift of tactics. The *Murphy*'s commander also shifted his hips, keeping the small detonation device from riding up his third point of contact."

"Yes, as per the reason we are having this conversation. I give you my word to allow you and your crew to live on this planet if you hand over the AI without further complications," Ran offered.

Dailey let the tension drain from his body in thought. "You know, the messed-up thing is, I believe you. But I don't believe the Prime Assembly will allow that. When they get here and you don't have their prize, you will be on the chopping block, won't you? Let me guess, they have someone shadowing you, ready to take charge at a moment's notice. Hell, you probably aren't truly in charge."

Ran's eye twitched lightly. There it was—the truth.

"Perhaps. I can assure you I am more than aware of my current position. I gave you a chance to walk away from this. The Prime Assembly will be here soon. I will let them decide your fate," Ran hissed. "One last thing. You have twenty minutes to choose. After that, I destroy one of your ships."

CHAPTER 25

THE TIME BANDITS

The *Murphy*'s bridge was a mix of controlled chaos and shuffling feet as Persius's voice came through the small translation speaker once mounted on Sparky. Bellman had only taken five short minutes, with Albert's help, to hook up the AI system.

"Connection protocol established," Persius hummed as Albert turned back to a console table, plugging into the ship's main communications port.

For this trick, they were simply transmitting data as if it was a Wi-Fi router of yesteryear. Albert had even gone as far as to program the signal to be picked up on board the *Crow* as soon as received. Even more impressive was Persius's ability to confine the signal to the diameter of a pencil. Even if the signal was intercepted, it would appear to be nothing more than cosmic radiation.

Pearl's voice came over the intercom in a mix of light static. While transmitting the data, they would be able to use the link to communicate through the same protocol that Albert had set up via an old video game chat lobby.

"Whatever you guys are doing, it's doing it on its own."

"Neat, huh?" Albert replied, slightly adjusting the signal. "Give it about five minutes, and we should have those pesky, nasty warheads taken care of."

Becket handed Lieutenant Commander Bellman a piping hot cup of go juice, a habit he often had with Captain Dailey. "How long till the warheads are far enough to no longer be a threat?"

Persius took this one. "I have already reduced the warhead's yields significantly. In order to not raise suspicions, we are slowly demagnetizing them. This will allow the warheads to slowly drift away. I have calculated three additional minutes to answer your specific question, for a total of eight minutes."

Pearl glanced out the open docking bay, seeing a small object, barely visible to the eye, floating off the hull directly under them. Being set up in the open bay, they had a clear view of not only several of the surrounding starfighters but also the planet and the *Waiting Sun*. The *Murphy*, on the other hand, was on the other side of the secondary moon, barely visible. It appeared like nothing more than a blinking dot in the distance.

"The sooner, the better," Pearl cautioned, knowing just how precarious of a situation they were in. While still unable to see the *Void Reaper* directly behind them, they knew its massive cannons were aimed directly at their ship. "If we direct all power to the shields, we should have about forty percent."

Persius spoke again. "I have calculated the probability between reducing the yields of the warheads, your usable shield status, and . . ." The Creare AI paused.

"Albert? What's going on?" Becket growled, swallowing the entire cup of piping hot coffee in one anxious swig.

"I think she found something. Standby."

Another thirty seconds passed before Persius spoke back up. "There is a fifty percent chance the *Crow* would survive detonation. There are also a significant number of mechanized battle droids on board. They appear to have no protocol loaded. Would you like me to do so?"

"Holy shit," Becket drawled out. "You're saying you can get those things up and moving without anybody in them?"

"Yes," was all Persius said. Mister Toaster's face turned toward the group, smiling.

"Told you," he gloated.

"How long will that take?" Pearl asked as several lights started flashing on the makeshift control panel on their secondary bridge.

"Protocol upload complete. The units are ready for input."

"I could kiss you," Becket said as Albert blew a raspberry.

"Rude," the AI followed, clearly taking a liking to the AI.

Unlike the *Void Reaper*, the *Crow* had the majority, if not all, of its lower bays completely full of battle mechs. The ship had been designed for orbit-to-ground combat operations, and it went without saying that the mechs were more than capable of space combat.

The battle mechs on board were significantly different than the Alurian battle droids they had previously encountered. Three times the size and capable of having an onboard pilot, the mechs were also fully capable of autonomous operations.

While in use, their functionality was fairly straightforward and effective. Once dropped through orbit onto a planet's surface, they would deposit their pilot on the ground as a separate assault infantry soldier while the mech did all the heavy lifting by their side.

Albert spoke up from his self-ordained throne. "The protocol is fully loaded. I suggest disconnecting the signal."

"Make it happen," Becket answered, walking back to the navigation table. "This changes things. Get Novak up here."

"Roger!" King shouted.

Bellman stared at the main viewscreen, also laying out the current situation. "What's the game plan?"

"The way I see it, Ran is going to blow up both of the ships, regardless of what he's promising Captain Dailey. We only have a few minutes before the *Crow* is safe, and if Albert's little timer is correct, those other ships will be here in about the same time."

"We still have a few little pesky things we need to figure out. We still have the team on the planet, and our gate drives are still a good bit away from being functional. Yes, I know. Before you say anything, I'm hurrying up," Albert added to the pile of problems.

"That's going to be our weak point. Our people on the planet," Becket growled, now back in thinking mode.

"What about Dailey?" Bellman asked.

Becket shook his head, not having a good answer. "We'll have to play that one by ear."

Lieutenant Jim Novak ran onto the bridge with his flight helmet tucked neatly under his arm, looking as if he had been in a schoolyard brawl.

"Top," Novak reported, looking eager to get back into the fight.

"You already heard most of this, but we're only going to have a limited amount of time to get people off the planet. Also, you remember those mechs on board the *Crow*?" Becket was asking a rhetorical question. "Persius got them all working. Albert has full control."

"Damn," Novak blew out. "What's the score?"

Bellman and several of the other engineers had taken weeks to get one of the mechs working. Novak had actually been into the mech bays, and had been shocked by the sight of the sheer amount of firepower.

"Albert, you have this all laid out yet?" Becket asked as he pulled up a schematic of the entire battlefield.

"Sorta, kinda. There's more going on here than in a Solarian mud bunny parade. Highly entertaining, but man . . . let me tell ya—" Albert stopped, realizing everyone was staring at him. "What?"

The main viewscreen erupted in a mix of ships and icons. The AI had included the warheads now floating out of what he had labeled the danger zone, a throwback to an old movie he had watched on Becket's personal entertainment files.

On Teras, an icon representing the inhabitants of the Vault, Jen, and the Nova Rangers of Third Foot was offset and further away from the Air Force base than the others realized. In orbit, the *Waiting Sun* and twelve other smaller craft were represented by what appeared to be old turd emojis. Albert had taken a liking to them when putting situational charts together.

Behind the *Crow*, the *Void Reaper* was represented by a larger piece of excrement that had seen better days. Used to this, Becket pressed the button, blurring the icons to their true form.

"Warning," Persius barked louder than the speaker needed, causing the words to distort. "Incoming Alurian vessels."

"How many?" Becket growled as several red dots started appearing on the screen. Even though the ships hadn't arrived yet, Persius had already computed their arrival location close to the *Waiting Sun*.

"Twenty-five," Persius stated. "Ten battle cruiser-class starships, five smaller attack-class vessels, seven support ships, two dreadnought-class ships—according to your classification—and a star carrier."

Eyes widened at the sheer amount of firepower about to arrive. This was an entire battle group. Albert chimed in, seeing it fit to do so. "They will be here in two minutes. I suggest we keep our current footing while we continue to bring the reactor online."

"Yeah, you keep doing that," Becket agreed, looking up at Novak. "I want you to have every attack fighter we have ready to go. Your mission is to secure the souls on the planet. With these mechs, I'm more than sure we can handle things up here."

For the first time since the mission to Teras had kicked off, Lieutenant Ponce and Master Sergeant Grantham, from First Foot, ran onto the bridge.

Grantham reached the group first, still in full ODA armor, not having removed even his helmet since coming back on board. Lieutenant Cardinali, better known as Card, was on board the *Crow* with most of Second Foot.

"Perfect timing," Becket stated, standing up straight. If something was going to happen, it would be the next thirty minutes that determined if they lived or died.

"Top, the team is ready. What are your orders?" Grantham asked before Ponce could get a word in.

"Go with the attack wing. Novak is in charge of the recovery operation. We have people on Teras who will need the support. All I can tell you is to be ready. This is going to be a close one. I can't tell you when, but the time is coming."

"Top," Novak cut in. "You trying to do this all at once?"

"Albert?" Becket turned the response over to the all-knowing AI. Albert, seeing the trust placed in him, stood up to his full height as Mister Toaster's lips flattened.

"I say we wait until the timing is just right and detonate those warheads. They're a safe enough distance away. Once the initial shock wave is out of the way, I say we release the mechs and cause as much chaos as possible. Once they've engaged, I say release the attack wing. One straight shot, moving like a bat out of hell. There're a hell of a lot of those damn tinker toys on board the *Crow*. I can't say what the other Alurian ships about to show up will do. From there . . . Well, hopefully we can get the ships on the planet aboard, and then we gate out of here."

Persius took this opportunity to bring down the feeling of hope. "There is a thirty percent chance of this operation working within the parameters provided. I . . ." The AI paused. "I don't see any other variables that improve that number."

Becket sighed. "Well, we've been in worse messes than this. Let's just play it by ear and use this plan as a general baseline. We don't launch the attack wing until the mechs are deployed. We don't do that until the gate drives are operational. Would it be better to somehow send those warheads closer to the Alurian ships? Maybe a few to the *Void Reaper*? We could use some of the mechs. Maybe get a few of the ones close to the *Murphy* as well?"

"We," Persius said, referring to both her and Albert, "can program the mechs to follow this line of thought. Doing so now. The probability of success has risen by eight percent on both factors."

Becket grinned at his stroke of genius. This was the thing with AIs, including Albert, who had gotten better at thinking outside the box. They were still, at times, linear in thought.

Albert put a timer up on the viewscreen, as was the norm. "We have another thirty minutes until I feel comfortable to use the drives. Persius, darling—" he corrected himself. "Persius, what is the probability of us successfully gating?" Like most of Albert's plans with Sparky, he was keeping the detonator to himself, knowing it would likely affect Becket's decision-making. If they went after Dailey, Albert knew they would probably not make it out alive.

"With all crew members on board both ships, fifty percent. Without . . . eighty."

"I can work with fifty," Becket spoke up. "Transmit the plans to Pearl. It's time to earn our paychecks."

The most telling piece of the entire conversation was Becket leaving out any mention of Dailey. He knew his friend—no, best friend would not want himself to become a liability. In reality, Dailey was front and center in the loose plan the team had just laid out.

Proximity alarms sounded as the Prime Assembly's battle group darted into orbit around the *Waiting Sun*. Albert nudged Bellman.

"Thanks for hooking Persius up. Here," he said, handing Bellman the vial of blood Remax had given Dailey.

"What's this?" Bellman asked, sliding it into his breast pocket.

"If we make it, things are bound to become much more interesting. That is a sample of Creare blood. I plan on making it, don't you? I mean, I have several seasons of a show called *Beverly Hills 90210* that I'm dying to rip into."

Bellman's eyes widened, the strobing red lights casting shadows on the science officer's face.

CHAPTER 26

TICK TOCK

Dailey pulled the small detonator from his underwear, holding it in his hand. The man didn't like being blind to what was happening, and hated even more not being in the fight he knew was about to take place. He knew his crew, and better yet, he knew Pearl and Becket would not go down without a fight.

The one thing the *Murphy*'s commander didn't know was that both his ships were no longer under the thumb of Ran's warheads, something he was pondering heavily. If he donated the reactors on board the *Waiting Sun*, Ran would probably not be able to send the signal to activate the warheads.

However, knowing Ran and knowing through their conversation that there were other minds at play here, the destruction of the Creare ship would likely give the signal to whoever was on board the *Void Reaper* to send the *Murphy* and the *Crow* to the same fate.

Dailey breathed out, pulling up his suit and zipping the front.

If he detonated the *Waiting Sun* while the Prime Assembly was on board, it would cause the most chaos. One question he had failed to ask Persius was just how large the explosion would be.

The sound of alarms rang through the hallway outside Dailey's holding cell, accompanied by the voices of several guards. "Shit," Dailey grumbled, slipping the detonator back into his drawers. Company. The fact that he hadn't heard the sounds of the ship's weapons systems firing or the shudder of concussions meant whatever plan the others had wasn't yet in motion.

Boots clicked in the hallway as the sounds of Ran's familiar cadence stopped in front of the door, followed by several more authoritative thuds. Whooshing, the door again opened to Ran shouldered by four blacked-out guards with their faces hidden behind helmets.

"Let me guess. The boss is here," Dailey yawned before standing up.

Ran didn't speak, motioning for the guards to muscle Dailey out of the cell. In classic fashion, the *Murphy*'s commander obliged.

As the first two guards disconnected his ankle braces, Dailey drilled down into one of the men's backs with his elbow. The reverberating thump was quickly offset by the fact that the guard acted as if a fly had landed on his back.

Ran smirked. Unknown to Dailey, there were programmed, mangled figures under the black uniforms. Once upon a time, they had been thinking, feeling people, but now, they were mindless, order-following shadows of a living being. Tortured and curated, the Prime Assembly's hover guards had been stripped of their identity and mind.

"Take him to the bridge," Ran instructed, leaving before Dailey could get within reach of the man. Additional restraints were slapped onto Dailey's arms, elbows, and neck. The mood of the conversation had changed.

Dailey was acutely aware that Ran hadn't yet destroyed his ships. The disgraced general was keeping Dailey and his crew as a backup. Backup for what, the *Murphy*'s commander was about to find out.

Kluvnew, Kelum, and Parox stood by the holoprojector, looking at a new scan of the planet. Persius had wiped the landing plan for the Vault inhabitants from the ship's tracking system, adding an overlay to further distract whoever went looking.

Dailey noticed Ran's displeasure with the close group. Only he would know the intricacies of Ran's actions. Even more telling was Kelum and Parox walking away as they entered the room. They had been having a conversation, and Ran was involved.

"Ah, the famed Captain Dailey," Kluvnew started. The guards pushed Dailey against a flat wall, magnetizing his restraints to the wall. "I was just catching up on current events. It appears you have something I want."

Ran stood resolute, not speaking. The tension on the bridge was palpable. Dailey glanced over, noticing a familiar face. Felix turned slightly, not wanting to engage the *Murphy*'s commander, who stayed silent as Kluvnew walked over. His green skin lightly glistened under the light.

"Not the talking type? I have a way to change that. I see General Ran has ensured that we have leverage in this conversation." Kluvnew held up a detonator. It was almost poetic that they'd both had the same idea, holding the fate of several ships in their hands. Dailey, though, was having to work not to let his leverage slip between his cheeks.

The last thing he saw before speckled stars was a black prod slamming directly into his face.

Blood reached Dailey's mouth, who spit it on the deck while working to get his vision readjusted. Kluvnew had slammed a kinetically enhanced rod directly into his face. The hammer prod gave a little extra push when making contact with a surface.

Stretching his jaw, it was clear that either Dailey's eye socket or jaw was broken. After another spit of blood, the *Murphy*'s commander heard one of his teeth hit the deck with a click. While Ran was an all-around killer and, as Albert said, an asshat, he also had a level of civility bred from years in the Federation, ensuring he wasn't ejected out of an airlock by his adversaries.

Civility. Something the human race took for granted in the deep reaches of space. Even the Moshans, who were now slowly becoming a more civilized society, thought nothing of exacting cruel and unusual punishment on their enemies, which, since the formation of the Federation, had slowly dwindled to age-old, on-planet disputes.

One planet in particular, populated by a race called the Severas, was so violent that the Federation had classified them as DNE—Do Not Engage. They were stuck in times similar to medieval days back on ancient Earth, and while contact had been made, sharing tech or off-planet travel was off the table.

Dailey stilled himself, looking the Alurian in the eyes with a small smile. "I see the Prime Assembly is sending its finest."

Kluvnew held in a chuckle, the right side of his green lips shifting slightly. "I see you have the book, but haven't read it. I know of you. You know nothing of the things outside your own little corner of the galaxy and your Federation. I am the Prime Assembly. It's clear by your eyes you don't know who I am. Where is the ship's primary AI?"

Dailey considered the statement, the thumping sting of the blow reminding him of his current situation. "On the planet." Dailey, while telling the truth, was not being concise enough. Kluvnew's hammer rod slammed into his stomach, and whatever he had in his belly was quickly ejected onto the floor. Kluvnew didn't move, the splatter of day-old food landing on his boots.

"Captain Dailey, I will start taking this level of conversation to your companions on board the *Crow*, as you call it next."

The Alurian wasn't bluffing. Dailey, shifting tactics, offered up something just as interesting, though not as useful. "There is a hibernation chamber on the surface. It's full of the crew. You'll find everything there."

Kluvnew, still not moving, tilted his head. "So you're saying you flew this ship and activated its scrubbers on your own?"

"No," Dailey huffed, still not able to get a full breath in. The burn of vile in his throat stung. He had been tortured before; this wasn't something he couldn't handle, but the threat to his crew had him measuring his words carefully.

Time. He needed to buy time. If Becket and the others hadn't acted yet, they were either doing something or waiting for something. Dailey even thought, for a second, that detonating the ship was such a signal. If he did it now, it would take out most of their assumed leadership.

They couldn't be that naive, Dailey supposed, letting his thoughts wander. Kluvnew took in the information, finally digesting it.

"Parox, pull up the surface scanners. Now that the atmosphere is clear, we can use normal systems," Kluvnew stated as the Alurian officer set another black box on the table next to the holoprojector.

A minute later, an image of the hibernation pod appeared on the main viewscreen before being transferred to the holoprojector. Parox pointed at the green lights flashing on the screen. "It's active. There are life-forms on board."

"Is the AI on board?" Kluvnew asked. Parox nodded.

"There are signs of active systems. It could be. This filth said the AI was no longer functioning. I agree. They didn't get this ship in orbit without some type of Creare system or training."

Dailey finally caught his breath. "Holan Remax."

"Who?" Kluvnew asked as Ran shuffled. This was new information.

"Check the infirmary's mortuary. Remax was brought out of hibernation somehow, along with a few others, and helped us." Dailey was telling the truth. He noted Kluvnew nodding slightly, knowing so. It wasn't lost on the man that other races had keen abilities to perceive things such as lies, something the human race had preferred to ignore in order to keep the status quo. Even Dailey enjoyed the occasional white lie, even if it meant going against direct orders.

Parox motioned two of the guards to follow him, and they stomped off the bridge. Kluvnew, now interested in this update, holstered the hammer rod.

"Why is this Creare in the mortuary?" He asked a good question. Dailey would have to be careful when answering it.

"He was injured or something." The something gave Dailey some wiggle room. "One of the last things he did was help us."

"Why?" Kluvnew pressed.

"They never meant to fully destroy the planet," Dailey breathed out.

Kluvnew's smug face was telling. "I see they got to you. They would enslave your people just the same as Aluria and every other planet in their way."

Dailey was getting the man to open up. Little did the Alurian know there was a deeper connection between humans and the Creare than he fully understood. What that truly meant was still a mystery for Dailey.

Just then, Parox ran back onto the bridge, nodding.

"General Ran, did Captain Dailey not supply this pertinent piece of information to you?" Kluvnew asked, danger dancing behind his gaze.

Ran's fists tightened. "No." He knew better than to make excuses. Dailey, while having played his cards right, had also probably just gotten the Alurian in a bad mood. He'd arrived without knowing all the details.

The disgraced general was right not to trust this group. If something had gone wrong, they would have simply taken the information learned and then gone to Teras. Ran was once again disposable, and he knew it.

Muscles tightened as Ran flexed his jaws. The familiar junior officer Dailey finally remembered as Felix shared a glance with Ran while Kluvnew walked to the command console.

"Send a battalion, plus air support, to the surface. Retrieve the hibernation pods and any systems on board. Once complete, find the surface team Dailey sent back to the planet, secure them, and . . ." he drawled out, "destroy them."

Dailey struggled against his bonds, the pain in his face amplifying as the numbness wore off from the strike. "I told you what you wanted."

"You think me gullible?" Kluvnew stated coldly. "I'll keep your ships intact as long as you cooperate. Ran was wise to keep leverage. As for your forces on the ground, or whoever else is there, I will use them as an example."

"Sir," Parox spoke up from the targeting station, now lit up with another of the black boxes sitting on it. "We have detected several power sources on the surface."

The main screen showed a map of the surface with a large cross over the Vault. "Good. We will save our ground forces the effort. Activate the rails guns. I think it's time to let Dailey know just how serious we are."

While he wasn't fully sure of their location, he understood they were several hundred miles away. The power source was the leftover remnants of the Vault. But even though Dailey knew his team wasn't there, he still struggled against his restraints, growling at the Alurian smugly holding his hands behind his back.

A hulking star destroyer named the *Blazer* turned as its battery of massive rail guns quickly shifted, triangulating on the surface target. From the time it took to locate the power source to the rail guns pounding in space, only two minutes had passed.

A live video feed of the Air Force base appeared on the screen, followed by a plume of destruction. Angry reds mixed with gray dust and chunks of buildings as the entirety of the base was wiped off the face of the planet.

"Sir, target destroyed. We will send the ground forces to confirm," Parox stated as Kluvnew turned.

"Continue scanning for power sources, and fire at will." The man was a monster.

Red spittle mixed with blood seeped from Dailey's mouth as he clenched his jaw. "You'll pay for this."

"Perhaps. Perhaps not. General Ran, I am leaving you in charge of this ship. The *Void Reaper* is now under the control of Executive Officer Hap. I will transfer your selected crew to help facilitate the return of this vessel to the shipyards. I am aware of your previous plan. With the Creare vessel already in orbit, we will send our shock troops to the surface."

Again, Dailey noted the glance between Felix and Ran. Anger swelled in Dailey, knowing that at some point, they would get a lock on Jen and the other's location.

With the forced conversation over, two of the guards pulled Dailey straight, muscling him off the bridge and back to his cell.

CHAPTER 27

THE COLD NOSE OF THE LAW

The familiar, cool metal surface was refreshing this time around as Dailey continued to pull himself together. His jaw, while still likely broken, had been mostly dislocated, and while painful, it had been fairly easy to reset on the hard surface.

His screams had been lost on the uncaring guards. His stomach, while not being able to see it, felt knotted from the strike. This wasn't going to be a simple play on time. He knew a killer when he saw one, and Kluvnew was the type who would rather destroy a planet full of millions of people than go to its surface to retrieve one single target.

With only a pin-size light allowing him to barely make out shapes in his cell, Dailey closed his eyes. He had a decision to make. A decision that could very well be his last.

Thoughts of Stella floated through his mind as he drifted into a peaceful calmness, steadying his nerves. He had been in situations such as this before, but as the thought crossed his mind, the countless number of souls also on the chopping block refocused him.

Drifting off into sleep, Dailey started dreaming about Kluvnew raking sandpaper on the black-and-blue sides of his face. The sensation morphed into someone pouring water on him, and he shifted. The numb swelling on his face slowly receded, making the once present throbbing turn into an almost real sensation in synch with his dream.

His dream shifted as the sound of a dog lowly chuffing and grunting in his head took him off guard. He never had dreams like this, and was starting to think his brain had also been as scrambled as his jaw.

Not able to reach up and rub his face, Dailey slowly opened his eyes, only to be greeted by a dark, lumbering mass directly above his face. He strained against his shackles, waiting for his inevitable death.

This was quickly replaced by the smell of Solarian jerky. And not just any Solarian jerky, but replicated jerky. Within a second of realizing this, the thick, heavy tongue of a lightly whining Sparky slapped against his stinging face, cooling every frayed nerve Dailey had ever lost.

"God, are you a sight for sore eyes," Dailey whispered, making the point to be quiet. Being that his eyes were literally sore, he let a smile crack his face, burning his jaw, as Sparky slapped his tongue on the man's cheek, letting it ride all the way to his hairline.

Unlike the others, Dailey had a connection with Sparky which was comparable to imprinting when they first met. He didn't need the translator to understand the glorious, bad-breath-having Alurian war hound.

A low whine came through as, "Safe now."

"How the hell did you get here, buddy?" Dailey asked. A light chuff answered in the Sparkiest way ever. "Magic. Must save boss."

"Look, I don't know how much time we have. They're going to kill everyone back on the planet. They are going to activate the warheads at anytime."

While Sparky had not been back on board the *Murphy*, he already knew Albert and Persius had removed the warheads from the *Murphy* and the *Crow*'s hulls. Albert had been keen to keep him informed. How that worked was still one of the universe's great mysteries.

"All safe. You next," Sparky replied, letting one more slurp of his tongue go before sniffing his restraints.

"Wait. I need to talk to Ran."

"King Asshat."

"Yeah, that's right. King Asshat," Dailey agreed. "Can you turn these things off? I just need to be here. He's up to something."

Sparky let a few sparks crackle, lighting the room, before Dailey felt his restraint uncouple from the metal surface. Another light crackle freed his hands and feet.

"We go now?" Sparky chuffed.

"Not yet. Listen, can you tell me when Ran is coming? He is going to want to chat after that shit show I just witnessed."

After a few sniffs, Dailey realized he was once again alone. The light smell of ozone told him Sparky had left the cell.

In a mix of utter joy and confusion on how Sparky had gotten there, Dailey situated himself as the familiar click of Ran's boots stopped once again in front of the door, followed by an eye-squinting flood of light from the corridor outside his cell. Dailey would blow the ship up just to get rid of the infernal cell he was in alone.

Every fiber of his being stilled, holding back the urge to strangle Ran, rip one of his arms off, and beat the guards outside his cell to death with the appendage. Meanwhile, Ran entered the room, turning up the lights to a reasonable glow. He knew Dailey was in rough shape.

Again, Ran pulled out the flatliner, making their conversation private. "I see you now understand what the Prime Assembly represents."

Dailey shuffled lightly, acting the part, spitting on the slab. "Real winners. Sounds like you are getting the tail end of this." Dailey took his time talking. In reality, he was struggling to keep his jaw from dislocating again.

"Within thirty minutes, the *Void Reaper* will be destroyed, and this ship will be out of the system. My offer has changed. Your friends on the planet will not survive, and neither will you. Where is the AI?" Ran asked, showing no emotion.

"On the planet."

"While you don't have to like me or even believe me, I know you. You would never give that information up that easily, even with your crew at risk. Yes, I know about your first command. Or do you forget who I am?"

Dailey stifled a chuckle, turning it into a gurgling mouthful of spittle dripping on the surface his face lay against. "No, I know exactly who you are. A murderer and a coward."

"And you aren't? I see why you would say that. Where is the AI? I will not ask this again."

Dailey quickly realized Ran no longer had the warhead detonator. A detonator that Sparky had made clear was no longer a threat.

"I don't know. If I did, I would, against everything I stand for, use it to work this out." Dailey was telling the truth, and Ran knew it.

"Very well. For what it's worth, I believe you. Once Kluvnew finds it's not in the hibernation chambers, he will tear your other ships and that planet apart."

"It seems to me you don't have anything else to offer other than my survival," Dailey said, also knowing Sparky wasn't there by chance. Either he, Becket, or Albert had a plan. A plan that he was figuring was waiting on something. Something he would supply in droves once off the ship.

"Letting you live just to have the pleasure to try and kill me is more than enough. Yes, I know that if I don't address you, you will kill me. Abandoning you on a derelict planet will do more than enough to keep you from reaching that goal. Trust me when I say there are more places like this in the cosmos than you could fathom."

To Captain Dailey, the thought of sacrificing so many others just so he could live turned his stomach almost worse than the beating he had just endured. With Sparky showing up, he also knew that the party was about to get started. In many ways, he was expecting Sparky to pop into the room at any time and fry the ever-living hell out of the man standing in front of him.

"My people on the planet likely know where the AI is. Yes, it is real. If you can stop Kluvnew from firing on them, you just might have a chance. There's one more thing I can tell you. The Creare are coming," Dailey said, the truth coming through in his words. While not as perceptive as Kluvnew, General Ran knew the man lying on the slab well enough to know if he was telling the truth.

"I'm hoping on that. If that is all, then your and your crew's time here is coming to an end. Just remember when you take your last breath, I gave you an opportunity. As for the Creare, I'll let the Prime Assembly handle that." Ran scowled before turning and walking out of the cell.

With that, the man was gone, the light slowly fading back to a depressive black. Two minutes later, the familiar stench of ozone wafted through the cell. Sparky once again appeared in the middle of the room. Dailey threw his legs over the slab, knowing his time was indeed limited.

"All right, what's the plan?" Dailey asked while Sparky let out a significant number of low yips, barks, and chuffs.

His message was simple. "Pick me up. We're going for a ride. Hold breath, and close eyes. Sparky to the rescue." A rough request for a lifetime supply of ham followed this.

"We're going to do that one thing you always do? Is it safe?" Dailey asked, referring to Sparky appearing and disappearing at all times through, oftentimes, mind-boggling distances.

Sparky's helmet clanked shut as his eyes started to glow white, filling the room with light. "Find out," was the last thing Sparky said as Dailey strained to pick up the dog.

Finally, locking his legs, holding his breath, and closing his eyes, Dailey froze as if suspended in ice. The feeling of a million needles being poked into a million pores swept over his body as if he were drowning.

CHAPTER 28

GOOD VIBRATIONS

Vomit splattered on the floor as stars danced in Dailey's eyes. Too dizzy to stand, Dailey dropped onto his side like a kid who had just been spun on a playground spinner for three hours straight at max velocity. The sounds of voices and footsteps rushing toward him forced the man back into motion, not able to focus on anything yet.

Unsure if he had been spread across the cosmos or simply been teleported into an even worse situation, Dailey scooted on the hard floor as far as he could until his back was against a solid wall.

A familiar voice rang in his ears as Jen rushed down, grabbing Dailey by the shoulders. His head bobbled loosely, still trying to figure out which direction was up. Her voice was quickly dwarfed by Janix's and several of the other Nova Rangers who had left the *Waiting Sun* for Teras.

"Ben," Jen insisted sternly, working to snap the man out of it.

As Dailey's eyes came into focus, he saw Sparky with his armor already retracted around his hind legs, now plopped over, scratching his two moons. A quick chuff affirmed the situation.

"Traveled a long way. May need food. Preferably ham," Sparky said, seeing Dailey start to focus.

A jarring thump echoed throughout the room, not helping Dailey's situation, as dust fell from the stone ceiling above. Kluvnew's rail guns were getting close.

"Water. I need water," Dailey insisted as someone scrambled off to oblige. After chugging the entire canteen, his entire body came back to life.

A bland old room started to materialize in front of Dailey's eyes. Several cots lay strewn around the room, with several old maps falling apart hanging on the walls, accompanied by a handful of barely recognizable posters of pinup girls.

"My God, it's you. You're safe. What the hell happened to your face?" Jen asked, seeing the signs of either a fight or, even worse, torture.

"I slipped and fell in the bathroom." Dailey grinned. The gap where a tooth once was made her grimace.

Janix kneeled. "We need to get off this planet. We've turned off all our scanners. We're pretty far underground, but if they keep hitting the surface like this, we won't last."

Dailey already knew they had also likely cut all lines of communications to the outside world to prevent anyone from triangulating their location.

The *Murphy*'s commander shifted his weight, pulling out the detonator.

"Uh . . ." Jen paused. "That's kind of gross."

"Our teams up there are waiting on a signal. This is that signal," Dailey said, holding it out. "Are the ships also underground?"

Jen took the lead, explaining their current status. "We're in an underground aircraft bunker. You could almost fit a cargo freighter down here. The ships are two levels up. They used this place for special, top-secret projects. I think the inhabitants of Teras knew a little more than what they were telling others. Tarik and the others had no clue this place was used for this. They simply knew it was here, and it was massive, based on all records. What's the plan?"

"The plan?" Dailey asked himself, rather than the others in the room. "I blow Ran to hell and kick this party off. We need to be able to leave as soon as that happens. Sparky here said our ships are safe. He doesn't seem to want to elaborate, but I'm betting as soon as that baby pops, we'll be good to go."

Janix spoke up this time. "What's going on with the *Murphy* and the *Crow*?" The Solarian knew there was more to his statement.

"They removed the warheads from the ships somehow. Sparky said they are safe," Dailey added. Everyone turned to Sparky for an explanation.

His translator kicked in after a few barks. "Now a problem for them." The message was clear. They had repurposed the warheads, likely at the hands of Albert and Persius, to take out the Prime Assembly's ships.

"We need to get to the ship to prepare to leave. Once that thing goes off, all bets are off. It's going to be like the damn Wild West out there," Dailey stated.

Janix stood up, barking several orders. "You heard the man. Get everyone loaded back on the ships and clear this place out," he bellowed. Even the people in the next room could hear the commotion.

Dailey, remembering the prize Ran and the others were after, finally stood. "Where's Persius?"

Jen glanced at Sparky and then back to him. "Yeah, about that. Albert decided to send us down here with a tin can full of nothing but some game on a drive with a plumber breaking bricks. He took her with him."

"That explains things. I'm not sure what they're cooking up there, but it had better be good. The Creare are coming. I don't know when, but it sounds like it would be better if we weren't here for that," Dailey said as Sparky let out a howl that didn't translate, meaning it was a cry of excitement, before turning and leaving the room at a quick trot.

"We figured that," Jen said, turning to see the others already out of the room. "Your face—what happened?"

The space between the two closed as Dailey felt her breath on his face. "I think my jaw's broken; it is definitely dislocated. There's an Alurian named Kluvnew in charge of what they call the Prime Assembly. Real nice guy. While he's an Alurian, it didn't seem he represented them as a whole. Well, not completely. Maybe a faction of them, but there are humans with them as well as Solarians.

"We wondered what drove the mining syndicates besides profits. Or at least what other faction was keeping things together. I have a feeling the Prime Assembly has something to do with it. I don't fully understand it, but it seems to fit."

Jen took a half step closer to Dailey. "Then why would Prescott send us here as the main representative of the Ocess Syndicate?"

"That's the right question to ask. I have a feeling they weren't getting the attention they wanted, or there were too many greedy hands in the Solarian cookie jar. Either way, they wanted us to see this. Maybe fix it. Remember, they played their hand in the open. As of now, they aren't on my shit list. Maybe for the trip here, though. But something big is brewing, and we are now part of it. I don't know, but at some point, if we make it out of here, we'll need to figure that part out," Dailey replied, finally standing to his full height.

Jen leaned forward, kissing Dailey lightly on the lips, forcing the man to wince slightly. Pulling back, they nodded at each other. Jen sucked in a breath. "That's not our biggest issue right now. Maybe they want to change the status quo. Either way, we need to get focused on the here and now."

With that, the two turned and walked toward the massive bay, now buzzing with activity. The Harpy rested under the Creare transport ship, showing its battle scars compared to the sleek vessel. The front of the vast cave was etched out of angular gray stone, giving the area a cool, damp atmosphere. Sitting on the far edges, several jets and other vehicles lay in a state of disrepair, awaiting people who would never come.

"Sir," Janix shouted from the ramp leading into the Creare ship. "What's the plan?"

Behind him, dozens of Teras's inhabitants glanced pensively at him, moving several crates of rations found in the sprawling underground facility. Dailey, realizing they were looking at his bruised face, motioned for Third Foot's fearless leader to join them out of earshot.

"The plan is to detonate the Creare ship in orbit and hopefully kick this thing off. I'm a little concerned they haven't moved, knowing the Prime Assembly is bombarding the planet," Dailey said, realizing he needed to get into a set of armor. "Dammit. While we're at it, do we have any extra sets of armor?"

Janix grinned. "I don't know how he did it, but Sparky over there"—he pointed to the war hound with his face buried in a bowl of something. The dog's jaw flexed as his rear end wagged—"left a few minutes ago and dropped your Armor in the Harpy. Said he was tired and couldn't take any more trips without refueling, or something like that. Damnedest thing when he does that."

"Wonder if he found anything else?" Dailey asked as Janix nodded.

"He said they were getting ready to do something and leave. I tried digging more, but he insisted on getting something to eat."

"He's earned it," Dailey said, pulling out the detonator. "I bet Becket and the others know we're safe. With Albert and Persius up there, who knows what they're cooking up."

A shout came from Specialist Jenna Jones from the far end of the transport ship. "We're all loaded up!"

Jen shouted back, seeing Coolio walking out of the vert rover in the back cargo hold of the Harpy. "Get everyone loaded up. We're leaving."

Taking a long, calming breath, Dailey nodded. "Once on board, I'm letting this thing rip."

Within five minutes, both ships were loaded and sealed shut, ready to launch. It had been ten minutes since the last blast had rocked the ground above. Tarik and Jen had both insisted the opening was still clear. When asked by Dailey, they simply grinned, knowing how shocked he would be when he found out they were, in fact, underwater.

While not nearly as advanced as most civilizations in either galaxy, the inhabitants of Teras had been able to build the entrance behind a massive set of waterfalls. The Plateau, as it was called, was an island on the main coast of Republica, several hundred square miles in size. The island sat nearly three stories above sea level, with a massive spring fed from the ocean in its center, creating massive waterfalls every couple of miles all around the island.

It blended in with the hundred or so other islands just like this off the country's coastline. One thing Teras had that was different from Earth was its aggressive elevation changes near all its coastlines.

Dailey, now having his armor back on, ran a self-diagnostic check, finding his jaw had a hairline fracture. While a brutal injury, it could easily be healed in one of the med beds aboard the *Murphy*.

Finally, coupling his safety harness, Dailey held up the detonator. "Once we clear the opening, I'm letting this thing rip. After that, I want an open line to the *Murphy*. We still have the communications protocol, so they will only know someone's trying to talk."

Jen glanced over, putting on a pair of old-style, gold-rimmed aviator sunglasses, before reaching back and patting him on the knee. Dailey, not caring who saw, put his hand on hers for a brief moment before giving the order. "Take us home."

From the back of the Harpy, several Nova Rangers sounded off.

"To the edge!"

Somewhere in the starting chaos, Sparky's light snore followed the call to either glory or death.

CHAPTER 29

THE END OF THE BEGINNING

The roar of thrusters rattled the Harpy while Jen powered the ship forward, gliding slowly toward the blue veil of water in front of the cockpit. The tunnel in front of the Harpy was a mile long and just as large as the main bay itself. It had been a feat of engineering with the technology the people of Teras had at the time.

This thought was thrust out of Dailey's thoughts when Jen slammed her right hand forward, fully throttling the engines. Luckily for the others, Albert and Persius had programmed what they called a follow-the-leader protocol on the transport ship. If the Harpy did something, the ship would follow its lead. Buckle had stayed on board just in case, having pilot training.

Every loose item in the Harpy rattled as the ship burst through the thick blanket of water, shooting out into the twinkling dark of night. The sky twinkled with stars, clouds, and several massive starships. On the horizon, the ominous glow of a burning countryside was drowned out by the brilliant flash of several pounding shots plunging into the planet like an angry knife.

Alerts started flashing red, warning of enemy ships in the general vicinity, while Dailey looked up to the heavens, pressing the detonator. The Harpy's ride smoothed out as Jen kept the ship only feet off the ground, turning toward open water to keep their profile low.

Dailey sneered as one of the massive ships hanging overhead like a circling vulture flashed in a blinding, catastrophic explosion. The ship was going supernova.

Jen leaned forward as if trying to push the Harpy to go faster before pulling up. They would get as far away as possible from the blast before shooting directly up and into space. While the explosion would mostly be contained in orbit, the chaos that was about to ensue, if timed right, would allow them to slip away unnoticed.

"Janix." Dailey turned to the man strapped into the small terminal behind the cockpit. "Open comms with the *Murphy*."

"Any Viper element, this is Viper Six. Do you copy?" Dailey, almost whispering, said into the mic mounted inside his helmet. The thought that General Ran had just taken his last breath had put the man in a calm, almost tranquil state.

"Hello—" Albert's voice replied just as Becket cut in.

"What the hell was that?" he asked, cutting off the AI. They were watching the massive explosion in front of them as it started creeping toward several other ships. A handful of those vessels activated their main thrusters, flying away from the massive explosion still building momentum.

Even with its thrusters at maximum output for suborbital operations, the sky above the Harpy glowed. "Ran's no longer going to be a problem."

"Jesus," Becket replied. "Well, if you thought that was a show, just wait to see what happens next."

Albert cut in before Dailey could respond. "So glad that Asshat is out of the way. Sending you the coordinates and a few tidbits of information." With that out of the way, Albert turned the conversation back over to Becket and Dailey.

A yellow light flashed in front of Jen, who pressed the button to upload the new coordinates. A location far away from the *Murphy* and the *Crow* appeared, as well as a guidance protocol. Several of the attack wing fighters would be meeting them as soon as possible to escort them away from the fight until things could be situated.

"Sir, we still have about thirty minutes to an hour before we can get the gate drives online. I'm sure you're aware of the warheads; watch this," Becket relayed, also having Albert and Persius detonate the now floating devices of destruction.

Over the last thirty minutes, they had schemed to position several of them at different locations, including having one hurled toward several of the Prime Assembly's main destroyers. While earlier than expected, they had indeed been waiting on Dailey to detonate the *Waiting Sun.*

Several more balls of popcorn smacked open in the skies and heavens above as the warheads started to detonate, once again proving just how much of an edge Albert gave in a fight of this magnitude. Dailey could only imagine the hellish parade occurring in the space between the moons and Teras.

"It's gonna take a little bit to get repositioned," Becket started. "I suggest maneuvering in orbit now—" The hazy fuzz of the warheads detonating finally cut off the communication, static trilling through not only the intercom but also their headsets.

"I don't think we're going to be able to talk to them for a little bit until everything calms down up there," Jen interjected.

Glancing out the cockpit above them, Dailey started to see the scope and magnitude of what was happening. The entire sky was lit up in a fiery bluish-red as the explosion from the *Waiting Sun* continued to grow.

Dailey shook his head. "You heard him. It's time to boogie." As the words left his mouth, several red proximity alarms started flashing.

"We have incoming!" Janix barked, seeing four signals pop up on the ship's radar.

"Talk to us," Dailey said while Janix continued to triangulate the incoming vessels.

"Looks like four small attack fighters!" the man shouted behind them, louder than needed.

With those words, Jen pulled the yoke back, causing the ship to go vertical. While they couldn't see the transport ship behind them, they were fully aware it was mimicking the same movement. A hundred souls were on board that vessel now, praying to some alien god that they wished they had stayed nestled in their beds inside the Vault.

"How long till intercept?" Jen asked, activating the Harpy's external turrets. The audible whirl of the two forward guns and the two back-mounted plasma cannons clicked into place, scanning just as the ship systems locked onto the incoming threat.

Janix didn't need to reply as the plasma cannons came to life. Flashes of red started darting in front of the cockpit, lightly rocking the ship. Blue afterburners scurried in front of the Harpy at blurring speeds while Jen continued to fully throttle the vertical ship.

"Buckle," Jen called over the radio. "What's going on back there?"

After a brief pause, Buckle's anxious voice replied. "Besides everybody swallowing their tongues, the ship just activated several defense mechanisms. I don't know what the hell it's doing, but it looks like it's about to fire. We took a couple of hits. It looks like they're coming around."

Unlike space combat, even attack fighters operating in a normal atmosphere followed the rules of Mother Nature. Gravity forced the fighters to make wider turns, unlike the pinpoint hundred-and-eighty-degree swivels they could do in the stars above.

More lights flashed in space as the explosions reached a crescendo. Several smacks from the Harpy's weapons found one of their targets. An explosion popped to their right, followed by a slurry of red lasers smacking into the small ship as it struggled to stay on its current trajectory.

"We're not gonna last long if those things keep firing at us. It's only a matter of time before they shoot a missile . . ." Jen's words were lost when several more alarms flashed, denoting they had been locked on and were, in fact, about to get shot out of the sky by a slurry of missiles.

Seeing no other course of action, Jen slammed the thruster throttle forward. The Harpy took a sharp nosedive back toward the now glowing ocean below them. The explosions reflected off its gleaming surface, creating an ominous glow, as if the entire world was on fire.

Gravity faltered in the brief few moments before they started their descent back to the surface. Three of the attack fighters zoomed by, surprised by the maneuver. Just as the Creare transportation ship launched a barrage of interceptor rockets aimed at the incoming missiles, several more pops crackled around both ships as the massive Creare vessel joined the nosedive.

While nothing more than a Creare transport ship, it was designed to protect its cargo. From what they, including Albert, had concluded, even centuries-old Creare tech was far superior to that of their own or the Alurians'.

Seeing her chance, Jen again throttled the engines, with an audible whine droning from the Harpy's thrusters. The sounds of someone retching were a telltale sign of Pickle getting sick, as was the norm. Even Sparky had been startled awake by the commotion. They would hear about awakening the great ham overlord from his slumber.

Jen focused on the glowing sky above, where the final chapter of not only Ran's but the *Waiting Sun's* story came to an end with a roaring final wave of kinetic energy. The Harpy rocked violently as the three remaining attack fighters darted in front of them, pushing the forward cannons to fire again.

If she was right, they were gaining altitude to turn and take them head-on.

"Buckle, if there is a red button flashing anywhere on that ship, press it!" Jen exclaimed.

Buckle glanced at the control panel, seeing that very thing. Seconds later, several purple streaks ripped around the Harpy, smacking into the three remaining attack fighters with a violence and speed that caught even Dailey off guard.

"I hope we don't run into the Creare in this mess."

A strained Jen replied, "We just lit the torch. Orbit reached."

The internal pressure normalized as the two ships continued to speed away from the planet. To Dailey's right, the massive afterglow of numerous crumbling ships around the once dormant *Waiting Sun* showed just how much destruction they had unleashed. Several of the larger Prime Assembly ships sat ominously in the far distance, working through what had just happened.

"It doesn't look like they're coming after us," Dailey noted, taking off his helmet.

Jen looked over her shoulder, having put the ship on autopilot. "We have about thirty minutes till we link up with the attack wing at the rally point. Comms should be back online soon. You see that?"

In the distance, several remnants of additional large explosions appeared next to the two moons where the *Murphy* and *Crow* were positioned.

"Yeah, they're busy." Dailey sighed. The roller coaster that had been the last fifteen minutes had frayed even the hardened crew's nerves. "Can we fit the Harpy on the transport ship?" he asked, thinking through their options.

"I don't think so. That thing is packed cheek to cheek," Jen replied. The ruffle of moving bodies caught Dailey's attention. He turned around, seeing the other Nova Rangers standing at attention.

Sparky joined in, holding his head and one front paw up. Dailey, figuring this was either a mutiny or some kind of mind control, stood up, finally seeing tears in Jones's and a handful of the other Nova Ranger's eyes.

"Present arms!" Janix barked as the entire ship snapped a salute. Even Jen was standing at attention, joining the group. "Order arms!" Janix finished before Specialist Jenna Jones stepped forward. She, like many—if not all—of the Rangers, had lost friends on the *Brightstar* and *Asher-5*.

"Sir," Jones said, wiping a drying tear off her face. "Thank you, sir."

"For what?" Dailey was so hyperfocused on getting back to the other ships that he had all but forgotten that he had indeed sent Ran to whatever hell was awaiting him and his cohorts.

"Killing that son of a bitch. I wish I'd pressed the button myself," she followed as the others all grumbled their approval of her statement, representing the team on board.

"Yeah." Dailey looked down at his feet, something the others rarely, if ever, witnessed. The *Murphy*'s commander shifted into his role as a leader. "Listen, it was all of us. We're all out here on our own, and the mission isn't over, whatever that now is. All of you have gone through something I still don't fully understand, but I'm not going—" he corrected himself. "We're not going to let anything happen to the people on board that transport ship. That's what we do. We're also getting every one of your asses back home. We can worry about what happens then later."

"Sir," Janix spoke up, his dark skin beaded with sweat. "If we don't make it out of here, we all want you to know we will follow you to the edge."

Everyone else echoed the statement as Sparky yipped.

RAN'S FINAL STAND

Ran dropped onto the con of the *Waiting Sun*, giving Felix the signal to execute their subprotocol aboard the *Void Reaper*. Felix turned, walking back to his seat just as a terminal alarm shrieked loud enough to raise all the dead in this system and the next.

The hum of the ship's alien reactors screamed louder and louder before Felix could make it to his station.

Ran looked up.

"Dailey!"

That was the last word to ever cross the disgraced general's lips.

CHAPTER 30

THE LONG AND WINDING ROAD TO NOWHERE

After another hour of pure anarchy, the Prime Assembly had lost over a quarter of their attack fighters and six of their larger ships, including one of the dreadnoughts, which had been parked next to the *Waiting Sun*.

Albert and Persius had ensured two of the warheads once mounted on the *Crow* found their way to the *Void Reaper*. While still in operation, the beast of war now found itself working to pull itself back together.

Becket stared out the main viewport on the bridge of the *Murphy* as the last attack fighter peeled off to secure the ship after escorting Dailey and the others on board. Realizing they had caused enough confusion to allow open movement, the plan had changed to get Dailey back on the *Murphy* and to follow up with securing the *Crow* with two sections from the attack wing.

The blast doors to the bridge opened to a round of cheers, whistles, and claps greeting Dailey, Janix, and Jen. After docking with the *Murphy*, Tarik, Bella, and Valen had also joined the group.

Already in shock from the level of technology and the fact that they were now in space, Tarik and his group of leaders became even more impressed by the organized chaos on board the *Murphy*. Dailey even caught Bella reaching for Tarik's arm as they stepped forward, pulling a smile from the man. Holding his hands up in a calming motion, Dailey held back a grin, his face stinging with pain.

"Sir," Becket stepped forward. Thinking he was about to give him a sitrep, Dailey was quickly surprised when he received a hug in front of everyone instead. Becket, realizing everyone was watching, cleared his throat, stepping back.

"Everyone, you have jobs. Do them!" he barked as smiles and cheers continued, the day-to-day of a Federation vessel in the middle of a war zone.

"Good to see you too, brother. I'd like to introduce Tarik, Bella, and Valen."

Becket bowed his head, reaching out and shaking Tariks' hand, then the others'. "Well, I guess you're part of the crew for now. Bellman will get you situated with quarters on board. It will be a little tight, but we will make it work." Becket smiled, knowing the happy reunion would not last long.

Albert stood up from his station after working feverishly to repair the ship. "We're getting the band back together!" he bellowed. Mister Toaster's eyebrows furrowed as he pointed to Persius. "We've been busy, boss."

"I'm sure you have. I'm just glad to see you," Dailey said, patting the AI on the plated shoulder. Albert's usually clean exterior was showing signs of the past couple of days, with pitting and burn marks from his trip back to the *Murphy* covering his metal exterior. "We have work to do. Everyone, listen up! Meeting in the briefing room in fifteen minutes. Becket, Jen, Albert . . . Well, Albert, you just listen in. My quarters. We don't have much time. I'm fairly certain the Creare will be here soon."

Persius took this time to chime in. "The probability of that happening is one hundred percent. I advise seeking shelter in the event someone attacks them. Time parameters are unknown."

The mood shifted as long faces went back to work. Dailey turned, the others following him off the bridge. Within five minutes, everyone was standing inside Ben Dailey's constricted quarters.

Without saying a word, and now out of his armor, Dailey opened his desk drawer, pushing two newer bottles of Bellman's rum out of the way to reach an old-school bottle of Bacardi. Not the crazy-good stuff, but the regular off-the-shelf spiced goodness.

Becket, seeing this, pulled out several cups from Dailey's small cabinet. Pouring numerous double shots, Dailey handed one to Tarik first. "Cheers," he said, not giving the reason for the event.

Tarik winced when drinking it, followed by a cool smile. The centuries had treated the once upon a time over-the-counter drink well. "What is this?"

"Rum," Dailey sighed, letting pounds of tension leave his body, joining Tarik with a small wince. "I want all of you to know what I'm thinking and to welcome our new friends. Albert, are you listening?"

"Well, besides missing the drink—which really, I just need an oil change—I'm absolutely not listening, duh."

"Perfect," Dailey started. "How long till the gate drive is operational?"

"We ran into a few complications; I'd say another two hours. Long enough to watch a few seasons of *Lo Yada Yada*," Albert replied, referring to another Solarian show.

"What?" Becket asked.

"Solarian crunch-monkey romance. Oh, the ignorance of lost youth. Anyway, we are trying to get them working. The issue, as I explained before Captain Dailey arrived, is the thrusters. We have to have them moderately working, or *poof.*"

"Poof? Let me guess, we don't make it through, and we all die a painful, agonizing death," Dailey said. Albert replied with a curt, "Yup."

Sparky chuffed. "The Ham Republic must live on."

"It will . . . I hope," Dailey drawled out. "Before we talk to the rest of the crew, I need to make sure we are all on the same page. There are a lot of unknowns here. One thing I think we can all agree on is that we need to take out the Prime Assembly's command ship. As much as I want to get out of here, I'm not leaving till Kluvnew joins Ran." Dailey had a score to settle.

The others all lifted their glasses, taking a sip. Even Tarik and his companions understood the motion.

With the side of Dailey's face still black and blue, the others realized the torture he had endured.

"Sir," Becket spoke up, finishing his glass. "With all the radiation, our long-range scanners are still foggy."

Nodding, Dailey glanced at the picture of Stella on his shelf. "We need to figure out what's going on, and not just here. I have a plan, but it's a little risky, and depends on what happens over the next couple of hours. Sparky, I think it's time we take another one of those trips," Dailey said as the dog let his tongue hang out. He had clearly already been treated by Thron since coming back on board.

"What's that?" Becket slowly asked.

"I'll explain it in a few. I want everyone here to get ready and fully stand up the attack wings, plus the Creare transport ship. We have to get to the *Crow*."

Nods peppered the room as they realized the truth of Dailey's statement. Becket grabbed another pour before speaking. "What is the game plan, sir?"

"Get to the *Crow*, and then we deal with the Prime Assembly. The Creare shows up, and we adjust. Albert, we will need to talk with Persius about that. Remax and Persius both suggested we could at least reason with them. For now, we need to get to the *Crow*. That's priority one. How many souls are on board?"

"Seventy-five in total," Becket recalled at the same time Tarik cleared his throat.

"What can we do to help?"

Pondering the ask, Dailey walked up to the man in the already tight quarters. "If we get the *Crow* up and running, that's where you and your people are going. There's more than enough room. For now, I would say not to get too comfortable. Top," Dailey shifted the conversation, "coordinate with Valen, and outfit his soldiers with armor, then get with Grantham on getting them some on-the-fly training. Tarik, Bella, if you would like, I want to set you up with our lead science officer, Bellman; he can give you a quick crash course on who is who in the zoo."

Valen looked at Tarik, nodding his approval. Jen spoke up next. "I called Casey on our way here. You need to go check in with her." Jen was, of course, referring to Medical Officer Casey Franklin.

"Fair enough," Dailey replied. "When we meet back in the briefing room, have plans ready on how to get to the *Crow*."

"You know," Albert chimed in. "Persius was just telling me that the probability of us reaching the *Crow* before the Prime Assembly takes additional action is extremely depressing."

"Numbers, Albert," Dailey replied.

"Thirty-five percent."

The briefing room buzzed with chatter, which slowly trailed off as the *Murphy*'s command team made their entrance. Over the past thirty minutes, Jen and Novak had gone over several different scenarios which included everything from avoiding the Prime Assembly to an all-out fight while trying to reach the *Crow*.

In the event they reached the *Crow*, they would use the attack fighters to push the vessel closer to the *Murphy*. With Albert and Persius on board, the USF *Murphy* was significantly ahead of the curve when getting the main thrusters online.

"Take seats!" Becket bellowed. Stern faces dropped into their places. "Everyone, this is the show."

Becket was referring to their slang term for a real life-or-death fight. Dailey and the rest of the leadership motioned for the room to relax as Albert and Sparky took their places by the holo-table.

"It's good to be home," Dailey started, to another round of claps and cheers. Everyone was high from the fact that he had sent Ran straight to hell. Someone in the back of the briefing room yelled, "Let's get some!"

"In due time," Dailey said. "Your team leaders have given you the plan for retrieving the *Crow* and leaving the AO." The acronym stood for area of operation. "I want it to be completely clear. The chances of this plan even getting past the front door is close to none." Asses rustled in seats as the *Murphy*'s commander continued.

"We owe it to Pearl and our crew members on the *Crow* to get them out of harm's way. The radiation will subside enough by the time this meeting is over to communicate with the *Crow*. As you all are aware, the *Void Reaper*, while likely damaged, is still an arm's throw away."

Albert stepped forward, activating the holo-table. "Hey, guys and gals. We, meaning Persius and I, have put together the best representation of the scenario possible."

A schematic of the *Murphy* and the *Crow* separated by what seemed to be light-years of distance appeared. To the far end of the representation, Albert had symbolized the Prime Assembly's fleet as several piles of crap.

Snickers followed before Grantham gave the rest of the team a shut-the-hell-up look from the front row. Once Becket retired or died in battle, Grantham would take on the mantle of the senior enlisted leader of Viper Company.

"Thank you, Albert." Dailey shook his head before getting serious. "I'm not going to tell you we are coming out of this together. I'm telling you we'll all make it. I'm not asking you to sacrifice yourself for the greater good. What I am asking is for you to make a sacrifice for the person to your left and to your right. Never leave a teammate behind. No matter the sacrifice."

A hand raised from the back of the room as Specialist Rebecca Dawn, Second Foot's trusty targeting specialist, stood up. "Sir."

Cardinali shrugged, knowing there was no controlling the young, vibrant woman.

"Yes, Specialist Dawn?" Dailey asked, holding back a grin. Dawn was the usual group-bullshit meter.

"Sir," she repeated, "what about the Creare?"

A nerve-racking pause followed as Dailey slumped slightly. While Franklin had fixed Dailey's face as much as possible, a light-blue blotch still streaked up his face, making the reality of the situation land close to home to the Nova Rangers.

"That's the reason I want to talk to all of you. What I can say just from seeing the transport ship in action is that they are in a whole different league; I want to make that clear. There's also something I want to say to drive this home. It appears Albert was conceived . . ." He paused, looking at Mister Toaster's face giving the go-ahead. "Albert was manifested, or whatever they call it, by the Creare."

Ohs and ahs came from the crowd. In reality, the truth had been in front of them the entire time.

Albert stepped forward.

"Totally not changing things. But I will say, I still expect birthday party invitations."

Sparky barked. "And oil changes!"

"Enough of that. We are against the clock. Team leaders, get your crews ready. We move out in thirty minutes."

CHAPTER 31

THE SHOT HEARD AROUND THE SOLAR SYSTEM

Ice-cold rage filled Kluvnew's veins as he stared at the chaos just outside the main viewport of the *Alpha Nova*. The vessel was two generations ahead of both the *Void Reaper* and the *Crow*, having been developed from human, Alurian, and a moderate sprinkle of Creare tech.

"Sir, we have comms with the *Void Reaper*. Executive Officer Hap is hailing us," a random bridge crew member spoke up.

Other occupants of the massive bridge mostly kept quiet, not wanting to experience the Alurian's wrath. As for Jelas Bonner, a young Alurian syndicate rep, this was the least of his worries. During the initial operation, he had been in charge of tracking and stopping any rogue signals from doing the very thing that had transpired. In all the confusion, his role had been mostly forgotten.

It didn't matter to the communications officer, as he had just lost several of his closest companions. This was a time to fight.

"Patch him through."

"Sir," Bonner spoke again. This time, an air of nervousness came through in his voice. "We also have an incoming message from the Alurian High Fleet."

Bonner had grown up as a proper Alurian High Fleet cadet. Raised in a traditional Alurian family, his father had been a politician pushing his son to be part of something greater. After years of fighting and a failed relationship, Bonner had chosen a different route. A route that would see the people against him and his family pay for their transgressions.

Not able to live up to his promise, Bonner had blended into the background for several years while working his way up to the bridge crew of the *Alpha Nova*.

"Hap, what's your status?" Kluvnew asked, razors coming through in his tone.

The *Void Reaper*'s executive officer looked out of sorts and, to a point, disheveled, something Kluvnew had yet to witness. "Our sensor and navigation systems are offline. Our thrusters are on manual control. Secondary weapon systems are functional; however, we have no targeting."

"Can you engage the dreadnought?" Kluvnew asked, seeing the blinking light of the incoming Alurian High Fleet message.

"Yes, sir, but we still need at least an hour to reposition the crew. Our entire weapons section was destroyed, including all personnel," Hap responded. The sounds of something being worked on in the background came through.

"The Alurian High Fleet is hailing us. They are probably on their way, and I would like to get rid of any tertiary issues before they arrive."

Hap nodded before Kluvnew turned off the communications link. "Receive the incoming transmission."

Two unfortunately familiar faces materialized on the main viewscreen. Vice Admiral Gray and Captain Stelt, with their full command regalia, stood on board the bridge of the main command star cruiser, the *Overseer*. A fitting name for a ship of such magnitude.

"Vice Admiral, Captain," Kluvnew greeted the two men. Flat lips and hardened stares beamed back through the view link.

"Kluvnew," the vice admiral replied, not using the Alurian's rank or status. "We have received several rather distressing signals and communications from your location. Your transponder codes were picked up by one of our outer scout ships in the Virgos belt. It also included a hyperdetonation that registered on several of our outposts. Would you care to explain?"

Kluvnew was well aware that the words he was about to speak had to be carefully chosen. While the Prime Assembly absolutely had their hands in the pockets of the Alurian High Fleet, attacking several Federation vessels where they weren't supposed to be was another story. Dailey had been correct in his assessment of the situation. The Alurians were not completely to blame for all the attacks on Earth. The Prime Assembly, on the other hand, was.

Kluvnew figured that the truth peppered with gaps in the situation would suffice. The two dark-skinned green Alurians stared back. "We recently encountered an older Creare vessel near Teras. When we arrived, there were multiple Federation ships in the system. They engaged, and we returned fire. The Creare vessel was subsequently lost."

Gray and Stelt glanced at each other, knowing the gravity of the situation. "And you didn't think to reach out to the Alurian High Fleet?"

The Prime Assembly, while an accepted entity, was only allowed to exist due to financial gain and their overall control of the mining syndicates. In many ways, it was an eyes-wide-shut situation.

The Prime Assembly fought proxy wars for the Alurians and also kept the peace so the Alurian High Fleet could focus on other threats on the opposite side of their galaxy, which included vacuuming up several other civilized planets in preparation for what they called the oncoming threat. The threat that the Federation had yet to encounter included the Creare.

"You will stand down your forces and prepare for us to secure the system until we have this sorted out. Might I ask who you cleared this operation with?" Gray asked, narrowing his greenish-black eyes.

"I did. With the situation surrounding General Ran, which I am sure you are aware of, we were made aware of Federation forces being gated here from one of the mining syndicates," Kluvnew stated matter-of-factly.

"Yes," Stelt spoke up for the first time. "We have been made aware that the Federation has acquired gating tech. Your orders, and those of General Ran, were to interfere with their development of long-range interstellar travel. We received reports of the *Brightstar* and the *Asher-5* being taken out of the equation. Are you saying that the third ship commanded by Captain Ben Dailey, is still operational?"

It was clear the two Alurians on the other side of the conversation knew significantly more than they were sharing. A voice spoke up behind Gray and Stelt. "We will be in the system within five minutes. This is not something that can simply be discussed. The High Assembly is aware of the situation. How many vessels do you have with you?"

This was news to Kluvnew. While he was aware the *Overseer* was more than capable of securing the location, regardless of their remaining vessels, he was not sure just what else they were bringing along with them. They had taken the ship out of a gate to communicate with Kluvnew prior to their arrival.

"We arrived with the battle group. Unfortunately, we have lost several of our combat ships." That's when Kluvnew figured out a way to work through the predicament. For once, General Ran had made the right choice in sparing both the *Crow* and the *Murphy*. "In order to avoid any problems, we only incapacitated the two Federation ships. They are still functional. However, they do not have thruster capabilities."

While used to being in charge, it was clear to Kluvnew that he was not at the top of the food chain in this scenario.

Or was he? The Prime Assembly's lead fleet commander could likely have the *Overseer* overran by its own crew with a few simple words. While this would most certainly call for him to be killed, it would also give him enough firepower to push back when the time came.

Vice Admiral Gray's demeanor slightly shifted. "That is good to hear. Please ensure they remain intact. I'll deal with the situation personally." With those words, the feed winked out of existence.

"Hail Executive Officer Hap. Let him know to stand down and await further instructions," Kluvnew ordered, motioning for his staff to follow them into the war room.

It wasn't lost on him that he hadn't acquired the AI, not to mention the likely probability of the Creare showing up. If the Alurian High Fleet was aware of the situation, so were the Creare.

CHAPTER 32

TWINKLE, TWINKLE

Albert leaped from his station in utter panic. Mister Toaster's face resembled that of somebody who had just lost their life earnings at a Solarian casino and was trying to figure out a way to explain it to his wife. Persius had been disconnected from the ship's systems even though she was probably still somehow listening in, still sitting on the navigation table that Pearl once occupied.

Dailey jumped to his feet, seeing the distraught Albert. Sparky had gone down to the drop bay with First Sergeant Becket to help prepare the attack wing. After finally being able to communicate once again, it had been suggested to wait and see how the Prime Assembly reacted. It had been extremely telling that the *Void Reaper* wasn't finishing the job that they had started.

"Albert?" Dailey asked as everyone on the bridge looked at the AI.

"I just intercepted a transmission from the *Alpha Nova*, which is the Prime Assembly's command ship. The Alurian High Fleet is coming," Albert spit out, clanking over to the navigation table, skewing Persius to the side.

"How long?" Dailey was in question-asking mode.

"Uh, now."

As soon as the words left his mouth, proximity alarms once again flashed to life on the main viewscreen. Albert redirected the *Murphy*'s cam system directly around Teras. Zooming in, still-energized sections of destroyed ships floated aimlessly around the remnants of the *Waiting Sun*.

"They're pulling all their attack ships in," Dailey stated just as the first of several gleaming, hulking ships appeared out of the dark void of space.

Dailey's jaw dropped while everyone on the bridge stood and watched as more and more Alurian High Fleet ships darted into orbit around Teras. It was almost too many to count as Albert started calculating the size of the fleet now on the battlefield.

"My God," Dailey breathed out under his breath.

"There are at least fifty ships in the system now. No, seventy-five," Albert computed as several more midsize destroyers appeared.

"Becket," Dailey's voice boomed over the intercom in the drop bay. This was no time for direct, private conversations.

"Sir, go ahead," Becket replied, looking concerned.

"We've got a problem. The Alurian High Fleet just showed up. I don't know how to put this, but it's more than one battle group in size. Keep everyone on standby. No one leaves the *Murphy* until we figure this out."

Becket and several other Nova Ranger platoon leaders walked up to the open drop bay's electromagnetic field, which gave them a clear view of the planet. While busy working, they had noticed the significant number of twinkling lights now surrounding Teras.

"That's not good," Grantham breathed out as the other platoon leaders and sergeants gathered around. "I'd feel a hell of a lot better if we had the *Crow* next to us with the rest of our people. I say we roll the dice and go get them."

Dailey was still listening in on the conversation through the intercom. Becket scratched his stubbled chin, knowing what his commander would say.

"We need to wait and see how this plays out. Either way, I agree with Dailey. We wait."

Frustrated groans and a few select cuss words were grumbled. Lieutenants Card and Ponce glanced at Janix. They would wait.

Nestled in the back of the drop bay was a companion viewscreen to the main one located on the bridge, so Becket brought up the entire schematic of the situation, where Albert had already listed out as many of the ships as he could identify. His eyes widened.

"They know the Creare are going to show up," Janix said, being fully aware of the situation. It also wasn't lost on Becket that a Creare ship had already been in the system over the past couple of days.

Becket again scraped his stubbled chin. "This is either a trap or something we have no business being involved in."

While it was easy to assume that they were the main focal point of the entire situation unfolding around them, it was becoming more and more evident that this was a play for the Creare. In many ways, they were nothing more than a small fly on a large animal.

Seeing the other platoon's leadership looking at him, Becket clarified his statement. "Oh, we're involved. And I can promise you, when the time comes, we'll figure that piece out. We just need to be patient. Pearl and the others on the *Crow* will be fine as long as nobody opens fire."

The politics of the interstellar situation unfolding in front of them was unmatched by not only his but also Captain Dailey's previous misadventures throughout the galaxy. For once, he would give anything to be able to communicate back with Earth and the council. The one missing piece of this entire puzzle was the lack of any representation from the mining syndicates. They themselves owned massive fleets of warships used to protect their territorial claims throughout space from pirates and the competition.

Dailey refocused, opening up a line of communications with the *Crow*. "Pearl, are you seeing this?"

"Yes, sir, a little too close for comfort. Are you still sending out the attack wing?" She was asking a rhetorical question, knowing it was better to stay put in overwhelming situations such as this.

"No, we're on standby. At this point, I recommend loading everybody on a transport ship and getting ready to leave. The gate drive on the *Murphy* is ready to go, and the thrusters are close to being operational. We could use the extra room on the *Crow* for the people from Teras, but we're good for now," Dailey replied, working through the possible scenarios. "Hang tight. This is either going to work itself out really fast or end in a blaze of glory."

Persius finally spoke up from the navigation table. "With this amount of vessels in the system, there is a one hundred percent probability of the Creare arriving in short order."

"Define short order."

"Within half a moon cycle at most," Persius relayed, giving them a twelve-hour window of time to work with.

For once, Captain Dailey was at a loss for words. With their previous plans off the table for now, it was a game of sit and wait.

"Albert?" Dailey asked, realizing the AI was preoccupied. "Albert!"

"Boss. Sorry, I was working through calculations of just how risky it would be to open a gate with minimal thrusters."

"You keep doing that. I need to know how long it would take the transport ship from the *Crow* to get here, and if those two are about the same amount of time, we'll need to be ready to move. This isn't the time for us to stand and fight," Dailey said.

After several seconds, Albert started talking with Persius again. "Yes. B-class engines. Not enough megajewels, but . . . Huh, we should have thought about that earlier. I see. That's why you make the big bucks. Brilliant." The conversation continued for thirty more seconds of eternity.

Albert finally stood to his full height. "Persius keeps reminding me we have the battle mechs, and there are three actual transport ships aboard the *Crow*. One appears to be damaged, but the other two could, in theory, nudge the *Crow* out of the way. It would, however, take too long. I won't get into the numbers, but we could cause a little distraction while we get the transport ship here."

"Time?" Dailey asked, working through the statement.

"The transport ship does have a hyperthruster. They could be here in five minutes. They could hyperjump. Persius says the highest probability would be for them to overshoot us, then it would be another five minutes. Persius states a seventy-five percent probability of success. This also means we could use the two docked ships to maneuver us through a gate."

Without asking any follow-up questions, Dailey put his new plan into motion. "Open up comms with the drop bay and Pearl. Pearl, you copy?" he asked as her strained voice replied.

"Roger, sir. We are loading the transport ship. Change of plans?"

Becket's voice broke in. "We hear you, sir."

"We're going to do this before the Creare show up. I'm going to give control of the transport ship to Persius and Albert. They believe they can do a short hyperjump without drawing too much attention after deploying the battle mechs on the *Void Reaper* to cause a distraction. They don't have to attack; they just need to be out there. The ship will overshoot us, but it will only take them five mikes to get to the *Murphy*. We let our transport ship go and let them dock on our hull." He was referring to the transport ship Senator Deborah Powell had installed on the *Murphy* before reclassing back to the Fleet as an admiral.

Becket didn't like the third change in plans, which, in reality, was needed with the ever-changing situation.

"Any questions?" Dailey was greeted by silence. "Pearl?"

"We are almost loaded and ready to go. I suggest letting Albert take control now. The sooner the crew is off this ship, the better," Pearl replied as the sounds of Dorax shouting, motivating people to move, echoed in the background.

"Albert, make it happen," Dailey ordered as he plugged Persius into the main navigation panel.

Persius spoke up next. "In the event I turn red, unplug me from the ship. That will mean I am being synced with the Creare."

"Got it. The Creare show up, we unplug you," Dailey noted, motioning for Specialist Kline to take on the task.

Within five minutes, dozens of battle mechs fluttered out of the *Crow* on low thrust, like droning bees slowly converging on their target. Persius was also keeping several in reserve close to the *Crow* in the event the Alurians sent attack ships, something that was likely going to happen once the plan was in motion.

"The transport ship is away," Albert spoke as they activated the highly calculated and dangerous short hyperjump. "Jump complete and successful. Uh-oh . . ."

Dailey nodded as an alarm pinged on the proximity screens. The *Void Reaper* and the Alurians were now very aware something was happening with the *Crow*.

Just as it started, the transport ship dropped out of its two-second-long journey.

"What's going on?" Dailey asked. The viewscreen shifted to several large Alurian destroyers maneuvering toward the *Crow*.

"The Alurians are sending three destroyers toward the *Crow*. They don't seem to be focusing on us. I suggest we keep comms off till docked. Persius has full control."

"I'm sure they know that's one of their stolen dreadnoughts," Dailey said as he stood up, now able to see the transport ship out of the main viewport. His heart pounded as it turned, starting external docking procedures. With two AIs running the show, the seamless ballet unfolding impressed the man.

A minute ahead of schedule, the transport ship docked as Dorax's panicked voice echoed over the bridge's intercom. "Pearl. I can't find Pearl. She said she would be the last on board!"

Dailey's stomach dropped while he tried to hail the *Crow*. No one replied. He turned to King. "What's going on?"

"Pearl's shut down the comms link. She had to do it manually. I don't know what she's doing."

Albert cut in. "There appear to be several batteries on the *Crow* energizing. Pearl deactivated the shields and looks to be transferring power to the *Crow*'s weapons systems.

"Shit," Dailey barked.

"She's opening fire on the *Void Reaper*," Albert added calmly.

"Why is she doing this?" Dailey asked the very air on the bridge.

Within seconds, the viewscreen shifted to the distant image of the *Crow* now firing every plasma cannon the ship had to offer. In turn, the *Void Reaper* started to return fire, a mix of flashes erupting on the screen. In the distance, the three Alurian destroyers also opened fire.

"Persius, activate the battle mechs," Dailey instructed. Several hundred twinkling lights burst to life all around the scene now unfolding.

The box with a speaker mounted to its side started changing colors, not only activating the battle mechs to attack but also seemingly piloting them all at once. The small twinkles of light shifted toward the three Alurian destroyers as several explosions dotted both the *Void Reaper* and the *Crow*.

Knowing they couldn't reach Pearl in time, Dailey made the only call he knew to make. Pearl was buying them time so they could gate out. Frustration boiled over in Dailey as he ordered Albert to activate the gate drive and exit the system.

Gritting his teeth, he knew that Pearl had just sacrificed herself for the greater good. To him, it was an unnecessary sacrifice that he would carry with him till his final breath. It wasn't for others on his team to make the sacrifice; that was his burden and his burden alone.

In the distance, the *Crow* and the *Void Reaper* exploded in a flash of finality. The three Alurian destroyers were holding their own as the battle mechs started thinning out.

As the space in front of the *Murphy* started to shimmer, Persius started flashing red. Kline, seeing this, ran from his seat, almost tripping over the rail behind his station, quickly unplugging the Creare AI.

"Problem!" Albert barked. "The gate is being remotely deactivated."

With those words, three massive shadows phased into existence between the planet and the *Murphy*.

The Creare had arrived.

CHAPTER 33

THE EVE OF WAR

Albert scrambled to reactivate the gate as the sheer size of the massive, sleek Creare ships came into focus. Overbearing and mind-bogglingly massive, even the largest Alurian star cruiser was a quarter of its size.

King stood up in frustration.

"Something has taken over the comm lines. All of them," King informed the bridge as Albert turned.

"They also have control of all external projection systems." Pausing, Albert clarified. "Scanners, shields, and by the looks of it, the gate itself. It's a projection system, meaning it's not physically attached to the ship—it's pushed out in front of the ship."

The one positive the *Murphy* and its crew had going for them was being on the far corner of the battlefield.

"We need to move away—" Dailey was cut short as the first volley of combined fire from the Alurian High Fleet and the Prime Assembly opened in a coordinated, planned attack.

Once again, Dailey started to feel as if he were several steps behind everything else going on around him. On the other hand, he also knew what was unfolding in front of the *Murphy* would have far-reaching implications even all the way back on Earth.

Lights and flashes traced in the distance as two of the three ships shifted position, letting loose a massive wall of purple fire from massive pounding rail guns. Several of the forward Alurian destroyers disintegrated, setting the stage for the starting battle. This wasn't a battle but rather an all-out brawl, as every ship on the battlefield, minus the two now clearly identified command ships, started ripping into each other.

Within another minute, hundreds, if not thousands, of drones and smaller attack ships launched from every corner and crevasse of the Alurian fleet. Not to be outdone, two massive arms, larger than the *Murphy*, jutted out of the rear Creare ship.

They all watched in awe as the arms further unfolded, followed by a swarm of ships ripping into the oncoming wall of Alurian drones and attack ships. Even though Creare tech was far superior, the sheer number of attack vessels the Alurians had brought to bear was crushing.

There were several gaps in Dailey's understanding of just how prepared the Alurians were to stand up against the Creare. Albert himself had proven to hold otherworldly powers. After witnessing Ran take over the Creare working vessel, he had come to an understanding that they knew enough to feel comfortable taking on the Creare in an ambush head-on.

With that string of thought, Dailey walked up to the viewport now facing the massive battle as the first lines of attack ships from both sides collided.

"Albert, can we tell if those ships have their shields operational?"

"Visual only. The Creare are firing their main rail guns into that mess of ships. Wait one."

Albert zoomed in on one of the dreadnoughts lurking in front of the *Alpha Nova*, the Prime Assembly's command ship. "There, look." Albert froze a frame where the reflection from a powerful deflector shield shone from the hit.

"Oh, that's not good," Albert added, switching back to the zoomed-in view. A purple blast similar to the ones they'd encountered on Teras smacked into the shields of the same dreadnought, followed by an unimpeded assault from the rail gun. Explosions erupted as the front end of the Alurian ship disintegrated in a bubbling round of explosions. Miraculously, while heavily damaged, the ship was still operational, maneuvering away.

The forward Creare ship was quickly enveloped by the fight as random fighters passed around its massive hull. Lurking from all directions were several other Alurian ships making their way to the fight, sacrificing several destroyers while doing so.

Dailey found it odd that the second Creare ship was staying slightly away from its partner. They were holding back. Stalking in reserve, the third and what was clearly the Creare command ship sat as if waiting to see just how much firepower the Alurians had in place.

"I think the Creare are a little hesitant to fully engage," Dailey stated as Mister Toaster's eyebrows furrowed.

"Seems as such. Let's check with Persius." Albert walked over to the AI, plugging her into his armor.

Albert's face screen went blank as the small box again started blinking red.

"Dammit," Dailey huffed quickly, grabbing and unplugging the cable. "Albert. Albert!"

"Hey, boss," his voice came out flat. "Need a minute. The Creare have total control of Persius. They know she's on this ship. They tried to pull me into their network; if you hadn't pulled the plug, I would not be here. That means she's gone."

Dailey realized this meant they also knew Albert was on board. As the thought passed through his mind, the main viewscreen erupted with a massive figure. The Creare wanted to talk.

The battle continued to rage as the size and scope of the fight unfolding continued to grow. On the monitor, the figure in front of them had the same smooth skin and complexion as Remax. Massive ornate shoulder armor panels connected to what appeared to be a cape, leading to an ornate medallion centered in the man's chest. Even more telling was the fact that he seemed completely unfazed by the encounter raging in front of him.

"I am Senior Originator Olan," the man's voice came through, calm yet strong. While he was speaking English, a translation system was making his words smooth out into an understandable cadence.

"Captain Ben Dailey of the United Space Federation vessel *Murphy*." Dailey was playing this by the books.

"Yes, we have uploaded the AI protocol on board your ship. That is the only reason you and your ship are still operational. You also have a secondary Creare protocol on board. We will need to acquire it as well."

Dailey glanced over at Albert, who shook his sensor pod. He didn't want any part of being uploaded. "Might I recommend we discuss this later? I understand you are currently occupied."

Olan didn't show any expression as he started talking again. "We are not here to initiate combat operations with the Federation. We are aware of humankind and, more specifically, of Earth."

Dailey didn't like the way he'd referred to Earth. "The protocol you mention is called Albert. And the one you uploaded, Persius."

At the mention of the AI, Albert stepped into the frame, walking beside the con.

Olan raised an eyebrow. "I see. The protocol you have onboard is not yours to have. I also need not explain how important the protocol you have is."

"My name is Albert," the AI added. Olan continued not to show emotion.

"Interesting," Olan stated flatly, almost indifferently. "Albert, as you are calling it, is one of the original protocols developed by the Creare monarch. I do not need to explain this to you any further, but he is the basis for all our other protocols and was lost many, many years ago while securing a very important artifact."

Dailey and the others already knew Albert had been on Earth, and stated he was from a planet that was no longer in existence. While even Albert admitted to having a massive gap in his memory banks, he had made it clear that he was involved in integrating tech into other civilizations. They now also understood this had been done in the name of the Creare.

"He was on Earth. What artifact?" Dailey asked, trying to unravel the statement.

"You know very little of your own history, human. You are not here by chance. Yes, we are the ones who provided Director Prescott with the gate protocol to bring you here. We also knew the Prime Assembly and Alurian High Fleet would soon follow. We fully projected you would locate the Creare ship. This conversation is coming to an end. We expect you to comply."

In the background, someone spoke to Olan as he stared up at the monitor, cutting the feed. Outside the viewport, several bubbling explosions rocked the forward Creare vessel. The fight wasn't as simple as the Creare had anticipated.

The truth of the matter was that the Alurians had been perfecting their attacks against the Creare. It was also becoming clear that the Alurians were the ones who had pressed the Creare to react. This still left a gaping hole in how the Alurians knew the *Murphy* would be there. The logic finally slapped Dailey in the face as the others watched the man chew on the inside of his lip, flexing his quickly healing jaw. Franklin had injected him with healing nanobots, rapidly increasing his healing time from weeks down to hours and days.

Dailey finally spoke. "I have a feeling Director Prescott wasn't working on our behalf. Damn syndicates. He has been working with the Creare to get everyone here at the same time. He's positioning himself with them. Someone get Sparky up here." Dailey reached down, clamping his chest plate on as it molded around his torso.

"That seems logical," Albert started. "Might I ask what you're doing?"

"What I'm doing? What we're doing," Dailey corrected. "Get your shit together. We're taking a little trip via the Sparky Express. Thron," Dailey called through the direct link to the galley.

"Sir," the gruff Solarian ex-warlord turned chef replied.

"I'm going to send Sparky your way in a few minutes. I need you to fill his tank up. Stuff as much ham in that pig as you can; we're taking a little trip." Dailey paused, thinking through what he was about to do. "You want to take a little trip?"

Dailey could feel the grin tightening on Thron's face. "If it involves fixing this mess, yes."

"Dust off your old armor. We leave as soon as Sparky gets a full belly." Dailey shifted to Becket. "Top, I need you to pick someone to go on a little mission. You're going to be in charge while I'm gone."

Becket chewed on the statement, glancing over at Grantham. He was the most experienced member of his team and, in all reality, the toughest. He had witnessed the man get shot ten times and still keep fighting while eventually having to resort to his ripper.

Sparky appeared out of nowhere with his armor on, visor slid back. It was clear the hound had been in the bay, ready to join the fight. "Sparky, I need you to listen up. We need to get on that Creare ship. When I say we, that means Albert, myself, and two others. If Thron lets you loose on the ham supply, do you think you can make that happen?"

Sparky contemplated the ask before holding his fat-necked head up high, followed by a growling bark. "Yes," came over the translator. "For the glory of the *Murphy* and the Ham Republic."

"Go to . . ." Dailey stopped talking, realizing only the smell of ozone remained. He was already in the galley. "Albert, are we going to need to do anything to make this work? Maybe loop us all together? I don't know how the hell he does it, but I made it in one piece."

Albert contemplated the ask, having a better understanding of the voodoo, as he called it, that Sparky used. "Perhaps. I'm going to break some news to you, boss. I—Well, we may have already taken a few trips. You know, for science."

"We can talk about that later. What do you think?"

"Well, if we supercharge my mini reactor and use bracers, we can be significantly more efficient," Albert replied, referring to the magnetic cuffs they used for prisoners."

"Kline, grab four sets of bracers," Dailey instructed as a full armor–clad Thron thumped onto the bridge. The sheer presence of the Solarian was crushing when he wasn't flipping pancakes in the galley. A gold sword hung off his hip as an old, well-used blaster rifle, coupled to his pitted armor, poked out from behind his back.

"How long are we going to be gone?" Thron asked. Dailey cocked his head. "If we're there longer than thirty minutes, it's . . . Well, we will see."

Albert spoke up. "The main thrusters will be back online within thirty minutes. Bellman and his team, now that everyone is back on board from the *Crow*, should make quick work of the manual side of the repair."

Becket joined the group on the bridge. "Sir, are you heading out now?"

"Yeah, we're going to get on the Creare command ship, then see where things go from there. If we can get Albert linked into their system, we might be able to shut off what they are using to keep us from gating. We run into trouble . . ." Dailey trailed off, pointing at Thron.

Both men grunted, knowing what the Solarian was capable of.

"Dorax will be on the bridge shortly. He's a little torn up over Pearl. Hell, sir, we all are."

Dailey was well aware of the loss of his second in command. He was also aware that even Sparky, using his little trick, would probably not have been able to react in time. The *Murphy*'s commander had already thought about all the scenarios that would have allowed them to save her.

"We will make this right. I don't know what that looks like, but we will," Dailey said, patting Becket on the back. "Keep the lights on for us."

Becket knew that meant he was to leave in the event they succeeded in shutting down the dampening system but were gone too long.

A flash went off in front of the *Murphy* as a spiraling Alurian ship flamed out in a large explosion.

The fight was getting closer.

CHAPTER 34

OUT OF HARM'S WAY

Cooler-than-normal air greeted the group as Sparky smacked his helmet back, panting heavily. The trip had indeed drained him. Albert handed over a small packet of ham meant to reenergize the hound for the trip back.

Sparky had landed them in a small, dark supply room stacked with lightly glowing green crates. Dailey, still on his knees like Grantham, looked up at Thron standing resolutely beside Albert, taking in the room.

"I think I'm gonna throw up," Grantham huffed, opening his visor, only to dry heave a handful of times before getting control of himself.

For some reason, Dailey felt significantly better than he had on his first trip over. It must be something that the body needed to get used to, or the distance traveled was significantly less. Either way, they had made the journey safely. Albert's suggestion to use the bracers had significantly helped Sparky energize the group with little effort.

"I wonder what's in these crates?" Thron asked.

Albert shrugged, the two Gatling lasers on his shoulders going up and down.

"If the ship is anything like the *Waiting Sun*, I should be able to plug in here to get a relatively good layout of the vessel, as well as the subsystems we need to adjust," Albert stated just as Grantham finally got to his feet.

"You think they know we're here?" Dailey asked. Albert cocked his head.

"They will absolutely know there was some type of power surge on board, but as with any spacefaring vessel, it all depends on who is paying attention or who is playing Moshan solitaire while on duty," Albert replied, walking over to a small panel by the door.

"I doubt anyone's doing that here," Grantham said, pulling his rifle up and following the AI to the entrance.

Scanning the supply room, Dailey found the sheer amount of stacked supplies curious. "You think we can open one of these?" he asked Albert as he held up a long digit.

"I highly recommend not touching anything until I can sort out what this subsystem is doing," Albert said, plugging directly into the console panel after pushing a small square cover away.

The silence in the room was crushing. If they didn't already know they were in the middle of a battle, they wouldn't be able to tell.

Thron walked the perimeter, ensuring there was no other type of surveillance or security systems in the room, only to conclude the door was the only viable security protocol in the small section they now occupied. The Creare clearly didn't expect somebody to voodoo themselves aboard their ship in the middle of a raging battle.

"Hello," Albert drawled out. "The ship's sectioned off much like the *Waiting Sun*. Lucky for us, we're not too far from their main relay reactors. For those curious, that means the systems that are powering whatever is dampening the space around us and also controlling their communications array."

Satisfied with their luck, Dailey continued to stand still, staring at the entrance door. If they could sneak in and out without being detected, it would be one of their luckiest breaks, if not the only luck the man had experienced over the past several days.

Albert quickly unplugged from the wall, turning to the group. "Good news, bad news? Now that we got that out of the way," Albert rambled on. "Bad news, they absolutely know somebody boarded their ship and are starting to scan the vessel. The other bad news is that Persius is definitely on the ship, but if I tried to upload her to my own data banks, things could get messy. If we can find the actual terminal she's loaded on, we could very possibly be able to temporarily utilize her to take control of the ship.

"Piling onto those two pieces of information, I would also be remiss not to mention that the navigation system tied to the local reactors is programmed for a direct jump to Earth in the event it's needed."

"For once, give me some good news," Dailey insisted.

"Well, their system is significantly easier to integrate into than I initially believed. I can't stay plugged in for long, or they'll be able to locate me. They know somebody is poking around for buggers. I suggest we move to another terminal so I can continue."

If they stayed in the supply room, they would be located; if they moved, they would be exposed to the interior of the ship. A ship that was likely crammed full of soldiers.

A light, jostling vibration caught the group's attention. The fight was getting closer to the Creare command vessel.

"All right," Dailey started, "we stay together. No one gets out of eyeshot. If things get too thick, we leave. Remember, we're not here to make enemies, so take it easy. Don't kill anyone. Sparky, how long is it going to be before you can get us out of here?"

The sounds of the others switching their weapons to various nonlethal settings rang out while Thron simply squeezed the handle of his sword tighter.

Sparky let a chuff out between chewing his ham. "Fifteen Earth minutes. Bring ham more often."

While he was serious in his calculation, the Alurian war hound was also making a play for Dailey and the others to bring ham along on missions.

The door slid open as Albert placed a thin sensor in the corridor, checking to see if they were alone or not.

"The coast is clear," Albert stated. "There's another port I can use one section down. It's another supply room that would be good for us to get out of eyeshot."

Without hesitation, the group stepped into the hall. Thron ducked, finally regaining his full height, pulled out his gleaming golden sword, a sword which had the ability to fire an extremely focused blast of energy.

The group quickly shuffled down two more uninhabited corridors, shocked by the emptiness of the area they were in. Sparky had somehow dropped them dead center of their supply stocks, an area often left unattended during a call to battle stations.

The sounds of a door opening somewhere caught everyone's attention as Albert worked to open the entrance to their next destination. Within seconds, the group piled into an identical supply room, the hiss of the door closing behind them. Dailey winced behind his visor, hoping they'd gone undetected.

Albert immediately plugged into the control panel by the door as the others stood ready for action.

"Albert," Dailey finally spoke up. "Can you tell us who's out there?"

"Yeah, I could, but you wouldn't like it," the AI stated as Mister Toaster's face winked with a flat computing pixelated screen. After a few brief seconds, Albert answered the question. "Some type of automated battle droids. Typical security protocol. They were sent here to see what the power surge was all about," Albert stated, turning back to the panel and shutting himself off from the conversation at hand.

Thron shrugged. "Not like we would be killing anyone, technically."

"Grantham, switch to EMP rounds. Sparky, if that door opens, juice the shit out of the hallway," Dailey instructed.

"Clarified juice?" Sparky asked.

"It's always something," Dailey huffed under his breath. "Shut them down."

Sparky nodded, taking several steps closer to the door. This the Alurian war hound could do.

Albert's viewscreen transitioned back to Mister Toaster's, at times, annoying face. "They just left the last supply room. They'll be here in two minutes. Once that occurs, all bets are off. I've triangulated the protocol drives to shut down the dampening field. I've also located Persius. You're not going to like it, boss."

"I don't like this new thing you keep saying about me not liking things. Let's hear it," Dailey said, readying himself for the upcoming encounter.

"Persius has been uploaded and sectioned off in that Olan fellow's personal quarters. He really doesn't want us to get our hands on her. Not like I was going to put my hands on her," Albert added as Dailey held up a hand, cutting him off. The sounds of clanking metal on the smooth floor were coming closer.

"Albert, as soon as they're before the door, open it. Sparky, you know what to do," Dailey instructed, signaling to Grantham and Thron to step back in order to provide cover.

Two heavy thuds *clomped* directly in front of the door, which immediately slid open. Sparky jumped forward, letting the electricity spider through the droid's legs, causing the six massive, hulking beasts of war to momentarily freeze. Dailey's targeting system identified the threats just as Thron leaped forward, crashing into the droids like an out-of-control space freighter.

The electrified, now glowing golden blade swooshed through the air with surgical precision, removing several arms and sensor pods from the droids while Sparky let up pumping energy into the robots in an effort to keep from knocking Thron unconscious.

This momentary lack of energy allowed the droid on the far end of the door to turn in a futile attempt to fire whatever weapons it had. Thron's golden blade whistled through the air, this time not only cutting off the droid's arm on the upswing but also slicing it down the center with the downward motion of the blade.

Dailey and Grantham both stood up, walking side by side with their rifles trained on the corridor door. The reading in Dailey's HUD panned, showing the droids had been neutralized. A voice from inside the supply room made the *Murphy*'s commander flinch.

"Yeah, no worries. I completely scrambled their systems before they could compute what was happening. Oh no, they are sending reinforcements to check on their little buddies. They must've had some kind of continuous link protocol, and if they lose communication, it automatically triggers some type of internal defense system." Albert's words were drowned out as a flat alarm screamed through the entire ship. Unlike the whooping *dings* aboard the *Murphy*, the Creare ship had a singular earsplitting tone.

"Don't say it. They know we're here," Dailey said, motioning the group to cover both ends of the corridor.

Albert stepped out of the supply room. "One section over and to the left. There's another room we can utilize. I've already unplugged. I only need one more data transfer to get this completed."

Without saying a word, Albert took off in a full-on sprint while the rest of the team followed. Dailey glanced over his shoulder, seeing the mess of mangled metal they had left behind.

Turning another corner, Albert immediately plugged into another panel, working with surgeonlike precision before the door whooshed open. Again, the group scurried inside and immediately clicked it shut. Unlike the previous two supply rooms, this one was completely different.

Row upon row, stacked six-high to the ceiling and as far as the eye could see, security droids, the same as the ones they had just encountered, sat dormant.

Another vibration reverberated through the ship as Albert went to work on the control panel. Dailey glanced nervously around the room before speaking.

"Albert, you think we can find another port?"

"Nope. Point of no return, boss. Oh, and there are several more of those clanky things coming. Wait, they're stopping at the end of the corridor. I'm gonna have to focus; ball's in your court. Five more minutes tops."

Dailey and the others all stood with their backs toward the room, staring at the unflinching army of death sitting in front of them, waiting to be awakened. Sparky, not liking the vibe of the space, backed up so far to the door that his butt clanked against the entrance.

While Dailey and Grantham were suited up, Thron had a helmet on with his regular armor. Two dots flashed on both of the men's HUDs from the far end of the room.

What happened next was pure, unadulterated nightmare fuel. Red lights started coming on in sequential order on the bottom row of droids like demons rising from the very pits of hell. Several clicks followed, then the second row of red lights also started activating.

"Albert, we gotta go," Dailey urged, not giving Albert or anyone else room for interpretation.

"Almost there . . . And good," Albert said, cocking his head. Mister Toaster's face reappeared on his viewscreen as Dailey started motioning everyone to circle around Sparky. "We better get—" Albert was cut off by the door swooshing open just as hundreds of security droids activated, snapping out of their charging bases.

There, standing in the corridor, was Senior Originator Olan. Significantly larger than Remax, the Creare was still dressed in the same ornate armor, dwarfing even Thron. The sheer crushing presence of the figure now standing in front of them caused them to pause long enough for the Creare to speak.

"Your weapons have been rendered inoperative. Please refrain from taking further action. I would like to talk with you, Captain Ben Dailey. Civilly," Olan said, louder than his previous radio voice, glancing down at Sparky, who was now standing in the middle of Dailey's team.

Dailey lowered his weapon, motioning for the others to follow his lead as the second round of security droids dropped from their stations.

"Okay, you have my undivided attention." Dailey glanced at Albert, noticing his viewscreen was now pixelated. Either he had also been taken offline, or he was up to something.

"Your droid will stay in this room, as well as that." Olan pointed at Sparky. "Yes, I am aware our AI protocol is loaded in that droid. We will sort through that later."

Olan motioned for Grantham, Thron, and Dailey to follow him as four Creare soldiers stepped behind them. With a parade of security, Dailey nodded toward the others.

The immediate change in the ship's decor was shocking. The bland supply stores quickly shifted to an ornate opulence. Gold lines flowed into black-and-purple walls lit by glowing yellow lights.

Dailey noted that the high-end finish matched Senior Originator Olan's just as flashy armor.

As the group passed through another set of doors, a massive catwalk opened into a bay full of ships, all the size of the *Murphy*'s drop ships, adorned with weapons. Large coil-shaped engines flowed into two ship-mounted rail guns poised for violence.

What confused Dailey was the sheer amount of power needed to operate rail guns on such a small platform. There was a reason they weren't installed on the *Murphy*. The Federation super carriers were the main ship class that utilized the weapon systems to protect Earth.

The elevator at the end of the walkway opened as several more Creare guards, wearing similarly ornate armor, stood at the ready with massive staffs. The Creare weapon contained a blaster on each end and, much like Thron's blade, several kinetic energy weapons.

Within five minutes, they were standing in a room surrounded by security droids and unflinching guards. After being directed to place their weapons and helmets on a table, Olan motioned for them to sit. Unlike Dailey and the others, the Creare commander sat on a throne at the head of the rectangular table.

A circular viewscreen hung overhead as a round section in the center of the table opened, exposing a holoprojector. Olan leaned slightly forward as two other Creare officers entered the room, sitting on either side of the man.

Dailey spoke up first, cutting through the thick silence. The low temperature in the room almost made his breath visible. "Are you concerned with the attack going on?"

"No," Olan replied, nodding to one of the officers to activate the holoprojector. "The forward vessel is automated. It is here to collect data on the Alurians' current capabilities. Our second vessel is here to keep them occupied. If they decide to destroy either of our ships, we will activate our combat forces."

"Those aren't your main fighters out there?" Dailey asked. Thron and Grantham were letting their commander do the talking.

"Very observant. They are defense units used to keep the Alurians occupied while we talk, and as previously stated, gather information." Olan's tone shifted. The translator modulating his voice kept it in synch with the Creare. Dailey was surprised he spoke a fairly understandable version of English. "I need you to understand we are not here to start a war, but we will if we deem it necessary."

"Then why allow this to happen? Why did you shut our ship down, and our weapons?" Dailey asked, making a good point.

"I already answered that question. I need you to understand I mean you no harm unless it's warranted. No, I need for you to help me deliver a message to your Federation. A message that those on Earth will understand."

Dailey nodded, so Olan continued. "Earth and the surrounding galaxy have been relatively unscathed by the dangers of the universe. Yes, the Alurians and the mining syndicates are a true threat, but one that is more of a symbiotic relationship. Humankind has yet to truly meet the Alurian High Fleet nor Aluria's actual leadership. Leadership that is well aware of the true nature of the cosmos."

Thron shifted in his seat.

"Yes, Solarian?" Olan asked. Dailey nodded.

"The Federation has not until recently encountered the Alurian Fleet. They don't know where Aluria is. That goes for the Solarians as well. Why now?" Thron asked.

"For years, the Alurians have believed they can best our kind—a foolish thought. Aluria is just one of dozens of civilizations capable of such thought. The Federation is also growing in such a thoughtless manner. Let me ask you something that I believe will reveal much to your eyes. Why do you think we haven't come to your system?"

"The Alurians have kept you away? Why, I don't know," Dailey replied as Olan showed the first sign of emotion since the meeting, lightly smirking.

"While the Alurians have been building their fleets to expand their reach and power, they, much like the Creare, understand the true threat. A threat that will one day reach their planet, then yours. Let me simplify the question. Why do you think we all have allowed Earth and the other planets in your Federation to exist and thrive?"

"We have something on our planet. Why else would Albert be there setting up star gates," Dailey correctly guessed.

"Yes, indeed. Many, many millennia ago, we occupied Earth. Buried under the sands of time, our civilization was visited by a race of beings that wielded unfathomable power. A race of titans with machines that would boggle even the greatest mind." Thoughts of the massive battle mech they'd encountered while running from the Alurians swept through Dailey's thoughts.

"Yes, I see you have some modicum of understanding," Olan continued. "The war that followed pushed us to the edges of this galaxy and the next, then the next. With every civilization we encountered, we found new ways to fight off this threat, and eventually, we did."

He paused to let Dailey ask questions. Olan was relaying information on purpose.

"You were so busy fighting, and the civilizations you passed by and utilized outgrew themselves and became a threat." Dailey was holding back from calling them conquerors.

Olan saw this in the man's face. "Some even forgot about our very existence, their governments wiping our history from their books, as you call them. Earth had been all but destroyed, covered in a layer of ash and rock. By the time we sent scouts back, things had changed."

"You found people survived."

"And thrived. We attempted to build gates to return, but this never happened, and then the plan was no longer considered a priority," Olan said, laying his large hands flat on the table.

"You can clearly go there. Why not just gate?" Dailey asked. Olan actually let the corners of his lips perk up in a weak smile.

"You are the right human to have this conversation with. Earth is not like other planets, nor are humans. Buried deep within the planet is a weapon that even we can't counter. A weapon that would eat your solar system in one swallow. With that, we have not wanted to draw attention to the planet. If we go to your system, we will bring the others. The Titans. I see by the look on your face that you're confused."

"Why not reach out to the Federation and work together?" Dailey asked. Olan's face flattened.

"Humankind has also proven to be dangerous, as the Alurians have learned. Yes, they could bring death and destruction to your planet, but why do so when they drain your kind for labor and gains? The Alurians are not your true enemy. The Prime Assembly and the mining syndicates are. The Creare are not your enemy. The Titans are. But that can change. Things can change."

"You want me to communicate this to the Federation," Dailey stated as Olan held out a small box.

"Inside, we have downloaded Persius, as you call it. There are certain protections included, but that is our ask."

Dailey let the term "our ask" roll around his mind. Olan was yet another fish in a much larger sea. "And you are just going to let us leave?"

"Yes. I also have something else that may sway your decision."

The holoprojector showed a random mech from the *Crow* floating aimlessly in space, bouncing off random pieces of debris.

"What's this?" Dailey asked, leaning forward.

"One of your people is floating in that mech. They are rapidly losing support systems and, from our scans, they appear to be unconscious."

Pearl. It was Pearl. Dailey immediately stood up.

"Sit down, Captain Ben Dailey. There will be time."

Grantham and Thron both nodded, easing Dailey back into his seat. There was more on the table. "Again, you have my undivided attention."

"We are going to leave this fight. When we do, it will be yours to finish. Remember, the Alurian High Fleet is not your enemy here. The Prime Assembly is. I will leave that up to you to interpret."

"You want us to destroy their command ship," Dailey stated flatly. In reality, he also wanted Kluvnew dead.

"If that is how you see it. The prize they seek, or thought they were after, is now in your hands."

That's when it hit Dailey. "You are taking Albert."

Olan nodded.

"I can't let that happen. He's part of my crew," Dailey said, working to keep his temper in check.

"What is done, is already done. We will escort you back to the supply room, and you can leave or not leave. If you choose to push the topic, this conversation will have been for nothing."

Olan nodded at the two officers, who stood up, walking out of the room.

Dailey looked down at the table before making his final decision. He understood that in times like this, reflecting could get others killed. "I accept."

Olan raised a smooth eyebrow. "What about your companions?"

"I speak for them. This is my decision, and mine alone. They will not carry the weight of leaving someone behind."

"You are an admirable warrior, Captain Ben Dailey. We are not that different, you and I."

With that, Senior Originator Olan stood. "The security detail will escort you to your ship. Your engines are now fully functional. The rest is up to you."

The team stood up as the guards and security droids once again surrounded them. One of the guards motioned for Dailey and the others to pick up their weapons as they made their way back to the supply bays.

Sparky stood in the supply room beside Albert's crumpled body. A red glow surrounded the Alurian war hound before one of the security droids clicked a button, removing whatever dampening field they had surrounded them with. Dailey held his hands up in placation, seeing the hound about to let loose on everything and everyone within reach.

A guttural, protective growl came from behind his mask as Sparky took several steps in front of what was once Albert.

"Calm down. It's time for us to go; we can bring what's left of him with us. If it's any consolation, we have Persius, and Pearl is still alive. We'll get your friend back—I promise."

One thing Sparky had learned was that Dailey always kept his word.

One of the droids moved beside him as Sparky snapped to his left, again pulling himself back from doing something that would cause more problems.

"Is that it? Are we good to go?" Dailey asked two of the actual Creare guards, who simply nodded.

Dailey led the rest of the team inside the room while two of the droids followed them. Thron looked down at the now dormant Albert, rage filling the Solarian's eyes as they all pulled out their bracers, connecting themselves together.

"Sparky, take us home," Dailey instructed before the familiar, vibrating sting of being ripped through time and space washed through his body. Just as the entire group was about to wink out of existence, a cold, hard claw from one of the security droids clamped down on Dailey's wrist.

CHAPTER 35

LINE IN THE SAND

The drop bay aboard the *Murphy* was a mix of excitement and sheer chaos. Dailey felt his arm being wrenched into the air as the Creare battle droid stood to its full height. Thron was already in motion, as was Master Sergeant Grantham, before Dailey was quickly released.

Dozens of Nova Rangers in their full orbital drop armor rushed to the scene, all taking in what was unfolding in front of them. One of the hulking Creare security droids was now on their ship.

In an odd show of restraint, the security guard held up both hands, as if telling everyone to stop. A gurgling, modulated voice chirped from its speaker seconds before Thron was about to slice the sleek, curved droid in half.

"Boss, must upload. No room," the screeching, alien voice boomed out of the amplified speaker, crackling as it did so.

"Wait!" Dailey barked, realizing something wasn't right.

As he did so, Sparky let out a howl, retracting the armor from his fat head. "ALBERT!"

"Son of a bitch," Dailey breathed out, letting the chuckle actually climb up his belly, through his lungs, and out his mouth. "What the hell did you do?"

It was clear by the strain of articulating actual words that Albert had somehow uploaded himself to one of the security guards. He hadn't been able to transfer all of himself, but it was enough.

Albert dropped to the ground beside his lifeless body, popping open the chest plate and immediately plugging in a cable left dangling from his cube. Not a word was spoken nor a breath taken as several alarms whooped in the background. Something else was happening.

Becket's voice blared over the intercom. "Sir, you better get your ass to the bridge."

"Albert, I don't know if you can hear me. Are you good?" Dailey asked, not knowing the breadth of the situation unfolding in front of him.

The group surrounding Dailey stilled again as the former Alurian battle droid's left arm flinched, morphing into a thumbs-up, followed by a blip on Mister Toaster's screen. They would soon be seeing the jolly purveyor of toast.

"Well, boys. That's three things off my list for now. Let's go get our girl and send Kluvnew to whatever hell he came from."

Grunts and the clank of boots started to echo as several cheers came from the support team and Nova Rangers alike. "To the edge!"

Still hazy on the whole situation that had just unfolded, Dailey ran into the bridge, dropping his helmet beside the con as Becket stood in front of the main viewscreen. Red flashes, blinking dots, alarms, and about every other signal that a sensor could possibly feed a ship were lit up like the Fourth of July.

"What's going on?" Dailey asked.

Becket snapped around. While he was happy to see the man, the look on his face was that of confusion and concern. He scraped his stubbled chin. "The Creare ships just vanished. It was like they were never here. On top of that, while you are away, they damn near destroyed half of the Alurian fleet, if not more. I'm not saying they blew them up, but they sure as shit shut them down. I can't really tell, but it looks like they took a bunch of them along."

Bellman ran back from Specialist Kline's targeting station. "They somehow pulled all the ships that were attacking them into some type of temporal field and just vanished. There are still two ships remaining. It looks like the Prime Assembly's command ship and one of their destroyers."

Unknown to Captain Dailey and the rest of the crew, the Creare had indeed taken the rest of the Alurian fleet with them. Instead of completely testing them and slinging them into the void of interspace, they had neatly deposited them on the other side of the galaxy.

"Pearl—we have to get Pearl," Dailey said. Confused glances landed on him. "She's alive. There's a battle mech floating out by the *Crow*. I'm almost betting that the Creare somehow tagged her. I don't know how, but she got on one of those mechs and hauled ass off of the *Crow*."

This put the wind in the sails of the crew, who all shifted back to their stations, focusing on the area and bringing up the schematic on the main viewscreen. There, in the center, was a flashing beacon of light in all the dark they had witnessed over the past several days. It was a transponder. If they hadn't known the look, they would have focused their scans elsewhere.

No more orders were needed as the *Murphy*, for the first time since being taken out of commission, activated its main thrusters at full power. If Albert were on the bridge, he would've been cursing them for pushing the ship to its limits after the repairs.

"Jen, do you copy?" Dailey asked over the main intercom.

"Sir, loud and freaking clear," Jen answered back.

"Attach assigned Rangers to their attack fighters and deploy," Dailey ordered, knowing a fight was coming.

While the *Murphy* was moving through space, it was common practice to launch the attack wing while fully activating the thrusters while in a fight. Dailey glanced out the main viewport, seeing several darting fighters scream out of the drop bay, ready for action.

Once they secured Pearl, they were going to unleash every living hell on Kluvnew. With or without Albert, they would accomplish the mission. Dailey sat Persius on the navigation table.

"What's that?" Becket asked as Dailey continued to focus on the viewscreen. It would be four more minutes before they reached Pearl.

"It's Persius. I'm not sure what they did to her, but we're not to hook her up to anything until Albert can talk with her. And that's another thing. They tried to upload Albert, and he somehow figured out a way to get into a damn Creare droid's body. I don't think he's gonna be much help for now, but as soon as he's ready, he'll be up here."

"Sir, I've seen that look before. What else happened on that ship?" Becket asked as Dailey simply continued to stare at the viewscreen.

"I don't know. But I do know we need to get back to the Federation. Something's happening, Becket. Something that I don't fully understand."

With those words, Becket knew that conversation would be for another time. For now, they needed to focus on the task at hand.

The next four minutes felt like an eternity as the main thrusters cut off, creating another barrage of alarms from the engineering section. Hontz, at one point, called up to the bridge cussing, using words that made even Dailey blush.

The drop bay's extraction claw slowly grabbed the battle mech, pulling Pearl on board the *Murphy*. Doctors were already in the bay, with Medical Officer Franklin ready to take care of the ship's executive officer.

"Where's Tarik and his group?" Dailey asked, realizing he didn't see any of them on the bridge.

"The majority of them are still on board the Creare transport ship. The rest are all in the briefing room, watching everything unfold from there. I asked them to stay off the bridge until we could figure this out," Becket said, refocusing the viewscreen on the *Alpha Nova*, now turning toward them in the distance.

"We got her," Dorax's voice came over the bridge. Smiles were quickly replaced by pissed-off faces as Dailey flopped onto the con.

"Intercept the command ship. Activate all forward batteries and prepare to fire long-range seeker missiles," Dailey instructed. The main viewscreen focused on the entire attack wing sitting between the two massive ships. To the left, an Alurian destroyer released its smaller yet still lethal attack drones. Drones they had encountered on their previous outing.

"Viper Six, this is Angel Six. Incoming bogeys. Advise," Jen asked.

Without hesitation, Dailey replied, "Engage and neutralize. Follow through to the destroyer. We have the big boy on the field."

The *Alpha Nova* was standing its ground, surrounded by the debris of other ships for protection. In reality, Kluvnew had been just as shocked by the events that had unfolded, including the disappearance of the Alurian High Fleet at the hands of the Creare.

Dailey watched while the *Murphy* forged ahead, the attack wing cutting into the drones like a buzzsaw. Spark and flashes popped as random laser fire streaked into the black of space. The deployed crew of the *Murphy* wasn't holding anything back.

Within seconds of the encounter, the Nova Rangers along for the ride decoupled from their assigned fighters, jetting forward toward the destroyer. This tactic was the new definition of shake and bake. Once engaged with the enemy in close quarters, the Nova Rangers would launch like a slingshot with a combination of momentum from the fighters and their boost packs. This, in turn, mitigated the risk of being sitting targets for the destroyer's close-range laser turrets, which had just sprung to life.

Not to be outdone, Kline turned. "Sir, I have seeker missiles locked onto their forward batteries. We can hit them before the team gets there."

"Fire," Dailey replied as the thump of several seeker missiles speeding away from the *Murphy* sounded off. "Oh, and Kline, sometimes it's better to ask for forgiveness instead of permission."

The targeting specialist grinned. "Does that go for everything else? Including when we're off duty?"

"Nope."

Was all Dailey replied as the seeker missiles quickly found their targets. Kline had even gone as far as to send a EMP burst missile ahead of the high-yield munitions. The man was well on his way to a promotion.

"Why aren't they firing on us?" Becket asked, now standing by the targeting and weapons stations.

"That destroyer looks like it was in the middle of the fight. If I were to guess, I'd say it's already beat up pretty bad." Dailey was right. While they were on board the Creare command vessel, the destroyer had taken several direct hits from a particle ion cannon. Similar to their own ion cannons, the weapon had the ability to take several systems offline while leaving the ship's hull relatively intact. It was often compared to burning a tree from the inside out. The starfighters now slowly being dispatched were there to secure the vessel and escort it to safety.

"Anything from the *Alpha Nova*?" Dailey asked as they lost sight of the battle raging around the destroyer. His Nova Rangers would make quick work of the ship in its current state.

"It's turning, sir," Kline replied as Dorax walked onto the bridge.

"You need any help?" Dorax said, beaming a thousand-watt smile.

"How is she?" Dailey asked. His green lips climbed further up the side of his face.

"Already kicking and screaming to get up here. Franklin told her to at least put some decent clothes on. The *Crow* was already at flash point when she jumped in the mech suit and had to drop her flight suit before closing it up." He paused. "She was on fire." The Alurian was being literal.

"Any burns?" Becket asked as Dorax grinned again.

"She has a tan for once." He chuckled as Dailey chewed over their next steps. Time was running out, and the *Alpha Nova* would be firing long-range missiles and plasma cannons within the next few minutes.

"Get with Tarik and Valen in the main briefing room. Get their people off the transportation ship. Figure out a place for them to go. It's going to get tight in here," Dailey instructed. Becket raised an eyebrow.

"What's the plan?"

"Plan? No real plan other than to burn that ship to cinders. I was thinking that transportation ship is pretty sturdy in comparison. We can use it as a battling ram or something," Dailey replied.

His logic was simple. Make one ship into two in order to draw Kluvnew's attention.

A red alert flashed as the proximity alarms started up.

"Sir," Kline spoke up, finding himself in the middle of the fight. "They've launched three long-range missiles, and it looks like they are powering up their rail guns."

"That means they don't want this fight to last long," Dailey started as a familiar and welcome voice piped through the intercom.

"Oh, everyone calm down, daddy's home. Yes, I'm here, and the party can start. Well, I'm technically in the drop bay till my body gets fully integrated, but hey, who am I to complain," Albert said. Smirking, Dailey nodded his head, finally clapping his hands.

"Albert, you sure you're good?" Dailey asked as "Iron Man" by Black Sabbath started playing in the background.

"Oh yeah, never better. I may no longer have several centuries worth of all that memory I had locked up, but I'm totally ready to rock."

Even Dailey didn't recognize the song. The younger members of the bridge crew slowly started nodding their heads. "All right, we get the point. Cut the music. Giving you control of our interceptor systems."

"Did you know they're trying to fire an orbital rail gun at us? The nerve," Albert said as Kline clicked the shiny green button on his control panel, giving the AI access to his targeting systems. The two had trained to work together with the *Murphy*'s systems. Albert would focus on the big stuff while Kline would take on the small to midrange targets.

Within seconds, several rockets launched from the *Murphy*'s interceptor systems, clashing with the oncoming fire with a surgeon's hand. Dorax, now in control of the ship's navigation, shifted the *Murphy* several miles, dodging two or three shots from the rail gun. Firing the thrusters back on, the *Murphy* started pressing into the massive debris field.

"Sir, is this one of those times to ask for forgiveness?" Kline asked, holding back from firing the ship's main weapons systems.

"Hold steady. I want to let it rip all at once. Let them keep firing."

And firing they did as several more blasts from not only the rail gun but the *Alpha Nova*'s plasma cannons started thundering in the area around the *Murphy*.

A bright flash forced Dailey to squint as the ship listed, briefly hit by one of the plasma rounds. Mostly deflected by the forward shields, the sheer inertia of the shot rocked the *Murphy*. Between the mix of debris and the *Murphy* facing the *Alpha Nova* head-on, next to none of the shots being fired at them had landed. In turn, Albert and Kline fired several volleys of interceptor rockets in response.

"We're not going to get a clear line of fire till we're damn near on top of them," Dailey stated as the ship rocked again. "Kline, hold steady; make sure the plasma cannons are fully charged."

Dorax and Valen ran onto the bridge, with Dorax taking the lead. "The transport ship is vacated. Do we need a pilot?"

"No need, sunshine," Albert spoke up. "I'm programming it now. I know Persius is on board; we could sure use a hand. It's not like that ship is ten times bigger than us or anything."

"Not till you get to see what they did. Get that ship moving at a forty-five-degree angle away, then turn it toward the *Alpha Nova*. Can you do that thing with its reactors again?"

"If you mean time it just right to overheat while it slams into the ship's hull—yes. Will it make it there? Not so sure. It would sure be great to know the probability of that," Albert added as Dailey shook his head.

"Nice try. Maybe next time. I want that transport ship—" Dailey stopped his order as the Creare transport ship blasted up and away from the *Murphy*.

"You were saying?" Albert asked. An alarm sounded just then, followed by the *Murphy* smacking into a large section of destroyed ship.

Lights flickered on the bridge as the deflector shields stabilized; they had received a direct hit from a plasma cannon. Becket pointed downward, meaning he was heading to the drop bay. In the event it was needed, the ship's first sergeant would grab a handful of standby pilots and take the Harpies into the fight.

"What's the status of the attack wing?" Dailey asked as Dorax shifted the *Murphy*'s course to avoid another volley of plasma fire.

Kline leaned back, running his hands through his hair. "The destroyer's gone. They're en route."

"Comms are open," Communications Officer King added.

"Angel Six. Status report?" Dailey asked.

"Sir." Jen sounded winded. "En route to your location. We have two angels down—no casualties. We'll have to recover them on our way back."

Dailey sighed at the positive assumption, then he quickly remembered Albert was back in the fight. "Good copy. Albert is back up and running. We will be fully engaged and out of the debris field in two minutes."

"We'll be there, sir. Just a little dicey with all this garbage floating around," she replied before the comms link cut off.

With time running short, the nose of the *Murphy* slid through the final layer of wreckage just as every weapon on the *Alpha Nova* erupted in one angry wall of fire. The deflector shields glowed as the power meter on the main display started shifting from a light green to an almost yellow color. The one saving grace was that Dailey knew they were now too close for the rail guns to be effective. As long as they approached the *Alpha Nova* from its topside, the ship would have to flip over to reach them.

"Kline, Albert—fire!" Dailey bellowed as every weapon system on the *Murphy* sprang to life in a chorus of hate. Hundreds of missiles bloomed into action while the close-range lasers of Kluvnew's vessel started snapping into them, followed by several continuous volleys for the ship's cannons. It was an all-out brawl as the significantly larger ship started rotating.

"Topside vector approach. Get us as close to that ship as you can," Dailey ordered as the *Murphy*'s thrusters once again flared.

"Hey, folks. Quick reminder. That ship has a nasty—and I mean *nasty*— forward ion cannon. One hit, and it's all she wrote," Albert informed the bridge as the *Murphy* started maneuvering out of the way. Being a smaller frigate, the slow-turning monstrosity of war could not keep up with the fast-approaching *Murphy*.

"Sir," Dorax spoke up, tracking the Creare transport ship with the help of Valen. "The transport ship is at the edge of the debris field."

"Oh man, they have that ion cannon almost fully charged. It would be super wicked if someone, you know, sort of flung that thing right into it as it was about to fire," Albert suggested to a very approving Dailey.

"Bait and switch. Albert, can you take control of the helm and see if we can get them to take the bait?"

Albert took several seconds to compute the trajectory.

"Yes, but I will say, the *Murphy* will probably take several direct hits in the process." While Albert replied, the *Murphy* shook again, hit by a missile. The shield's energy meter started dipping into orange as Dailey gave the go-ahead.

Glancing over to the main viewport, several long-range missiles, reset to point detonation, lurched into the *Alpha Nova*'s hardened exterior. They were so close to the ship they had entered its deflector shield's release range. Simply put, this was the range at which kinetic weapons fired from the ship would be able to detonate to protect the vessel from blowback. It also allowed things such as missiles to pass through and then activate a delayed detonation sequence.

A rocking explosion bloomed from the surface of the sleek ship as several of its forward plasma cannon batteries erupted, causing several secondary explosions inside the ship. Dailey, in a move of either ego or pure rage, hailed Kluvnew. Another direct hit slammed into the *Murphy*, causing several control screens to wink out.

"No worries, I can still see everything. Man, this is getting exciting," Albert guffawed as a massive streak of plasma fire skimmed the bow of the ship, causing more of the systems to waver.

Just as the viewscreen flashed on with Kluvnew's highly agitated face staring back at Captain Dailey, the attack wing joined the fight. The one thing they immediately noticed was that the massive ship had launched and subsequently lost all of its attack fighters during their encounter with the Creare. A rookie move even Dailey found himself currently doing.

The Alurian didn't speak, the signs of a strained bridge crew showing in the background. Whatever they had hit with their previous volley of missiles had hit close to home.

"Kluvnew," Dailey started, buying time while the massive ship moved into position to fire its massive primary ion cannon. Albert had put a trajectory chart on the main viewscreen, which flickered. As much as the crew of the *Murphy* thought they were indestructible, the fact of the matter was that they had also sustained damage to their main core reactor. While not enough to affect the thrusters and the gate drive, several of their systems were transferring power to the forward shields.

"One last chance to stand down and surrender your ship."

Kluvnew smirked. His eyes shifted to an obvious chart showing how long till they were in a position to fire. The Alurian growled. "I am offering you the same opportunity."

Dailey stepped down, picking up Persius. "And destroy this? I feel like I have something you want." The *Murphy*'s commander was buying time.

"I see. But that is of no consequence at this point. You will stand down," Kluvnew stated as another volley of plasma fire smacked off the now red-flashing shields of the *Murphy*. A few more direct hits would put an end to the *Murphy*'s main deflector shields.

Albert blew an audible raspberry. "Pfft. Fat chance. I'm sure you would like to know what happened to the other ships. Oh, don't know anything about that. Well, that just means you're not one of the cool kids."

Kluvnew, not fully understanding the statement, smiled at the same time Albert's chart flashed red. They were about to fire. "See you later, Kluvnew."

"No, Captain Ben Dailey. I'll be seeing you—" A nod from the Alurian gave the signal to fire.

"Yeah, in hell," Dailey mumbled to himself, cutting the comms line.

Several things happened all at once, with the attack wing launching every remaining ordnance they had and Albert activating the Creare transport ship as Dailey switched over to the attack wing. "Angel Six, get your running shoes on." The phrase was an age-old message to haul ass out of the area.

Blue thrusters screamed overhead at the same time Albert activated a short-range hyperjump on the Creare transport ship. Every warning light wailed like a newborn child as the ion cannon fired. But unknown to Kluvnew, Albert had hyperjumped the ship directly into the massive cannon's opening, so instead of firing outward, a brilliant flash of light swallowed the ship, bubbling from the inside out.

Dailey wasn't able to give the order to leave before the ship lurched into maximum thrust, shooting directly up and away from the quickly faltering *Alpha Nova*. The last signs of lights flickered as the rearview cameras appeared on the main viewscreen, showing the last breaths of the ship and crew on board.

The first explosion flashed just as quickly as it was pulled back in. The reactors were going supernova.

A bead of sweat formed on Dailey's forehead as the explosion lit the space in front of the *Murphy*.

"How close is this going to be?" Dailey asked, gritting his teeth.

"Time to do that pray thing, boys! We can't jump out of the debris field," Albert announced.

A blinding flash snapped as the blast shields slammed shut over the main viewport. Heat radiated from the hull of the ship as the thrusters shut completely down, listing the ship helplessly.

Dailey took a deep breath as he opened his eyes, no longer hearing the roar of the explosion.

They had survived.

CHAPTER 36

HOME AGAIN, HOME AGAIN

Sparky never left Albert's side while he was pulling himself back together. The attack wing hummed into the drop bay as the scars of battle stood out proudly on the fighters. With the Nova Rangers and pilots alike having been in the fight of their lives, there was a mix of exhausted faces and high fives.

Dailey stood in the drop bay beside Becket as they watched Franklin treating several wounded Rangers, including Dawn and Card. Grantham sat on a bench inhaling a vaporizer, his hair matted to his head.

Albert stood just as Mister Toaster's face morphed back into existence. Jen walked over to Dailey, not holding back as she jumped into his arms to a deafening round of ohs and ahs.

"That's unprofessional." Dailey leaned back before she pulled him into a kiss. This time, a round of claps followed.

Albert looked down at Sparky. "They're totally bumping uglies." Sparky didn't reply, simply slurping a lick on Albert's leg piston. "Enough of that. People will talk, you know." Albert paused. "I don't know if this is an emotion, but I missed you too. I thought there for a minute . . . Well, I thought a few times today it was over."

A quick bark and chuff followed. "The Ham Republic never dies." As the translator kicked off, Thron and the entire mess crew barged into the bay, handing out bags of Solarian chips and actual beers. Thron had kept them tucked away for an occasion such as this.

Becket breathed out of his nose. "So, what's up with the Creare?"

"They want us to send a message to the Federation. I think it's uploaded on Persius—Albert will get that figured out. We can hook her back up to that ugly-ass speaker." Dailey grinned. The stress of the day had weighed heavy on him, but he would be bringing his entire crew back.

Cheers started from the far end of the bay as Pearl slowly walked into the bay. Dorax ran up to her, and the two leaned into each other, touching their foreheads together.

"Those are going to be some ugly babies," Albert said to Sparky, who nodded his thick neck.

Pearl walked up to Becket and Dailey, saluting the two men. They returned the snapping motion. Dailey leaned forward, hugging the Solarian executive officer as she smiled.

"That was a close one."

"There will be more," Thron butted in, handing Pearl a beer. "Sir, with all due respect, it's time to have a drink," he said, smacking two in both Becket's and Dailey's chests.

"I'm never one to argue with the chef," Becket growled, downing the cool beer in one impressive gulp.

Dailey followed while the celebration continued, but was unable to keep up with Becket. Bellman and Chief Engineering Officer Hontz entered the bay with a crew of engineers and massive tool pods. They had work to do on the ship.

"Sir," Hontz grumped. "Everything's pretty much broken. It's going to take a couple of days, maybe weeks, but we can get her back in order. She's a good ship."

"Keep us informed. It took everyone here to make this happen," Dailey followed, patting the man on the shoulder.

Tarik, Bella, and Valen walked out of the main elevator, seeing the utter shit show of a celebration in the drop bay. They were all ignoring the fact they were covered in carbon and pit marks from direct hits from close-range lasers.

"Seems like we made it," Tarik told Dailey with a smile.

"Seems that way. So what's your plan?" Dailey asked, still taking in the ragtag group of warriors around him.

"Plan? After seeing all that . . . probably getting my head checked to make sure this is all real. For my people? I believe you are right. There will be more problems on Teras than we can handle. I already saw some reports of other signs of life on the planet. I was going to ask if we could travel with you to Earth, I believe you called it. Maybe we can come back with some help," Tarik said as Bella cut into the conversation.

"What he's trying to say is we want to come back with you. When we're ready, we can figure out a way to return home. We've been in that Vault and in that rain our whole lives. It's time our people got out into the sunlight."

"Valen, what about you? You're a soldier. What about sticking around after we get back? Janix could use some help."

Valen nodded as Janix motioned the man to join and meet the rest of his platoon. "I can do that." He paused, glancing at Tarik.

"I think it would be good to have one of our representatives on your team," Tarik allowed as Valen grinned, jogging off.

The adrenaline started wearing thin on both Becket and Dailey as they both realized they still hadn't worked through what Director Prescott and the Ateris Syndicate were doing.

"Olan said something interesting. I believe he speaks in the literal sense." Dailey shifted topics as several other crew officers started talking to Tarik and Bella.

"Sir?" Becket growled, grabbing a beer from a passing Nova Ranger.

"He said that Director Prescott was part of this, but he also said the mining syndicates are our enemies, not the actual Alurians, minus the Prime Assembly."

"Try convincing the council of that. They have their noses so far up in the mining syndicates' asses they wouldn't care if they smelled shit."

Dailey huffed out a laugh. "Yeah, you're right. We just need to keep that in mind. This isn't over."

Dailey walked over to the dynamic duo taking in the scene. "Albert, what the hell did you do back there?"

"Nothing special. I just split my personality, so to speak, in two, then let them download just enough to think they had me. Once you left, I simply jumped into the battle droid that had me hooked up to the drive they brought in. Boring stuff, really, and those droids . . . Let me just say, I wouldn't want to piss them off. Plus, I got a new party outfit." Albert pointed at the slumped-over Creare security droid.

"I see that. Listen, I need you to check Persius out. We can't take any chances after Prescott's little trick. See how she's doing, and when we get done presenting whatever message she has loaded, we can take the next steps," Dailey promised as Mister Toaster grinned.

"On it, boss. In case you're wondering, I gave them all the old, dusty stuff. The phrase 'they don't make them like they used to' applies here."

"Agreed. Just get yourself pulled together, and we can talk. We're heading home, and I need you on the gate drive. Oh, Sparky, one more thing. I have released the rest of the ham and something we like to call sausage rations to you. It's a donation to the republic," Dailey stated before walking back to join the party.

Sparky kicked his back legs up in excitement, seeing Thron making his rounds. Before Dailey could speak again, the hound had already taken off at a brisk pace toward the warlord turned chef.

CHAPTER 37

WELCOME HOME

The scene was a mix of a welcome-home celebration and an inquisition. Dailey, Becket, Pearl, Jen, Dorax, Tarik, Valen, Albert, and Sparky all stood lined up in front of the Federation's main leadership council, which included representatives from all the Federation member planets, as well as the ones hoping to join soon.

The massive hall aboard the space station was capped with a transparent dome looking out into the reaches of space. Two star carriers sat in wait directly above them, hovering beside the dwarfed *Murphy*. The USF *Murphy* looked as if it had been to literal hell and back. Dark burns from the *Alpha Nova*'s explosion tarnished the once pristine exterior, accompanied by several large gouges in its hull.

In the large hall, a delegation of Moshans ensured they were the loudest in the room as Admiral Deborah Powell called the assembly to order, a word Dailey and his crew no longer appreciated.

The crew of the *Murphy*, minus Tarik, Valen, and Dorax, were in their full dress uniforms, and both Becket and Dailey had more medals dangling off their chest than they could almost comfortably carry. This was only outdone by the jinglejangle of awards hanging off Sparky's now shined armor. To be fair, Albert and the hound had created many of them in the name of the Ham Republic.

After hours of grueling debrief after debrief, a meeting and celebration had been called.

Powell walked in front of the motley crew standing before them. At no time in known Federation history—or any other history, for that matter—had a group so diverse been assembled.

"We are here today to honor Captain Dailey and the crew of the USF *Murphy*," she started to a round of cheers and applause. "Your actions are an honor to every being in the galaxy. Even though we have learned of more troubles ahead, we have also been offered a path to peace, and a broader understanding of the order of things. As of today, we are designating several of the mining corporations as enemies of the state and this Federation. Captain Dailey, step forward."

Dailey walked in front of Powell, who beamed a smile at the man. After a quick salute, she motioned for a large tray of medals before starting again. "For bravery and heroism above and beyond the call of duty, you and your command staff are hereby awarded the Federation Cross, the highest honor we can bestow."

She walked with Dailey as they draped the ribboned medal around his crew members' necks. Once in front of Tarik and Valen, she smiled, continuing to bestow the award. She paused in front of Dorax, not knowing how she even felt about bestowing the award on the Alurian. Last in line were, of course, Albert and Sparky.

Mister Toaster's face had been modified with a cleaner-than-usual haircut. Albert bent down slightly as she draped the award around the former toaster. For Sparky, she kneeled, placing a smaller version around his neck, joining the four other medals already in place. As she pulled her hand back, Sparky snapped his thick tongue out, licking her hand.

Dailey, knowing the drill, ordered the team to turn toward the gathered group as another round of applause greeted them. After bringing the room to order, Powell again took center stage.

"It is hereby also decreed that Dorax Flam is appointed lieutenant of these Federations," Powell added, to Dorax's shock and confusion. A feeling of true pride for once in his life and a true sense of belonging followed.

Pearl squeezed his hand as the moment passed.

"Lastly," she continued, "we have been given a message from a race of beings called the Creare. In this message, there's also included an invitation. An invitation to not only meet with the Alurians but also to broker peace.

While this is a celebration, it is also a warning of things to come. The galaxy as we know it has changed."

Gasps came from the audience; most of the representatives in the room had yet to be briefed on the situation. She was taking this time to do that.

Knowing she had talked enough, she turned as Persius, now loaded in the Creare security droid, activated the message. For the next thirty minutes, the story of the Prime Assembly and the true nature and history of Earth was laid out in a clear, organized manner that even the drunk Moshans could understand.

Dailey and his crew walked out of the hall, all standing in a side room for senior Federation members. Dailey looked at the team they had assembled with pride, knowing the celebration would be short lived.

"What's next, boss?" Albert asked as Sparky walked over to a mirror meant for the military officers to check their uniforms, posing with his new medal.

"I have a few promises to keep. A little R and R for the crew. Get the ship refit. Make sure Tarik and the others are settled. Then . . ." Dailey paused to think. "Then we take Sparky back home, and from there . . . Well, from there, we go to Aluria," Dailey stated as anxious nods and smiles beamed back at him.

EPILOGUE

Angry voices bellowed before the sounds of someone finally bringing the chaotic conversation to order boomed. In the room, a main representative from each of the mining syndicates sat with rage in their eyes. A plain, unassuming man from Earth turned to the group.

"While this is concerning, it doesn't change our focus. Just our path. The Alurian High Council will undoubtedly work for peace with the Federation after this recent setback with the Creare," Chancellor Abraham said calmly. His voice was flat and without emotion.

"What about our main fleet?" an Alurian officer said at the far end of the table.

"What about it? We have other means available to us. Means we have been aware of for some time," Abraham replied.

"If you're talking about the Titans, we don't have the resources," the Alurian followed.

Abraham picked up a remote, turning on the large, monolithic monitor on the wall. There, a live feed of the Titan they'd encountered while chasing the *Murphy* came into focus. Sparks and dozens if not hundreds of constructo ships sat attached to its hull, working on the gigantic machine. Two offset moons sat beside the Titan looking like basketballs, showing the true size of the ancient machine of war.

"There is always a path forward," Abraham said as he started going over several up-to-now hidden projects.

AUTHOR'S NOTE

I hope you have enjoyed the first three-part story of the Descending Worlds series. Your support and kind words have helped to make this series into a new world for readers and listeners alike to enjoy and live in. While this is just the beginning for Dailey and his motley crew aboard the USF *Murphy*, it's also a time to get back to writing their next misadventure. Thank you again for joining me and the crew of the *Murphy*.

Cheers,
Justin S. Leslie

ACKNOWLEDGMENTS

To all the new fans of the *Murphy*'s crew and their antics, thank you for joining us at the start of this epic journey. You ain't seen nothing yet! Thank you to all my friends and family who have supported this effort! That includes you, the reader or listener—you're fam now.

For our audio listeners. Luke Daniels, thank you once again for lending your voice to this crew of misfits. You are a master of your craft and an amazing person. It has been a true honor working with and meeting you.

This book is ultimately dedicated to all the brave men and women I served with, and in some cases, lost in dire times of hardship, and the friendships also shared.

Halfway down the trail to Hell,
In a shady meadow green,
Are the Souls of all dead troopers camped.
See you at the Fiddler's Green.

ABOUT THE AUTHOR

Justin S. Leslie is the bestselling author of the Max Abaddon, Sinking Man, and Descending Worlds series, as well as a retired Army major who served several combat tours. When he isn't writing, playing music, or spending time with his family, Leslie can be found at his home in Doctors Inlet, Florida, immersed in his latest urban-fantasy or military sci-fi project or a well-made cocktail. Visit www.JustinLeslie.com for more info.